To Tael & Laura,
Enjoy!

Elif Howard

The
Chaos Chip

The
Chaos Chip

Gil Howard

Glenbridge Publishing Ltd.

Library of Congress Catalog Card Number: LC 98-70864

International Standard Book Number: 0-944435-46-7

Printed in the U. S. A.

To

Thomas Bedell
who helped me hone
my writing skills
and encouraged me.

Linda Tidrick
who edited the first draft,
and whose incisiveness
and brutal frankness
frequently jerked me into
reality.

Ruth Z. Tresner,
my eldest daughter,
without whose unrelenting
push, the word processing
program might never
have been loaded.

with ceaseless gratitude

Prologue

Part of the northern spine of the Alps forms the border between the Austrian province of North Tyrol and the German state of Bavaria. One of the vertebrae of that spine is the Zugspitze, a peak that rises 9,721 feet (2,963 meters) above sea level. It is perpetually snowcapped. Geologists believe that, in eons long past, as the Earth's primeval crust crept slowly northward, the cracking and folding of that crust pushing up from the bottom of the sea released molten rock that formed Zugspitze. Today, melting snow generates innumerable swift streams that scamper headlong downward, swirling around and across sedimentary rocks, cutting through bleak wastelands where only mountain wildflowers grow, dropping in mini-waterfalls, cascading below the timberline and slackening as the slope slackens. On the Bavarian side of the Zugspitze, one of these streams, the Liederbach, slices through a woodland and meanders across a broad meadow before spilling into a sparkling, clear, cold lake. The meadow is surrounded by tall beech and larch, now bleak and leafless. No sound disturbs its tranquility, except the occasional song of birds and the incessant lullaby of the gurgling stream. In the concave of one of the meanders, where in warmer months the tiny white edelweiss bloom among the high grasses, is a brown lump. A closer inspection reveals a coarse woolen garment encrusted with ice — a monk's robe with a cowl. Inside is a body of what had been a man, before a bullet had pierced his heart. When that body had contained a mind, it was the mind of a monk, albeit an unusual one. He had been called Brother Stephen. He is dead because there are people who can no longer suffer him to live. They have great power. And he, like most of us, was incredibly easy to kill.

The sun, sinking into the upraised bare branches of the trees, gives warning that darkness will shortly hide the icy lump. But the warning is futile. There is no one to warn. Except for a few birds and wild animals, the meadow is lifeless. The monk no longer cares. A chill wind is blowing. Storm clouds far off, advancing southward from the North Sea, will bring snow by late morning. Then the lump will be white.

Monday
November 17

⊰ 1 ⊱

To awaken in winter amidst a world of lingering darkness that was cold everywhere except under the covers of his bed did not perturb Murdock McCabe. Had it been a work day, it would have. But today he was beginning a two-week expense-paid skiing holiday. Dry road was forecast. Driving from downtown Munich to the Zugspitze Hof Lodge in the Bavarian Alps would take less than two hours. His watch read 6:10 A.M. The city was quiet. In minutes he loaded his ski gear into and onto his new BMW 528i. His six-foot-two frame fit comfortably—but just barely —into the driver's seat. He inhaled the new car aroma. As he inserted the ignition key, his mind turned to Karen. The death benefit from Karen's life insurance had paid for it. Theirs had been as near perfect a marriage as two people could hope for—until the kidnapping and shoot-out that destroyed it. *So many dreams were destroyed by that bullet, he thought. But she would have wanted me to buy this car.*

As he fastened his seat belt, he reminded himself that he had been neglecting his abs. He promised himself that he'd use the weightlifting room at the Lodge. With his handkerchief he wiped a fingerprint from the broad walnut door trim and unconsciously ran his hand through his thick mop of red hair. The mirror reflected the mischief the wind had done. He ran a comb through it.

Murdock turned the key. In spite of a temperature well below freezing, six cylinders instantly purred into action. The sound of a finely crafted piece of machinery pleased him. Quickly putting the early morning traffic behind him, he headed south on the autobahn. Miles of residential neighborhoods zipped past him on both sides. He hadn't liberated himself from the rat race yet, but at least the rats were wearing softer-soled slippers.

A coquettish sun peeked over the eastern horizon and, having been seen, withdrew into a shroud of dark clouds that stretched westward across the winter sky. He knew that a blizzard was moving southward from the North Sea. Murdock was determined to outrun it. Behind him, beyond the horizon, heavily moisture-laden black clouds were blanketing the Rhine Valley with snow, in preparation for slipping across the Black Forest and the Bavarian Highlands, and descending into the valleys of the Danube and the Isar Rivers, before shrouding the Alps. It was the valley of the Isar that he sought to escape.

A vague feeling of guilt haunted him. *It's what she would have wanted, he repeated to himself.*

He accelerated to 150 KPH. There was no speed limit. The farmland changed to lifeless grazing pastures without animals. In Bavaria cattle are fed in the villages during the winter. Murdock passed a lumber mill on his left. On the right he caught a glimpse of the frozen waters of the Starnberger Sea. His favorite restaurant, the Hefeweissehaus, stood on its shore. Murdock was starved, but he decided to wait for Zugspitze Hof. Frau Bayer's famous croissants and jams were worth the wait.

The darkness of the sky deepened, enshrouding the countryside in gloom. The road sliced through fields of stark, dreary patterns of the ghostly stubble of dead plants. But presently the icy bucolic scene began to surrender to the tall conifers that clothe the foothills of the Alps. *More like it, he thought.*

As the conifers lined the highway in increasing numbers, a recurring memory gripped him. Time leapt back two years. He saw himself — a stark, lonely figure — standing at a grave — Karen's grave — his wife's grave — the grave that buried his love. He had returned to the cemetery at twilight, long after the family and guests had finished the post-funeral lunch — said their final regrets and departed — after he could no longer pretend to himself that what had happened hadn't. A dusting of fresh snow blanketed the loose earth that covered the coffin. Offshore, Lake Erie was choked with ice. A March wind, unmercifully cold, ascended the slate cliff, sliced through the silent cemetery, and chilled him. The grass, which surrounded the tiny mound and thousands of grave stones, was brown and lifeless. Flowers — hundreds of flowers — final tender offerings of those who had loved her — contrived an incongruously cheerful halo encircling the mound. Standing there with no fragment of cheer in his heart, silently, he agonized to understand how anyone could shoot and kill a woman so young, so kind, so loving, so vibrant, so utterly delightful. He shuddered. He didn't notice the color of the sky. If there were a god above in heaven, he was either heartless and cruel or, to be kind, impotent. Desolate, he felt coldness gnawing at his bones. Since the day of her death, Murdock had struggled to understand how Joe Carlyle could have conducted the FBI raid on the kidnappers so wantonly and recklessly, unless he had absolutely no regard for Karen's life. He remained standing there, motionless, until he felt as cold as he imagined

Karen. When he left, something that was trusting in him remained behind.

But this isn't New York State. Up ahead are the Bavarian Alps. I can't keep thinking about Karen, he resolved. I have a reasonably happy life now, and a few good friends. I've got the dream car both Karen and I wanted. I've put my FBI career behind me. I'm an investigator for an outstanding international agency. I have some wonderful memories. What more can anyone expect from life? He was tempted to say *plenty*, but he didn't.

As a bonus for solving one of Veritus' most urgent cases, the Baltic Insurance fraud, his boss, Richard Laplatenier, had given him two expense paid weeks at his favorite ski lodge in the Bavarian Alps. It was the first vacation he had taken in almost two years. *I'll do nothing but ski and drink and eat and sleep, he thought. The slopes will be perfect by morning. Why was she kidnapped in the first place? If it were to keep me from testifying, as the ransom notes said, why didn't they take me instead? Was she easier to get?* He felt that he had squandered eleven years with the FBI and had ended up with a dead wife. *Karen was right. Our friend Allison made the right career move. She joined Veritus Investigations International right out of college. Now she's assistant station chief in Munich, one of the world's largest international detective agencies, and my superior. Allison warned both Jerr and me that there was a slim future with the FBI. We should have listened. But, fresh out of law school, we were too macho to listen to our women. When Jerr and Allison married, Karen predicted that diverging career paths would pull them apart. It did. Sadly for Jerr. Fortunate for me, he thought. Allison has been a rock. Every time I feel low, we have dinner, and she lifts my spirits. She knew Karen longer than I did. She's an extraordinary woman. I wish I could think of her other than as Jerr's ex and my boss.*

Silence reigned, except for the purring engine and the hum of the road. He listened. There were moments when the need to hear Karen's voice was intolerable, when the air was so crowded with memories that it was barely breathable, and he felt suffocated by it.

The autobahn gave way to a two-lane road, one lane in each direction. The faint outline of an old monastery high on the mountainside came into view. The ski slopes and Zugspitze Hof Lodge would appear around the next curve. He reduced speed. The mental shards of city life began to disintegrate. He relaxed. The narrow side road which leads to the Zugspitze Hof came into view. He slowed, turned left, and pointed the nostrils of the 528i up the winding road. It meandered with tortuous twists among naked white beech interspersed with the dark green of spruce and fir. The 528i was stable on the switchbacks. Its six cylinders delivered urgent response on the inclines, and its suspension allowed an almost fluid ride over the rough spots. The road narrowed into a one-lane bridge. He approached cautiously. A sharp, blind curve to the right just beyond the bridge hid oncoming traffic. Beneath the bridge surged the furious waters of the Liederbach Creek. A few feet beyond the road, the creek reached a sheer bluff of three hundred feet and transmuted itself into a glistening waterfall. Murdock had driven past it many times, but never had he noticed the beauty of it — until now. Beyond the right turn, he encountered a wide spot in the road. He parked and stepped outside. *God, this is beautiful. Why haven't I ever really seen it before. Karen mentioned it, but I was driving. She would have enjoyed stopping here, but I was always anxious to get to the ski lodge. We never took the time.* He looked down. Far below the bluff, the creek meandered through the tall grasses of the alpage, a broad Alpine meadow. *It is wonderfully wild, he thought. No blade of grass has been trimmed. No effort's been made to conform the course of the stream. No brush has been cleared. Not a jot of concrete anywhere. Just pristine beauty. How could I have been so blind or so unkind to Karen that I'd never stop?*

The meadow below looked cold, misty, and remote. Feasting on the serenity, he stood there without moving for several minutes. Ground fog, which had been creeping across the meadow below, now started mounting the slope, drifting upward toward the road. No wind stirred the naked branches of the white trees. Murdock listened for a bird's song, but he heard only the sound of water falling and striking the rocks below. An eerie feeling overcame him. He strained to listen, as if the silence itself had something to say. A chill ran up his spine. The meadow below was now hidden in fog. He turned up his collar and shoved his hands in his pockets. *What mysteries does it hold? he wondered. How much history has happened on that very meadow?*

His reverie was abruptly interrupted by his stomach reminding him that he hadn't had breakfast. He never failed to listen to his stomach. He decided to move on.

*   *   *

Zugspitze Hof Lodge is located on a middle elevation of the north slope of the Zugspitze massif, Germany's highest mountain, not far from the village of Hammersbach in Germany's largest state — Bavaria. Although constructed at the end of the 19th century, it was renovated under American suzerainty after World War II. For four decades the lodge had been used by the U. S. military for R&R.

As Murdock rounded the final curve, the main lodge came into view. Since he had been there last, the eaves and soffits had been given a fresh coat of light blue paint, causing them to stand out delightfully against the bare wood exterior. New flower boxes graced the under-sill of each window, replacing those that had needed tender loving care. Colorful flowers were painted on them. In the summertime, he knew, they will become alive with red geraniums and impatiens. He checked in and headed for the restaurant.

His eyes feasted on the ambiance. Murdock admired the ancient woodworking. He had a sense of history. Ripples on the hand-hewn timbers reminded him of the skill of woodworkers long dead. He could picture them chopping the logs with a broadax, and smoothing them with an adze. He admired their ability to integrate the towering roof, which slopes up over the restaurant and cocktail lounge to a central high point, and creating a harmony with the mountain itself. The timbers were massive. Along with the stone-buttressed walls, they were designed to withstand wild Alpine winds, and the weight of deep snow. Smooth glaciated stones, carefully selected from nearby valleys and hauled by oxcart to the site over a century ago, had been chiseled into shape and fitted by expert stonemasons to form an enormous, magnificent fireplace. Blacksmiths had heated iron, exciting the fire with bellows made of hides, tooled it into shape, and formed the handwrought light fixtures and the andirons of the fireplace. This morning it radiated and crackled with a cheerful warmth.

Murdock had met Hans and Matilde Bayer, its present owners, shortly after they had bought the lodge in 1985. They renovated the guest rooms, de-Americanizing them and converting them into central European ambiance with a distinct Bavarian flair.

For Murdock one of the main attractions was the special pride the Bayers took in their restaurant. Along with traditional Bavarian fare, they offered American beef — a rare commodity in a Europe, which long ago had invented fancy sauces to disguise poor meat. To Murdock, the jovial personalities of the Bayers themselves added an effervescence and hauteur that made Zugspitze Hof a truly exceptional lodge.

"Please wait to be seated" the sign said in four languages. The hostess was occupied elsewhere. There was one man ahead of him. All tables were occupied. *Drat, Murdock thought. But no reason not to be friendly.*

"Good morning," Murdock said, guessing from the cut of his clothes that the man was American and would respond to English. "I'm Murdock McCabe."

"Good morning to you," the older man responded easily. "I'm Professor Otto Klugman from Cannon Beach, Oregon. Most folks call me professor. I'm not certain whether it's to honor me or humor me. What part of the States are you from, Mr. McCabe?"

"Please, call me Murdock. Actually, I've been living in Munich for the last two years."

"Ah, yes," the professor replied. "I've visited Munich many times. A beautiful city indeed. I take it you are employed there?"

"Gentlemen," a strange voice interjected. "Please join me at my table. There are none other available. I'm alone and would immensely enjoy your company."

Murdock and the professor turned to see an olive-skinned man whom Murdock estimated to be in his late thirties or early forties. A dark black mustache formed a brusque chevron under his nose. Half-glasses highlighted an intelligent face. The corners of his mouth turned ever so slightly downward, between smiles, giving him a look that vacillated comfortably between joviality and stolid patience. But his most striking feature was his eyes — dark brown Spanish eyes — shining in anticipation. "I am Jose Enrique Perez-Krieger from Chile. My friends call me Enrique. I hope you will too. Please . . . join me." They followed him across the room. "You are?"

"Murdock McCabe."

"Professor Otto Klugman."

The table was set for three. "Please be seated," he insisted. A sterling silver coffeepot dominated the setting. "Please, will you try my personal blend of Colombian coffees? I bring it with me. Frau Bayer is so kind to brew it for me." Both nodded in agreement. Two empty cups waited on the table. Fine Bavarian china, Murdock observed. Enrique poured with a graceful flourish. "Cream and sugar?" he offered. "This is fresh local cream, not the imitation. Tell me please, professor, are you the Otto P. Klugman who wrote *The Amoral Universe*?"

The professor stared at Enrique for several seconds. "I'm shocked, Señor, that you have heard of such an obscure and esoteric treatise?"

"Please call me Enrique. I'll feel more comfortable. I hope you will too. I've not only heard of it, sir . . . I have read it." Enrique smiled warmly. "In fact, professor, I have reread it twice and made copious notes. I have many notebooks. They are my real treasures." Enrique sipped his coffee. The professor was speechless. "I admire your blend of intellectual disciplines, professor. You are both a renowned philosopher — a seeker of truth — with complementing expertise in astrophysics."

"I'm happy you think they are complementary," the professor injected.

"I know that you taught philosophy at a university. Did you teach astrophysics also?"

"One elementary course per year. Unfortunately, many of my colleagues don't find my interests complementary at all. I do not pretend to be an astrophysicist. It is a collateral interest."

Enrique nodded in understanding. "You must be here to visit Brother Stephen and Brother Antonio at the monastery."

"Yes, but how did you know that?"

"I merely surmised," Enrique replied. "I don't mean to pry, but it is curious that you meet with monks. From your book I concluded that you are not a religious man. Is that not true?"

"That's most certainly true. Other than a few hundred scientists, you're a member of a rather exclusive club. Or perhaps you too are a scientist?"

"No. I'm a mere businessman. And you, Mr. McCabe, what do you do?"

"I am an investigator for Veritus International. Have you heard of us?"

"But certainly," Enrique said, smiling confidently. "Now I understand why your name seemed familiar. You solved the Baltic Insurance fraud. The result benefited one of my companies—Siegfried Insurance. May I call you Murdock?"

"Of course. I'm more comfortable with informality." Murdock watched Enrique's eyes. They were a closed book. "You seem to know many things, Enrique. How is it that you know that I was involved in the Baltic case?"

"I keep informed about all organizations with which I do business, or in which I invest. Siegfried was a silent coinsurer with Baltic in several deals."

Murdock decided that Enrique was playing a game—that he holds his cards close to his chest and invites everyone else to show theirs. Murdock considered the possibility that this meeting was not accidental. But, he wondered, if it was not accidental, was his purpose to meet him or the professor? "You mentioned that you are a businessman. What business, Enrique?"

"My family is into several businesses in Chile and elsewhere—primarily copper, nitrates, and agriculture. The fresh blueberries that you buy in winter may have come from our lands. But I'm mainly into finance and investment. Are your wives with you, or are we three bachelors on the loose?" Enrique refilled their cups as he spoke.

Murdock, casually sipping his coffee, observed Enrique. *He's relaxed—supremely comfortable with himself, he thought. Not smug . . . not self-centered . . . comfortable . . . complex . . . and shrewd. I'd rather have him as a friend than as an enemy. I'll make it my business to get to know him better. I'll look for a hook."*

"I've never married," Murdock heard the professor respond. Murdock turned his attention to him. "I never found a woman who could tolerate an egghead like me. I have a tendency to talk women to sleep with demonstrations of logical syllogisms craftily worded, or esoteric images of a dynamic universe in a state of constant flux. If one of my lady friends told one of my former lady friends that she slept in my apartment, the former would nod knowingly and say that she knew exactly what she meant. Philosophy is my wife and astrophysics is my mistress. No woman that I ever dated would buy one of my books. My books that are boring to normal people. No offense. You said you read *The Amoral Universe.* Frankly I'm amazed that you found it interesting. But I've heard your name before . . . seen it in *The Wall Street Journal.* I suspect that you are a very interesting man yourself. Not an average person. Average can be exceedingly dull."

Murdock noticed that Enrique responded to the last remark with a wry smile.

"And you?" Enrique continued, turning to Murdock.

"I'm afraid I have not read it," Murdock replied. "I imagine it appeals to a distinctive audience of scholars. I have never considered myself a scholar. However, I have admiration for scholarship. It must give you a great deal of personal satisfaction, Professor, to know that your books have challenged the minds of your peers. I have never had the honor of meeting a distinguished author before. I say that sincerely. When we get to know one another better, and I hope we shall, you will learn that I am not a flatterer."

Enrique injected: "And your wife, Murdock? I see you're wearing a wedding band."

"My wife is dead." Enrique noticed that Murdock lowered his head ever so slightly and rubbed his thumb and forefinger repeatedly over the slender handle of the coffee cup.

"I'm sorry," Enrique continued compassionately. "It was recent?"

"Two years," Murdock replied.

"Cancer?"

"No. An apparent kidnap and murder."

Enrique engaged his eyes. "I sense that you loved her very much, and there's an uncertainty about her death that troubles you acutely." Enrique paused. "Forgive me. Now is not the time to talk of such things. Please, will you both allow me to treat you to Frau Bayer's famous breakfast? I would be honored."

Before either could answer, Frau Bayer arrived with a huge silver serving platter overfilled with fresh croissants, rich local butter, and her famous homemade jams, including Murdock's favorite — plum. Enrique again assumed the duties of host. *He is more than polite, Murdock thought. Polished . . . finely polished . . . genuinely considerate . . . but underneath, I suspect, a brass door handle.* He sensed that they could be friends. *He was right about my uncertainty about Karen's death. The FBI report was complete. At least that was something. But it was too damn complete. The brass usually don't admit their misjudgments, especially when their misjudgments contribute to the death of an agent's wife. Why in Karen's case? Out of deference to me? No. I'm a little fish. It's too neat,"* he thought. *Like Enrique. So neat that there might be some intrinsic messiness to hide. Did the Bureau shelter me from something? What is Enrique's agenda?* The other two were staring at him. "I'm sorry," he said. "My mind wandered. Please forgive me."

"Of course," Enrique assured him, smiling broadly. "I understand."

After a patter of small talk, professor Klugman finished his breakfast, excused himself, and departed. Murdock noticed a leather jacket draped over the fourth chair. "Is that yours?" he asked Enrique.

"Yes," he replied.

Murdock noticed a National Drag Racing Association membership patch. *This may be my hook, he thought.*

"It's unusual to find a Chilean interested in what is almost an entirely American motor sport," he said. "You fellows usually get into the Indy type cars."

"So, you recognize the patch," Enrique said, brightening. "I have a business associate who has owned a top fuel car for several years. I have been with him at many races. Last year I was with him at both the Winter Nationals and the World Finals."

"Ah. The alpha and the omega."

"Yes," Enrique chuckled, "the beginning and the end."

Murdock watched his eyes again. There was a genuine sparkle that he hadn't noticed before. "When I lived in the States, I followed the sport on television," Murdock said.

"I'm putting together a crew. It's rather exciting. Just came from Indianapolis. Bought a shop there."

"Do you own a car?" Murdock asked.

"No. First I'll find the right crew chief. Then we build the car."

Murdock sipped his coffee. "Smart man. It's been done ass backwards a few times with mediocre results."

Frau Bayer approached, walking briskly.

"Herr Perez-Krieger, you have a phone call from Cyprus. Will you take it in your room?"

"Yes, Frau Bayer. You are most kind. Please excuse me, Murdock. We must talk again soon — about drag racing, if you like." Enrique disappeared as quickly as he had appeared.

Have I just hooked him or has he just hooked me? Murdock wondered.

* * *

Snow had begun to fall. Murdock's room had a fireplace, and a roaring fire had been prepared in anticipation of his arrival. He opened his travel bag and took out a book bought three months ago, which he had not yet found time to read. Settling into a comfortable chair, he passed the afternoon reading. The scene outside changed. Through the huge picture window, he watched a blizzard capture the Alps. An ever-deepening carpet of white covered the ground and clung to the branches of the conifers creating an illusion of huge ghosts half hidden in the gloom. He was glad to be here, off the road, already indoors, and warm and comfortable.

At supper he noticed that neither Enrique nor the professor was in the dining room. *Perhaps they dined earlier, he thought.* He saw three men at the table nearest the fireplace. They were dining, all dressed in dinner jackets with formal shirts and black bow ties. *Rather unusual for a ski lodge, Murdock thought.* One, a Hollywood image of an aristocrat, commanded the waiter and was obviously the host. "Who is that," he asked Frau Bayer, discreetly pointing.

Her face flushed. "That is Baron Rupert von Richter," she whispered.

"The monarchist?"

"Ja, ja," she replied. "I don't trust him." She turned quickly and walked away.

Murdock watched them discreetly. They were engaged in animated conversation. The acerbic expression on the Baron's face showed no hint of a smile. Murdock had met men whose eyes, even when mitigated by a smile, conveyed an image of evil. He pictured the Baron with such a smile. *Shouldn't prejudge, he decided.*

The Baron gestured flamboyantly with his arms, his guests acquiescing to his domination of the conversation. Murdock decided that he wouldn't want the Baron as an enemy. He recalled that his close friend, Rudi Benzinger, had mentioned the Baron. Murdock couldn't remember the context, but he remembered vividly the impression that this man might be dangerous. Rudi was a high administrator in the Bavarian State Police. He would know.

Murdock's meal was his favorite — roast pork, bread dumplings in gravy, and red cabbage sweetened in the Bavarian style, hard rolls, and fresh, sweet butter. He didn't like eating alone, but he'd gotten accustomed to it since Karen's death. Supper completed, Murdock rose to return to his room. The Baron and his two cronies were leaning over brandy snifters, the Baron smoking a large black cigar and still talking conspiratorially, as Murdock characterized his demeanor. He chuckled to himself. *Maybe they're hatching up some asinine plot to restore the Bavarian monarchy.* But it was none of his business. Or so it seemed.

Tuesday
November 18

2

Guest rooms at the Zugspitze were bone-chilling cold during the night. The Bayers reduced heat to save energy. Frost covered the windows from top to bottom except for small portholes in the center. Murdock moaned in his sleep. His six-foot-two frame barely fit in the bed. Curled into a fetal position, he had pulled the feather bed up around him, but his feet were still exposed.

The phone rang.

Murdock turned onto his back, his flaming red hair disheveled and half buried in a huge downy pillow. He pulled his feet under the feather bed. "Why do they make beds so blasted short?" he asked himself, half wake. His bare left arm (he didn't believe in pajamas, even in winter) reached out from under the feather bed and grabbed the offending phone. With his right hand he turned the lamp on so he could read his watch. It was 5:23 A.M. "Yeah?" he said gruffly.

"Glad to catch you in your room, Murdock." It was the voice of Richard Laplatenier, who was in charge of the Munich office of Veritus International.

"Where would you expect me to be at this hour?" Murdock demanded.

"We won't discuss that now," Richard replied matter-of-factly. "I hate to interrupt your vacation on the second day, but I need you to look into the disappearance of a monk."

"A monk? Are you kidding?" Murdock injected.

"Not at all. His name is Brother Stephen. He's been missing two days from the monastery near the Zugspitze Hof. St. Luke's. Check with the local police. Meet Allison at T3 at noon for further instructions." *T3* was code. Only the three of them, Murdock, Richard, and Allison could decipher it. It was based on a code that Karen had developed in college. Codes had been her bag.

"Why the cloak and dagger?" Murdock asked.

"Just do it, please. I'll fill you in later."

"Aren't we abrupt at this hour of the morning?" Murdock replied sourly.

"T3 at noon," Richard repeated, ignoring Murdock's mood. "The Bavarian State Police are already investigating. Check it out. See what you can learn before you meet Allison."

Murdock tried to shake the sleep out of his brain. "We're getting involved in an investigation of a missing monk? Who is paying for this? Who is our client?"

"I don't know yet," Richard replied. "I got a phone call from head office in Chicago ten minutes ago putting us on the case, and another from Frankfurt five minutes ago summoning me to one of Harvey's famous staff meetings. But Harvey is not supposed to know anything about this assignment. We are under instructions from Top Dog himself. I think two phone calls in a row at this hour of the morning are curious, don't you?"

"Curious is not the word," Murdock replied. "Top Dog, in Chicago, knows about some obscure monk who has been missing in Bavaria. And he cares. *Weird* might be more appropriate."

"You've assumed the monk is obscure. Is he? We don't know. Let's just get on it," Richard replied.

Murdock detected consternation in Richard's voice. It wasn't like Richard to be devious with his operatives. Richard had not been a peerless investigator, but he was unexcelled as station chief. Management was Richard's expertise. Murdock respected his candor, and the fact that he never failed to have his ducks all in a row. His agents humorously referred to him with no disrespect intended as Sir Richard the Boss. Murdock esteemed candor as one of the more noble human virtues. Honor and loyalty were a close tie for second — or maybe reflections of the first. He had always been honest with Richard and felt that Richard had always reciprocated. The voice on the phone was strained. It didn't sound like the Sir Richard that Murdock knew. *And, Murdock thought, it was not being candid.*

"We *do* have a client, don't we?" Murdock pressed uncomfortably, not entirely convinced that he wanted to know the answer. "The state police are going to ask."

"I think we can assume that we have a client," Richard replied with an uncharacteristic chill. "Now please get to it."

"Assume?" Murdock felt even more uneasy. "Why can't this investigation be handled by someone who is not on vacation? Why couldn't you wait until sunrise to call?"

"The company jet is waiting for me at the airport now," Richard replied impatiently. "I'm off to Frankfurt and to Humble Harvey who probably needs to show off his power again — or he's got wind that we have a confidential assignment from Top Dog, and he wants to discreetly bleed it out of me. Top Dog has made this investigation super confidential, which is like fanning a fire to the information percolators. By the way, Benzinger is on the case."

"Rudi Benzinger?" Murdock was shocked. "Who is this monk that he should attract such high brass from the state police? Rudi doesn't get out of his office suite in Munich any more except to have a few beers with me. And he never hunts for missing persons. He's pretty close to top brass. I can't imagine a scenario that would put him on the search for misplaced monk."

Richard was silent for several seconds, and when he spoke, it was in his old sincere voice that Murdock knew well and trusted. "Answering that question should make it more interesting for you, my friend. Our orders are simply to find the monk, and if harm has come to him, find out who did it and why. And, before you ask, I don't know why we don't leave it to the police. To satisfy my curiosity, see if you can find that out too. Find out why Rudi is there."

"Company policy requires that I have written authority to conduct an investigation."

"Meet Allison at T3 at noon. She'll deliver it to you. I'm out of here. Be careful. Goodbye." Click.

T3 was a castle near Oberammergau, and about a half-hour's drive from Zügspitze Hof. Murdock dressed quickly. Unconsciously, he turned on his pocket police scanner and recognized the voice of his friend, Rudi Benzinger. Murdock was fluent in German, having learned it from his mother. "What have you found, Georg?"

A voice he didn't recognize replied, "A body, Herr Benzinger. It appears to be the missing monk. We are in the meadow by the Liederbach Creek, approximately 1.5 kilometers from the road. It appears that he died from a gunshot wound at close range. Perhaps, sir, you could give us some assistance before you return to Munich."

"Ja, ja, Georg. I am almost there now. I shall join you in a few minutes."

Murdock descended the stairway to the first floor and the door to Bayers' lodgings. He knocked. Herr Bayer, already dressed, opened the door.

"Good morning, Murdock. You are arisen early?"

"Yes. And a good morning to you, Herr Bayer."

"I see you are in a hurry, Murdock. What can I do for you?"

"A monk has been found dead in the meadow, and I've been assigned to investigate. May I borrow one of your snowmobiles?"

"Of course," Herr Bayer replied without hesitation. Take any one of the three. The keys are in the ignitions. Be careful, Murdock. These are dangerous times."

"You're the second person to warn me in the last ten minutes. Thank you."

Arriving at the snowmobile shed, he noticed that the engine was already warm on one of the vehicles. He wondered who had used it at that hour of the morning. He chose it, fired up the engine and roared off. *Who the hell would want to murder a monk, Murdock wondered.*

*   *   *

At first light, the source of the Liederbach Creek, high up the slope of the mountain, was hidden by low, gray clouds. From out of the clouds, the rushing stream cascaded wildly downward, relaxing only after it reached the meadow, where it casually meandered among tall grasses. Ice covered the rocks on both banks. Rudi Benzinger, standing in the meadow with his hands on his hips, breathing deeply, took it all in. He loved every square inch of what he saw, and the smell of the fresh, cold air. His imagination transformed the undulating water, gurgling and splashing over rocks, into childlike voices of water nymphs chanting a bewitching "good morning" to their sisters, the nymphs of the deep woods. Cold water glittered as it caught rays of the early morning sun flickering through tiny breaks in the clouds. Strong winds aloft were chasing the clouds southward into Austria. *It's a splendid morning, he thought.* The Alps, majestic in their picture postcard white from base to the peak, vanished into the clouds. Boughs of tall spruce, pine, and larch sagged under the burden of glistening new snow. *Too much. It almost takes my breath away.* The scene was familiar to him, but he had never become accustomed to it. He thanked God for that. He stared into the cryptic shadows of the deep woods and imagined the Bavaria that the Romans had found when they came as would-be conquerors 2,000 years ago. The woodland floor had been almost unfathomable, hidden in enigmatic shadows. *My ancient ancestors venerated trees. Love of the deep woodlands is seared into the soul of Bavarians by history.*

Unlike the upper winds, the air in the meadow was crisp and almost motionless. Nothing stirred. *So quiet, Rudi mused, that Mother Nature, having painted this scene, must have stepped back to assess her canvas and, startled by what she saw, held her breath in awe of her own creation. Could such striking beauty of sight and sound have created itself accidentally by some random meeting of molecules? No. Wood spirits are merely legends. Perchance there is God.*

Rudi had been born and raised Landshut in lower Bavaria. He and his family had skied the Alps every winter as far back as he could remember. But even to a native who has seen it countless times, the clean, sharp beauty of each first snowfall was still startling. But, alas, he was not an artist come to paint the pristine scene, but a policeman standing at the scene of a crime. And a policeman who was hungry. His stomach told him that it was time for breakfast.

Georg noticed the enigmatic smile. "What is it, Herr Benzinger?" he asked.

"I was thinking about having breakfast at Zugspitze Hof Lodge, Georg. You shall be my guest . . . please?"

"Ja, ja. Thank you. At my pay grade I cannot afford such luxury, Herr Benzinger. Thank you. You are most gracious."

"Pay grades change. Do not be discouraged. You are young and a good policeman." Rudi smiled. *And a good politician too, he thought.* "You are learning investigative work quickly. You have a talent for it. I have heard your name mentioned favorably in Munich. I am certain your career will advance directly."

"Thank you, Herr Benzinger." Georg was embarrassed by praise. His face turned serious. "What do you make of it, sir?"

"It is rather curious, I think. When did you arrive, Georg?"

"Half hour before you, Herr Benzinger." He looked down at the body wedged in the rocks at the edge of the stream, almost hidden by snow and ice. "It is difficult to estimate how long he has been here, sir. I found the body as you see it. Most of it under water, as now. Ice formed around it. The left profile of the face was above the water, as now. Notice, Herr Benzinger, that the water in the left ear is frozen solid. I found those cross-country skis leaning against that birch in orderly fashion, and his coat over there, under that spruce, open, lying in the snow as you see it now." He turned to the photographers. "Are you finished?" he asked. They affirmed that they were. Georg rolled the body onto its back. "He was shot through the heart. Close range. No wallet. Robbery is the obvious motive. He appears to be the missing monk . . . Brother Stephen, I believe. I met him once. There is a small notebook in the pocket of his robe," he continued, officiously handing it to Rudi.

Rudi flipped through it quickly. It was a small, leather-bound holder in which pages could be inserted. Most of the pages were covered with mathematical equations in pencil. One page appeared to be partially ripped out. He couldn't tell whether the removal was recent. Perhaps forensic could tell. "So, Georg," Rudi probed, "it appears to you to be robbery and murder."

"Ja, ja, Herr Benzinger. It seems so to me." He was discomforted that Rudi had asked a question that demanded such an obvious answer. "But — "

"But what?"

Georg cocked his head. "Murder and robbery is what it appears to be, yet, would a monk be carrying much money, sir?"

Rudi kept his thoughts to himself. *If only things were always what they appeared to be.* After twenty-three years as a criminal investigator for the Bavarian State Police, he knew better than to jump to obvious conclusions early in an investigation. But then again, sometimes the truth is the obvious. Sometimes it is so obvious that you cannot see it. "It is invariably wise to look beyond the obvious until the obvious becomes so compelling that it cannot be ignored, Georg."

"We are indeed fortunate to have you here, Herr Benzinger. Your lecture on motive yesterday was unequaled. And it was good of you to come out here this morning in the cold. Perhaps you can remain and assist us." Georg hoped that he could not. This was *his* big chance.

Rudi frowned. "I wish that I could," he replied. It was no longer his job to do the actual criminal investigations, only to supervise the local supervisors. *I appreciate the larger salary, he admitted to himself, and the comfort of a warm office on a cold day, but I miss the action. There's little excitement behind a desk.* His instincts were tingling. "There's more here than meets the eye, Georg. I can't put my finger on it, but I advise you not to jump to effortless conclusions. Alarm bells are ringing. Not all robbers want money. Taking the wallet may be a cover. What was this monk carrying? Someone at the monastery must know."

"Ja, ja, Herr Benzinger. I shall make prompt inquiries."

"I would like to help, Georg, but unfortunately I must return to Munich. Commander Weiss has set a conference for early morning — one of those that we must attend when we arrive at the point where we can afford breakfast at the Zugspitze Hof Lodge, Georg."

Georg laughed.

They heard the sound of a snowmobile approaching from the trail that leads to the slopes and Zugspitze Hof. It came to a stop on the other side of the creek. A man warmly bundled, his face hidden by a ski mask, killed the engine and dismounted.

"Hey, Rudi. Good morning. What the hell are you doing here?"

"Murdock?" Rudi exclaimed half to himself and half to a puzzled Georg. Murdock pulled off the ski mask. "Ja, ja, Murdock," Rudi shouted jovially. "Good morning, my friend. What are *you* doing here?"

Murdock leaped the stream.

Rudy laughed. "You are more agile than I thought."

Murdock curled up the right corner of his mouth into his patented half-smile. "Maybe the snow nymphs of your legends gave me a goose," he chuckled.

"Ja, ja. Maybe that could be," Rudi said, still laughing. "I thought for sure Georg and I would have to pull you from the water. I confess I'm somewhat disappointed. That would have been a sight to see."

"For you but not for me. Good to see you again, Rudi, my friend."

"And I you," Rudi exclaimed sincerely, turning to Georg. "Georg, please meet my good friend Murdock McCabe, late of the FBI, and now with the Munich office of Veritus Investigations International."

"Please call me Murdock." He offered his hand, which Georg accepted.

Georg smiled a professional smile, and bowed ever so slightly. "Herr Benzinger has frequently mentioned your work in his lectures. It is a great privilege to meet an eminent investigator."

"And I've heard your name mentioned in Munich," Murdock replied, sensing that flattery might buy a friend that he might need later. However, the remark was met with a dusty smile. Georg detested private detectives.

"Murdock has been with Veritus for two years, since he resigned from the FBI. When he was with the FBI, I was a detective. We worked on several cases together and we became close friends. He is a man worthy of your trust. If he discovers criminal activity during his investigations, he does not hold back from the police. You can count on that."

Georg did not ask why Murdock left the FBI. *I shall withhold judgment, he decided, until I know why.*

A vigorous snow shower enveloped them and then dissolved as suddenly as it had begun. A few more rays of sun danced through the holes in the clouds. One fell upon the unfortunate monk's body.

Rudi turned and walked along the Liederbach Creek, motioning for Murdock to follow. When they were alone, Rudi said: "Tell me Murdock, my friend, why are you here, and how is it that you're here so soon?"

Their eyes met.

"What do you mean?" Murdock asked casually, but inwardly on guard. He wished that he knew the answer.

"I mean that, in this weather, it is a long drive from Munich at night. The body was discovered two hours ago. You arrived here only fifteen minutes after I did. Such facts are the essence of mystery, are they not, my friend?"

"Well, Rudi old chum, this mystery is easily solved," Murdock answered firmly, exhibiting more confidence than his knowledge justified. "I'm a guest at Zugspitze Hof, as you already know. Sir Richard the Boss called at an ungodly hour this morning and asked me to cut short my vacation and investigate the disappearance of a monk. I rolled out of bed, turned on the police scanner, and heard my old friend's voice. I guessed that you had made my job easy by finding my missing monk. Was I correct?"

"Ja, ja. I think so. With a bullet through his heart. Georg met him once, and has tentatively identified him. His name is Brother Stephen."

They returned to where Georg was standing.

Murdock shook his head. "I'm sorry to hear that. He *is* the man I'm looking for. What was he doing here? Do you know?"

"You will recall that the monastery is not far from here — across the meadow and up the slope to the tree line. What do you know about him, Murdock?"

"Very little. Richard didn't have much information. What can you tell me?"

Rudi looked at Georg.

"Not much," Georg responded. "He had been a scientist and industrialist. Before he came to the monastery, he made a fortune in semiconductors, in the Silicon Valley, I believe. I have heard that all of the monks are scientists, except the abbot, Brother Martin, and Brother Gustav. Martin may be the only theologian, and Gustav had been a professor of classical literature. A highly unusual group of monks, I would say. We shall ask Brother Martin to formally identify the body. He may be able to tell us what Brother Stephen was doing here."

Turning to Georg, Murdock asked: "If they're scientists, why are they monks?"

"I only know the rumors in the village, sir," Georg replied. "Apparently these monks believe that scientific research is frequently morally irresponsible, and that it often inflicts great evil on the world. They evidently pray for the world and do what they consider to be morally responsible science."

A cynical smile crossed Murdock's face. "That's interesting. Couldn't they do that without becoming monks?" He stared down at the rough brown woolen cowl that partially covered the dead monk's head. "Who would want to kill a monk?" Murdock wondered out loud. "What did he have worth killing for? There's no profit in killing the average monk. Find the motive and we narrow the list of suspects — a list that right now includes the whole world except us — hopefully."

Rudi laughed. "Ja, and I cannot be sure of you."

"Maybe," Murdock continued, "somebody's wife was sneaking under the robe. Could you really suspect me?"

"Tell me, please, who pays Veritus its huge fee to find a missing monk?"

"Really, Rudi, I don't think Richard knows yet. You know how straight he is with me — and with you too. He got orders from someone over Harvey's head. I know you're uncomfortable with that. I'll try to find out today."

"From over the head of the district manager? But, my friend," Rudi asked, looking distractedly upstream, "does this not complicate the puzzle?"

"Is there movement there?" Murdock asked, following Rudi's gaze into the thicket at the far edge of the meadow.

"Perhaps it was a deer," Georg suggested. "I shall investigate immediately, Herr Benzinger, if you will excuse me."

"Perhaps it was a deer wearing a green nylon jacket," Rudi said. Take my snowmobile, Georg. See if this deer has left any droppings. I shall ride with our American Sherlock Holmes. Join us for breakfast at Zugspitze Hof Lodge, if you are able. Come, Murdock. We shall leave the unfortunate monk to the medical examiners — and to the proper local authorities. Besides, it is not civilized to go without breakfast."

Deftly, they both leaped across the creek. Murdock fired up the engine of his snowmobile. Rudi seated himself behind him, and the machine roared off toward the trail. Quickly the meadow disappeared behind them. Surging up an incline with power to spare, they soon were encompassed by the tall conifers. Murdock slowed. The trail narrowed to where it was barely wide enough for them to pass. Murdock was concerned by Rudi's suspicions. Last Saturday night, over a few beers at Hofbrauhaus, Murdock had told Rudi about Richard's offer of a two week skiing vacation at Zugspitze Hof Lodge. Rudi knew Richard well. Richard was seldom generous with the company's money.

Rudi wondered how much Murdock knew and wasn't telling him. He remembered a twenty-five watt light bulb in the security hall that led to Richard's office. *Richard is frugal, Rudi acknowledged. Maybe he just likes Murdock. But would he open the door? Now everyone will expect the same treatment. Richard believed his people were well-paid. Successful investigations were what they were paid for. Why would he give a bonus to Murdock for what he was already paid well to do? Was the vacation offer a deception? Did Richard put Murdock on station here? Did Richard know the monk would be missing? If the assignment came down from Veritus headquarters in Chicago, is it not unusual that it was routed directly to Richard without going through Harvey's office in Frankfurt? Does Murdock really not know? Is he holding out? No. Our relationship of trust is too important to Murdock for him to risk it. Unless this is really big. How much really big would it take?*

*   *   *

Georg eased back the throttle of the snowmobile. The movement had come from brush at the south rim of the meadow. He stopped and dismounted. Slogging through thick underbrush, Georg found an area where the snow had been disturbed. No footprint could be distinguished. The person had come on skis and gone on skis. *Possibly a casual observer, but I should not leap to the obvious conclusion.* Georg searched the immediate area. *He—or she—was careful. No droppings. No cigarette butt. No match. No mitten. No anything. Almost too careful for a casual observer.*

Georg remounted the snowmobile. Revving the engine, he crushed through the brush and followed the trail left by the skier. Presently, he came upon the open area of the first slope. Several people were riding the ski lift. None wore a green jacket. One was descending, but his jacket was orange. Beyond this point there was a myriad of ski tracks. Pursuit was hopeless.

* * *

The trail widened again as Murdock and Rudi neared the lodge. Rudi turned the coincidences over in his mind. *The coincidence of Murdock's being here is but the first of several curiosities. Commander Weiss has never sent anyone of my rank to the provinces to give seminars to the troops. That is the second curiosity. Herr Weiss told me that no one could teach the subject as well as I, but that was not true. And Weiss knew that I knew it. The Commander is sometimes obscure. If I should receive orders to stay and take charge of this investigation, which would be the third curiosity, this might be the beginning of a very fascinating day. How could Herr Weiss have known, when he gave me the assignment, that the monk would be missing? He couldn't have. But what if he did? That would pose the most curious curiosity. By far!"*

Murdock brought the snowmobile to a stop near the restaurant door. The clear, cold, fresh air had made them famished. Without another word, they both dismounted and made for the door.

⊰ 3 ⊱

Snow had begun falling shortly after noon on Monday, and by late afternoon Munich was in the grip of a blizzard. Near dawn on Tuesday, the snow relented and moved on. The streets of the old city sparkled like fields of diamonds in lamplight. Except for a few automobiles snaking their way among a labyrinth of vehicles stranded in awkward positions overnight, the streets were deserted. A light wind, brutally cold, swirled the snow into mini-blizzards, which occasionally reduced visibility to near zero. Few pedestrians were in sight. Allison, dressed warmly in a silk-lined cashmere full-length coat with a cashmere scarf wrapped around her head and shoulders, trudged cautiously through deep snow past the Augustinerkloster and eastward on Kaufingerstrasse. She was tall for a woman, two inches short of six feet. She had bought the coat in Montreal where they know what winter is. She was warm. In the Marienplatz city workers were clearing walkways with determined German efficiency. Her incisive brown eyes peered out from under her scarf as she rearranged it to keep the flurries from wetting her shoulder-length brown hair. Knee-high brown leather boots provided protection from the snow-devils that swirled around her. *I'm glad I took the hotel room, she thought. If I'd gone to my apartment in the suburbs last night, I would've been stranded there this morning. Besides, the company picked up the hotel bill.* Richard had phoned at 5:45 A.M. Within a half hour she was in the hotel elevator calculating that the walk to the office would take thirteen minutes. When she maneuvered herself through the revolving door and assessed the condition of the sidewalk, she revised her estimate to eighteen minutes. *Too much hurry, hurry, she thought. I must kick that habit of forever calculating time estimates.*

Her progress accelerated when she reached an area where city workers had already cleared the snow. *Perhaps sixteen minutes will do it. There I go again.* She rounded the corner of the Rathaus — a city hall which, in her mind, wore its almost two hundred years with ineffectual grace. To Allison, the Rathaus, the seat of Munich's city government, is a profoundly ugly building. But then, neo-Gothic architecture held no charm for her. To her, its only redeeming feature was an open-air café where she spent many pleasurable hours lunching with friends during the warmer months. But not today. There would be no street musicians today, nor the myriad of artists around the fountain entertaining crowds. Few tourists will gather at noon as the carillon chimes. Today it is winter, and Allison didn't much care for it.

She passed the Alter Hof, and, in the middle of the block, came upon the crystal-clean glass double doorway, which opened into the company's elegant Munich office. It crossed her mind that Veritus Investigations International was not for the impoverished. The office normally would not open for two hours. She had called ahead. Josef, the doorman, was waiting for her. He unlocked the door promptly and welcomed her with his usual flourish and decorum. He had been doorman for twenty-six years. His military style uniform was impeccable, and he took great pride in it. Her four years experience in the country had taught her that Germans love to wear uniforms. Josef promptly locked the door behind her.

Passing the main bank of elevators, she turned down a narrow corridor marked "Employees Only," stopped in front of a single smaller elevator, and quickly tapped her PIN into the keypad. Rattling doors opened begrudgingly. The compartment had space for two people only if they had watched their diets. Encapsulated, she began counting aloud in German to salve her claustrophobia. *Why are elevators in this town so lilliputian and so damn slow? They're worse than London's.* She was fond of brooding before breakfast — it was best to get it over with for the day. Mercifully, the "muscle," as she called the management offices, was only two floors up. She estimated forty-four seconds. In fluent German she counted 42, 43, 44, 45. The elevator stopped. For another five disconcerting seconds nothing happened. Inexorably, the doors, like a kidnapper loath to release his victim, slowly opened. Allison sighed and exited promptly. After its doors closed behind her, she was encapsulated again — now in a small hallway barely five feet by five feet, with a table and a lamp having only twenty-five watts of illumination. It had no window. Next to an imposing solid oak door was another keypad. Again she tapped her PIN. A random number appeared on a digital readout. She subtracted her age, thirty-six, from that number, and tapped in the result. Last month she had been impressed when, on her birthday, the contraption had reacted correctly to her age change. The door unlocked. She walked in and closed it firmly behind her. On the intercom she called Peter at the night desk to inform him that she was on station.

"Hi, Al," he said brightly.

"Hi, your own self, night bird," she retorted, slightly disgusted at his unfailing cheerfulness this early in the morning.

"We don't sound like we're awake yet, do we?" Peter went on.

"We? Speak for yourself. It isn't normal for a human being to be cheerful this early in the morning."

"I hear rumor," he continued, "that there's a bit of snow outside."

"Yes, Peter. As usual, you are most adept at the art of understatement. That's like saying that you heard a rumor there was a fire in Hell," Allison bantered, grumpily. She hadn't had breakfast yet.

"Now that you mention it, I've heard that rumor too. Did you keep your room?"

"Yes, Peter. The company is hitting for two nights."

"You got two beds?"

"Sure. You want to borrow one?"

"If you don't mind, Al. I'll be out of there and back to work before you'll need the room again," Peter proclaimed enthusiastically. Peter was a child of enthusiasms.

"The exuberance of youth. How can you get so excited about sleeping in a hotel? You're not planning on entertaining company in my room, are you?" Allison chuckled to herself. Last week he had met a *Jungfrau* about his age with golden hair and two *grosse Busten* that invited young men's eyes to bulge, and produced pure envy in some more normally endowed women.

"I've never holed up in a fancy hotel like that before. Can I charge meals to the company?"

"What do you mean by 'holed up'?" Allison asked suspiciously.

"Huh? Oh. No pun intended. That would've been a crude one at that. She is with her parents at their home on the Chiemsee this week. They'll be skating on the lake. Besides, we haven't done anything like that yet," Peter replied matter-of-factly.

"And you have known her a whole week? Sometimes I worry about you," Allison said in mock concern. "The innocence of youth. Maybe you work too hard. I'll phone the hotel and tell them to give you my key. But be out of there by six."

"*Ja, ja, meine Kapitan.*"

"Don't give me that *Kapitan* crap. Just be out of there by six. And when I walk past your office, stop ogling my buns behind my back. I'm too old for you, Sonny."

"How did you know that I ogle your buns?"

"I didn't. I do now. Bye." She hung up the intercom.

The office of "Sir Richard the Boss" adjoined hers and the door between the two was never locked. Allison entered and seated herself behind his desk. His window faced the street. Trucks were being loaded with snow with determined efficiency. She drew the drapes carefully, making sure they overlapped in the middle. The safe was hidden behind a hinged painting of the Zugspitze, the highest mountain in Germany. She turned the painting on its hinges, dialed the code, and opened the door. Inside on top there was a sealed manila envelope with her name on it. She removed it and then reversed the procedure. She unsealed it. A note from Richard was inside.

Allison:

Please listen to the enclosed tape. It's the conversation that I had with Murdock just before I called you. I must run. Harvey wants me in Frankfurt immediately. The Company jet is waiting for me at Riem. Must be big stuff! The tape will tell you all I know. Sorry about the mystery. I'll phone you by 11:30 on your encrypted cellular and fill you in on what I have learned. We have to tell Murdock something or he'll be furious. Probably is anyway. He thinks I'm holding out on him, but I'm not. I received instructions from Top Dog through the head office in Chicago, with instructions to keep it top secret — even from Harvey. I don't know why. I'm in the dark so far.

Top Dog wants Murdock to do a complete workup on the missing monk, Brother Stephen, and also Brother Antonio. If Stephen was kidnapped, Murdock should find out who did it and what we can do to set him free. If he is dead, Murdock should find the killer. Meet Murdock at Schloss Linderhof at noon. Deliver to him written authority to investigate. If you can, convince Murdock that I don't know why we are involved in a criminal investigation. I'll tell him as soon as I know. I'm to communicate the report only to Top Dog. Communicate these instructions face to face. I have to run. Be good. It's a blue dog day. Bye.

Richard.

P.S. Tell Terry as little as possible. Just enough to minimize his mouth.

By tradition, Terry was third in command in Munich, after Richard and Allison, although it was not included in his job description. His regular job was the agent in charge of the information desk, which handled all intracompany communications. Allison and Murdock called him The Weasel — behind his back.

Lucky Richard, Allison mused sarcastically. He gets to have one of those famous lunches with Harvey Specter, that disgusting little slug of a district manager in Frankfurt to whom Richard reports. Only last month, while she had been attending a conference in Frankfurt, Harvey had treated her to one of those fabulous two-hour lunches and then, on the way back to the office, stopped at a fashionable boutique on Frankfurt's Goethestrasse so that she could help him pick an alluring night garment for his mistress — even though she knew his wife. Harvey had explained that her participation in this activity fell under the standard company policy of confidentiality. On the good side, she had decided at the time, he had accepted her as a person he could trust. On the bad side, she had feared, she might receive the garment herself by messenger later in the day. She hadn't. To his credit, Harvey had concurred in Richard's appointment of her as assistant station chief. Harvey didn't have a reputation for enticing subordinates, but no woman had ever owed a management position to the fact that he had acquiesced to her appointment. Allison never felt comfortable in his presence. It wasn't anything he said. It was just Harvey. He had dirty eyes.

A sly grin crossed Allison's face. She wondered where Harvey took Richard after those lunches when he's in Munich. Wherever it was, she'd noticed that Richard never complained. There were elegant whorehouses down the street near the Hofbrauhaus, which were reputed to cater to any lifestyle one could afford. She wondered if everyone, like herself, had a secret urge to see what those places were like. She resolved that some night she would ask her friend, Moira, to take her on a sight-seeing tour. But she couldn't picture Richard in one of *those*. Harvey yes. A whorehouse seemed like part of the essence of Harvey.

Which brought to mind Moira. She was more than a friend. She was an extremely capable agent. Allison remembered that Moira's report was locked in her top desk drawer. She extracted it. *It's handy to have a lesbian as an undercover agent, she reflected. And Moira's salary reflects her special skills. She learns the peccadilloes of her targets. Targets always seem to relax their guards in the intimacy of the love nest, so Moira latches on to their co-nesters, and literally trains them as subagents. When money talks, secrecy walks.*

Allison returned to her office and slipped into the comfort of her rich, Spanish leather executive chair, dialed Otto's across the street, and ordered her usual croissants accompanied by margarine and raspberry jam. Josef knows. He will send them up on the dumbwaiter labeled "Documents Only." She searched the eastern sky. Dawn had not yet made its appearance.

She switched on her desk lamp, unlocked her top desk drawer, and extracted Moira's report.

Moira's primary assignment for the past three weeks had been to hang out at the Mädchenhaus Café — a popular gathering place for Munich's lesbians, and become amiable with one Patti Dale. The immediate goal of the assignment was to develop a confidential relationship with Patti and take the time necessary to become her confidante. *Moira's suave. It should work. The puzzler is that Richard, who had the highest clearance from the company headquarters in Chicago and could receive the most confidential information, didn't know the reason for the liaison, nor did he know who the client was. He was blindly following orders from Harvey. Richard didn't know whether Harvey knew, or whether Harvey had concocted this as one of his personal projects.* She opened the envelope.

To Allison

From Moira

Patti has taken a liking to me, but she's holding me at a distance. For the first few days, I worried that I'd lost it. I put out the word that I don't wear panties under my dress. Maybe that will soften her. The thought of it turns some on. Unfortunately, Patti and I haven't exactly become pals. We have a conversation in passing occasionally. I must move discreetly with her. She says she works as a librarian in the English language library at BMW. I don't know whether that's for real, or whether it's a fancy name for a file clerk, or if she even works there, but that's what she says. Do they have an English library at BMW? I suggest that you make a discreet inquiry of your contact there.

I hear that she'll be out of town until Friday, but I'll continue to hang out at the Mädchenhaus so that my presence looks cool.

Patti has a part-time lover who hangs there. Naturally, the lover will become jealous of me if I get too close. I need to smooth that out. In order to handle the lover or Patti when she gets back, I may be expected to do more than I want for sanitary reasons if nothing else. Does Richard understand that there are limits to my commitment, or is the company offering an extra-attractive hazardous duty package?

Please try to convince Richard that I need time off to do some skiing. Meanwhile, for the next few days I'll be in Regensburg working on the Herzog Insurance matter. See you Friday. By the way, in regard to Patti Dale, what are we looking for?"

Allison shook her head, a slow smile crossing her face. *I wish I knew. Now we have two mysteries.*

She filed Moira's report, sat back in her chair, and mused. *In all of the years I've been with Veritus, I've never supervised a single investigation in which I didn't know the name of the client and the purpose of the investigation. Now I have two—Patti Dale, and the missing monk, Brother Stephen. Coincidence? I don't believe in coincidences. Always assume that it is not a coincidence until the investigation leaves no other conclusion. How could there be a connection between this lesbian and that monk? And why is Murdock's investigation of the wandering monk to be kept secret from Harvey?*

Allison made a notation that she and Richard should sit down with Moira when she returned from Regensburg. Although he admired her skill as an investigator, Richard felt uncomfortable with Moira. He had placed her under Allison's supervision. *I think he tries not to be bigoted. Sexual orientation is his exception.*

She fired up her computer and ran through the items on her daily reminder. "Phone Rudi Benzinger." *I'll phone him this evening and invite him to my house party this weekend. He's a delightful man—so polite and gentlemanly. He doesn't seem to have any lady friends. Maybe he was hurt badly once. Actually, I think he's shy. That's odd for such a successful policeman. Maybe he's just shy with women. Murdock is tight-lipped about Rudi's personal life, though.*

Murdock is special. He has everything a woman could reasonably want. It would be easy for the old flame to be ignited again—at least on my part. I don't know that he ever had a flame for anyone other than Karen, and she was my best friend. If I had met him before Jerr—. Or if he had met me before Karen—. I guess we can't build a life on what might have been. I suspect he's interested in me. But never mess with the hired help. If ever he makes a career change, or if I'm no longer his supervisor . . . Oh well. I'm reasonably happy. I have a well-paying job with plenty of responsibility. Veritus is an equal opportunity outfit. I should move up soon and have my own station. She noticed that there was another page to Moira's report—a postscript.

"P.S. If you talk to Murdock, tell him that I have the information that he wanted."

Allison smiled. As co-workers, Moira and Murdock got along fine. When Richard had first considered putting them together on a case, he had asked Murdock what he thought of Moira. "Great. No problem," had been Murdock's instant response. Murdock respected ability.

The bell on the dumbwaiter rang. She opened the door to the dumbwaiter and extracted her breakfast. Reaching into the bottom left drawer of her credenza, she extracted a red gingham tablecloth—laid it over her desk—spread out the breakfast fare—and dug in. The coffee was black, strong, and very hot. She luxuriated in the first sip. *Wonderful, she thought. Brood no more.*

The "blue dog" in Richard's message was a code that meant there was another message—hidden in case Terry had gotten the combination to Richard's wall safe. Palm up, she reached into the shallow center drawer of her desk—the blue dog location. A thin envelope was taped to the bottom of the desk top. She extracted it. Addressed to Murdock, she was to deliver it personally. Richard hadn't sealed the envelope, which meant she could and should read it. Allison extracted the memo.

Dear Murdock:

Brother Stephen was working on a highly secret project that Top Dog feels must be protected. He didn't tell me what it was, if he knows. Talk to Brother Martin, the abbot at St. Luke's Monastery, which is located near Zugspitze Hof. When he feels comfortable, ask him about the chip. I don't know what that means. Our client wants to know whether Brother Stephen had the chip on him when he was kidnapped. And he wants Stephen found.

Report your results to no one except Allison or myself. We have instructions from the highest authority to keep this even from Harvey. Mention the chip to no one.

Richard

Allison returned the document to its envelope. *The message was written by hand so that we can feel secure that each word had actually come from him. Richard was retired from Swiss military intelligence, so he's good at cloak and dagger.*

Her watch read nearly 7:30. Terry would arrive soon. *He always arrives early and leaves late,* she mused. *The little weasel doesn't want to miss anything. He's Harvey's weasel. And who knows who else's—higher than Harvey. He's after my job or Richard's. Or maybe even Harvey's, if he could compromise him. Harvey deserves him. He forced Richard to make Terry responsible for contacting and coordinating with other Veritus offices worldwide—an ideal position for a master rumormonger and back stabber to do the most damage. And, I must admit, the little weasel is good at it. He focuses on it with deliberate intensity. Carefully crafted half-truths are his ammunition. I must never let him know about my background with Murdock. It would only induce his vulgar smile, and he'd insert some dirty innuendoes on his own little worldwide misinformation web.*

Allison had fallen hopelessly in love with Murdock during their freshman year at the State University of New York at Buffalo—hopeless because he fell in love with Karen, her roommate and best friend. Murdock introduced Allison to *his* best friend, Jerrard Blair, who promptly fell in love with Allison. The four were inseparable through the remaining three years of college. A double wedding followed graduation. Murdock and Jerr went to the University of Michigan law school. Karen followed Murdock and worked on a master's degree in linguistics. Fascinated by encryption, Karen had made up fun codes that the four of them used to confound their friends. Allison had gone on to Michigan State for a master's in law enforcement administration. After law school Murdock and Jerr went into the FBI. Jerr had been assigned to Seattle. Jerr had wanted Allison to come with him, but Allison had accepted an offer from Veritus Investigations International in Chicago. After two years of almost total separation, she and Jerr decided to call it quits. They parted best of friends, but Allison knew Jerr was hurt very deeply. That troubled her. But if Terry knew that she had been in love with Murdock in college, he would manufacture dirty reasons for the divorce, and his version would take legs worldwide.

I shall be especially pleasant to The Weasel today. That'll aggravate him. She poked his number on the intercom. He answered.

"Good morning, Terry. I'm glad that you found your way through the blizzard."

"Good morning," he replied cheerfully. "I believed the forecast so I took a hotel room last night."

"I'm certainly glad that you did," Allison said brightly. "We could be the only ones here today, and I have to leave when the roads clear a bit."

"Where are you off to?" Terry asked, trying not to seem too curious.

"Richard is meeting Harvey in Frankfurt, but you probably already know that." No response. "He's sent me on an errand. I'll be gone most of the day, so it'll be up to you to keep the office in operation. Do you feel comfortable with that?"

"Yes. No problem."

"Good. It'll be a useful experience for you to be in charge, even though there may be no one here to be in charge of. We must keep communications with Frankfurt and our other offices open. It's good that we have someone like you that we can rely on."

"Allison, because you and Richard leave me in charge when neither of you is here, it'd be helpful if I knew the code that you and Richard use. Murdock understands it. I'm his boss when you guys aren't here. Shouldn't I know it?"

"What code?" Allison asked coolly.

"The word code. The one Murdock's wife developed when you guys were in college." He sounded like a hurt puppy.

Already he knows too much. "Someone has been telling you cloak and dagger stories. Why would Richard, Murdock, and I have a code? Why would we need one? And, if such a code existed, why wouldn't we share it with you — our number three man? I'll let you know when I leave. Bye." Beep.

By 10:30 the road condition reports suggested that she could get through to Linderhof. She might be late, but Murdock would wait. She put on her coat and wrapped the cashmere scarf around her neck. Before taking the elevator to the company garage, she beeped Terry on the intercom."

"Yes," he answered pleasantly — almost sweetly. He was already feeling a sensation of power.

"I am leaving now," Allison said. "By the way, Terry, if Richard calls, will you give him a message for me?"

"Sure."

"Just tell him that I said it was a blue dog day. He'll know what I mean."

⤎ 4 ⤏

The restaurant at Zugspitze Hof was comfortably warm. Fresh beech logs fueled a bed of hot coals, and excited whirlwinds of sparks playfully chased one another up the chimney. The professor, Murdock, and Rudi were seated at the same table, which the Baron Rupert von Richter had occupied last night. A buzz of skiers' voices filled the room. Rudi was getting acquainted with the professor. Murdock, who had been staring across the room, suddenly excused himself and, without waiting for a response, abruptly left. Rudi and the professor looked at each other blankly.

"Murdock can be impulsive," Rudi said. It stretched the truth. Rudi knew that Murdock was seldom impulsive, but he felt he must say something. "So, how long have you known him, professor? I do not believe he had mentioned your name."

The professor smiled warmly. "No. He wouldn't have. We met yesterday. Here in the restaurant. For breakfast, as a matter of fact. I hope we shall become better acquainted. And you, Herr Benzinger, what is your occupation?"

"I am an administrator — a division chief of the Bavarian State Police — at our headquarters in Munich."

Rudi observed that the professor appeared flustered. The older man had fixated on the fireplace. Their eyes met. The fluster was gone.

"Ah," the professor said, brightening, "I have never had the pleasure of meeting a policeman socially — not that I have anything against policemen, you understand. Policemen are usually pragmatic people — I suppose — and I wouldn't think they're interested in the arcane debates of dull intellectual types. But meeting you is most interesting. I know little about policemen except the stereotypes portrayed on television. Are you here on vacation, or are you investigating some dark deed?"

"Yesterday, I gave a seminar to the local detectives in Garmisch-Partenkirchen. I knew Murdock was here, so I decided to take a day's vacation and surprise him. We are close friends going back to the days when he was with the FBI."

Murdock returned. "Excuse me," he said. "You two, please sit a little closer. I'd like to take your picture."

They moved closer.

"Smile!" he commanded in such a loud voice that everyone in the restaurant looked at him.

Rudi observed that the camera was pointed slightly over their heads.

Murdock re-seated himself. "Professor. Please. Discreetly look at the man in the green plaid sport shirt next to the stairway sitting with the two women."

"Yes. I see him."

"Do you know him?"

"No."

Rudi spoke in a low voice. "Obviously you *do* know him, Murdock. Who is he?"

"Doctor Frederick L. Bauer from Huntington, Indiana. Last week, when I tracked him in Stuttgart, he was wearing a neck brace and getting about in an electric wheelchair. He claims he was grievously injured — crippled — in an auto accident. The other driver is insured by one of our clients."

"He doesn't seem all that bad," the professor injected seriously.

Rudi chucked. "I agree."

"The trial is next month. It's a stroke of luck finding him here. I need to take some photos of him on the slopes and e-mail them to Chicago. Unless I miss my guess, the jury won't buy a miracle cure — especially when he returns to the neck brace for the trial." He turned toward the professor. "I'm afraid it's my job to make this a cruel world for some of its inhabitants."

Rudi grinned. "Tell your client's attorneys that I will make a good witness if they will buy my airline ticket to America. Besides, you may need my protection when you testify. Doctor Fraud may pick up his wheelchair and throw it at you." Rudi turned to the professor. "Are you a skier?" he asked.

"No. I've never skied. Judging by the clothing, I may be the only nonskier in the restaurant this morning. I've come here to visit a friend."

"Is your friend staying here at the Lodge?"

"No," the professor replied. "He lives in the monastery beyond the ski slopes. Are you familiar with it?" They nodded in the affirmative. "I have an appointment to visit him in a few hours."

"You need an appointment to visit a friend?" Rudi probed.

"Under the circumstances, yes. He's a monk."

"And his name?"

"Stephen Armbruster. Brother Stephen as he likes to call himself. He's gotten into that religious stuff." Rudi and Murdock stared at each other.

Rudi's eyes met the professor's. Rudi calmly inquired, "I take it you are not a religious man?"

"No," the professor replied abruptly.

Rudi smiled kindly. "Forgive me," he said. "Being a policeman makes me irresistibly nosy." Without waiting for a response, he continued. "You are an interesting man, professor. How is it that a nonreligious man became friends with a monk?"

Murdock watched the professor's reaction. This is a police matter, so it wasn't Murdock's place to speak. Rudi will drop the bomb when he's ready. Murdock wondered whether the professor knew about the murder. He couldn't read the answer in the professor's face. *If he knows, he's unnaturally composed. If he doesn't know, we may learn something from how he takes the news.*

Murdock refilled their coffee cups. Rudi calmly added cream and sugar. The professor added sugar. Murdock took his black.

Frau Bayer appeared with a basket of steaming pastries. "We have croissants fresh from the oven," she announced cheerfully. "You must eat," she said placing warm croissants on their plates. "It is such sad news about the monk."

"What monk?" the professor asked.

Frau Bayer's eyes met Murdock's. His signaled for her to leave.

Rudi put his hand on top the Professor's hand. "I am afraid your friend is dead." The professor's hand didn't move.

"Dead?" he exclaimed. "Dead? Impossible. When I saw him Monday morning, he seemed to be in very good health. Yes, indeed. Excellent health. He seemed the picture of health. We talked amiably for over two hours. He didn't mention any illness. This is totally unexpected. He is — was — thirty years younger than I. Was it his heart?"

"Yes," Rudi said. "His heart suddenly stopped. So you think he was well when you left him Monday?"

"Why, yes. Perfectly. As much as I could tell. He was the picture of health, as I said — didn't I?"

Rudi extracted a small note pad and a pencil from his inside coat pocket. The professor's eyes followed his every move. "That was on Monday — yesterday — you say. And what time did you leave him?"

"About 11:00 or 11:15," he replied. "Am I being investigated?"

"No," Rudi replied. "But you can help, if you will."

Murdock concluded that the professor was genuinely surprised, but he wasn't certain that Rudi had reached the same conclusion.

"But why would a policeman need to know these things?" the professor asked. "Is there something you're not telling me?" He turned toward Murdock. "Please. What's going on?"

Rudi watched him closely. "A bullet stopped his heart."

The professor's arms went limp. His head lowered. He shook it back and forth. A tear ran down his cheek. His lips moved but no sound ventured forth.

Murdock leaned over to Rudi and whispered, "Unless I find he's been active in community theater, this man is at the bottom of my list of suspects."

Rudi nodded in agreement, and turned toward the professor. "I'm sorry to ask you questions at this time, but you may have been the last person to see him alive."

"Except for the killer," Murdock injected.

Rudi continued. "We are told that he did not appear for midday meal at 1:00 o'clock. Did he tell you his plans?"

The professor was silent, his face a blank.

"Ah, yes," the professor said. "I *do* remember. Yes, indeed. He said that he would ski into the village and post a package. I offered to post it for him, but it seemed important to him that he do it himself. He insisted that he needed the exercise. He is — was — an accomplished cross-country skier, you know. He said he was sending something to America. California, I believe. No. That's not correct. The destination was my home state — Oregon. He said it was already in his backpack."

"He had a backpack?" Murdock injected.

"Oh, yes."

"Can you describe it," Rudi asked.

"Yes. It was forest green. About 24 inches high and 14 inches wide. I'm sorry. I should give it to you in centimeters."

"Inches are fine," Rudi said kindly. "Did he tell you the contents of the package?"

"I don't believe we discussed that. It's not my habit to pry. I'm sorry that I can't be of more help."

Rudi wrote in the notebook for a minute or more, and then took a casual sip of coffee. "It is possible he told you and you don't remember?"

The professor appeared confused. His hands shaking, he took a sip of coffee, reached for a croissant, broke it open, buttered it, and added raspberry jam. "I don't remember that we discussed it at all," he said.

Rudi stopped writing. "Did he mention that he would see anyone else that day — anyone other than the monks?"

"He said he might see Michael. He wasn't certain whether Michael would come."

Rudi tapped on his pad with the eraser of the pencil. Murdock took the ball. "Have you met his friend Michael?" Murdock asked.

The professor looked at Murdock, shifted uncomfortably, and turned to stare briefly out the window. The clouds were dissipating, and the day had brightened. A few puffy stratocumulus were catching the top of the mountain. Turning back toward Murdock, he replied: "I wouldn't call Michael his friend," he said.

"What would you call him?" Murdock pushed.

The professor held his chin in his right hand, the left tapping on the arm of the chair. "Mind you, I am not saying that Michael wasn't his friend. I don't know. Michael was a colleague. They were engaged in research together, I think." He looked outside again. "I'm not certain exactly what their relationship was."

"What do you think it was?" Murdock asked effortlessly.

"I'm sorry. I don't wish to speculate. I guess I can't help you much, and it may lead you far astray. Besides, to me Michael is an enigma. And don't ask me why. If I knew, he wouldn't be an enigma in the first place. Earlier this year, Stephen had mentioned him on several occasions. He had described Michael as an incisive scientist and an interesting personality. I first met Michael this past July. It was a brief meeting. We talked small talk. I didn't find him particularly interesting. Rather dull, as a matter of fact. I'd the distinct impression that he had little interest in talking to me. I admit that I was offended. Michael trivialized our conversation to the point where Stephen was embarrassed."

Georg had come up behind the professor. "Can you describe him physically?" Georg asked, walking into the Professor's view. The professor's body suddenly became rigid.

"My associate, Georg Brüner," Rudi injected.

Murdock observed that the professor was shaken by the appearance of the second policeman. Murdock knew that was Georg's intention. Putting a witness off balance often produces revelations. But the professor's equilibrium quickly returned.

The professor arose, formally shook hands with Georg, and then replied. "He was an inch or two taller than Murdock, but with blond hair and blue eyes. Muscular, but not overly so. I think he avoids the sun — his skin was almost albino — unhealthy looking. He walked too erect — so straight that it seemed unnatural — and spoke with a voice too firm for its softness. He left me with the impression that he was one of those scientists who is almost totally detached from reality. By *reality* I mean the usual social intercourse one enjoys among human beings. I think of myself as an egghead, but this guy came across like the king egghead of us all — what my grandniece would call a super-dork. But then, I'm prejudiced. Pure and simple, I plain didn't like him."

Murdock pondered for several seconds, baiting the air with dramatic tension. Rudi and Georg remained silent. "That was your *first* meeting? How many meetings were there?"

"Just one more. Last month."

"Did you find him interesting then?" Murdock asked. "And incisive?"

"Oh, yes. It was like meeting a different person — the difference between mass and force in physics. In describing the second meeting, *incisive* becomes an understatement. He was the most intellectually penetrative person I've met. But I had a vague feeling that there was more to our conversation than appeared on the surface. I searched for a reason. Little things in his conversation were discomforting, although I can't remember a specific example. He had mannerisms that were foreign to me. Several times he stuck his fingers in both ears for no apparent reason. He made allusions to facts of which I was unfamiliar, and then drew back awkwardly when I questioned him. Frankly, I wondered whether he was faking brilliance, if that's possible."

Rudi looked puzzled. He interrupted. "What was it he said that put you off?"

"I wouldn't say I was put off. *Amazed* might be a better word. I had never conversed with a man as tranquil or candid as he, nor with a scientist as comfortable with his theories as he. Many of his theories were remarkable. He emphatically insisted that each would be confirmed by experiment. He spoke boldly, but this time I discerned a gentleness in his boldness. He didn't wear a watch and never looked at a clock. When I suggested that it was time for lunch, he stared at me as if I had said something totally devoid of significance."

"Was he interested in your opinions?" Murdock asked.

"Yes. When I spoke of scientific matters, he hung on every word. I had the impression that he was feeding — grazing on every theory proposed by both Stephen and me — not so much because our theories were interesting, but the fact that we held them was."

"Why did you mention your lunchtime remark?" Murdock injected.

The professor thought for a moment. "As I said, I find him difficult to describe with any degree of precision. It wasn't so much that he wasn't interested in eating. It was more as if the thought had never occurred to him."

"Most curious," Rudi added. "Most curious indeed. Perhaps it was a language problem. Did you speak English or German?"

"English. But he is fluent in English. I understand that he's fluent in at least five languages."

"He strikes me as otherworldly," Murdock suggested.

"An extraterrestrial?" Georg injected, rolling his eyes.

The professor took both remarks seriously and pondered them. The others noticed and stared at one another blankly.

"No," the professor decided. "Terrestrial, I think, but unique. Perhaps *unique* is an understatement. It's difficult to find words to describe Michael that are not understatements."

"Maybe a little deranged?" Georg chimed in.

Murdock chuckled. "I dread the possibility that those we think are deranged are the only ones who see the world as it really is."

The professor shook his head thoughtfully. "Not deranged. He may be one of those supreme geniuses who shape human thinking. Few have heard of him because he's an extremely private person — recluse might be a better word."

"In any event, I would like to meet this man," Rudi said with finality. "Please remain here for a few days, professor. Georg may wish to speak to you again."

"I'm reserved for a week."

"Good."

The professor excused himself.

Georg sat down next to Rudi and poured himself a cup of coffee. "Herr Benzinger, Commander Weiss has directed you to remain here and to take charge of this investigation. He says the request came from the Minister of Justice. The commander did not seem happy about it."

Rudi looked puzzled. "I am surprised. Government ministers usually do not interfere with police administration."

"I do not know about such things," Georg said. "I only pass on the message. He asks you please to phone him before 11 o'clock this morning."

Rudi and Murdock looked at each other. Neither spoke. Both knew that a man at Rudi's level would be placed in direct charge of only the most sensitive investigation. What was so important about this monk? Maybe the phone calls to the commander and to Sir Richard the Boss would shed light. But detective's intuition caused both to wonder if it were mere coincidence that had brought them together at Zugspitze Hof on this brilliant winter day in November. And if it were not coincidence, who had sufficient power to command both Veritus and the Bavarian State Police? *No one*, each concluded without conviction.

Coincidence, Rudi decided conveniently. Murdock reached the same conclusion. But he was less confident.

Rudi broke the silence. "I have things to do, Murdock. Shall we meet after you've spoken to Richard? Perhaps cocktails in the lounge at five?"

"That's fine," Murdock replied. He had not mentioned his scheduled meeting with Allison. "If I turn up anything, I'll share it with you." *Anything, he thought grimly, that the law compels me to share.*

⊰ 5 ⊱

Murdock adjusted the telephoto lens on his camera. Centered in his viewfinder was Doctor Frederick L. Bauer from Huntington, Indiana. An attractive young woman stood — unnoticed — next to Murdock. He hadn't taken serious notice of attractive young women for some time. He was still in love with Karen — or at least Karen's memory. He had loved Karen almost from the moment Allison had introduced the two of them.

Bauer was speeding down the slope, zigzagging from side to side. His neck brace was missing. Its absence didn't seem to handicap him. No electric wheelchair awaited him. Murdock observed that his grievous, crippling injuries appeared to be less grievous today, but he knew that when the good doctor appeared at the courthouse, his injuries would magically reappear. He adjusted the telephoto lens and snapped several shots. *Too bad the trial won't be in a German court. He'd have to pay our costs. There's no justice for the unjustly sued in American courts.*

He glanced at his watch. There was still plenty of time before he had to leave to meet Allison. He regretted that she and Jerr had divorced, but he knew of few long-distance marriages that had worked over the long term. *They're both marvelous people. Jerr can be hardheaded. He's a purist and fanatically loyal to the FBI. He didn't agree with my leaving the Bureau, but it was a good move. Photographing jerks committing insurance fraud may be less glamorous, but it's less likely to get one's wife killed.*

"Excuse me," the young woman said. "Is that one of those new digital cameras?"

Startled, he turned to face her. *Stunning, he thought.* After a momentary loss for words, he stammered: "Yes, it is." Awkwardly he stuck out his hand. "I'm Murdock McCabe."

"And I'm Diana Crenshaw. Taking pictures of the slopes?"

She was about 5'10" he estimated, and neatly packaged with a pleasant face and a slim figure, as best he could imagine under the ski garb. A wisp of blonde hair curled upward from under her hood. Her full-ish lips gleamed red without lipstick. Her eyes, a bluish hazel, were agreeably deceptive — somewhere between erotic and demure. "Yes," he replied, attempting to recover from his surprise. "And the mountains. They're dazzling after a new snowfall. Diana, you say? Goddess of the hunt."

"I'm impressed, she responded. "You are a scholar of the classical myths in an age where such people are scarce. And I believe you're right. Diana was goddess of the hunt in Roman mythology, wasn't she? But I'm no hunter — just a mere predator of candor and wisdom."

Murdock smiled. "Mere? Now those are hard to find. I hope you're not easily discouraged."

"It seems we *do* live in a deceitful age," she responded with a broad smile. "Actually, I'm a very determined person. I persevere until I find what I want. I see you're using a telephoto lens. Catching anyone is particular? Like a wife?"

He chuckled. "You come right to the point, don't you? I respect candor too. It's not easy to find it in either sex these days. I'm not married. My wife died two years ago."

"I'm sorry," she responded. "I come to the point because I detest women who steal the affections of other women's husbands. And so that you don't feel compelled to ask, I'm not married. Might I see it?"

"Pardon?" *About thirty-three, he guessed.*

"The camera. I've not seen a digital."

"One last shot." He focused on Doctor Bauer carrying his skis to the lift. "There. That does it."

He handed her the camera. She looked through the viewfinder. "I presume that the advantage over other cameras is that the picture is captured digitally and can be saved on disk."

"Exactly. I can print it on a color printer, or transmit it by e-mail. By the way, I'm not really a classical scholar. When I read translations of classical Greek and Roman literature in college, I thought Diana was interesting. My mental picture of the beautiful goddess fits you perfectly."

"Pretty neat," she said, handing back the camera. "Are you normally a flatterer?"

Murdock feigned an innocent grin. "No."

"You were focusing on the man in the royal blue and white ski suit. He's a handsome man. Do you and he have a romantic attachment?"

Murdock laughed. "No. I've never met him. Just wanted an action shot. Join me for a quick brandy in the lounge?"

Diana smiled warmly. "I was just a tad concerned that you might not ask."

Murdock was astonished and pleased with himself. Diana was the first woman, other than Allison, that he had invited for a drink since he had met Karen — twenty years ago — and the invitation was a pleasant impulse. Karen had been the only woman he had ever needed or wanted.

They walked together toward the lodge. He noticed that she wasn't carrying skis. *I need to turn off the detective. I've almost forgotten how to do that. I've buried myself in detecting since Karen's death. Rudi constantly reminds me there is a beautiful world out there. This woman has an enchanting lilt to her speech and a devilishly charming smile. Is this what Karen would have wanted? There I go again.*

In the restaurant lounge, most tables were empty because most of the patrons were still on the slopes. They shed their ski clothing and took seats around the corner of the bar. Murdock decided his assessment had been correct. *Slim and trim as I guessed, he thought. "Neatly packaged" would be an understatement. She has a Marlene Dietrich body. Everything is tidily stacked in all the right places.*

They both ordered brandy to warm themselves. The bartender promptly complied and placed two snifters of the amber liquid in front of them. Diana sipped hers, smiled comfortably, and began to relax. "I have some business I need to take care of over the lunch hour, but would you like to join me on the slopes after lunch? I hate to ski alone."

"I wish I could," Murdock replied. "But I have some business, too, and it will take me away from the lodge. Are you a guest here?"

"Yes. Room 107."

Do women give out their room numbers so casually these days? "I'm 115. How about dinner tonight, and maybe we can do the slopes tomorrow?"

"Sounds great," Diana replied. "Knock on my door about seven?"

"It's a date," Murdock exclaimed, hardly believing what he'd said. He felt pleased with himself.

"She caused a Christian riot, you know."

"Pardon?" Murdock stared blankly at her.

"The goddess, Diana. In the first century A.D. In Asia Minor there was a silversmith named Demetrius who employed many people making images of Diana. Saint Paul and his followers tried to lay waste to his shop. It caused an awful riot. I don't recall who won. That's your trivia for today."

"Are you a biblical scholar?"

"Hardly. What do you do?"

"I'm a private investigator. Have you heard of Veritus Investigations International?"

"Yes. I'm with Seneca Financial. Have you heard of us?"

"You're an investment and insurance firm."

"Correct. We've used Veritus on several occasions, but none of the agents I've dealt with has been as jaunty and cultured as you."

Murdock grinned but couldn't help adding: "My culture is limited. Which Seneca? The Indians or the Roman?"

"God! I don't know," she replied in mock surprise. "No one has ever asked me that before. I wonder why? Probably because no one except you is that perceptive or gives a turd. Is it important?"

"Only to the Indians, I suppose. With all of their gambling income they must have plenty they could invest through Seneca Financial. They've finally learned how to get even with the white eyes."

Diana grinned. "Well, let's just say we're not Indians."

"Are you a money manager or an insurance agent?"

Diana pondered before answering. "In a manner of speaking, you could say I'm a surrogate money manager. I manage the people who have the money. You could even say that I roll the high rollers."

Murdock frowned.

"But not in the way you think," she continued. "Or perhaps I shouldn't presume to know what you think. To the point, I'm responsible for courting potential clients and getting them to invest huge gobs of money through our organization. Big money bird dog — that's what I am."

Murdock felt uncomfortable. "How do you convince them?"

Diana brightened and smiled effortlessly. She lifted her brandy snifter and stared into it, studying her reflection in the amber liquid. "Needless to say," she began coyly, "details of our marketing techniques are highly confidential business secrets, so I'm afraid I can't tell you much more than that. I'm sure you understand. I can assure you, however, it's honest business. The folks we deal with aren't easy to hoodwink. They have millions that need to be placed somewhere. We help them decide where and draw a fee. I have a client here at the lodge now. I handle all the little details, pay all the bills, and see that he has a fabulous week."

Murdock frowned again. *What's included in the detail, he wondered.*

A slow, easy smile crossed her face. "But I'll be free for dinner tonight. My client must fly off in his private jet to Cyprus this afternoon. He'll be back tomorrow. So, while the cat's away, I can play. And if your frown indicates that you think that sex is part of my job, it isn't. At least not directly. I write the checks, so to speak, when sex is necessary. And it sometimes is. Business is business . . . boys will be boys . . . broads will be broads . . . and whatever other cliché fits."

Murdock laughed, searching her eyes to see whether she intended the humor he saw. He wasn't certain. She finished her brandy so quickly that he was disappointed. It felt good to be around a woman again in a socially pleasing setting — a woman with whom he could imagine being romantically involved. He had been to dinner with Allison many times, but that was different. She was his best buddy's ex.

"Sorry," she said. "I've gotta go now. I need to check his accommodations and make sure he's content. But I'm looking forward to dinner. See you."

"Might his name be familiar to me?"

"Probably. He is a rather well-known Chilean businessman."

"Enrique?"

Diana had turned to leave, but the question stopped her. She turned back. "Do you know him?"

"We met at breakfast yesterday." Murdock detected a barely noticeable sigh of relief, which passed quickly.

"I really must run."

She offered her hand. Murdock shook it. She had a firm, sincere grip. "I'm too poor," he said. "I'm not a potential client."

"I know," she replied. "See you later. Don't forget. I'm really looking forward to dinner." She turned again, walked confidently through the doorway, and disappeared.

*   *   *

Diana swept through the suite. She checked the bar for liquor and ice. "I believe we have included your favorite scotch."

"You have indeed," Enrique replied.

In the bathroom she checked the adequacy of towels and toiletries. In the bedroom she assured herself that the silk sheets and pillowcases were in place. "You prefer silk, don't you," she asked.

"I do."

Diana stopped, breathed a sigh, and smiled warmly. "I can count on the Bayers to have everything right, but I like to satisfy myself. I understand that you will not be here tonight. Is that true?"

"That is true," Enrique replied. He noticed the fluidity of her body motions. Not a move was wasted.

"Shall I arrange dinner for tomorrow night?"

"Yes, I would be pleased."

"Would you like company?"

Enrique walked over to the picture window. The ski lifts were filled. Five stories below, in the parking lot, his limousine awaited him. The road to the highway looked clear. The airport at Garmisch-Partenkirchen was about one-half hour away on dry road. With his back toward her, he said: "I would very much enjoy your company for dinner tomorrow. Would you be pleased to join me?"

"Yes," Diana replied. "I would enjoy your company too. But there would be a downside of which you need to be aware."

"And what could that be?" Enrique inquired, still with his back to her.

"I'm afraid my company ends with the dinner. But I could, instead, arrange company with more stamina."

He turned to face her. "I imagine that a charming woman like you would have more than ample stamina for my humble needs. But what is it that you can arrange?"

Diana donned her professional smile. "You are a first-time client, and I don't know your preferences. Will you please help me?"

A faint grin crossed Enrique's face. "Most assuredly. What do you need to know?"

"Do you prefer male or female company?" she asked matter-of-factly.

"Female."

She never put notes on paper in a client's presence. It could make them gun-shy to think that someone was recording their peccadilloes.

"Intelligent? Is that important?"

"Of course."

"Physically attractive?"

"That would be most agreeable."

"Any particular physical attributes like—"

"No."

"I know a young woman who is working on her Ph.D. at Heidelberg. She is writing her thesis on the transition of the Roman era into the Dark Ages in Burgundy. Oddly enough, she is Japanese. You can expect nothing from her except a pleasant social partner and intelligent discourse. If she does anything else, it's for love. And I don't know that she does anything else. So, if it's sophisticated romance you have in mind, she would be a fascinating challenge. Frankly, if you lay her, I'd like to know what argument swayed her."

"I admire you, Miss Crenshaw. You come to the point. Unfortunately, however, I never reveal such secrets. But, perhaps for you, because you are so considerate, I can make an exception. If I should choose her, and if it should be convenient for her to join me, and if I should plant in her mind the seeds of thought from which dreams are made, and if they should blossom into a beautiful flower that blooms for one evening and dies, I shall share with you the argument that persuaded her. I promise. There are other choices?"

"Endless. I can find ladies of guaranteed pleasure."

"Do they work for you?"

"No," Diana said, "but I know the people they *do* work for. I have contacts all over the world. By tomorrow night I can procure a virgin from Bangkok or a woman with almost any skill you desire. Two women if you prefer. If you prefer voyeurism, I can provide two lesbians. You are our guest, of course."

"They are volunteers?" Enrique jested.

"Hardly, but confidentiality is guaranteed."

"Yes, Diana. I have heard that I can trust you in such matters."

Enrique had heard that from several friends who had been quite impressed by her. Their enthusiasm had been so rabid that he wondered if they were being entirely honest, or whether she had some power over them? Such power can be dangerous. *I suspect that this beautiful young woman has a thirst for it. But then, again, I could be wrong. Sometimes I'm too suspicious, but that's a fault I can live with. Besides, I like women who have a thirst for power. Real power.*

"You are most generous, Diana," he said. "Do you approve of such behavior?"

"It's not my place to judge," she replied, watching him casually.

"Do you enjoy your work, Diana?"

Her eyes met his. "Most of the time," she replied. "I look forward to getting to know you. You impress me, and I don't say that to pat your fanny. That's not my style. I meet a lot of wealthy men, but not many are fascinating. Most are just interested in what I can do for them. Some get really pissed when I won't go to bed with them. I know a little about your business, and I especially admire you for creating the College of the Caymans."

"You know about that?"

"Yes. You've created a super opportunity for bright Latin American young people to learn the free enterprise system, to become entrepreneurs, and to network when they return to their own country. I understand that you keep the classes small and charge no tuition."

Enrique smiled. "You're well-informed except on one point. I *do* charge tuition. I don't believe in welfare. It demeans people and cripples them mentally. Paying tuition gives students incentive to not waste *their* money. It would be easy for them to waste mine. However, I give a 100 percent tuition loan when needed. They must repay it when they are able — and I know when they are able — into a revolving fund that provides tuition loans to those who follow them. I have not had one nonpayment because I prudently select our students. I don't care whether they are rich or poor, so long as they have ambition, academic ability, and a deep sense of personal honor and truthfulness."

Diana's eyes met his. She smiled. "Meeting people like you is the pleasant part of my job. I look forward to spending some time with you."

"That feeling is mutual," he replied.

"After you enjoy the slopes for a few days, perhaps we can sit down and talk business."

A broad smile crossed his face. "I would be pleased to do that."

"However, in the meantime, I need to provide for your entertainment, if that's what you want. Of course, if you prefer to be alone, that's fine. What will please you?"

His smile became serious. "I have made some new acquaintances here — some gentlemen. Perhaps you could arrange a dinner for tomorrow evening with a Professor Klugman and Mr. Murdock McCabe. And you, please, must join us. You will add radiance to the table. Is it convenient for you to arrange such a party?"

"If they are agreeable, it shall be arranged. Shall I arrange for two more women?"

"I think that would be too bold a stroke. I hardly know them. Your charming presence should be sufficient, unless, of course, my guests would like to invite women on their own."

Diana made a mental note. "And the evening after that?" she inquired.

There was a knock on the door. Enrique opened it to his driver who picked up the travel bag and departed. "The next evening we shall plan tomorrow, please. Now you must excuse me."

"Yes. Of course. Have a safe trip." She bowed slightly, turned, and departed.

Now the death of the monk has changed the picture, Enrique thought. Murdock may learn or the professor may know the monk's secret. They must be my focus. I'll meet the abbot in a few days. Diana doesn't know the real reason I chose Zugspitze Hof Lodge, but her entertaining me here has provided useful cover. And Diana's company at dinner tomorrow will make an interesting cat and mouse diversion. In the meantime I must learn what Linda has prepared for me.

*   *   *

High over the Alps, a biz-jet climbed through the tops of the clouds, thrusting itself into the severe clear of the upper troposphere. Enrique eased the throttles back, trimmed the nose for level flight at 25,000 feet, and listened to the engines spooling down to cruise RPMs. He was struck by an attack of nostalgia. *Level at two-five-zero, he thought.* When he had first obtained his instrument rating, those words would have been his report to Vienna Center to inform the air traffic controller that his aircraft had reached its assigned altitude. Now a black box — the transponder — did the talking for him. Ground radar automatically asks the transponder every few seconds, "What's your aircraft ID number, your ground speed, and your altitude?" and the transponder automatically answers. *Too easy. For us part-time pilots it takes some of the fun out of it, and you don't pay attention as closely.*

Enrique was flying from the right seat — the copilot's position. Frank, a professional pilot who was much more experienced with jet air-craft, was in the left. Though Enrique owned the airplane and was rated to fly it, Frank was the pilot-in-command. Years ago they had agreed that Frank would always be in command so that, in the event of a sudden emergency, there would never be any doubt as to who was to control the airplane.

Enrique turned to Frank. "Your turn to fly the bugger."

"Got it," Frank replied. "Send Ozzie up."

"Will do."

Enrique opened the door to the main cabin, and motioned for the copilot to come forward. Ozzie nodded, shifted his feet from the confer-ence table to the floor, stuffed his girlie magazine into his back pocket, dragged his eyes across Linda DiStefano's blouse, and moved into the cockpit.

"I think we should find a new copilot," Linda said as she handed Enrique a scotch and water. "I never feel comfortable back here alone with him."

"I'd better not drink," he said, waving away the scotch and water. "When we land at Limassol, I want to fly the instrument approach for practice. Alcohol and shooting an approach don't mix. But please enjoy one yourself. Oh, and replace Ozzie anytime you want."

"Thank you," she replied.

Linda added a little more scotch and settled into a chair across the table from him. A divorcée pushing forty, she was intelligent, loyal, pleas-antly attractive, superlative in attention to detail, and a competent lawyer. Turning toward a mirror on the wall, she painstakingly brushed her short, dark-brown hair, combed her long bangs, and then swiveled to the right where her laptop computer was mounted on a credenza. She tapped a few keys, pondered the screen, sipped her drink, and then turned to Enrique.

"The landing strip at Boris Romanovsky's villa is too short for jet traffic. You'll be met on the tarmac at Limassol by a pilot who will fly you to the villa in a twin engine Cessna 310. You two will confer until dinner is served at 8 P.M. After dinner it will be cognac and cigars — no women. No men either. Boris is straight. He retires at ten. You'll stay overnight at the villa — finish your conference in the morning — join us here at 11:30 A.M., and we take off for Garmisch-Partenkirchen. I'll prepare lunch for you in the galley. Don't be concerned about your dinner engagement for tomorrow evening. You'll arrive at the Zugspitze Hof Lodge in ample time to shower and dress. Diana Crenshaw has confirmed that professor Klugman will be happy to join you. She's having dinner with Mr. McCabe tonight and will invite him at that time."

"Diana is having dinner with Murdock McCabe tonight?"

"Yes. She's confident he'll accept your invitation for tomorrow night."

"Find out whether the evening ends with dinner."

A wry smile crossed Linda's face. "It will. She's the kind of woman who holds out hope, but her puppies end up without a treat."

Enrique laughed aloud. "I am not a puppy."

"Okay. I've checked with our sources in Oregon. The professor is the genuine article. A copy of his book will arrive before noon tomorrow. You may want to refresh your memory." She reached into a drawer in the credenza and extracted a multipage document. "This is a dossier on Mr. McCabe's wife, Karen, and the circumstances of her death. You'll want to read it on the flight back. My gut feeling tells me that the FBI report has been discreetly massaged. I ask myself why anyone would want to do that . . . and who had the power to do that and get away with it? It has been reviewed by Joe Carlyle. As you know, he's only two steps down from the Director. He signed off on it."

"Who indeed," Enrique exclaimed. "Our man in the Cayman police doesn't trust him. It could have been him."

"Yes. It could have. In regard to Diana, I haven't been able to discover much. Information from Seneca Financial indicates that she was born in a defunct coal mining town in central Pennsylvania. Her parents were middle class. Her father owned a pharmacy . . . not a particularly successful one . . . but their lives were comfortable. You like her, don't you?"

"Yes, as a matter of fact, I do. But you need not be concerned. You'll always be my most trusted administrative assistant. Your position is secure."

"That wasn't my concern."

"Ah, yes. Romance. Linda, I am not a Latin lover easily suckered by a pretty face, or a supple figure."

"The qualifier *easily* is interesting. She has plenty to go along with that pretty face and lithesome carcass."

"Like what, Linda?"

"From observing her yesterday, I think she has a gift for subtle theatrics."

"What's bothering you, Linda?"

"Can't put my finger on it. Maybe I'm just being a woman."

Enrique laughed roundly. "You? Just being a woman? Never! I can't imagine that. Your mind is too incisive to ever permit you to just be a woman."

"I don't bother you with rumors. I get the facts first."

"I know. Bother me just once."

She stared out the window for several seconds. Ethereal ice crystal clouds swept across the sky close above the aircraft. The sun set them afire. Particles of ice sparkled like millions of glittering rubies. "There is a rumor that Diana Crenshaw is a principal in Seneca Financial — not a mere agent."

"She makes no pretense of having any proprietary interest."

"One rumor says she holds a majority of the equity. If that's true, she has come a long way from a defunct coal town pharmacist's daughter in a very short time. She's thirty-four. Mind you, I'm not convinced that it's true. It's far-fetched. If it were true, why would she be working at a rather menial job?"

"Her job is important. A business such as Seneca Financial can't exist without high roller clients. She recruits them. And if it's true that she worked her way up from mediocre pharmacist's daughter to majority shareholder in a substantial corporation, is not such success to be admired? Is that not what your America is all about? Rags to riches, and all that? If the rumor is true, I admire her. She certainly doesn't boast about it. Besides, she's rather charming."

Linda frowned. She tapped on her laptop's keys, making an entry in the things-to-do file. "We need to look at her more closely, right?"

"Right," Enrique replied — his face incandescent. "Yes, indeed. I need to know all about her. She is a most interesting woman." He noticed Linda frown again and decided to change the subject. "And the dead monk. We must know exactly what he was working on."

"We've not been able to crack the monastery. There's a wall of silence. I don't think the police have learned much from the monks — at least not much about the dead monk's projects. Before they entered the monastery, most of these men held positions, or owned businesses, in which they were extremely sensitive to the threat of industrial piracy. They'll not disclose more than they're compelled to."

"This wall of silence must be cracked," Enrique urged. "It's absolutely critical. I need answers before I meet with the abbot, Brother Martin — if we are to succeed."

⤙ 6 ⤚

A century and a half ago, King Ludwig II of Bavaria had been con-demned by his government ministers as a crazy castle builder. Today, those same castles are the leading tourist attractions in Bavaria. They provide income to the state. The king's favorite was Linderhof. He had lived there. It had been built for him from 1869 to 1878 by Georg von Doll-mann. The king, an admirer of the court of King Louis XIV of France, insisted that it be patterned after the Petit Trianon palace at Versailles. It was Allison's favorite.

Allison arrived at Linderhof fifteen minutes before noon. Hers was the only vehicle in the parking lot. Few tourists are attracted to the site in November. Back on the road, as far as she could see, no traffic was moving. She was satisfied that she hadn't been followed. Exiting the car, she wrapped her scarf snugly around her neck and walked to the ticket booth. It was unoccupied. She surmised that the guides were selling tickets inside the castle. The asphalt path, which leads a quarter mile to the castle, had been cleared of snow, and as she walked its gently curving route, she noted with pleasure the tall still-green conifers on both sides. On her right, framed by the conifers, was a small lake. She calculated that one could walk around it in five minutes or less. It was frozen, but no children were skating. They were in school. There was no wind. Arriving in a large open area, she stopped. In its center, bathed in brilliant sunshine, stood the old castle. The fountains were turned off for the winter, and the reflecting pond, which occupies almost as many square feet as the building itself, was covered with snow. There are no thick high walls . . . no turrets . . . no moat . . . no drawbridge . . . and no portcullis. It was more a smallish palace, a jewel of rococo design, and built for comfort. She loved it.

Opening one half of a huge double door, she stepped inside. A man dressed in a formal nineteenth century military-type uniform welcomed her. His name tag indicated that he was a guide. She explained that she was waiting for another party. He offered her a seat and disappeared. Allison's minor in college had been European history. She thrived on it and, sitting there, she had the pleasant feeling of being surrounded and enveloped in it. She determined that someday she would write a period novel, specifically middle and later nineteenth century when Ludwig II of Bavaria reigned. She was determined to expose the politicians of that day and show how little politics has changed. *They, along with the religious hardheads, have caused endless barbarous wars and ghastly death to millions, almost beyond imagination.* She felt herself ascending the moral high ground. It was a familiar climb, although she felt uncomfortable when she became judgmental. She would expose the unspeakable evils that the combination of religion and politics can foster. *My book will expose the lies that Ludwig's political enemies foisted upon history. One would be the lie that King Ludwig II was insane. The king was crazy like a fox. His government wanted to form a German Empire by uniting with Prussia and Saxony. Then they would make war on France and regain territory that, the politicians claimed, had been rightfully German since Charlemagne. Of course the French politicians felt it had been French for the same period of time. The moral high ground is always paid for with the lives of innocent young men—and now women too. The king neither wanted to form a German empire nor to make war on France, so he spent the public treasury on building castles, and thus, he hoped, make it impossible for his government to fund a war.*

But she knew it hadn't worked out that way. Ludwig lived at Linderhof, far from Munich. He feared the politicians would have him killed in the capital. Finally, tired of his obstructions, the government had him declared insane and made his uncle regent. A week later the king took the bait. He set off for the capital so that his people, most of whom loved him, could see that he was not insane. *He was half right, Allison thought. It would have worked, except halfway to the capital the politicians, through resourceful agents, murdered the king. He was drowned in the Chiemsee, a beautiful lake within sight of the Alpine peaks he loved. My sympathies are with the king. If the politicians hadn't killed him, and if Germany hadn't been united, the world might have avoided two world wars. He was a tragic figure, and I'm a hopeless romantic.*

The grand door suddenly opened, followed by a gust of cold air and Murdock. A shiver went up her spine, only partly from the icy draft.

"Good to see you," she said. "Were the roads dry?"

"Not bad considering all the snow that fell in the mountains. Did you have any trouble getting here from Munich?"

"There were some slippery spots. Are you having a good time?"

"Yesterday I did. Today started off poorly."

Getting directly to business, she handed him the message from Richard.

"Please read it before the guide comes back."

Murdock sat down beside her and read Richard's instructions. He nodded. "I've already begun the investigation," he said. "This doesn't tell me much more than he did by telephone. I guess he wanted me to have it in writing. Keeping it from Harvey is new."

"What have you learned," Allison asked.

"The monk is dead. His body was found in the Liederbach Meadow before sunrise. Rudi is on the scene."

The guide reappeared and announced he would start a tour at 12:30, then disappeared again.

Murdock was puzzled. "When will you talk to Richard?"

Allison motioned for him to step outside. They could see no one near the building or on the pathway. Although the doors were thick, and it was unlikely they could be heard through them, she motioned for him to walk straight ahead to the reflecting pool thirty feet from the door, directly in front of the building. It was surrounded by open air. From there they could see anyone who might hear them.

"I have disturbing news," she said. "While I was driving here, Harvey reached me on my cell phone. Richard didn't arrive in Frankfurt. Harvey was furious. He acted like a little boy whose candy had been yanked from his hands. He likes to hold those meetings where he can lord it over Richard. He knows that Richard's a better administrator than he — and he knows that we know it — so he likes to remind Richard who is at which end of the leash. I checked with our company pilot. Richard's car was found parked next to the fixed base operation at the Munich airport, but Richard was nowhere about. He said that there were signs of a scuffle next to Richard's car. Fresh tire tracks gave indication of an all-terrain vehicle. I don't like any of this. Not one bit. The man we were assigned to find immediately comes up dead. Our boss is missing. And why is Rudi at the Zugspitze Hof?"

Murdock filled her in with the little that he knew. She agreed that it was strange for Rudi to be assigned to the case. He mentioned the person — he thought it was a man — in the green nylon jacket whom Georg couldn't trail. Their eyes met for several seconds.

"I have a few questions," Murdock said. "Like, isn't it Rudi's job to find the killer, not ours? And if we *are* to stick our nose in where the police belong, what do I tell Rudi? He's a little peeved that he doesn't know who our client is. I'm not sure he's going to believe that we don't know. I hate it when the truth isn't believable. And whoever our client is, why is he — or she — interested in the monk? I'd hate to become a subject of Rudi's investigation. We need to give him some answers."

She noticed the castle door was open, and standing just inside was the uniformed tour guide. Murdock was alert and abruptly watchful. The guide moved away, closing the door softly.

"I don't have any answers," she responded. "With Richard missing, whom do we ask? I don't have access to Top Dog. I wonder what he'd say if he knew we called him that. Anyway, Richard says that Harvey and his Frankfurt boys are out of the loop. Weasel would probably know how to get Top Dog's attention, but I dare not ask."

"Yeah. Terry probably has something on him too but, judging from Richard's note, Terry's to be kept as far out of the loop as anyone can get. I guess it's your call, Allison. Where do we go from here?"

"Well," Allison hesitated for a moment, and then replied decisively. "Find out *why* Brother Stephen was killed, without stepping on police toes, if you can help it. Start with Brother Martin. Use your imagination with Rudi. If I can think of a story without lying, I'll get back with you. We'll go from there. By the way, Brother Martin wrote a book called *The Deceptive Innocence of Science*. I stopped in a book store in Garmisch and found two copies — one for you. We both need to read it as soon as possible. I'll be at the Bayerisher Hof Hotel again tonight. I took the room for two nights, not knowing how quickly the roads would be cleared. Phone me between 10 and 11, if you can. See Brother Martin tomorrow, if at all possible. Do you feel comfortable with this plan?"

"Very."

Murdock looked up the trail. Loud voices were coming from the direction of the parking lot. "Do you think you're in any danger, Al?"

"Maybe we all are, and the scary thing is — I don't have the foggiest idea why. That makes it scarier. So, let's both be cautious. We confide only in each other — and Moira. She's solid."

"And Rudi?" Murdock injected. "He's our good friend as well as being a policeman."

Allison hesitated. "But he's *all* policeman, isn't he. Tell him what the law demands. The rest, play by ear. I trust your judgment. I'll do the same."

A gaggle of school children were coming down the path next to the frozen lake. "Come on," she said. "Let's walk back to the cars. It's cold out here. Any interesting people at the lodge?"

Murdock mentioned meeting Enrique and the professor. She had heard of Perez-Krieger, but not Professor Klugman. He neglected to mention Diana.

"Have you ever heard of a Baron von Richter?" he inquired.

Allison frowned. They had reached the parking lot. She motioned toward her car. Inside, she started the engine and set the heater blower to high. "Baron Rupert Karl Hermann Otto von Richter? Yeah. I've met him. Have you?"

"No. I saw him at dinner last night. When I asked Frau Bayer who he was, she replied rather brusquely and walked away. He was having a serious conversation with two confederates, but they did most of the listening. What do you know about him?"

"He's a pompous ass. He leads a group who believe he can restore the Bavarian monarchy."

"That's crazy," Murdock injected. "I take it he wants to be the king."

"You take it correctly." The heater was beginning to produce some warmth, but the windows were fogging. Allison made no effort to prevent it. "If he's at Zugspitze Hof Lodge, he's probably up to no good. Frankly, I don't like the man."

"You say you've met him?"

"Twice. At cocktail parties. He is much too unctuous. And, if I interpreted his courteous offers correctly, he was willing to allow me the privilege of going to bed with him. I thanked him for the proffered honor and told him that I hoped that someday I might find myself equal to his expectations. He responded with a supercilious grin. But, in fairness to the jerk, I have to confess that — intellectually — there is logic to his politics."

"What politics?"

"He wants Europe to adopt more than a common market — he wants a federal Europe. He argues that only federation can prevent the endless wars that have ravaged the continent continually for almost two thousand years, but he claims that a federal Europe can never be achieved among the present nation-states. But he doesn't want a federal union made up of the present nation-states. He sees too much opportunity for politicians to invoke nationalist jingoism — the curse that has killed untold millions of young men. He suggests that the nation-states be broken up into their constituent parts — their states or provinces. For example, Bavaria would not be one of the states of Germany, nor Scotland one of the units of the United Kingdom. Both would be states in a United Europe. The states could choose their form of government — republic or monarchy. Sovereignty would be divided between the federal European government and the constituent states in much the same way as it originally was in the United States."

Murdock shook his head. "It's too logical. Do you think that sufficient political will could be mustered to accomplish it?"

"Not until goats can fly," Allison replied. "Politicians don't like to see their political base dissolve in a metamorphic transposition. But some folks listen. Do you think he's tied in with the monk's death?"

Murdock shrugged. "I haven't the foggiest."

"If you find a connection, give me a call. I've got more background information on von Richter." Allison turned on the defrosters. "Well, I've got to get back before The Weasel becomes too comfortable with power. But, Murdock, I want you to be extremely careful. There appears to be a great deal of power at play — more than seems appropriate over a monk. Use the Karen codes, if you think it necessary. And remember — Richard's missing — and we don't know what's out there."

"Do you worry about me?"

"Of course. For old time's sake."

Murdock stepped out of the car, and as he closed the door, she revved the engine and took off across the parking lot — disappearing down the road.

*   *   *

Back in his room, Murdock phoned St. Luke's Monastery and set up a meeting with the abbot, Brother Martin, for 8:00 A.M. tomorrow. Convinced that the professor could shed light on the monastery, he phoned him. A meeting was arranged for 3:00 P.M. Murdock estimated that Rudi would be back about 5:00. He wondered how often Allison worried about him. So far as he knew, she hadn't worried about him on his previous assignments. *She just likes to have all her ducks in a row, and, without a known client with a known bias, this investigation is unstable. That must be the reason.* The only other reason he could think of, he felt that he had to deny.

⇥ 7 ⇤

Two brandy snifters enriched with Irish Mist sat on the end table. As Murdock entered the room, the professor picked one up and, with a congenial smile, offered it. "Most of the year we have gloomy damp days on the Oregon coast. This is my prescribed medication for gloom cutting. Besides, my mother was of Irish descent. She had red hair like yours. Welcome. Please be seated."

Murdock accepted both offers. Yesterday, his first impression of the professor had been favorable. Over the years, he had learned to rely on his instincts, which had seldom failed him. He prided himself on his keen sense of character. The professor wasn't a suspect high on his list, but he had learned never to write one off totally until the mystery was ultimately solved.

The older man reached into a humidor and withdrew a cigar. "Cuban," he said. "You have to get out of the United States to buy a good cigar. I think they taste better because they're contraband in America. The forbidden fruit, you know? Care for one?" Smiling warmly, the professor held out the humidor.

"No, but thank you. I smoked cigars in college. My wife Karen — we weren't married then — thought they had a manly aroma. Her father smoked them. I quit when I entered the Bureau. The Bureau came down heavy on cigar smoke."

"The Bureau?"

"I was a special agent for the FBI for over ten years, but please don't hold that against me." Murdock was accustomed to receiving either of two responses to that disclosure. Some were impressed. Some, including many local cops, were more circumspect. Murdock felt that recent history lent credence to the circumspect group. But then, he had his own reasons for a lingering personal bias.

The professor replied: "I won't. I judge each man individually. You haven't personally shot up anybody's wife in Idaho, have you?"

"No," Murdock replied, awkwardly. "Nothing like that, fortunately."

Leaning back in his chair, the professor blew three perfect smoke rings and watched as they drifted across the room and dissolved. Murdock waited. Silence was a device he often used to discover what was on another man's mind. After the better part of a minute, the professor inquired distractedly: "Are you assisting the police investigation of the death of my friend, Stephen?"

Murdock studied his face. He read the face of a distraught pedagogue quizzing a student. "Not directly. We have a client. However, if we come upon evidence necessary to the police, we share it with them."

"Do they share with you?"

"If it suits their purpose, and if they trust us."

"I assume your visit isn't entirely social. How can I help?"

"Because we are not police, you don't have to answer my questions. If you feel uncomfortable answering any question, please let me know and I'll try to raise your comfort level."

"Please proceed, Murdock. I'm quite willing to do anything I can to assist in finding my friend's killer."

"Brother Martin has agreed to meet with me in the morning. If you can, I need some background on the monastery."

"My knowledge is limited. What would you like to know?"

"Are you part of the monastic organization in some way, professor?"

The professor chortled. "You certainly haven't read any of my books. Quite the opposite. I'm a humanist. And an odd old duck. I have a Ph.D. in astrophysics and another in philosophy. Are you a religious man?"

"No." Murdock assumed that answer would keep the spigot open.

"People like these monks, who believe in a god who created and governs the universe, simply delude themselves. I'm not sure why. I believe in the scientific method. The pathway to truth twists through thickets of theorizing and experiment. Reasonable people discover truth logically. I confess, though, that I have a mixture of disdain and envy for people who can believe in a god, unburdened with an ounce of empirical evidence that he, she, or it exists."

"Envy?"

"Yes. The universe is a much simpler place for them. Much easier to explain. Dogma fills in answers for anything they can't explain. Alas, I've never been capable of enjoying that luxury, although, I admit, some scientific theories border on dogma. All my adult life I've studied and researched. Each new discovery produces more questions than answers. The more I learn, the more exciting the unanswered questions become. And, believe me, I've searched for God. I've looked everywhere—almost back to the Big Bang. He comes up absent."

"How did you and Brother Stephen become friends?"

"Indeed. That's really a good question, isn't it? I admit we are— were—an unlikely pair. Please understand that, whatever your mental picture of a monastery is, Saint Luke's doesn't fit it. About seven years ago the abbot wrote a book that decried the amorality of today's scientists. For example, we doggedly research and develop atomic bombs and the ability to clone without accepting the responsibility for what either can, and probably will, lead to. Martin's book touched some scientists' nerves. Martin organized a conference in Munich that brought together several hundred scientists who were Christian."

"Were you in attendance?"

"No. I don't suffer from the Christian persuasion. I read his book, however, and wrote a critical review in a scientific journal. Martin and Stephen are members of the small breed of readers who read my review. Although they thoroughly disagreed with my conclusions, they expressed appreciation for my scholarship and insight. That led to their reading my last book, *The Amoral Universe.* Even though they disagreed with many of my postulations, they discovered that we share a commonality of concern. Stephen arranged for me to fly here last May at his expense. He was an extremely wealthy man. Before joining St. Luke's, he'd made a fortune in the Silicon Valley. That's when we first met. This is my second trip."

The professor fell silent, deep in thought. Murdock decided not to interrupt. The professor refreshed their drinks, puffed on his cigar, and they both sipped the liquor. The sun was setting. The professor switched on the lamp. It was he who broke the silence.

"My friend," he began hesitatingly, "we are dealing with a fire that could consume us — that has already consumed Stephen — and threatens me. It will burn you if you get too close. I like you, Murdock. I regret that we didn't meet under more congenial circumstances. Because of that, I would like to help you. But also because of that, I must advise you to leave this alone. You are not being paid enough to get involved. It's police business; let them handle it. But unless I have grossly misjudged you, you will pay no heed to my advice."

Murdock read a look of grim concern. "I can't run away because the going is tough. What's fueling this fire?"

The professor hesitated, staring out the window, watching the afterglow paint the clouds brilliant orange with strands of fuchsia. "You could say computers. The Internet."

"Could say?"

"Today the world is literally being inundated with new knowledge. Information — data as the computer folks call it — is cascading down upon us at an appalling rate. When I was a boy, I walked to the library and, often tediously, searched through an encyclopedia. Now recorded knowledge is expanding exponentially — at a rate barely imaginable even ten years ago. It floods into databases that can be accessed on screens in our homes. What's frightening is that the technology that makes it possible becomes obsolete after only months — sometimes days. We used to talk about the 3x5 card index. Now it's web browsers. I can fire up that little laptop over there and pull up a picture from the Louvre in Paris in seconds."

"In your opinion, is this bad?" Murdock inquired.

"It's neutral. And therein lies the problem."

"Aren't scientists supposed to be neutral?"

"Yes. The real question is whether the world can afford the neutrality. In the past, if a group of scientists wanted to study something, a small group of them would come together at some prominent university for a few years. Today they can stay put. There's no necessity for them to come together. They share their research by the Information Highway."

Murdock looked puzzled. "That sounds like progress to me."

"It is. But let me illustrate the problem as simply as possible — I

tend to run on. Today a team of a hundred or more scientists can work together on a project without ever meeting. Each team member is highly
specialized and studies his or her infinitely small part. Other members do
nothing but collate thousands of small parts into a whole, which those
who study the small parts often cannot foresee. Still others interpret it.
Their intermingling by computer, it seems to me, fosters remoteness and
detachment — impersonal science on a compelling scale. In the next ten
years we may learn more about the elementary particles that make up
matter — if matter exists and some doubt it — than we have learned since
the beginning. We may become capable of commanding awesome powers unimagined today — power that will demand frightening responsibili-
ties. Whom shall we trust to exercise such spectacular power? What
restraints are possible? Will this kind of power inevitably lead to despot-
ism? What if some twenty-first century Hitler decides to clone a real
master race? Could he be stopped? *Should* he be stopped? Or should
every nation compete? Should the power unleashed by our science be
given to the control of a committee of scientists? Who would choose the
committee? When the inevitable politics within that committee turns into
its inevitably deadly competition, who will bring it under control? Finally, is control possible? There are so many things we need to learn but
may not heed because this impersonal, Internet-connected team is not
structured to bother itself with moral questions. In that failure there is a
danger, not only to everyone alive today, but to every future generation.
You look skeptical, Murdock McCabe."

Murdock considered his response. "I'm sorry. I've never given
much thought to such things."

"Most folks haven't — and won't. Most people have no concept of
the potential danger. There aren't any easy answers. Even an attempt to
understand the problem requires more thought than many people are willing to give."

"Can you focus the problem for me?"

"I believe there are two focuses necessary to understand it. The first
I've just explained: abuse of power. The second deals with what is happening to the integrity of the process. Such grand scale collaborations encourage consensus among scientists, but make it difficult to achieve
because of the size of the group. Some large groups contain over a thousand specialists contributing parts of the research. Sometimes a large
group consisting of representatives from dozens of universities may hesitate for months to publish a new theory because there is disagreement
whether they have achieved compelling proof. This can be inefficient and
counterproductive. By publishing and sharing promptly, compelling
proof may be obtained more quickly by another mind or groups of minds

testing the same theory from a different perspective. Precious time is lost in trying to protect the proprietary interest of the original group. Often groups are reluctant to share with one another because each wants credit for the discovery. Usually the taxpayer pays but has no idea of the true purpose for which the tax money is being spent." He paused. "I'm sorry. The dormant lecturer in me often reawakens and I become orotund."

"Not at all," Murdock insisted. "Please go on. Was Brother Stephen concerned about this issue?"

"Yes. Of course. All the monks are. It's their primary focus. Every one of them, except Martin and Gustav, is an eminent scientist. Martin is the only theologian. Gustav is a classical scholar. I don't believe you've met him."

"Brother Martin is their leader?"

"Yes. They elected him abbot, like the Benedictines do. But they're not Benedictines. They're not even Catholics—most of them."

Murdock interrupted. "How can they be monks if they're not Catholic?"

The professor smiled patiently. "You don't have to be Catholic to be a monk. There are Eastern Orthodox monks. I've met some Lutheran monks in Michigan. Surely you've heard of Buddhist monks in the Far East."

"How many of the monks are Catholic?"

"I'm certain that Antonio is Roman Catholic. I'm not certain what my friend Stephen was, other than a computer chip genius."

"Please tell me more about him."

"He made a fortune in the Silicon Valley. Stephen joined them when Martin invited Christian scientists to form a brotherhood of monks and dedicate their lives to both prayer and science and to making the world cognizant of the moral imperatives compelled by science."

"Why did they locate on the Zugspitze?"

"Martin knew of an old, ruined monastery sitting on the slope, which had been abandoned for over two hundred years. Its grounds had been seized by King Ludwig I, the father of the crazy king, and held until some monks were willing to put it to use again. Martin's group pooled their vast wealth and convinced the politicians in the Bavarian state government that they were the monks who should revive the monastery. They rebuilt it, restoring the medieval architecture but making the inside a hive for buzzing computer bees. Martin calls them God's electronic bees."

"Is this some sort of secret cult?"

"Not at all. They welcome guests. The monks are free to leave."

A thin smile stole across Murdock's face. *Perhaps they're reactionaries fighting progress. There are always some people who knock progress. Science has certainly changed our lives for the better over the last 150 years—and I suppose in some instances for the worse. If Gottlieb Daimler hadn't perfected the gasoline engine not far from here, there wouldn't be over 50,000 people in the United States killed by drunk drivers every year. Air would be purer. The Los Angeles basin might smell of horse turds, but the smog would be gone.* "It's pretty radical to turn your back on fame and wealth to become a monk," he said.

The professor recharged the snifters and offered Murdock the humidor again. This time Murdock accepted. The cutter and matches were lying on the end table. Murdock clipped off the end and lit it. "This *is* a mighty fine cigar," he acknowledged. He managed one lacerated smoke ring.

"Thank you. These monks didn't turn their backs. Just the opposite. There are no vows of poverty — or chastity either. Not in this monastery. They continue to function as scientists. Some of the monks in one year make more than I have in a lifetime. One of their goals is to demonstrate that socially and morally responsible science, if one can make a distinction between the two, can be profitable. Profit is the only real god worshipped by many people."

"How do you feel about all this?"

A shrewd smile crossed the professor's face. He laid his head on the top back of his chair, looked up at the ceiling, blew three more perfect smoke rings, and chuckled. "I don't believe in God," he began, speaking slowly, "but I give the monks credit. They have identified what I see as the crux of the problem. The grants and profits that the fruits of science produce often obscure moral consequences. For example, if I learn how to bend a particular protein in a certain way and insert it into a gene, where will it take us? Do we know? Do we want to know? Do we want to go there? And, who is this 'we'?" Would Oppenheimer and his colleagues have completed the Trinity Project and produced the first atomic bomb if they had first been required by the politicians and the military to answer the 'what if' questions? I don't know. What if *we* fool around with bent proteins and other things that haven't even been named yet, and learn to perpetrate catastrophic biological destruction far beyond what Oppenheimer in his wildest dreams could have imagined only dimly? Or, if we progress beyond cloning, whom shall we trust with the power to reform life?"

The alcohol was beginning to warm and relax Murdock. The taste of the cigar brought back pleasant memories: sitting on the back porch with Karen — smoking a cigar — cocktail in hand — she, scrunching up her face — playing with some new cryptograph — her long auburn hair caught by the breeze. He needed to forget, but couldn't.

Murdock chuckled inwardly. *The professor was right about himself.*

He tends to fall into the professorial lecturing mode. He was also right about most people not wanting to concern themselves with the potential consequences of scientific research—probably because they feel impotent. I'm one of them. Leave those problems to the experts. But who are they? Do they have names? The professor has a point. This is all very interesting, but where is this going? "Does all of this have something to do with Stephen's death?" he asked finally.

"I think so. I'm coming to that. As best I can."

"Do you share the monks' concerns?" Murdock injected.

"Oh, yes. Most certainly. But we are worlds apart on the solution."

"In what way?"

"The bottom line question is: If we're to judge the morality of our research, by whose morality do we measure? Stephen and his brothers believe that God's laws provide an authoritative basis. I think they delude themselves. God simply doesn't exist. There's no extrinsic evidence to support the belief that he does. These so-called laws of God are merely creations of men. Religion is a bogeyman. As soon as you insert some superhuman spirit, whose existence you can't ever prove, science ends. For centuries religion kept people ignorant. Look what the theologians did to Galileo. They persecuted him unto death, even though they knew he was right. They were afraid that the truth would expose the silliness of their notions of the universe, diminish their power, and destroy the good life they enjoyed, living off the backs of simple peasants whom they manipulated through fear of hellfire and damnation."

"And you? What would you use as a standard?"

"I'd review the parallax of human experience and adopt those standards that have been the most enduring."

Murdock smiled. "Doesn't that beg the question? It sounds as if you haven't thought it through. In fact, your answer has a sinister quality."

The professor's eyes met his. "How's that?"

"By whose judgment do you choose the standards most enduring? Communism has endured. So has slavery, and the persecution of certain classes of people. What would give you the moral authority to make such decisions?"

"Not I," the professor exclaimed. "Perhaps the decisions could be made by a panel of prominent philosophers from around the world."

"My friend," Murdock interrupted, "it sounds pretty arrogant to assume that only philosophers are qualified to proclaim what is moral and what is not. If the choice is between some elite humans and God, I'll take God."

The professor cocked his head. "Murdock, I didn't have you figured as being religious."

"I'm not, but the Ten Commandments seem to say it all." Murdock deposited the cigar in an ashtray and pushed the brandy snifter aside. From his coat pocket he extracted a notebook, adopting a demeanor befitting a detective. "It's probable that Brother Stephen was killed because of something he was working on. Was it something he kept secret because of its potential moral or ethical consequences?"

"I can't say."

"Because you don't know?"

"That's what I told the police."

"Was the answer truthful?"

"Yes. It would have been more candid if I had said that I can't say exactly and don't want to guess."

"So, you have some idea, and you didn't want to share that idea with the police. Is that accurate?"

"It's possible my guess might be accurate. But if it were inaccurate, it would lead them far afield."

"Will you share your guess with me? I'll accept the risk of going far afield."

"As much as I can. I want the killer found before someone else gets hurt—especially if that someone is me. I'm more trusting than Martin. I think you can be trusted."

"And the police can't?"

"I think your friend, Rudi, is trustworthy. But he reports to superiors who report to politicians. I don't have one iota of trust in any politician, especially when it comes to acutely sensitive matters."

"You and Allison both."

"Pardon?"

"My supervisor, Allison Spencer, feels the same way about politicians. In spades."

"Then I admire her." The professor put his cigar in an ashtray. Standing with brandy snifter in hand, he walked to the window and stared into the fading light. A bright full moon peeked over the eastern rim of the mountain.

Murdock jotted down a few notes, closed his notebook, and inserted it in the inside pocket of his sport coat—useful body language in situations where an interviewee appeared on the verge of sharing some confidence. Often they would speak more freely when they thought the interview had terminated.

The professor turned to face him, his back against the window sill, the moon silhouetting his right shoulder. "I made a pledge of secrecy to Stephen and Martin. I'm an honorable man. I can only say so much. You must promise to disclose whatever I say to no one, unless it is absolutely necessary in order to find and prosecute Stephen's killer."

Murdock offered his hand. "I shall be discreet unless the law compels me to disclose. I'll not commit a crime to protect these monks and their secrets." The professor took his hand. They shook.

The professor sat down and relaxed. "May I assume that a young man like yourself is computer literate?"

"To a point," Murdock replied.

"Do you know what a central processing chip is?"

"Yes."

"This is merely hypothetical. I am not suggesting it's true. But let's suppose someone developed a chip that would operate at the speed of 50,000 megahertz at room temperature. Would that be valuable?"

"It would mean instant fortune to the inventor," Murdock exclaimed.

"And what would it mean to the world?"

"I can't begin to imagine. Things that we think are impossible might become possible—like artificial intelligence."

"Might such a chip produce sufficient wealth to kill for?"

"People kill for much less," Murdock observed soberly. "Did Brother Stephen develop something like that?"

"As the price for allowing me to share in some understanding of what he developed—or was developing—I had to pledge not to reveal even my assumptions to anyone. I belong to a generation to which personal honor is still important. Brother Martin, and possibly Brother Antonio, can answer your question, if they choose. Martin is the key, though. He can open or lock the door. I doubt that he will open it unless he knows who your client is and why he wants to know."

"Do you have a suspect in mind?"

"No," the professor replied without hesitation.

Murdock looked at his watch. Rudi might be waiting for him at the bar. Besides, it appeared that this conversation had come to a logical ending, and he needed to digest some of it before he questioned the professor further.

"Thank you, professor. You've given me a motive. That's indeed helpful."

"I've given you nothing. A hypothetical is merely a story . . . possibly an invitation into a blind alley."

"Let's just say that my intuition tells me that the motive for Brother Stephen's murder was commercial, and that very big bucks are involved."

The professor turned again toward the window—his back toward Murdock. "And," he said, his voice slightly quivering, "let's also say that your imagination is infinitely small."

⪥ 8 ⪤

The sun slipped behind the Alpine landscape to the west. Evening shadows crept across the depopulated slopes. The frosty air was calm. Inside the Zugspitze Hof Lodge dim lamps, aided by candles at the center of each table, set the mood for the cocktail hour. A table had been reserved for Rudi next to the huge picture window. Both Herr and Frau Bayer have great respect for policemen, but Rudi Benzinger was special. He and his wife, Angelika, had stayed at the lodge frequently before her accident — a tragedy that the Bayers remembered well. Two years ago, on a clear, cold morning like today, as the restaurant was preparing for the first breakfast customers, Angelika had poked her head into the kitchen and breezily wished them good morning. She and Rudi were anxious to be one of the first on the slopes.

"You will have apple strudel for lunch, yes?" she had pleaded. "You make the best strudel in all of Bavaria."

"Ja, ja." Frau Bayer had assured her. "You know we will. Have a good time. Be careful. The slopes will be fast this morning."

They were. About halfway down a run designed for only the most experienced skiers, Angelika missed an "L" turn and struck a tree. Rudi had found her lying in the snow, her blonde hair red with blood, and her skull fractured. There were no signs of cognition. He had accompanied her as she was airlifted to a hospital in Munich where she arrived in a coma from which she has not awakened. Since that fateful day, he had prayed for her upon arising every morning and upon retiring every night. Nothing but death could steal his hope.

Frau Bayer stood silently as Rudi considered the menu.

"I do not know why I look," he said. "I always order your pork schnitzel with a fried egg and potato salad. But hold the order, please. Murdock will join me for a couple beers. I do not know what his plans are for dinner. For now bring a stein of dark beer, please.

She spoke softly. "How is your wife? Do the doctors have optimism for Angelika?"

"The doctors cannot say when, if ever, she will come out of the coma. She is still on life support systems and does not respond to stimuli. I have noticed the merest hint of a smile when I play her favorite folk music, but the nurses tell me it is wishful thinking. But as long as I can think, I shall wish. She is my life, Frau Bayer. Without her I feel like a violin that is broken so that the tension of its strings cannot be adjusted. One can play it, but what comes out is not music."

Frau Bayer shook her head slowly. "That is heartbreaking. We pray for her every day. She is in the hands of God. He is waiting for something — something we do not understand. I feel it. Do not give up hope. He will awaken her in his good time."

"Perhaps." He *had* given up hope. Almost.

"Now, please relax and enjoy the view. Herr Bayer is drawing a big stein of the dark beer for you, and one for Murdock. I'm sure he will join you presently. He is never late."

Murdock arrived just after the beer. Rudi arose and offered his hand, which Murdock shook firmly. "Good to see you again, my friend," Rudi said.

"Likewise," Murdock replied warmly.

The first stein washed down comradely small talk. With the arrival of the second stein, Rudi became serious.

"I interviewed Brother Martin and Georg interviewed Professor Klugman. We both felt that they genuinely wanted to help, but neither was particularly helpful. They claim to have no idea who wanted Brother Stephen dead. Somebody did. And somebody has some idea who that somebody is. We do not believe it was a chance killing. Incredibly, neither of them could — or would — give us Michael's last name. They both say they never heard it. I find that curious. Do you? Would not Stephen have introduced him using his last name?"

"It would seem so," Murdock answered distractedly. He noticed Baron von Richter and another man seated two tables from them. They were engaged in animated conversation, oblivious to those around them. *If two men ever looked like they were hatching some grand conspiracy, those two do.*

Rudi followed Murdock's stare. "Have you met him?" Rudi asked.

"No," Murdock replied. "Allison believes that he wants to restore the Bavarian monarchy."

"He is a foolish man," Rudi replied.

"It's uncharacteristic of you to put a label on a person."

"Ja, ja. But there's no other way to describe him. Bavarians love their kings, but kings wear better from a historical distance."

Murdock smiled. He enjoyed a good argument. "But Rudi, you can buy likenesses of King Ludwig II in shops all over Bavaria today, even though he's been dead for over one hundred years. There must be some yearning there—some latent desire—some thirst for things royal—things that, perhaps, can sparkle and glitter in this unostentatious age."

"Ja, ja. Ludwig is wearing well. But you know, Murdock, in every country the most respected heroes are dead. It is not so much the hero who is praised, but the myth that emerges after his death. In any event, it appears that our Baron came here two days ago, also to meet with the popular monk now dead. Martin tells me that von Richter wanted to invest in a new computer chip that Stephen was developing—an advanced C.P.U., whatever that is. I have no idea what was special about it. I'm a computer ignoramus when it comes to opening one of those boxes and looking at its innards."

"C.P.U. means central processing unit—the main brain."

"In any event," Rudi continued, "Martin cannot imagine Stephen being interested in accepting von Richter as an investor. Apparently Stephen spurned his offer by letter, and von Richter came here to—shall we say—persuade him."

"Are you giving the word *persuade* a menacing connotation, Rudi?"

Rudi smiled wanly. "It *is* a disturbing thought to apply that word to such a man. Von Richter is extremely wealthy. Wealth and power incessantly interact. I cannot always be certain exactly where the power has been bred. My advice, Murdock, is that you try to stay out of his way. If our investigation should perchance focus on him, it is better that I handle him. The minister of justice urges that we deal with him most gingerly."

Murdock noticed that the two imagined conspirators were preparing to leave. Von Richter paid the check in cash. The other man bowed, turned, and departed through the door to the parking lot. Von Richter moved to the bar, sat down alone, and imperiously ordered a drink. "I agree," Murdock said, "that the Baron must be on our suspect list, but it's interesting that he's still here. How many killers remain so near the scene of the crime—unless he's an exceptionally shrewd one. Is he shrewd?"

"Ja, ja. I think so. I also think this Brother Martin is very shrewd. The abbot knows more than he is willing to tell me. He refers me to Brother Antonio, who was not present in the monastery today. Antonio was Stephen's assistant, or, perhaps, collaborator is a better word. Von Richter has asked for an audience with the abbot. He will get it. I understand that in the morning you too will meet with Martin.

Yes," Murdock said.

"He may tell you more than he has told me. Brother Martin is uncomfortable with policemen. I do not know why, but I assure you that I shall find the answer."

"Or," Murdock suggested, "he may be between a rock and a hard place, trying to protect a commercial secret. Professor Klugman believes that Stephen was on to something big — something that could produce a fortune — probably in patent licenses. That can be done in the computer business in a very short time. Look at Microsoft."

Rudi leaned forward, his forearms flat on the table and his hands folded. "Please, ask Brother Martin what type of computer chips were in the package that was stolen from Stephen in the meadow."

"It contained computer chips?"

Rudi shrugged. "I bluff. Watch his knee-jerk reaction, if the knee jerks. If it opens a door, walk through it. But if you do, I want to know what is on the other side. Ja?"

Murdock grinned. "Ja."

"One other thing." Rudi extracted a photocopy from the inside pocket of his suit coat. "The medical examiner found a date book amongst Stephen's effects. Stephen had used it more for writing notes than recording dates. In the slot for last Sunday he wrote this." He handed Murdock a photocopy. "It had been under water. Forensics has restored the page. Can you make it out?"

Murdock strained to read it. He moved it closer to the candle in the center of the table. "It doesn't make much sense," Murdock observed.

Rudi leaned forward and spoke almost in a whisper. "What do you think it says?"

Murdock strained again. "It looks like 'Odin has found the wolf, and its name is Hecate.'"

"That's what I think it says. What does it mean?"

"I don't know. In your German myths, of course, Odin — or Woden — was king of the gods. I recall that he had something to do with a wolf. Do you recall what it was?"

"No," Rudi replied. I have not read the legends since grade school. Hecate is not a German name."

"I agree. It sounds Greek. I'll talk to Allison. One of her ambitions is to become a writer. If she doesn't know, she won't be at peace until she finds out. She's my word mole."

"She is much more than that, my friend." Rudi smiled wisely. "She is a vivacious and thoroughly delightful lady. She invited me to a party at her apartment this Saturday evening. Would you mind if I attend?"

"Why, no," Murdock replied, a blank look on his face. "Why should I mind?"

Rudi grinned. "Ja, ja. Why indeed. Then I shall attend. Have you mentioned anything to Allison about Angelika?"

"No. That's your private matter. I've always respected that privacy. I tell no one."

"Then she doesn't know that I am married."

"I have suggested that you were at one time. She sensed that I was protecting some private information and backed off."

"Ja, ja," Rudi said, folding the photocopy and returning it to his pocket. "A beautiful, charming woman, engaged in the information business, but respecting the privacy of even a casual friend. Truly admirable, wouldn't you say?"

Murdock smiled. "To her, you're more than a casual friend. I've known Allison for about fifteen years. She's a straight arrow. She and Karen, you know, were roommates in college. There's been many times since Karen's death that I've needed a friend, and she's always been there, as you have, Rudi. And Jerr. I hope I've been there for you guys, too. It was easier to lose Karen than to go through what you are. I'm at least free."

"Are you?"

"Pardon?"

"Sorry, Murdock. That's *your* private business. How is Jerrard? He's still with the FBI, is he not?"

"He's still agent-in-charge in Omaha. In fact, there was a telephone message from him in my mailbox — I picked it up just before I joined you." Murdock reached into his shirt pocket and, extracting it, read it out loud: "Phone me after you have talked to Jose Enrique Perez-Krieger." Rudi looked at him blankly.

"Well," Murdock said, "that's weird. How did Jerr know I was here at the Zugspitze Hof? I spoke to Allison at noon. If she had told him, she would have mentioned it. I doubt that she phoned him on her cellular on her way back to Munich. It's not company business. What does Jerr have to do with this opulent Chilean? Is the FBI investigating him? If it were, Jerr would want to talk to me *before* I talked to Enrique again."

Rudi laughed. "It seems that the more we investigate this affair, the more the mysteries deepen. I find the message not so much weird as ominous."

"Ominous?" Murdock injected quizzically. "An interesting choice of words."

"Jerr, in Omaha, seems to be cognizant of what is going on here. He even knows that you are going to meet with a potential suspect — and knows his name. The monk was killed only yesterday and his body discovered only this morning. It's one more piece of evidence," Rudi said somberly, "that suggests to my mind that a number of people know much more about this than we do, and I think that Richard did not send you here for fun. He positioned you. Now he is missing without a trace. How many people knew this monk would die? To my mind the presence here of both Señor Perez-Krieger and Baron von Richter confirms Professor Klugman's assertion that high stakes are involved. And von Richter's stakes always have a political mix. The world never changes — the chain links are never broken — money, politics, religion, and death."

"Wow," Murdock exclaimed with mock horror. "What a normal combination. But what about sex? Where is the woman in the plot?"

"And please do not forget a would-be king," Rudi added. "So, Murdock, what is your gut feeling? Was the motive economics or politics?"

"When it comes to big stakes, is there a difference?"

Rudi chuckled. "You are a wise man, Murdock. Do you have plans for dinner?"

"Really sorry, Rudi. I am dining with a lady tonight. I would invite you to join us, but you know how it is."

Rudi raised his stein in a toast. "Splendid."

"Her name is Diana Crenshaw. I hope she's not on your list of suspects. I'd like to have some conversation with someone not involved in this case."

"She is on our list of guests at the lodge. She arrived the day of the crime, but many others did too, of course. We will question her, but we have no reason to suspect her. Perhaps you could help us."

"No. Not tonight, Rudi. I have a date. Can you believe that? I need to freshen up. See you tomorrow."

Rudi was delighted that Murdock was finally dating. He knew that the dinners with Allison were platonic. Or so both insisted. Rudi felt that neither could see the obvious. *Allison being Murdock's supervisor stands in the way. And, of course, there's his friendship with Jerr.* Rudi stepped outside onto the porch, glanced down onto the moonlit snow fifteen feet below, and then up toward the severe clear blackness of the night sky, dotted with stars and washed by a rising full moon. Breathing deeply the fresh, cold air, he turned up the collar of his suit coat. He too needed to get his mind off the case and relax. A chill ran through him. He decided to flatter Frau Bayer so that she would give him an extra bread dumpling with his pork. The air was cold and crisp — the stars sharp. Near the far end of the veranda stood a young couple, their arms crossed behind one another. They looked very much in love — standing at the very place where Murdock and Karen and he and Angelika had once stood — on a night very much like this one. *Now Karen is dead and my Angelika lies in a coma. But I am content—happy that the Holy Mother in heaven prays for Angelika—happy that I lit a candle to St. Jude after mass last Sunday —happy that Murdock has a date—happy that this young couple can take pleasure from the same visual experience the four of us shared here.* He left them to their reverie and returned to his table.

If the lovers had listened to anything other than themselves, their solitude would have been violated by the barely audible sound of a snow-mobile engine coming from the direction of the far-off meadow. The machine approached a branch in the trail. Moving tentatively, its headlight caught the waters of the Liederbach Creek. Its only occupant, a man wearing a ski mask and a green nylon jacket, chose the trail leading to the monastery.

⇥ 9 ⇤

The shadows created by the setting sun had been replaced by those created by moonlight. As Murdock looked out the picture window, he could barely make out the slopes. He saw a young couple, their arms crossed behind them, standing on the porch, and a dark figure watching them from behind. Diana sat across the table from him. Frau Bayer had seated them in the corner farthest from the fireplace. Diana was wearing a cherry-red lipstick. His mind wandered to the bright red cherries fresh from the trees along Grand Traverse Bay where he and Karen had spent a summer vacation. *Karen's dead. This is Diana, and she deserves better company than a man mooning over his lost wife.* Discreetly he noticed that her breasts rose unpretentiously under a blouse that glimmered in the flickering candlelight — the neckline enticing but not immodest. The half-light conferred an aura of mystery to her face and golden hair. When she smiled, dimples appeared on both cheeks. He noticed that she employed minimal makeup, and used it expediently as Karen had. Her eyes were bluish hazel, as Karen's had been. Her graceful movements reminded him of Karen's. There was an exactness about her that reminded him of Allison. In the candlelight she appeared chaste and beautiful, but — at first he couldn't put his finger on it — passionless. He noticed her looking at him — her smile imponderable — her stare level — communicating nothing. Her face changed, softened. Diana broke the ice.

"The woman who seated us must think we're lovers. This is the most private table in the dining room."

Murdock smiled. "I think not. Frau Bayer knows me. I've stayed here many times."

"With your wife?"

"Yes."

"So, Frau Bayer thinks you wouldn't be a lover? That would be rather uncomplimentary for a man of your age whose wife passed away over two years ago. Maybe she thinks that it's perfectly natural for you to have a romantic encounter. Not that this *is* a romantic encounter, but it would be natural for her to think that it is. Obviously she chose this table especially for us."

"You may be right," Murdock acknowledged.

Diana took his hand. "Do you plan to remain celibate for the rest of your life? I'm not hustling you. I'm just asking. And, I guess, it's a rhetorical question anyway, so don't answer."

Murdock didn't *know* the answer. It's not that he didn't want to have a romantic relationship. The fleeting, inadequate sensual pleasure from casual sex didn't appeal to him, and he wasn't ready for commitments. Besides, he still compared every woman he met with Karen, and they all came up short. But tonight there was something about Diana that intrigued him. He'd been illogical. Diana had confronted him with it, just as Karen had. That was good. He wasn't fond of mealy-mouthed women. *She's strong and comfortable with herself, like Allison. She's the kind of woman who could not respect a weak man, and yet she respects my weakness—or else she sees my loyalty to Karen as a strength.* He sensed that she didn't want casual sex either, but her job must put her into situations where it's unavoidable.

A waiter arrived to take their dinner order. Murdock withdrew his hand from under hers. She handed her menu to the waiter and turned to Murdock. "Please order for me," she said. "I shall enjoy your favorite."

Murdock smiled, pleased. "In that case," he said, turning toward the waiter, "we'll both have roast pork, bread dumplings with pork gravy, red cabbage, and bring a chilled bottle of Riesling, please." The waiter filled their glasses with mineral water, bowed, and retired. Murdock turned toward Diana. "Tell me more about your work," he urged. "Do you look after the pleasures of your clients?"

"You don't approve of my work, do you?" She continued without waiting for an answer. "Wining and dining is a big part of my job, and frequently I must procure other services — whatever bait it takes to land the fish."

Murdock felt uncomfortable with the word *procure*. It had a pejorative connotation. It didn't fit the picture of the woman he had held in his mind since their morning encounter. It's a judgmental word, he thought. Is she a *procurer* or does she procure the procurer? He wondered whether there was a moral difference. Perhaps society had become less judgmental to the point where assessing such a thing as culpability was politically incorrect. *Have I become less judgmental? What do I believe? Since Karen's death, I'm not sure that I believe in anything or anyone, except Jerr and Allison and Richard and Rudi. By what right can I judge Diana?* He looked into his soul, but the answer didn't look back. *She arranges a dinner or sex—or maybe provides the sex herself—whichever is necessary to get her job done. It's that plain and simple.* He noticed that Diana was staring at him.

"If you're wondering whether all high rollers are debauchers, the answer is no, but the majority like to play. Probably the same percentage as among the low rollers. But, so what. It's the genuine sport of kings. If you look at the history of England, most of the kings had extramarital relationships. Some of the most impressive families in the realm are descended from royal bastards. And the poor people love to read about the sex scandals of the rich and famous. In that sense, the rich and famous perform a service for the common man — they provide fodder to feed his lust for scandal and color his otherwise gray life. But scandal is not *my* purpose. My assignment is simple. I recruit and hold clients with big bucks. In order to do that, I must meet their expectations. If they want *me*, as they often do, and I don't say that to brag — I substitute some smashing young beauty in my place."

"What do you think of these men?"

"What I think of them is unimportant. If my client wants a ski trip, I arrange that. If he wants a fancy dinner and exotic drinks, I arrange that. If he wants to invest with us, I arrange that. If, in order to clear his mind so that he can make a decision, he needs to satisfy some primal urge, I arrange that. I'm not ashamed of it. I produce millions in annual income for Seneca Financial."

"Do you handle women clients?"

"Only in the figurative sense," she said, grinning. "I have to be prepared to respond to their peccadilloes. They're generally more demanding than the men."

"Do you enjoy your work?"

"I can think of a lot worse jobs. I don't place land mines or blow up buildings and airplanes, both of which appear to be increasingly popular vocations. Nor do I cheat little old ladies out of their husband's life insurance proceeds."

"Are there limits?"

"Absolutely. I don't tolerate barbarity or outrageous behavior. I fulfill reasonable desires, so long as they're gentlemanly — or gentlewomanly — about it. That's the real world, my friend."

Presently their meal was served. The waiter opened the wine and poured a sample. Murdock swished it about in his glass, tested first its bouquet and then its flavor, and nodded approval. He was not a connoisseur of wines, but he had learned the proper ritual. Roast pork with the knödel, or bread dumplings, had been his favorite meal since he was a child. His mother had learned the secret of making the dumplings — the technique that prevented their falling apart during the boiling process — from her mother in Germany. He had taught Karen. A curious and rather unsettling perception crept over him. Behavior that he and Karen would have considered immoral seemed less reproachful in Diana. He felt that some last semblance of naiveté had evaporated. *Am I abandoning the values that Karen and I held sacred? Am I becoming infatuated with Diana to the point of devil-be-damned? Does it really make any difference anymore? Hasn't the Christian concept of morality become old-fashioned and politically incorrect?* His mind was packed full. *She's more a woman of the world than Karen, and that's probably the understatement of the day. I suppose that's what makes her exciting.*

Diana ordered a brandy ice. She watched him unobtrusively. *Karen would not have taken an alcoholic beverage.* He noticed Diana glancing toward the von Richter table. He had noticed nothing that would have invited her glance. *Does she know von Richter? Is he one of her clients? Eyes wander. I'm probably reading too much into it.* His mind raced like the propeller of a ship when it's out of the water. Her voice caught his attention — she had been talking to him, and he hadn't heard her. Her face had changed. He no longer judged it passionless. She spoke sensitively.

"You must have loved her very much. You still miss her, don't you?"

"I'm sorry," Murdock replied. "Is it that evident?"

"I'm afraid it is."

"I'm not very good company, am I?"

Diana smiled affectionately. "You *are* very good company. Am I the first woman you've dated since her death?"

"Other than Allison Spencer."

For a second, a modicum of affection disappeared from her smile, but quickly reappeared. "Who is she?"

"She's an old and dear friend whom I sometimes lean on. But Allison and I don't really date. We sometimes stop for a few drinks and a snack after work."

"Then I am flattered to be your first dinner date," Diana replied affectionately. "But I'm a big girl. I have no pretensions. We've broken some ice. We're trying to become friends. I'm pleased."

A waiter, interrupting them, and begging forgiveness, delivered a note to him. Murdock's eyes quizzed Diana.

"Don't be concerned," she said. "Please read it."

He recognized Rudi's handwriting.

Murdock,

Georg has obtained information that Brother Stephen was working on a project called "Codex." When you meet with Brother Martin, please see whether he volunteers that information. If he doesn't, please ask him. Find out what "Codex" is.

Thank you.

Rudi.

He carefully refolded the message and placed it in his inside coat pocket.

"By the way," she said, her eyes following the note until it disappeared, "Enrique would like you, and Professor Klugman, to join him for dinner here tomorrow evening at seven. The professor has already accepted. I'll be there too. Will you please join us?"

"Certainly," he exclaimed without hesitation. "I look forward to it. But I need to talk to Enrique before then. Do you know when he'll be back?"

"Not later than tomorrow at 3:00 P.M." Diana smiled compassionately. "Her name was Karen, is that right?"

"Yes." The name coming from her lips seemed indecorous. *But why shouldn't she ask? She wants to know whether my head is on my shoulders when it comes to women. She's talked to someone about me—perhaps the Bayers. She knew Karen's name.*

"Have you kept anything of hers?"

Murdock hesitated. He thought it a rather personal question. *But maybe I need to talk about it. Maybe she knows that I need to.* "She didn't have much," he replied diffidently. "She wasn't interested in accumulating material things. She didn't care for jewelry or expensive clothing. Other than photos, the only thing I saved was her code books."

"That's incredible. Code books?"

"Karen enjoyed making up and cracking codes. She became a professional cryptographer—even did encrypting for the FBI. Secret codes used on the Internet weren't secret for long when Karen tackled them. It was possible for her to listen to a lecture on classical Roman literature and, at the same time, devise a new code, never missing a point that the lecturer made."

"She sounds like a remarkable woman. Have you looked through these notebooks?"

"No. Not really. They don't interest me. I saved them because they are something tangible that she created. Her intellect lives on in those notebooks. Does that seem crazy to you?"

"No, not at all." Diana shook her head. "It's really an incredible coincidence though. I'm interested in encryptions too. I'd love to see her code books. Maybe, when we get to know one another a little better, you'll show them to me—if there's no secret FBI stuff in them, and if you don't think it would make you feel disloyal to her. You still do feel a sense of loyalty to her, don't you?"

Murdock mellowed. "They're just a bunch of stuff on floppy disks, I guess—nothing really important."

"I'd like to see them. Actually, I'm quite good at it too," Diana continued. "Karen and I may have met in a Usenet discussion group. Her ideas might be very helpful to me."

His face was a closed book. She took his hand again. "Can we ski together tomorrow?"

His face came alive, electrified with a broad grin. "You bet. I should be free between noon and three o'clock. I'll look you up when I get back from an appointment, if that's okay with you."

"Super," Diana replied. "I've got to read some briefing reports before I sleep, so thank you for the dinner. My treat next time. I do very much look forward to seeing you tomorrow."

She turned to leave.

"By the way," Murdock injected, "is the term *Hecate* part of any code you've come across?"

She frowned. "Not in any code that I'm aware of," she replied. "It's the name of the ancient Greek goddess of the hunt, I believe. But you're my classical scholar. You should know about her. Bye, now."

She passed the professor who entered the room as she left.

⇥ 10 ⇤

Murdock was pleased. Diana had not expected more out of the evening than he was prepared to give. They'd ski in the morning. Entering the cocktail lounge, he saw the professor waiting for him at the bar. Murdock took a stool around the corner of the bar and faced him.

"First one's on me," the professor said, flashing a kindly smile.

The bartender awaited his order. "A manhattan-on-the-rocks," Murdock said. The professor already had a brandy.

When the drink arrived, Murdock raised his glass toward the professor. "Thanks," he said.

The professor lifted his glass in Murdock's direction and nodded.

"Have you been retired for some time, professor?"

"Almost ten years."

"Do you miss teaching?"

"I miss the students. I miss trying to teach."

Murdock suspected that *trying* was a buzzword invitation to another lecture. Wanting to know the professor better, he took the bait. "Trying?" he inquired. The professor's posture stiffened. His expression became solemn.

"We live in a wretched age. Teaching is subordinate to research. There's a high altar. University administrators prostrate themselves before it. Across its front the word *GRANTS* is inscribed in gold. In my department — philosophy — we were lesser gods. Neither the government nor industry was interested in us. It was difficult to attract graduate students."

Murdock interrupted. "What kind of research are you talking about?"

"Any silly thing the government is willing to pay for. After devouring millions of dollars, they discover what common sense had already taught the average taxpayer. Skill in the art of politics is helpful. One's conclusions should agree with those of the bureaucrat writing the check . . . or the politician who got the money appropriated. It's a little more subtle than that. I mean . . . we all know that a person who agrees with us is intelligent."

Murdock shifted his weight uncomfortably. "That's a rather cynical assessment, my friend. Some professors still teach, don't they?"

"I've heard professors complain that the time spent teaching impeded their research. Research advances them. Does that attitude lend itself to highly motivated teaching? I think not."

Murdock wondered as to what precisely was the professor's agenda. He decided to push. "It sounds like you enjoy grinding *that* ax."

The professor hesitated, not certain at first how to respond. After several pensive seconds, he decided to be direct. "I'm disturbed. Good teaching is important. It requires great skill and dedication."

Murdock was tiring of the subject, but didn't want to seem rude.

"Of course," the professor continued, "some students are unaffected . . . the ones who just want a degree because it opens doors. Some come to learn. Effort may be rewarded by a slot in graduate school, kissing some professor's butt so that he'll be anointed to assist in some abstruse piece of research that he can list on his résumé. A symbiotic relationship is born. Mediocrity feeds on mediocrity," he said, throwing his hands in the air.

Murdock was amused by the passion of the dissertation. "As Shakespeare might say, methinks you exaggerate."

The professor shrugged, grinning sheepishly. "Some say that I have that skill."

The lecture had made Murdock dry. He ordered another manhattan. While with the FBI, Murdock had investigated the misuse of federal funds in research projects, so he wasn't unfamiliar with the subject.

"We produce few educated people," the professor rambled on. "We produce autotrophic beasts who spawn ideas out of a vacuum to prove some politically acceptable truth. Traditional courses are still offered in Plato, Aristotle, St. Augustine, Shakespeare, and even Thomas Aquinas, but all too often these are taught by deconstructionists."

Murdock cocked his head. "What are 'deconstructionists'?"

"They are professors who dissect Plato's ideas for political incorrectness, demonstrating how foolish Plato was compared to the all-wise professor who is teaching them. And a student had better agree. It's more dangerous to think on a college campus today than ever before. You could be branded an extremist. Forty years ago you would have been branded a communist. Only the killer words change."

"And you?"

A wry smile crossed the professor's face. "Oh, I'm a certified crackpot."

Murdock laughed. "Why is that?"

"I wouldn't permit my students to accept the theory of evolution by natural selection on face value, even though I firmly believed it to be correct."

"Why not?"

"They had no right to accept it unless they had thoroughly studied the theory of creation and considered the possibility that there could be a third, undiscovered theory that could explain the universe."

"That sounds logical," Murdock suggested.

"But, I also warned my students about the consequences of independent thought. They could endanger their chances of success in our conformist world." The professor grinned broadly. "Because listening to me might compromise their futures, I decided to retire and save them."

Murdock laughed out loud. He enjoyed an astute sense of humor. The lecture had ended. He had persevered. "How do these monks fit into all this?" Murdock inquired.

"I'd gotten to know Stephen fairly well. With Martin and Antonio, I've a passing acquaintance. Some of the others I know only socially. Of course, the monks don't teach. They're interested only in research. I think it's important that we separate teaching and research."

"I agree," Murdock inserted. "How do you feel about these monks?"

"I respect them. They don't give a damn about political correctness. They don't take money from any government. Their science is authentic. I just can't understand why they feel that they need to be monks."

"You're an atheist, are you not?"

"I confess."

"The monks seem to have taken you into their confidence."

"Some have."

"Why?"

"Because they need me for balance. We—all of us—need to disagree."

"I'm afraid it's not clear to me."

The professor was thoughtful for several seconds. He sipped his brandy and lit a cigar. "Would an example help?"

Murdock sipped his drink. "Sure."

"Have you heard of the Anthropic Principle?"

"No. Please try not to be too technical."

"It's a fairly simple idea, actually. You've heard of the Big Bang theory?"

"That the universe began with a Big Bang?"

"Yes. The bang created four forces. We call them the Gravitational Force, the Electromagnetic Force, the Strong Force, which holds elementary particles together in atoms, and the Weak Force, which is responsible for certain types of radioactive decay. In order for the Big Bang to produce the universe, each of these forces had to have the right strength—not too strong—not too weak. They had to fall within a window of opportunity. For example, let's consider the Gravitational Force. We think that atomic nuclei formed from protons and neutrons colliding with each other in the primeval soup about three minutes after the Big Bang. If gravity were too strong, the universe would have fallen back into itself in less than three minutes. If it were too weak, the expansion would have been too rapid, and the collisions so infrequent, that matter, as we know it, could never have come together. Do you follow?"

"Yes," Murdock responded, "I think so. It sounds logical. Where does it take us?"

"Ha," the professor exclaimed. "That is where the monks and I can't agree. Remember, each of the four forces had to have the necessary strength—not too strong—not too weak—or the universe, including us, couldn't have happened. The big question is how the Big Bang produced the correct strengths for each force so that our universe could form in such a way that life could exist. Two hypotheses have been put forth. One we call the strong Anthropic Principle. It postulates that the universe was arranged so that life could develop, that it demanded that life develop, that it was fine-tuned for that purpose. Stephen accepted that principle."

"But you don't?"

"No. There's another hypothesis, which we call the weak Anthropic Principle. Is postulates that there is no explanation. The forces of nature are what they are by chance. I subscribe to that."

"Isn't that a reach? I mean . . . that all four forces turned out with exactly the right strengths accidentally."

"There may have been millions of Big Bangs that fell back in on themselves before this one got everything right."

Murdock shook his head. His knowledge of scientific matters depended largely upon his recollection of his ninth-grade science class. "Are any of the monks—or anyone else—testing these hypotheses by experimentation?"

The professor lifted his hands despairingly. "How can it be done? There are only two ways to test it. If we could go backwards, before the Big Bang, and if we could see thousands of previous universes and determine whether they contained life, that would be one way."

"Is it possible with radio telescopes, or whatever, to look back beyond the Big Bang?"

"No."

"What's the other way?" Murdock asked.

"The only alternative is for someone to write an equation that would explain the whole universe—what we call the 'grand theory of everything.' Short of either, the principles are untestable."

Murdock sipped his drink. He hadn't thought about such things. Anthropic principles didn't affect his everyday life. "If they're untestable, where does science go from there? I mean, if the question is unanswerable, shouldn't we just forget about it?"

The professor smiled broadly and raised his glass ceremonially. "There we have it," he exclaimed. "As long as it remains untestable, it will linger *outside* the realm of science and *in* the realm of philosophy. That's *my* major field."

"And the dead monk's field?"

The professor hesitated. Murdock watched his face. The professor folded his lower lip under his upper, and held it there for several seconds with his teeth. He released it. "Stephen was *curious* about philosophy, but his major interests were electromagnetism and semiconductors."

"Curious?"

"He thought that theology was a form of philosophy."

"And you don't?"

"Hardly," the professor responded shaking his head for emphasis. "Theology gets in the way of philosophy. A philosopher searches for the truth. We employ logic. Theologians assert that they have found the truth . . . that it's encapsulated within the dogmas of their religion. The door of inquiry is slammed shut. Bang. That's it."

"Was Stephen dogmatic?"

"Stephen feels — felt — that evolution by natural selection is undeniable. He believed it is inherent in nature. At the Big Bang, God stirred the pot and created the laws of nature. He believed that God still stirs. Needless to say, he hadn't proved his theory. I don't believe it can be proven. Besides, it's wrongheaded."

"How did you feel about Brother Stephen?"

"I had great respect for him. He had the guts to advocate the creation theory in the face of ridicule. Fellow scientists branded him a fool. He was proud to be *God's fool,* as he called himself. I think he took that phrase from the carving on the lintel over Brother Martin's doorway. Therein lies the bond between us. He searched mightily and found God. I searched mightily and found nothing but happenstance. We respected each other because neither of us came by our persuasions easily. Neither of us gave a damn whether they were *politically* correct. His believing in God didn't soil his work in electromagnetism and semiconductors, and my disbelief never dissuaded me from teaching creation theory."

"And your work? Has your disbelief closed out areas of philosophical inquiry?"

"I think not. But it has had one undesirable result."

"What is that?"

"My rejection of religious superstition has made me politically correct." The professor chuckled. "I resent that."

Murdock laughed. "Let me buy *you* a drink," he insisted. He liked this man.

The professor thanked him, and then stared at the amber liquid in his glass in silence for some time. He cocked his head and looked directly at Murdock. "A couple of years ago I read a story in the *Oregonian* about an FBI agent whose wife was kidnapped to discourage him from testifying in a mob-related case. I don't mean to pry, but was that you?"

Murdock took a sip of his manhattan. "Yes."

The professor frowned. They were the only people sitting at the bar. Noise emanating from a crowd gathered around the fireplace afforded privacy. "As I recall, the FBI located her, raided the place, and she died in the firefight. I'm truly sorry. I don't know what else to say."

"There is nothing to say," Murdock responded, "but thank you. It's been over two years now. I've gotten over it."

The professor put his hand on Murdock's shoulder. "I think not. The story didn't tell whether you knew beforehand they were going to conduct the raid."

"I didn't."

The professor kept his hand on Murdock's shoulder. "And you feel that you should have been consulted?"

"I'd been promised that. But one of the big boys in Washington overrode the promise."

The professor looked astonished. "Why? Did he give you a reason?"

Murdock stared at the liquor bottles neatly arranged in front of the mirror behind the bar. For the better part of a minute he was silent. "Those guys don't give reasons," Murdock replied, "or when they *do*, their reasons have been thoroughly schmoozed."

"When did you learn about it?"

"Three hours later," Murdock replied angrily. "And it wasn't the guy who gave the order that told me. He made my friend Jerr tell me. I was appalled. Karen was dead before I had any idea that it was going down. If those bums didn't want me to testify, why didn't they take *me* out? Why kidnap *her*? Taking me out was a sure thing. Taking her out wasn't. You'd think they'd be smarter than that. I've never understood it."

"Was it really a mob kidnapping?"

"The mobsters denied it, which was natural. But there was something in their denial that rang true. And why did Joe Carlyle and his brigade just rush in shooting without trying to talk them out? It was worth a try. It was standard procedure to talk first. Why didn't they follow standard procedure? The sheer audacity of the whole affair defies understanding. That's why I don't work for them anymore."

Their eyes met. Murdock shook his head.

"Why am I bothering you with all this? I'm sorry. Really. Please forgive me. We're here to enjoy ourselves."

"I started the conversation. Nothing to forgive," the professor insisted. "A couple hours ago I noticed you were having dinner with a very attractive young lady — the same lady who invited me to dine with Enrique tomorrow night."

"Diana Crenshaw."

"Yes. That *is* her name. But, forgive me, it didn't look like it was she who was on your mind. You looked like you needed to come to terms with something. If you need one, you'll find I'm a good listener. I could be trite and say 'life must go on,' but you already know that. I don't think you'll ever be at peace until you find out why they didn't follow standard procedure."

It was getting late. They finished their drinks and strolled back toward their rooms, parting at Murdock's door. Murdock entered his room and locked the door behind him. It was time to phone Allison. He sat down next to the phone. It felt good to be alone. Closing his eyes, his mind wandered. He pictured Diana. *She is similar to Karen in some ways —the very opposite in others. But it was the opposites that made her interesting. She's a chaste woman cast into an immoral job situation, if the terms "chaste" and "immoral" aren't anachronisms in modern idiom. How easily I fall into cynicism. I wasn't a cynic before Karen's death. The professor's right, of course. Peace won't come until I know why that brassy son of a bitch Joe Carlyle ordered that raid. Well, in government service men don't get promoted as high as Joe Carlyle for their brains. Except Rudi.*

Murdock unlatched the double-glazed sliding door that opened onto a balcony. He stepped into the night. Behind the lodge, the land sloped downward into a shallow ravine. Stimulated by the cold night air, he breathed in deeply and exhaled. Near its zenith, the full moon crowned the peak of the Zugspitze. But the balcony itself, beneath an overhanging roof, was in darkness. He listened. Nature seemed hushed. He listened more intensely, as he remembered doing the previous morning when he had stopped along the access road. *The monk's body had to have been there when I glanced down into the meadow yesterday.* He listened again. *It's as if the darkness itself could articulate, but chooses not to speak—or if it's speaking, it needs to raise its voice. My imagination is just overactive.* But the silence seemed to throw that argument back in his face. In one of their late evening confabs at the Hofbrauhaus, Allison had described a similar experience—when silence seemed to be literally gripping her. She had listened patiently for several minutes and heard what she described as a distant, beguiling echo. When she'd listened again, it was gone.

Enough of this. My mind will play tricks if I let it. I need to call Allison, and then to bed. I meet Brother Martin early in the morning. Perhaps he holds the keys to the puzzle.

Looking into his pocket notebook, he retrieved the number of the Bayerisher Hof Hotel in Munich and keyed the numbers. Allison would be waiting for his call. *Maybe Richard has turned up, and I can find out who our client is, and why Veritus is involved.*

⇥ 11 ⇤

When Allison arrived back at her office in Munich, it was already late afternoon. She was greeted by Terry's benevolent-cat-greeting-pathetic-mouse smile. He asked how well her meeting with Murdock had gone. She wondered whether The Weasel knew about Murdock and Linderhof, or whether he was testing to see whether a change of facial expression would confirm it. She had learned to be stolid in his presence. "Come up to my office," she commanded, "and give me a report on the day's events."

Terry frowned. Sporting his patented wounded puppy expression, he followed her as she walked quickly across the foyer. The small private elevator swallowed them. Regurgitated into the petite hallway, Allison keyed the security pad. The door opened into the private offices. They marched into Richard's. Allison sat behind his desk. He took a seat on the employee side.

"Well?" she demanded.

Terry was ruffled by her sudden assumption of Richard's authority.

"Well," he replied, fumbling for words, "there is still no information on Richard's whereabouts." He paused, searching his mind for some way to gain the upper hand. "I talked to Harvey several times." He smirked, composing himself. "I thought you would have wanted me to."

Wanted? she thought. Expected would be more accurate. I'm sure the employees knew about those calls, and that the regional boss and he are tight. He probably gave the impression that Harvey was running the office through him because he didn't have confidence in me. Allison knew his tricks.

"What did you learn from Mr. Specter — Harvey — that might be helpful?"

Terry's lips curled into a satanic grin. "He said that, if Richard's not back by tonight, he may have to come here tomorrow to take charge."

Not a muscle twitched in her face. "That certainly is one of his options," she said calmly. "But I'd hate to see it happen for your sake."

His cocky grin changed to bewilderment. "For *my* sake?"

"If Mr. Specter doesn't come tomorrow, I'll need to depend on you for some extra help."

He flashed his patented patient-cat-playing-with-foolish-mouse smile. What Terry hadn't told her yet was that Harvey had finally decided that he couldn't get away tomorrow. What he would never tell her was that Harvey's wife was in London, and his mistress was demanding attention in Frankfurt.

"As you know," she continued, "I'm scheduled to go to Regensburg tomorrow to confer with Erik Müller of Siegfried Insurance. The meeting could result in an important new account for Veritus. He's giving consideration to our handling all their Stateside investigations."

Terry grinned again.

I hate his goddamn grins. Life would be much more pleasant if this little prick were transferred.

"Just before you returned," he continued, "Harvey called again. He said that he wouldn't be able to get down here tomorrow after all." She gave no reaction. "What do you want me to do while you're in Regensburg?"

"I won't be in Regensburg," she shot back. I need you to go in my place."

His grin, along with the blood in his face, disappeared. "Me?"

"Yes, Terry. With Richard gone, I need to be *here*. You're the best person I've got to sell Erik Müller. You handle all our contacts with our Stateside offices. You know the people over there. If anyone can land this account, you can."

His customary cockiness dissolved. He stammered: "But . . . but . . . you know . . . I've never done any sales work. That's never been my job. I don't have any ex . . ."

"Experience?" Allison interrupted. She took pleasure in interrupting Terry. He didn't think well on his feet. "I know," she said. "You need experience. Lack of direct customer contact can limit opportunities. You've been with Veritus for fourteen years. You need to be noticed." She had a habit of crossing her fingers when she told white lies. Fortunately, Terry couldn't see under the desk. "I want you to succeed. Nothing is more important to the future of this company than new clients who can send us the amount of business that Siegfried Insurance can. I've talked to Erik Müller on the phone several times. We're on a first name basis. He's already taken the bait. I think you can hook him and land the fish." She pushed a file across the desk. "You may leave immediately and review this on the train. Take my hotel reservation at Regensburg."

"But what about my communications desk?" Terry stammered.

"I'm switching Peter's shift. He needs experience at what you're doing."

"But I . . ."

"There's no need to thank me. I've been watching you for some time. You're good at communications desk, but it's a dead-end job, Terry. Am I correct to assume that you want to advance?"

"Well, yes, but — "

"But nothing. I'm confident you can handle it. The skids are already greased. Close the deal tomorrow and you'll be a hero." *Or*, she thought more likely, *you'll fall flat on your ass and I'll bail you out.*

Terry recovered his composure, but just barely. "Before I leave, I need to complete the duty log and prepare the daily report. What case were you working on today?"

"Don't be concerned about the duty log. Peter will complete it. Siegfried Insurance is important. Leave the little stuff to Peter. You have bigger fish to fry."

"But Harvey . . ."

"Don't you worry about Harvey. Get cracking. You have a lot of preparation to do in a short time. You're free to leave the office now. Good luck."

In a way she felt sorry for The Weasel. *The poor bastard doesn't see through Harvey. Harvey's the consummate politician, like Joe Carlyle at the FBI.* She flipped open a spiral notepad in which she kept notes for her book and wrote: "Power bought by guile and subterfuge ultimately turns back on you and destroys you, because truth cannot be hidden nor justice denied forever." *I'll work Terry into my book too. Everybody knows someone like him. When Harvey finishes using him, he'll spit him out like a melon seed. Terry may lose his cherry tomorrow. Maybe it'll open his beady little eyes.*

*   *   *

After getting her ducks in a row at the office, Allison walked to the hotel. After dining in the hotel restaurant, she took a long walk in the cold night air. Her mind turned over the events of the day. She wondered where Richard was. No ransom note had arrived. No terrorist had made a claim. She knew of no one who had an agenda against Richard personally. *Could it be a vendetta that went back to his years with Swiss Army intelligence? Did he decide to disappear for some reason? What reason?* She knew him well, but she couldn't imagine one. *Maybe Murdock has learned something.*

The warmth felt good in her room. She changed into flannel pajamas and a warm robe, curled up in a chair next to the radiator, and opened the newspaper. The evening passed quietly. At 10:30 she recalled that she hadn't passed on Moira's message to Murdock. As she reached for the phone, it rang. It was Murdock.

"What's new, Al? Did you have a good day?"

"Yes," she said, "but before I forget, Moira asked me to tell you that she obtained the information that you wanted."

"Super. That'll save me some time. She's an efficient gal, Allison. I could use Moira."

"She's tied up until the weekend. I'll send her Saturday. Unless Richard materializes. Then it's his call. What have you learned since we met at Linderhof?"

"Not much. The professor is more complicated than I expected. We talked over a few drinks. He gave me a lecture on the quality of teaching in our universities. He's beating around the damn bush, Al. I think he wants to tell me something, but he doesn't know whether to trust me yet."

"Trust you? You're investigating the murder of his friend. Why should *he* need to trust *you*?"

"I haven't the foggiest."

"If he's involved in the killing, he must know you couldn't withhold evidence."

"I don't think that's it. Maybe it's my imagination. He mentioned the anthropic principles. Do they mean anything to you?"

"I've read about them."

"He and Brother Stephen had agreed to disagree about them. How's that for progress? I'm getting nowhere."

"The professor sounds like an interesting man. I'd like to meet him."

"Then you shall," Murdock replied. "I'm certain he'd enjoy meeting you. I don't know how long he'll be here. This is only Tuesday. Can you get down here before the weekend?"

"I doubt it. Not unless Richard returns."

"No word on him, Al?"

"No ransom demand. No threats. Nothing. Not a clue."

"Getting late, Al. I'm meeting Brother Martin in the morning. Talk to you tomorrow night. Okay?"

"Okay, Murdock. Have a good night." Click.

She climbed into bed. Her spiral notebook was lying on the end table. She fluffed the pillow and placed it against the headboard. Sitting up in bed, she placed the notebook on her knees, opened her fountain pen, and began to write: "smashmouth politics, tough and uninhibited by scruples . . ." She stopped. *What if Harvey gets wind there's some secret investigation in progress and that he's out of the loop? He might still come in person tomorrow because, by now he knows his weasel won't be around to spy for him. But I can manage him. I'll show a little leg and schmooze him with flattery.*

* * *

Alone in his room in the Zugspitze Hof, the professor extracted his laptop from its carrying case, placed it on a table near the fireplace, and pushed the start button. While the computer was booting, he walked over to the door, locked it, and shook it to make certain it was secure. Reaching into the pocket of his parka, he removed two floppy diskettes bound together with a narrow rubber band. The disks, given to him by Brother Martin, contained memoirs written by the murdered man, Brother Stephen — disks that Stephen had made specifically for the professor. To the best of Martin's recollection, Stephen had begun them late in September. The professor hoped they would explain the urgency in Brother Stephen's invitation that had brought him to the monastery. A feeling of uneasiness mixed with expectancy came over him as he inserted the first disk into the drawer and brought its contents onto the screen — an uneasiness borne of being the first to read the words of a man whose life had been cruelly ripped from him by a bullet. He read slowly, hoping to detect a clue to the murderer or the motive.

> I, Stephen, a child of God, offer this memoir as a chronicle of what I have done, and as a suggestion of a context in which my work may be justified. Many times during my calculations and experiments I have wondered whether the Church was right when it tried to silence Galileo. The epoch of science and social thought which he, four centuries ago, helped bring kicking and screaming into the world has, especially in the last century, proven how easily Man can become more brutish than the wildest animals. How can anything that my work might unleash produce events more reprehensible than those the politicians contrived that exhaustively dehumanized the killing fields of the twentieth century? I pray that my work will not permit such chaotic horrors to leak into the cosmos.
>
> I look forward instead to a new epoch, more gentle and more rational than the present, where an unspoiled wisdom will nurture a less arrogant race of men — an epoch that my work may help to kindle. If it does, I shall take no pride in it, because I am merely an empty vessel that God has filled as He pleased. All praise be to God. If, instead, my work contributes to a new dark age, then may God forgive me for I have misread His mind.

The professor clicked to the next page. There began pages of esoteric mathematical formulae mixed with symbols and electronic diagrams. Avariciously, he devoured them, sometimes in disbelief, checking them on his handheld calculator, until finally, mentally expended, he fell off to sleep.

$$\rightleftharpoons \; 12 \; \rightleftharpoons$$

As the sun had set beyond the west coast of Cyprus, the airport at Limassol was not busy. Enrique taxied the jet to the general aviation ramp. He came to a stop near the fixed base operation and cut the power. As the engines spooled down, he released his seat belt and carefully placed his approach charts in his flight bag.

Frank turned to him, smiling. "Nice approach and landing, Boss."

Enrique returned the smile. "Thanks. I should shoot approaches more often. I want to keep sharp."

"Will you take the controls on the return trip?"

"I think not, Frank. Linda will want to debrief me."

Enrique climbed out of the copilot's seat, turned, closed his flight bag, and stored it in the main cabin. Linda was busy at the laptop. He paused and turned toward her. "What are your plans for tonight, Linda?"

Linda swiveled her chair so that she faced him, her smile pensive. "I plan to remain on board."

"Are you sure? Wouldn't you be more comfortable . . ."

"The sleeping quarters here are more comfortable than some foreign hotels. Besides, I want to monitor the communications equipment. From the information I already have, Boris Romanovsky is a complex character. I'm trying to obtain information from a source I've just discovered in the Ukraine. Be cautious, Enrique. I recommend that you make no firm commitments until after we talk again."

"Thank you. I don't plan to."

She looked out the window. A Cessna 310 taxied over and parked next to them. The pilot exited and waited next to the aircraft.

"It looks like that's your transportation to the villa," she said pointing.

Enrique peered through a port. "The pilot looks like he could use a shave and a haircut. This could be an interesting flight."

"Should I arrange an air taxi instead?"

Enrique hesitated. "No," he said. "It might insult my host. If this character is reckless, I'll take the controls."

The right side of her lips curved upward incredulously. "How long has it been since you've flown an aircraft with reciprocating engines?"

"Not since I obtained my jet rating seven years ago."

Linda's eyes met his. "Are you still legally qualified to fly that type of aircraft with a passenger on board?"

Enrique shook his head. "No. Of course not. But it would only require a few hours flying the aircraft and a check-ride with an instructor to requalify."

Linda turned back to her laptop. "Have a good evening," she said without looking back.

He hesitated. "Likewise," he replied. He considered himself properly admonished but not to the point of changing his mind.

As Enrique exited the jet, the pilot of the Cessna walked toward him. They spoke briefly. Enrique climbed on the wing, opened the cabin door, and deposited his overnight bag on a back seat. He lowered himself into the copilot seat and placed his briefcase on his lap. The pilot went through his preflight checklist. In spite of his slovenly appearance, Enrique was impressed by his thoroughness. The pilot obtained the necessary clearances by radio, and in a few minutes they taxied to runway nine, which faced into the east wind. The pilot placed the RPM controls at high, the mixture controls at full rich, and then pushed the throttles full forward. The plane lurched ahead. Once airborne, the pilot made a sharp climbing 180° right turn to the west. The sun had set. On their left wing, along the coast of the Mediterranean, lights shown from seaside homes. The sky was clear except for some high cirrus in the west, colored fuchsia by the rays of the hidden sun. They followed the coastline. After a fifteen minute flight, the pilot eased back on the throttles and commenced a descent. Enrique noticed a dirt landing strip pass beneath them, roughly paralleling the Mediterranean Sea. The pilot made a descending 180° turn into the wind, and dropped the flaps and the landing gears. After a smooth touchdown, the aircraft rolled to a stop near a line of tall Italian cypress that formed a demarcation line between flight operations and the villa. Enrique observed a tall rotund man standing in the half-light near the trees, waving toward him. *That must be my host, Boris Romanovsky, he thought.*

As Enrique stepped from the aircraft, Boris shouted a greeting, ran toward him, shook his hand vigorously, and grabbed Enrique's overnight bag.

"Señor Perez-Krieger," he shouted jovially, putting his arm around him in a bear hug, "it is good to meet you at last. I have heard much good things about you . . . mostly that you have big money to invest . . . and I, Boris Iliovitch Romanovsky, like money. Perhaps as much as you do. But so. We make much more money . . . together. You will see."

Enrique estimated him to be six-foot-four, broad shouldered, and with massive hands like an outfielder's glove. A green silk shirt opened at the collar to reveal a jungle of chest hair. His head was totally bald. Upon being released from the bear hug, Enrique responded with a genteel bow and an amiable smile.

Boris motioned him toward an opening in the tree line, which revealed the beginning of an asphalt pathway lighted by foot lamps. Boris led and invited him to follow. They descended among thousands of red bougainvillea, which met in arches overhead. A garden on both sides extended as far as Enrique could see in the dusk. They descended to a lower terrace. The garden changed to long grasses and blazing orange geraniums. They passed an oval reflecting pool. In its center, a fountain pulsated a single column of water, alternating from five to ten feet high. Marble colonnades and benches graced both sides. On the next lower terrace, another pool sported three large marble fish, each spewing a fountain of water. The final terrace contained the villa and an Olympic size swimming pool. A low cliff dropped off to the Mediterranean.

"You enjoy my gardens?" Boris asked.

"Yes," Enrique replied. "I look forward to seeing them in the daylight.

"Actually," Boris said, without having been asked, "I have four gardens, each different. One is Japanese. I have imported Japanese experts to design and care for it." They turned toward the villa. "This house is built in the Roman tradition of the *villa urbana*, a country house with city comforts, as opposed to the *villa rustica,* which was essentially a Roman farmhouse with a kitchen and stables. I admire the Romans. Their architecture is strong and clean. There is no evidence of Roman presence at this precise spot, although I'm sure they were here. Cyprus was part of their empire for hundreds of years. I think they took it from the Egyptians." He pointed to an old tower at the far side of a vineyard. "That is what remains of a crusader's castle dating back to the twelfth century A.D. That's when crusading orders of knights ruled Cyprus. Interestingly, only the subterranean cells and dungeon remain intact."

Enrique was impressed with Boris's knowledge of history. They walked into a large open space, which terminated abruptly at a cliff. Twenty feet below, the sea pounded against huge basalt rocks. Surrounded by the open space was the living quarters of the villa—a magnificent structure of high white stucco walls with bright orange roof tiles. Heavy oak double doors opened into a large hall—a two-story arcade of white stone. The second story was ringed by a walkway with a finely crafted wrought iron railing. In the center of the arcade, open to the sky, was a bright circular courtyard with a gentle fountain, which sounded like a stream in a meadow. The courtyard's circumference was accented by a colonnade of Corinthian columns. As they entered the court, Enrique noticed a second two-story arcade perpendicular to the first, thus forming a cross with arms of equal length. The courtyard formed its axis. In the four wings, on either side of the long halls, were rooms of generous proportions. One was assigned to him. It contained a covered bed with delicately hand-carved posts and festooned with the finest Spanish lace. *Fit for a queen, Enrique thought*, somewhat uncomfortably. Handsomely handcrafted armchairs, end tables, a dresser, and a wardrobe, completed the furnishings, all of which appeared to be late Renaissance Italian originals.

"I'm afraid they are not originals," Boris confessed, guessing his thoughts. "They're expertly crafted fakes. But so, the average man does not know that. A common man might think they have great value. But a cultured man such as yourself has already recognized their lack of genuineness. Boris knows he could not fool you, my friend. With you I am honest. Please make yourself comfortable. If you need anything, please dial one-one on the phone. After you freshen up, please join me in the den. When you leave your room, turn right. Third door on the left. The only double door."

*   *   *

They dined on a spacious veranda, which overhung the cliff. Moonlight revealed puffy clouds low on the southern horizon. Panfried fish with loaves of fresh-baked breads and spanakopita suggested to Enrique that Boris had had his preferences investigated. Conversation was lighthearted. After dinner, Enrique edged the conversation toward commerce.

"Tell me, Boris, what brought you to Cyprus?"

Boris grinned expansively. "In the former Soviet Union I worked as tractor repairman on collective farm. Then I join the Communist Party. Soon I became a minor official in the Ministry of Agriculture. They gave me a two-room apartment in Kiev. A good room. Sometimes it had heat in winter. I worked hard. When I became assistant to the third deputy minister, I was given a three-room apartment with a private heating unit, and an automobile that usually ran. I observed and learned how things work. I learned how people work the system. I learned who screws who and who gets what. I learned to screw first deputy minister, even though she was very ugly — so ugly her husband didn't screw her. He had a pretty mistress at Polish embassy. So I kept on screwing the first deputy minister and got a better car. I learned that a better car made her look less ugly. It ran all the time. When the Soviet Union drowned in its own slobber,

the smart ones in Communist Party — like me — next day become capitalists. We keep same connections — 'network' as capitalists say. Now, look
around you. I live better than under the communists. Nyet? Because I'm
smart and I learned how to get things done in new Russia and Ukraine. I
make much money. I screw pretty girls now. You will see."

Enrique raised a snifter of cognac, which a servant had placed before him. "A toast to my most gracious host," he said. A cool breeze
drifted off the Mediterranean. He sipped the liquor. It warmed him. "I
compliment you in your choice of leisurewear, Boris. You have good
taste, and you wear the hottest brand names. Are these available in
Moscow, or did you acquire them in Cyprus?"

Boris roared with laughter. "Neither, my friend. Don't you know?
We jump in jet and fly to Lebanon. One hour. We party in Beirut. It's
coming back to life, you know. Soon it'll be playground of Middle East
again. We enjoy an evening with imported French cognac and imported
French girls who make you hotter than the cognac. You will see. I shall
take you. Next morning we throw women out of bed and rent car. We
drive to Aleppo in Syria."

"Isn't it quite difficult to do business in Syria?"

"Easy, once you learn that laws are made for suckers. For example
banks in Syria can't exchange money. In hills of Lebanon, near border,
men sell us bags filled with Syrian pounds — black market exchange
rates. In Aleppo we get big bargains on the best brand names. Every al-
leyway has an unofficial currency trading office, but exchange rates are
not so good as along road in Lebanon. But, if you cannot buy enough
Syrian pounds, merchants openly accept American dollars. It is illegal,
but who cares so long as police get their share. If they don't, you die from
sickness in jail. Syrian policemen need American dollars so they too can
rent French girls in Beirut. No good whores in Islamic countries. It's
against their religion." Boris roared with laughter. "The system works.
Not complicated. I load a truck in Syria. My men drive goods back to my
plane in Beirut. We fly back to Cyprus. I keep what I want and sell rest in
Munich or Paris or Prague at huge profit."

"How do the Syrian merchants obtain these brand names so in-
expensively?"

"Very good question. I like you. Not afraid to ask a dumb question.
But, forgive me please, I'm not yet ready to answer. Anyway, you knew it
was a dumb question. You're just testing me." He roared again with
laughter. "But, anyway, tomorrow I shall reverse all that. I have compelled their source to sell to me cheaper than they sell to the Syrians. Tomorrow I shall cut off their supply and absorb it myself. By end of week,
merchants in Aleppo will be begging to buy from me. And I will sell to

Aleppo merchants wholesale. But *I* will set wholesale price."

"How will you get paid? As you said, private banking is illegal in Syria."

"Boris is smart. Transactions of 10,000 U.S. dollars can be arranged in an unofficial 'textile' trading office in the center of the commercial district of Aleppo. I deposit Syrian pounds with the 'textile traders,' and two days later I pick up German marks from trader's account in Munich."

"You're amazing, Boris. How do you stay out of jail?"

"Jail? What do you mean . . . jail? Who would want Boris in jail? Boris helps Syrian policemen and judges live better. Is that not good? Sure it is. They like it. French whores don't have the same religion. They like to make money from Syrian judges and policemen. Everybody is happy. Boris likes to make people happy."

"Do you miss your home in Russia?"

"I have a wonderful life here. To hell with Mother Russia. Here it is warm and convenient. Most leading Russian banks have branches here. It is good place to make business. You will see."

"Where do you obtain these brand name fashions at such a low price?"

Boris impatiently ran his huge right hand over his bald head from front to back. "Why do you ask? Buyers in Paris and Munich are too smart to ask. That is why we sell to them." A broad grin crossed Boris's face. "Ah. You make joke, yes?"

Enrique held his cognac up to the candlelight and enjoyed the amber glow refracted by the glass. "Yes. I'm pleased that you appreciated my joke. But isn't it difficult to obtain a dependable supply of discount brand names?"

Boris roared. "I like your jokes. You are very astute man. Of course, we make labels in Russia. It puts Russian people to work. That is what you like, nyet? Russians produce labels that look exactly like real thing. Then, in Lebanon, we remove cheap labels and sew on better ones. The value of the goods jump. That's smart business. I'm a good businessman. You will see."

After dinner they retired to the den and settled into American-made recliners upholstered in silk. A servant offered Enrique a Cuban cigar, which he accepted. Boris lit a pipe and savored the sweet taste and aroma of Turkish tobacco. He kicked off his shoes and reclined. "Enrique, my friend," he began, "you want to do business in Russia. Good. But you must remember always that deals with Russians are unconventional. I know Russians. I am Russian. Maybe half Ukrainian. Some say my father was a yak. No matter. If you wish to succeed in Russia, first you must find the right partner. Nothing else matters. I will assist you. That is my business. I'll find best partner for you. Second, you must remember that, when you negotiate with Russians, it is expected that you buy the same horse twice. Allow for that."

Enrique flashed his most engaging smile. "Of course, Boris, but I worry that you may be the silent owner of the horse."

Boris roared again with laughter. "Here, friend. I like you." He pushed a bottle of rare Swiss brandy across the table. "Enjoy."

"You have expensive tastes."

"I don't like vodka. That's for peasants. I'm descended from royalty. My great, great, great, et cetera grandfather was the bastard son of Alexander I, Czar of all the Russians. So now, I'm the latest and most successful descendant of my royal ancestral bastard. Do I not look the part?" Boris laughed. Without waiting for a response, he continued. "Of course I do."

Enrique nodded politely. "Has the commercial law and the court system in Russia been modernized to the point that business disputes can be resolved with a high degree of predictability?"

"You listen. In Russia you avoid conflict. Never use courts or police. Resolve problems behind scenes. I know the behind scenes. I'll guide you straight shot. You'll make money. I'll make money. Our bastard sons will make money . . . please excuse . . . *if* you have bastard sons. We will fashion a good relationship between the two of us. In our spare time we'll long enjoy good cognac and sizzling women. What more can life offer? I know you Chileans appreciate fiery women. No? Yes. Of course. You don't have to say. I know. All men are platoon buddies when they talk about women."

Enrique was becoming impatient. The hour was late and not much had been accomplished, other than gaining insights into what made Boris Romanovsky tick. "Perhaps we can talk about some specifics," he suggested.

"We shall make an agreement in morning," Boris suggested. "Plenty of time then. After you leave, smart-ass Cypriot lawyers will put it into writing. Come back next weekend to sign. I'll have woman for you. She will make love like never before. You will not want to leave." He laughed uproariously, spilling cognac on his slacks. "After I help you, you will need to do nothing but count money and make love. You will be sheik of Grand Cayman with finest harem." Boris chuckled under his breath, his eyes rolling. "Young women. You bet. But not tonight. Tonight we learn to enjoy each other's company. Good talk. Good drinks. Funny jokes. Then we'll always be friends. In morning we'll make deal."

Wednesday
November 19

⫸ 13 ⫷

Enrique slept well. He awoke at six. Arising, he slipped into a robe and walked over to the window. His room faced east, but there was no sign of dawn. He noticed that, off to the left, the lights were on at the pool. Stepping into his slippers, he opened the double doors, stepped outside, and walked in the direction of the light. Upon reaching the pool, he saw Boris swimming laps. Boris noticed him, stopped, and grabbed the edge of the pool.

"Good morning, Señor Perez-Krieger."

"Good morning. Please call me Enrique."

"Good morning, Enrique. There is a suit on that chair," he said pointing. "It will fit you. Please join me. I must do twenty more laps. You can change right there." Noticing Enrique's hesitation he added, "And don't worry. There's no one around to see."

Quickly donning the suit, Enrique gladly joined Boris. After twenty laps, they toweled and headed back to the villa where breakfast awaited them on a terrace facing southeast.

"Perfect place to view the dawn," Boris said. "As you can see, the first hint appears now on the horizon. Within minutes the sun's rays will catch those cumulus clouds in the east and set them ablaze. They shall reflect beautifully on the water."

The rising sun, slinking over the mists where the sea met the sky, performed as if it had been scripted for a Hollywood movie. Its light caught the whitecaps, and colored them orange-red with patches of yellow. Creeping upward until its entire circumference was above the horizon, its brazen redness flooded the terrace with light. The two men relaxed and enjoyed a leisurely breakfast. A sterling silver serving platter in the center of the table contained warm, fresh-baked croissants. Beside it was sweet butter, a selection of jams, thin slices of ham, and blocks of Brie and feta. Strong Greek coffee completed the menu.

Boris half filled his cup, added a like amount of heavy cream, and three spoonfuls of sugar. Withdrawing a pad and a fountain pen from a briefcase learning against a table leg, he placed them on the table and looked up at Enrique. "Whatever you need, I get," he said. You want me to steal a Russian company for you? It can be done. Cyprus is Russia's financial gateway to the world. We have direct flights to Moscow every day. The government welcomes us and taxes our money. But that's okay. We lie to them about amounts of transactions. We keep three sets of books. They know, but we take good care of tax collectors and police. Politician's campaign accounts have good balances. Already I curse well in Greek, so I can deal with local merchants and fancy women."

Enrique refilled his cup and turned his chair toward the sea. Three gulls soared effortlessly, riding upon drafts of a gentle sea breeze ascending the cliff. Offshore, four fishing boats bobbed in a lazy sea, their crews preparing nets. The morning was cool. Boris watched Enrique out of the corner of his eye and waited for him to speak.

Enrique sighed. "How can I convince you that I'm genuinely looking to invest capital in companies that will provide decent-paying jobs for Russian workers? My partners and I are dedicated to helping improve conditions in Russia."

"But so. We pay correct bribes to politicians. You make it look like you want to help Russian peoples. That helps politicians to look good. You smart man indeed."

Enrique noticed that Boris's English was deteriorating again. "I don't want to throw money away, you understand. I'm not interested in handouts. They make people lazy and irresponsible. I'm not a socialist in capitalist clothing. I want to either find or form companies that can be profitable with proper capitalization and responsible management, and I want to send deserving young Russians to my business college in the Caymans."

Boris roared with laughter. "But so, my friend, it is hard to believe you. One should invest to make money. To hell with rest. With your family's wealth, you should know that. You invest in Russia. I see you get good return. You give me — say 25 percent — of return. I happy. You happy. If someone get in our way, I kill them. That is how business works in Russia. I kill only when is necessary. No more. You want to do business in Russia, you listen good to Boris — the great etcetera grandson of imperial bastard."

Enrique frowned. He stared out to sea. A cluster of stratocumulus clouds were forming near the horizon. The sun painted their bottoms blood red. *An omen, he thought.* "You make murder sound respectable. I won't be a party to killing anyone over money."

"Maybe you are religious?"

"Maybe I am."

"Good. I am religious too," Boris said donning sunglasses and turning his lounge chair more directly into the sun. "Many religious people believe that 'Thou shalt not kill.' Some are willing to kill to prove it. The crusaders, who built the dungeon over there, were Christians. They were sent by the Roman pope to kill 'infidels' in the Holy Land, and to rob them of their lands. On the way to the Holy Land, they killed many of my Eastern Orthodox Christian forebears. These soldiers of God raped Christian women and young girls and threw them in dungeons like that one until they were finished playing with them. The Roman pope promised that all sins would be forgiven upon their return from the crusade. But so you see, it is not wrong to rape and kill, if you rape and kill the right people at the right time." He looked out to sea and laughed under his breath at the irrefutable logic of his wisdom.

Enrique shuddered. "You're a irreclaimable skeptic, my friend. I wouldn't want to be your enemy."

"So, be my friend," Boris insisted good-naturedly. "I know how to stay alive. You remember the first deputy minister whose husband wouldn't screw her because she was too ugly?"

"Yes. I remember your telling me the story last night."

"Well, when her husband discovered that I was screwing her, he decided to kill me. It was a matter of honor — not love, you see. But you can also see that he did not kill me." He laughed under his breath. "I knew his young mistress. She was tired of him. One night when he visited her, he drank some vodka, which was not good for him. He died. It was ruled an accidental death."

"Did you . . ."

Boris smirked. "I have good judgment," he interrupted jovially. "Whenever someone dies over deal, it is never Boris. It will never be you. The long arm of Russian Mafia now reaches the Cayman Islands and Chile, but you needn't worry. You will survive if you stick with me."

Enrique stared out to sea. He'd never done business with a man like Boris. *What price might I have to pay? he wondered.*

"I like you," Boris chortled. "But why you pick such nasty place to do business? Maybe there are workers somewhere else in world that you should help. Why Russia?"

Enrique resolved to push forward and see where it would take him. He turned to face Boris directly. "I and my backers believe that everyone is better off in a stable world. If Russia's economy crashes, and if its progress toward integration into world commerce fractures, it may trigger worldwide instability. Businesses and their employees everywhere will suffer. But instead, if people perceive that their standard of living is improving or likely to improve soon, that perception is good for them and good for business. We want to see the expansion of a comfortable law-abiding middle class in Russia. That is the best guaranty that democracy will thrive."

Boris's expression lost its joviality. "I would too, my friend. But such things may not be possible. The problem with Russia is that it is full of Russians. For centuries we have thrived on suffering. We are very good at it. Russians expect to suffer. If you tell Russian people you want to relieve their suffering, they will laugh. They will ask why would you want to do that? Suffering — he is an old friend to us Russians. You must not kidnap him. He is our soul."

Enrique was silent for several minutes as each sipped his coffee. Finally, he spoke haltingly. "I agree, Boris," he said without looking away from the sea. "We will tell them nothing." He raised his glass and sipped the brandy. "We will just *do* it." He smiled, and their eyes met. "When we get results, the results will speak for themselves. Will you help me?"

Boris was pensive for the better part of a minute. He shook his head. Leaning toward Enrique, he held up his drink as if he were offering a toast. "I think you mean it. Maybe you're idealistic, but that's not totally absurd. Perhaps it's my royal blood that makes me hope that you can succeed. Yes, indeed. I shall help the man who wants to be loved by Mother Russia."

"That is *not* our purpose."

"Forgive me, Señor Enrique. Even if it were your purpose, you would not succeed. Mother Russia loves only her own."

Enrique shrugged off the remark. "So that we may talk details at our next meeting, what do you need to know?"

"I need direction. What kind of business? Russians are good at making guns and bombs. If we build modern factory, we can employ many Russians making guns and bombs and sell them all over world. Big market. Big dollars. Guns best merchandise."

Enrique smiled. "I'd rather not think about businesses that are illegal."

"But so," Boris injected with mock pain, "if they are made legally in Russia and sold to a legal government, how can this be illegal?"

"Just to governments?"

"Well, sometimes to a government just before it becomes a government. Can we help if we sometimes anticipate history?"

"Are you talking about elected governments?"

"Sure! Of course, Enrique, my friend. But you know even in your own country, not all ballots have been made of paper. Some have been made by generals. Besides, peace comes when there is a balance of terror."

"Do you make gun deals here in Limassol?"

"No. Buyers and sellers from all over the world meet in Munich. Sometimes even at Zugspitze Hof." The jovial expression returned to Boris's face. "But so, I understand. You don't like guns. I find some other choices for you. You give me today ten thousand United States dollars for what Americans call bird-dog fee. You come back Saturday. Sunday I take you to Orthodox Church. Priest will pray for the dismal state of our poor souls and for the success of our enterprise. Then we go forth and practice new golden rule for twenty-first century — do others before they do you. But so, you'll find I'm good bird dog. Find many birds for you to choose from. You be happy. And Saturday night I have hot women for you who will arouse the fires in your Chilean soul. Sunday morning the priest will forgive your Saturday night sins. I pay him."

"Will the priest pray for the women too?"

"I don't pay for that. They smart girls. Don't worry. They pray for themselves."

"What if, after I give you ten thousand dollars, I'm not happy with the prospects you find for me? Do I get my money back?"

"Boris never gives money back. I make you happy — don't worry — or you refuse to do business with me again. Ten thousand dollars is not much money. Take a chance on Boris. Good result. You'll see."

Enrique looked at his watch and arose. It was time to reboard the Cessna for the flight back to Limassol. Enrique had seen enough of Boris for now, and he didn't want to make commitments until he had had time to better assess the man and to share his impressions with Linda.

"By the way," Boris said, "I understand that you are staying at the Zugspitze Hof. Is that correct?"

"Yes," Enrique replied. He offered his hand to Boris who arose to take it.

A sly grin crossed Boris's face. "Have the police learned who killed the monk?"

"I don't believe so — at least not when I departed yesterday."

Boris put his arm around Enrique in a bear hug and then released him. The grin turned to inquisitiveness. "Do you know what the killer was after?"

"No," Enrique replied. "Do you?"

Boris roared with laughter. "No! Of course not! How could I?"

Neither believed the other.

*   *   *

Enrique's jet lifted off the runway at Limassol at precisely 10:15 A.M. local time. When they achieved level flight, Linda poured two coffees, handed one across the table to Enrique, and poked a key on her laptop. She studied the screen.

"We will be cruising at flight level 320, airspeed will be mach .83 in level flight, and we'll arrive at Garmisch-Partenkirchen shortly after 1:00 P.M. All of your dinner guests are confirmed for tonight. Our mole at FBI headquarters in Washington reports that the Bavarian State Police have inquired about you and that woman, Diana Crenshaw. I got in touch with our mole in the Bavarian State Police. He confirms our FBI source and reports that the Bavarians have made an inquiry to Cypriot Police about Boris Romanovsky. Our mole in the Cypriot police believes his last name may be fake. He suggests that Boris may be descended from a long line of bastards but not necessarily from Czar Alexander I as he claims. I think our Cypriot mole is reliable as long as we continue to pay him more than Boris does."

"Make sure we do that."

He filled her in on his meetings with Boris. She listened intently and said little. Occasionally she tapped the keys of her laptop. When he finished, he asked if there was anything else he needed to know.

"That woman has had your favorite Chilean wines flown in to surprise you tonight."

"Her name is Diana Crenshaw."

"I know her damn name. She's arranged for the cost of the dinner to be charged to her account, although you will appear to be host. My gut feeling is that the professor is not as benign as he looks. I suspect he has knowledge of what went on at the monastery that led to the death of the unfortunate Brother Stephen. You will want to warm up to him tonight. And, finally, before that woman, Diana Crenshaw, charms you to the point of silliness, if you want my female intuition, which you always politely listen to and invariably ignore, Murdock McCabe is working at falling in love with her, and she's not discouraging him. She doesn't discourage you either. I think she's shrewd and scheming. That's fine for any man who likes to diddle vipers."

Enrique laughed. "You haven't met her and you don't like her?"

"Excuse me," she responded. "I need to type your conference summary."

They said little to one another during the remainder of the flight.

⅔ **14** ⅖

First light penetrated a cold, clear night sky over the peak of the Zugspitze, dissolving the stars clinging to the eastern horizon. Cautiously, Murdock navigated a snowmobile, its single light revealing the path through an ice mist and up a serpentine trail walled in on either side by the pitch-blackness of the deep woods. Presently, the trail spilled into a clearing. In the gray-dawn twilight, he saw it. Thick stone walls rose twenty-five feet on all four sides. To Murdock, St. Luke's monastery looked more like a mighty fortress than a place of prayer and meditation. He smiled inwardly. *If Satan were to attack these monks, the old evil one had better use modern firepower. Pitchforks or even small arms won't cut it.*

He brought his snowmobile to a stop near an eight foot high heavy oak door which slowly opened as if expecting him. A man wearing an ankle-length dark-brown woolen robe, secured by a rope around his girth, stepped out. He was a tall, confident, muscular, slightly overweight man, maybe an inch shorter than Murdock, but with a heavy graying black beard. A cowl covered his head.

"Good morning. You must be Brother Martin," Murdock said as he shut down the motor and disembarked.

"God be with you, Murdock McCabe, and welcome to St. Luke's."

"I am grateful that modern monasteries have telephones, and that you had the time to see me this morning."

Brother Martin flashed a broad grin. "It's God's will and my pleasure to obey."

They shook hands and proceeded through the door and into a large open yard in which the snow was mostly undisturbed. Brother Martin closed the door behind them and slid a heavy bolt into place. Murdock estimated that the walls were at least five feet thick at the base. They walked past a stone chapel topped with a traditional Bavarian onion dome. Beyond the chapel lay a two-story, square wooden building that reminded Murdock of the quadrangles at Oxford. Its bare dark-brown wood formed a contrast to the dazzling white snow. They walked through an archway, the second floor providing its top. A dusting of light snow was still falling. There was no sound except the squeaking of snow under their feet. Murdock felt isolated. He had an eerie feeling, like the world outside had passed away, like he had been transported into a place of deep peace.

They passed into an open courtyard. A covered walkway lined the outside walls of the courtyard quadrangle. In the center stood a fountain, silent, surrounded by wooden benches, all snow covered. Snow on the walkway showed recent evidence of many feet.

"We use it for morning prayers," Brother Martin explained. "We rise at 5:30 and walk there in silence for an hour. It may seem fatuous, but it is the way of peace. We speak only to God."

"Not fatuous at all," Murdock replied. "I admire dedication."

Brother Martin walked briskly. Murdock, athletic as he was, had some difficulty keeping up. They breezed through a door and into a long, dimly lit, somewhat heated passageway. Brother Martin lowered his cowl disclosing a carefully shaved tonsure. Near the end of the first quad, Brother Martin stopped and opened a door.

"This is my chamber," he said, motioning for Murdock to enter. "I hope you will find it comfortable."

The room was sparsely furnished — a cot, a rather large desk, a computer table with a computer on top, and two stuffed chairs. Brother Martin invited him to choose one. Light poured in through a tall, narrow window. The rising sun had caught the peak of the Zugspitze and ignited into a blaze of brilliant orange-red. The room radiated in the fresh light of the new day. Under his feet, Murdock observed flat stones, carefully hewn by expert hands and, he assumed, burnished by thousands of feet over hundreds of years.

Over the doorway through which they had entered, Murdock noticed a massive lintel. Carved into it in a magnificent ancient script was a sentence in Old German. Murdock paused to read it, but its idiom eluded him.

Brother Martin followed his eyes. "Ah, my friend, I see that you too are enchanted by the inscription. When I first read it, I knew immediately that this must be my room."

"You don't often see workmanship of such skill. Who carved it?"

"We don't know, but it must be quite ancient."

"Its inscription is in a more ancient German than I'm familiar with. What does it say?"

"One cannot easily translate it. If I were to capture the thought that the antiquated words bring to mind, I would read: 'If I must be a fool, let me be God's fool.' It's an absurd sentiment by today's standards, I suppose, but I find empathy with it. You see, I am a profoundly foolish man.

But, forgive me, you have not come here to talk of me, or the inscriptions of fools more ancient than I. How may I help you?"

They seated themselves. Brother Martin folded his arms across his chest, over a rounding belly. Murdock took out his notebook. "You've already talked to the police," Murdock began. "You're not required to talk to me but I . . ."

Brother Martin interrupted. "Don't concern yourself. I wish to talk to you."

"Thank you." Murdock glanced down his list of questions — some contingent upon Brother Martin's response. "First, I find it curious that a monastic order is made up mostly of scientists. Are not science and religion diametrically opposed to each other?"

Brother Martin chuckled. "That is a misconception."

"Then it's a misconception held by many."

"Well," Brother Martin replied, smiling, "I can't argue with you. But like so many popularly held misconceptions, I believe the truth is quite the opposite. A great deal of knowledge is hidden from us. Does God have his reasons? I could only speculate. Mind you, it's not forbidden. It's merely hidden. For example: Let's consider the truth about elementary particles and superstrings. Are there particles even smaller than the quarks and the leptons that make up the protons, neutrons, and electrons that make up the atoms? A good question. God has given us the ability to find the answer. Scientific research is merely searching the mind of God."

Murdock would have liked to have continued the discussion. Since boyhood, he'd been fascinated by stories about the origin of the universe. But he moved on.

"Did you see Brother Stephen on Monday morning — the day he was murdered?

"Yes. He stopped by my room just before he departed for the village. We spoke briefly — nothing important — just small talk. He said that he was mailing a package to his manager in Oregon. He didn't say what was in it and I didn't ask. He often shipped packages to Oregon. I didn't think anything of it. Other than that, our conversation was inconsequential."

Murdock suspected that Martin knew more than he was willing to say. He wondered what he was hiding. "Do you know who killed Brother Stephen?" he asked bluntly.

"No."

"Do you know why he was killed?"

"The killer took the package from him. I draw the same inferences as you."

Murdock was chafing. "My time is valuable, as I'm certain yours is. Forthright answers will save time for both of us. Please share with me, if you will, the remainder of the inconsequential conversation with Brother Stephen?"

Brother Martin shrugged, exasperated. "Stephen told me he would ski to the village. He was an expert cross-country skier. He planned to have lunch there and then phone Professor Klugman at the Zugspitze Hof to make plans to meet with him. He said he would return by 3:00 P.M. unless the professor invited him for dinner."

"Do you know what project he was working on just before his death?"

"Oh, yes. For the last week he and Brother Gustav were working on what I thought was a rather innocuous project—they were setting up a web site where students and theologians could access the Sinaiticus Codex. Have you heard of it?"

Murdock shook his head. "I've heard of Mount Sinai where Moses was said to have received the Ten Commandments. I don't know what you mean by a codex."

Martin smiled. "First a story. Not long after the crucifixion of Jesus, monasticism was born. In the days of Roman orgies, Gregory of Sinai taught that mankind had become, in both soul and body, senseless animals, prisoners to whims of anger and lust. He taught that by discipline and mortification of body and soul, men and women could escape this condition. He believed that the soul was created without passions and will be resurrected without passions. Gregory believed that the fastest method of overcoming the lusts of the flesh was giving one's self to the monastic life. The dispassion and discipline of monastic life became, to him, a martyrdom not unlike the martyrdom of our Lord. A monastery was constructed on a ledge high up the steep slope of Mount Sinai where, as you mentioned, Moses had received the holy law over one thousand years earlier. The monastery took the name St. Catherine's. It's still there."

"But what's this got to do with this codex that you mentioned, or with Brother Stephen?"

"I am coming to that. St. Catherine's is fortified. For seventeen centuries one could enter it only by being pulled up in a bucket on a rope. Inside is a library containing manuscripts that date back to the time of Christ and beyond. No one paid much attention to the monks. They were irrelevant to the ebb and flow of history. And the monks paid little attention to the contents of the library."

"Are they Catholic monks?"

"Orthodox. The monks follow the rules of St. Basil. They possess nothing and live in physical solitude. They're disciplined in dress, conversation, and even tone of voice. Their rules require them to eat silently and never be obsessed with food or drink."

Murdock shook his head. "How could the monastery survive all these years—the Muslim hoards—the crusaders?"

"That's easy. They had nothing anyone wanted. And we here at St. Luke's have nothing more than ordinary people have—simple furnishings, simple food, and a few computers. No one bothers us."

"Stephen was bothered," Murdock shot back. "Are many of your monks Americans like Stephen?"

Martin lowered his head. "Over half."

"Why didn't you choose a site in America?"

"We're more secure here. If law is supposed to be a predictable rule, you have little of it left in America. Your presidents appoint politically oriented people to your Supreme Court. Any five *can* and *do* amend your constitution by decree when it suits their purposes. Your IRS can intrude into the privacy of anyone for unpredictable reasons. Here in Germany the constitutional court is better insulated from politics. We feel as safe from governmental interference as if we were in St. Catherine's on the cliff at Sinai. I'm not saying that we *trust* the German government more than the American. I'm saying we have less need to."

Murdock jotted down a few notes. Martin watched.

"I'm sorry," Murdock said. "I interrupted your train of thought. You were about to tell me about a codex."

Brother Martin smiled. "Feel free to interrupt. You can't distract me from what I intend to tell you. A little over a hundred years ago a German Lutheran theologian, Professor Tischendorf, was permitted by the monks of St. Catherine's to browse their library. He discovered a complete manuscript Bible of second or third century origin—the oldest complete Bible known. He literally stole it. Now it's in the British Museum."

"Don't the monks at St. Catherine's want it back?"

"I suppose, but they won't *do* anything. The effort would disturb their contemplation."

"Do you think that all of this has something to do with Brother Stephen's death?"

"It's possible. You must meet our Brother Gustav. He's not a scientist. He's a classical scholar. We don't want our brotherhood to be insular, so we have included a few liberal arts men. Brother Gustav insists that this old Bible—or Codex—is a valuable piece of classical literature. He asked Brother Stephen to prepare a web site so that anyone on the Internet could read the original, as long as they could understand classical Greek."

"There may not be many who can. Why is this Codex of any importance?"

"The Bible has been translated and retranslated many times. Each translation elicits shades of meaning. Some shades have been used to justify, not only many opposing points of view, but often unspeakable crimes. Some say the Bible is like a work of art because it means all things to all people. The Codex sidetracks those shades of interpretation and takes us back close to the original sources. It's not the original New Testament, but it is closer to it than most. Fragments of the New Testament have been found in earlier sources, some going back to the first century A.D. But this Codex is the earliest complete Bible with both old and new testaments. Its text is consistent with fragments quoted in letters written by St. Cyprian, a bishop in the Balkans, who lived circa 250 A.D. It's important, not only because of what it says, but because of what it doesn't say. For example it does not contain the last fourteen verses of the Gospel according to St. Mark. That's important because St. Mark's was probably the first written of the four gospels. The later gospels show the influence of Mark. The last fourteen verses, as we read them in modern Bibles, tell the story of Jesus' appearances after his crucifixion. How did these verses get into St. Mark's gospel if they were unknown to the monks who copied the Codex and got everything else right? Are these verses interpolations? Are they later revelations? Are they simply wrong?"

"Who cares?"

"Touché. Admittedly, these aren't burning questions for the non-Christian, nor for the simple faithful, but they are cogent topics for those who *teach* the simple faithful. St. Jerome, when he prepared the Latin Vulgate Bible around 380 A.D., accepted the last fourteen verses of St. Mark as accurate. But the question remains. Why don't they appear in the Sinaiticus Codex? This is a most intriguing question and Brothers Stephen and Gustav wanted the Codex in its original form available to the world exactly as Herr Tischendorf found it."

Murdock pointed to the Bible lying open on Brother Martin's desk. "Is that a copy of the Codex you have been talking about?"

"Oh, no," Brother Martin said, reaching over and picking it up tenderly. "This one has its own claim to fame. Examine it closely. It's a manuscript copied by a monk in this monastery in the twelfth Century A.D. Monks preserved the ancient literature for us by patiently recopying old manuscripts by pen and ink. We wouldn't be able to read Plato and Aristotle if it weren't for them. When they copied the Bible, each monk was assigned certain chapters. But this monk, in his spare time, copied the Bible in his own hand from the first chapter of Genesis to the last chapter of Revelation. He copied it painstakingly on this parchment, tiny letter by tiny letter. Look." He thrust the book upon Murdock. "Each letter is so perfect and consistent in style that it appears to have been printed on a modern printer. I can't discern any change from beginning to end. Can you?"

Murdock examined it. "No," he said, thoroughly impressed. "His eyesight must have survived the project — there were no eyeglasses then, were there?"

"No," Brother Martin answered. "But you are not sufficiently impressed. Here, quickly," Brother Martin urged, handing him a magnifying lens, "before the sun gets too high and the light is lost. Look at this illuminated letter. It was common in the twelfth century to draw tiny pictures around the enlarged first letter of each chapter. See the three maidens dancing around the red 'T'?"

Murdock held the magnifying glass to the tiny picture, one inch by one inch. "Exquisite detail," he exclaimed in amazement. "Even their tiny fingers are perfect."

"Look at the finger nails," Brother Martin prompted.

Murdock's eyes widened. Each diminutive fingernail was also perfect. "Absolutely amazing," Murdock exclaimed. "How could he have done it?"

"Infinitely carefully, I should imagine," Brother Martin postulated mischievously, a smile curling the corners of his mouth. "A work of love. A love of work. A love of God. A love of each of God's creatures who would hold this amazing thing in his or her hand and be amazed that one medieval monk would do this."

Murdock shook his head as he gingerly turned the pages. "To be accomplished so painstakingly, it must have taken an unbelievable amount of time."

"I understand that it took him thirty years working in his spare time. Monks had precious little spare time. Almost everyone died before age fifty, so it took most of his life."

Murdock felt overwhelmed by the enormity of what he was holding. Hard-pressed for words, he asked: "How much is this worth?"

Brother Martin shrugged. "A very American question. I have no answer. Could the most accomplished appraiser give you the answer? There are no comparables. It's priceless. Perhaps the real gift that the scrivener gave to us is the contemplation of the intensity of faith that drove him to it."

Murdock shook his head. "To me it seems foolish to spend your whole life copying the Bible."

"Perhaps that was his joy — to be God's fool."

"So," Murdock injected, "there is wisdom in foolishness."

Brother Martin placed his right hand on Murdock's shoulder and smiled. "You *are* a wise man, my friend. Such foolishness as his is like a half-opened door. God dares us to peek through."

"Ah, an enigma. Do I find something on the other side of the door? Or do I find the same emptiness that Professor Klugman found?" Murdock chided. "Do you really believe in God?"

Brother Martin was shocked at the question. "Why must you ask? Can't you see?"

"I see a robe and crucifix and an opened Bible on your desk. I see forms and symbols. I'm impressed by what everything appears to be. I'm not certain where to draw the line between reality and illusion. I'm not certain what your real agenda is in this—forgive me—rather peculiar monastery. I see that your Brother Stephen is dead—murdered—and a story about the Codex seems to offer no motive. Who would kill to prevent a web site?"

"Our people are accomplished scientists from many nations, all well recognized and respected in their fields. None is poor. Some are exceedingly wealthy. Our agenda is to do science in a responsible way and to encourage all scientists to do the same. By responsible, I mean science that produces results that serve to better humankind, not to demean it. Science that is God-pleasing—not destructive, either physically or morally. We focus the moral issues that scientific discoveries raise and define the problems they engender using a Christian frame of reference. We present recommendations to fellow scientists for their consideration."

"Why haven't I read about St. Luke's or seen something on TV?"

Brother Martin sat comfortably in his grand chair, his hands casually folded in his lap. "We are fortunate to have escaped attention. Our message is to the scientist. If we take it to the public, the media will politicize it as they do most everything else. We're not politicians."

"Yet there seems to be power at play surrounding the murder of your Brother Stephen. The Bavarian minister of justice has taken an interest. It's difficult to imagine how a multinational group of ethnicist monks could draw the attention of so much power, and the people who control it, without drawing the attention of the public media. Do even your enemies conspire to keep your work secret?"

"Perhaps it suits their agendas too."

"Was Brother Stephen working on some project other than the Codex web site?"

"He always worked on several projects at once. He was a brilliant man who was fascinated by all of the natural world. Frankly, I can't tell you all of his projects. I'm not a scientist. I don't understand much of what he talked about."

"How long had Brother Stephen been with you?"

"A little over three years."

"He was not one of your original monks?"

"No. He came to us a few years ago after becoming a billionaire at a very young age. Stephen rode the crest in the Silicon Valley. He became deeply concerned that electrifying advances in research would result in an accretion of knowledge at a speed much faster than humankind might be able to assimilate it beneficially. There is a potential for destructive power inherent in some of the science being done. Particularly in genetics and physics."

"Was Stephen married?"

"Divorced."

"Did he have any contact with his ex-wife?"

"Yes. None of it pleasant."

"Any of it give her reason to want him dead?"

"I seriously doubt that."

"Children?"

"None."

"Enemies that you know of?"

Brother Martin smiled wryly. "I'm certain that any man who made so much money so fast must have left a trail of enemies, but I don't know who they are."

"Where is Brother Antonio?"

"I can't say."

"Or you won't say?"

Brother Martin frowned. "Perhaps we can talk again, but now you must excuse me. It's time for matins and I must conduct the service. Will you join us in the chapel?"

"No. Thank you. I understand that tomorrow is the funeral. Could we meet again Friday after matins?"

"It'll be my pleasure, Mr. McCabe. Shall we say at 9:30 A.M.?"

"Fine. But one final question for today. Why were Brother Stephen and Professor Klugman so close? Klugman is a died-in-the-wool atheist."

"Our brother Klugman may not be what he thinks he is. He claims he will believe only what the conscious mind can prove by experiment. Ask him about his views of consciousness, and why he has not shared them with his colleagues. Our professor friend acknowledges that many scientists believe that rational consciousness is but one type of consciousness and that, all around it, parted from it by the filmiest of screens, lie potential forms of consciousness entirely different. I agree. Now come, walk with me toward the chapel and I will see you out."

They retraced the route that had brought them to Brother Martin's room. In the open area Murdock saw monks entering the chapel. Martin unbolted the large oak door and, as Murdock was about to walk through, Brother Martin gripped his left arm. Murdock turned to face him.

"I have a question for you, Murdock McCabe," he said somberly. "Do you believe in evil?"

Murdock stared at him quizzically. "It depends on what you mean by the word."

"Simply put, do you believe that things exist that are inherently virtuous and others that are inherently venal, no matter what spin people put on them?"

"Are we talking about some sort of generic sin?" Murdock asked, smiling. "Some pure, unadulterated essence of nastiness?"

Brother Martin smiled whimsically. "I'll accept that definition."

"I'm sorry," Murdock replied. "I'm not sure that I do."

"Then you're not certain that you don't. Good."

Murdock offered his hand. Brother Martin shook it. "Is there some secret in the Sinaiticus Codex," Murdock asked, "that would upset the religious world to the extent that someone would be willing to kill to conceal it?"

"No," Brother Martin replied. "The Sinaiticus Codex has been available in the British Museum for almost a century." A slow smile crossed his face. "Until we meet again, God be with you, Mr. Murdock McCabe."

"Thank you."

Murdock roared off down the trail. Brother Martin watched. When Murdock had disappeared from view, a man in a green nylon ski jacket came up from behind Brother Martin and stood next to him in the doorway.

"I'm not certain you've measured him correctly," Martin said.

"How far did you bring him?"

"Only the first step."

"Did he ask about Michael?"

"No. I didn't give him a chance. But he will."

*   *   *

The professor, lying on top his bed, fully clothed, a blanket wrapped around him, had awakened just before sunrise. His computer was still on, the screen saver drawing contorted lines dancing in full color. He moaned and sat up, staring blankly at the blackness outside the window for several seconds. Arising, he turned up the thermostat, ordered breakfast from room service, showered, and shaved. The room was still drafty so he donned a blue flannel shirt and ski pants. His toes were cold. He moved the table close to a heat radiator and sat down in front of the computer. Just before he had fallen asleep, he had come to a page break where the text had changed from mathematical formulae to narrative. He had wearied of equations and welcomed the change.

> On October 5th I received a phone call from Mac Townsend. He has been the general manager of my chip manufacturing plant in Westwood, Oregon, for sixteen years. Normally, Westwood had very little crime, yet there had been two break-ins at the plant in the last month. Strangely, nothing had been taken. Mac believed they were looking for something in particular and suspected that they were looking for the schematics and notations for my new super chip. Mac had been keeping them in his briefcase and taking it home with him at night. I doubt that that could have been the reason, however, because, I believe, the only ones beside myself who know of their existence are Mac and our abbot, Brother Martin. If the schematics get into the wrong hands, and if those wrong hands learn their intended function, the result could be catastrophic. Not only might a great scientific discovery be put to a devilish purpose, but the political balance in the world could be upset.
>
> Of course, we don't know as yet whether my chip will function. Brother Antonio and his people in Spain will have the software completed in a few weeks. They're frustrated because they can't imagine how a dynamic, quantum program could be useful. They suspect I'm a bit *loco*. Sometimes I wish they were correct. Please read on and decide for yourself. It is best not to skip to the end. You must make the difficult journey if you are to understand.

The text reverted to a plethora of numbers. The professor turned on his calculator and began making notes in a spiral notebook. It was slow going. Many of the terms and symbols were unfamiliar and required research, but he was enthralled and eagerly devoted himself to the project.

⇥ **15** ⇤

Rudi Benzinger, the number three man in the Bavarian State Police, was getting accustomed to his temporary office in Garmisch-Partenkirchen. Georg, the previous owner, had generously loaned the cubbyhole that had constituted his kingdom. It was a far cry from Rudi's spacious office in Munich, but he was happy to be involved in a hands-on criminal investigation again. Being an administrator paid better, but he missed being a policeman. Regardless of which function he was performing, Rudi was a precise man. He opened his daily journal and wrote:

Wednesday, November 19, 9:00 A.M.

The man in the green nylon ski jacket still eludes us. Georg has questioned every guest at the Zugspitze Hof Lodge. Several saw such a jacket but paid no attention. Three own one. Georg is checking their backgrounds. Of course our mystery man may have merely been a spectator, curious about the scene of a crime. That is not unusual.

This morning I spoke with Commander Weiss by telephone. Headquarters is operating on the assumption that the disappearance of Richard Laplatenier is connected with the investigation of the murder of Brother Stephen. They suspect a grand plot. Perhaps they are right. The Swiss police in Zürich have checked Richard's relatives and friends. No one has heard from him since the weekend. Brother Stephen's body was discovered early Tuesday morning. He had been dead since Monday morning. Richard disappeared from the airport on Tuesday morning. The investigating officers are not convinced that the signs of struggle are genuine. Richard may have known the person or persons who took him. Headquarters is checking all aircraft departures and their flight-planned destinations. I recommended that they consider the possibility that he may have been removed by auto rather than aircraft. They have no witnesses.

I expressed my concern about Murdock McCabe arriving on the scene so soon after we learned of the crime. I believe his story that Richard sent him. Richard is a good man. Murdock has not told me who is their client. Maybe he does not really know. I am not convinced that Veritus should be involved in the case. I expressed that concern to Commander Weiss. He knows Murdock and I are friends. I need to protect my posterior. Commander Weiss says that I am not to fret—that I should treat Murdock as though he were one of us until I am told otherwise. The Commander received this order from the Minister of Justice. Why?

I inquired as to why the minister was interested in Murdock. The government wants to know what is going on at the monastery. What are they doing that someone would be willing to kill for? Brother Martin jealously guards the monks' privacy. The Bavarian state government has no probable cause to believe the monks are involved in criminal activity, so there is no authority to investigate. It seems the government will trust Murdock, and also Allison Spencer, but not Harvey Specter. The minister believes that Murdock will find out what the monks are doing and confide in me. I am confident that the minister is correct. If Murdock does confide in me, then I must sort loyalties. One cannot cross a bridge until one comes to it.

Commander Weiss indicated that a mole in Baron von Richter's camp reports that he, and several of his fellow rakes, staged a risqué lesbian show last week at the Baron's castle. He used women recruited from the Mädchenhaus Café in Munich. Some men like to watch women doing it to each other. The women were not professional; some men prefer amateurs. Big money can lure big debauchery.

A woman by the name of Patti Dale is seen frequently at the Mädchenhaus. She is an American who may have a protector highly placed in the government. Commander Weiss believes she holds some power over several women at the Mädchenhaus Café. Possibly over the owners too. She bears watching. Rumor suggests it was she who arranged the women for von Richter's party.

Headquarters is running a check on Señor Jose Enrique Perez-Krieger with Chilean police, as well as with Cayman authorities and the American FBI. His biz-jet departed Garmisch-Partenkirchen for Cyprus yesterday afternoon. Five minutes later another biz-jet took off from the same airport for the same destination — Limassol. The second has made eleven flights to and from Limassol in the last month, landing in Bavaria at either Garmisch-Partenkirchen or Munich. The aircraft has Austrian registry. I have directed Georg to talk to the airport manager at Garmisch-Partenkirchen. We need to know the names of its passengers and the nature of its manifest. Headquarters is checking with Austrian authorities to determine the registered owner. There are many Russian opportunists in Limassol. Is there a Russian connection in Brother Stephen's murder? The Russians buy and sell anything, including death.

Murdock is meeting with Brother Martin as I write. Will he share with me everything that he learns?

Rudi closed the journal and glanced at his watch. The phone rang. It was Commander Weiss again.

"Bad news, Rudi. The Austrians tell us that the aircraft is registered to a Liechtenstein corporation. We will check with the police there but, as you know, the identity of the true owners may be elusive. Talk to you later."

"Thank you, sir."

As he hung up, Georg entered the office and sat down facing the desk.

"What have you learned?" Rudi inquired.

"Not much, Herr Benzinger. The airport manager reported that no goods pass through customs. In the past week the same passenger passed through immigration police three different times. Our officers indicate his name was Boris Romanovsky. He has a Ukrainian passport, which appeared to be in order. Shall I have our officers at the airport check the pilot's credentials?"

"No. We will not let them know they have our attention. Come. We will go now to Zugspitze Hof and talk to Diana Crenshaw. She is playing hostess to this Señor Perez-Krieger. He flew off to Limassol yesterday. Recently, she played hostess to the Baron von Richter. I have asked Headquarters to check into her employer, Seneca Financial Company."

Georg looked puzzled. "What is a financial company?"

Rudi smiled paternally. "In America they have companies who invest money for clients. Ms. Crenshaw is what the Americans call a bird-dog for Seneca. She wines, dines, and otherwise entertains wealthy prospective clients."

Georg frowned. "Is she a whore? I would never trust the word of a whore."

"I think not. But I suspect she could easily find whores if that is the wiggling bait needed to lure the fish. You have much to learn about whores. Whores are often more trustworthy than their clients. Come. Let's see what this fisher-lady knows about two of the fish in our pond — Señor Perez-Krieger and our rakish baron who would like to be our king."

Georg directed him to an unmarked police car in the parking lot. Rudi entered the passenger side. Before pulling out of the parking lot, Georg handed him a copy of a report. Rudi glanced at it. As they entered mid-morning traffic, Georg said: "You are aware, Herr Benzinger, of the pistol found by Grüber 500 meters down the Leiderbach Creek from where we discovered the monk's body?"

"Yes, Georg. I've seen the report. It contained too little detail. Do we know more?"

"Sir, the murder weapon was a Grozski pistol like those issued to Polish army officers. Its caliber matches the monk's wound."

"Polish army officers must often buy their pistols in the black market, Georg. One month ago over five thousand guns were stolen from an armory in Krakow. In Munich you can buy them in wholesale lots. Thousands disappear into central Africa. Transactions are done in Munich, but the money doesn't change hands there. It usually passes through Russian banks in Limassol, and the Cypriots happily tax the transactions."

Georg turned up the narrow road that led to the Zugspitze Hof. The surface was dry, except for icy patches in the shade of the trees.

"Herr Benzinger, does all the money pass through Cyprus?"

"Cyprus, or banks in the Cayman Islands or Antigua."

"Do you think we are dealing with gunrunning monks, sir?"

"I truly don't know what to think, Georg. I suspect that if we can find Richard Laplatenier alive, or this Michael character whom the professor described as being rather strange, we will know better what to think."

"Ja, ja, Herr Benzinger. Or the person in the green nylon jacket who watched us in the meadow."

"What have your investigators learned about this Michael?"

George shook his head. "I'm sorry, Herr Benzinger. Nothing. Absolutely nothing. We have circulated the sketch made from the descriptions of Professor Klugman and the abbot, Brother Martin. Michael could be a woman disguised as a man. The artist fudged his sketch to postulate what he would look like as a woman. No one has seen such a woman. We checked with the reservations people at the railway station. Nothing. He may have traveled without a reservation. I suspect that is the case. Our officers in Munich checked the airlines. We have found dozens of Michaels. We are attempting to obtain photographs of each through police at their destinations in Britain, Canada, Australia, New Zealand, and the United States."

"If he does not have a criminal record," Rudi suggested, "there will be no photograph available. Have you checked rental car agencies?"

"Ja, ja, Herr Benzinger. We have had no success."

Georg brought the car to a stop in the parking lot at Zugspitze Hof. They exited and walked toward the front door.

Georg looked discouraged. Rudi placed his hand on his shoulder.

"You are doing a fine job," Rudi said. "You don't need me, but I must stay."

Georg smiled. "Thank you, Herr Benzinger. You are most kind. I am pleased to have an opportunity to work with an investigator of your stature and experience."

Rudi was puzzled. His mind meandered over the facts of the case. *This Michael is an enigma. I'm not convinced Martin is untruthful—just less than candid. Perhaps Martin will be more open with Murdock. The atheist professor seems incongruent with these monks. It is difficult for me to trust monks who are not Catholic. I must not allow that to cloud my analysis. And professors can be a dangerous lot—they have been known to foment revolutions. I wonder. Is this one as harmless as he appears?*

⊰ 16 ⊱

Sitting behind Richard's desk, Allison reviewed Tuesday's daily report. The phone rang. She answered. A male voice greeted her.

"Good morning, Allison. This is Karl. Karl Kunkel at BMW. How are you?"

"Good morning, Karl. I haven't seen you for weeks. Please phone the next time you're in Munich. I'll spring for dinner."

"Spring?"

"Buy"

"Ja, ja, Allison. I like the sound of that word and look forward to your company. It is not easy, you know, for a European gentleman to become accustomed to a lady buying dinner. In my country it is the man who buys. The tradition was begun by some suave Frenchman as a diplomatic method for inviting a woman to his bed, if she were not too concerned about her husband. But I am too old, or you are too young, so I must assume the dinner invitation is business."

Allison laughed. "No. Not business. Just friendship with a charming European gentleman whose company I enjoy."

"Thank you," Karl said. "You are most kind. And how is your true love?"

"My true love doesn't know that he's in love with me."

"Ja? Then he is a foolish man. If I were thirty years younger and single, I would try to steal you, Allison."

Allison laughed. "What a sweet thing to say. If he doesn't wake up soon," she taunted, "then, perhaps you and I could do something really wild, if you can get your wife's permission."

He laughed merrily. "You know her, Allison, so you know you are safe. But I called because I have the information you requested. I checked with my personnel manager. We have no one by the name of Patti Dale working in our English language library, or anywhere else at BMW in Bavaria. In fact, we have no Americans in the library — just two Brits. I am sorry I cannot help you. What has she done?"

"She's been less than candid with one of my operatives. Now we know she is lying. You have been a great help, Karl. Thank you so much. And thank you too for helping Murdock get a fantastic deal on his new car. He's like a boy with a new toy. Maybe it'll help him out of his funk."

"Is he the true love?"

Allison hesitated. "He and I have been friends for many years. Please remember to give me a call when you come to Munich."

"I'm sorry, Allison. Truly. It was none of my business. I shall phone soon. Goodbye."

She turned to her keyboard, brought up "Patti Dale," and entered Karl's information. Moira had made an entry late last night. An airlines check disclosed no Patti Dale booked to anywhere. *Had Patti lied to Moira? Or was she using a false name either at the Mädchenhaus or with the airlines? Did she also lie about visiting her parents in Chicago? And if so, why?* She got Peter on the intercom and instructed him to request that Veritus's Chicago office do a low profile check of Patti's parents. She returned to her computer screen. Moira had noted in her remarks:

Allison:

> Rumor has it that, a couple weeks ago, Patti was cruising — trying to find three or four women to stage a lesbian love-orgy to satisfy the peccadilloes of some nobleman. According to the best rumored authority — the barmaid at the Mädchenhaus — she had big bucks at her disposal. Several patrons decided that they might as well take a bundle for doing what they were going to do anyway, so they negotiated the fee vigorously and successfully. They didn't pussyfoot around.

Moira.

Allison smiled at Moira's kinky sense of humor.

The phone rang on her private number. She answered.

"Hello, Ms. Spencer. This is Harvey Specter. Have you heard anything from Richard Laplatenier?"

Allison cringed. His voice alone made her flesh crawl. "No, Mr. Specter. I've heard nothing. If I had, sir, you would have been informed immediately. The Bavarian State Police think that he may have known his captors because the scene of the struggle appeared staged to them."

"What made it appear so?"

"I don't know. Rudi Benzinger is my best contact. I shall speak with him before the day is out."

"Please make certain that you do. Was it your decision that sent Terry Crawford to Regensburg?"

Allison stood and walked over to the window, stretching the telephone cord to its limit. "Yes, sir," she said, looking at all the fortunate people in the street below who could go through life without ever having to deal with Harvey. "Richard authorized me to take full charge whenever he was absent. Siegfried Insurance will be a substantial account for us. I felt it was important to keep the appointment in Regensburg and also important for me to be here in Richard's absence. So I sent Terry. It'll give him an opportunity to have client contact experience."

"You should have consulted with me," Harvey declared, obviously irritated.

She decided he had asked no question so she didn't respond. Besides, she took pleasure in irritating Harvey. Harvey broke an extended silence.

"Did you hear my question?"

"I didn't realize it was a question, sir. I made a routine decision. I knew you had more important things to do. I believe Terry has a bright future with the company, but he needs hands-on contact with clients. His desk is being covered by Peter Loxley, whom I moved from the night shift."

She spoke the truth. Terry had a bright future with the company, she felt, because blowhard, unscrupulous, step-on-anyone-in-your-way unadulterated pricks often do.

"Yeah. Yeah," Harvey replied. "And chickens can talk. I'm trying to get a replacement for Richard, but the head office isn't cooperating. I can't get my calls returned. They must be on another efficiency kick and cut staff." Her respect for the head office increased. Sitting on a windowsill, she watched the customers lining up before the doors of the department stores, their breaths showing in the clear cold air. The doors would open presently. Allison didn't like to shop. She was quite happy to be where she was on this early Wednesday morning — inside and warm and in charge of the Munich office. "You needn't worry. I can handle it, Mr. Specter."

"Call me Harvey."

"Harvey."

"That son of a bitch has never sold anything in is life. Is the account in danger?" he growled.

"I gave him my file. He's had plenty of time to review it. I think we need to have confidence in him. I'll follow up. I've developed a pleasant relationship with Erik Müller, the main man. Terry knows our company well enough to answer questions. Wouldn't you agree that he has potential?"

"Yeah. The little fart has his moments."

They're not as thick as I thought. Not even as thick as Terry thinks. She laughed inwardly. "I realize that I'm making a sacrifice by not closing the deal myself, especially with a performance review coming up, but I feel good when I help a junior employee. Don't you?"

"Yeah. Yeah. I'll do your review if Richard doesn't show up. Why haven't I gotten a ransom note? I expected the sons of bitches to send me one. Do you know who would want to kidnap him?"

"No, sir."

"No, *Harvey*," he growled.

"No, Harvey," she responded dutifully.

"Good. You and I need to get to know each other better. In a few days I'll come down to Munich and take some of the burden of running the office off your shoulders. I'm not certain that you've had enough management experience to handle it alone, regardless of what Richard instructed."

He gets nervous when his little spy-fart isn't here to keep him informed.

"Was Richard working on something I don't know about?" he inquired.

"Everything goes into the daily report. I've not known Richard to keep secret files. He's quite straightforward, don't you think?"

Harvey grumbled. "I don't know what to think. I'll take you to lunch when I get there, so we can talk free of the office. Goodbye." Click.

"Goodbye." *Oh, wow. Now maybe I'll find out what the boys do on those three hour lunches of Harvey's. Now I'm not sure that I want to know.*

Peter knocked and entered. Allison arose from the windowsill and cradled the phone on her desk. Peter grinned. "Now that my secret's out, I want to tell you that you have nice buns."

"Oh, thank you, Peter. My day is complete. What do you have there?"

He handed her a computer printout. "It arrived a few minutes ago," he said.

Allison took it and glanced at it. "Why didn't you decode it?" she asked.

"I tried, but the cryptography is different from any in our code book. It came on a secure line from Veritus in Chicago. Why would they use an alien code?"

She took a second look at it. "Don't worry about it, Peter. It's Okay. I'll handle it. Thank you."

"And thank you, Allison, for letting me borrow your hotel room yesterday."

"*De nada*, as the Spaniards say. Bye-bye."

Closing the office door behind him, she stared at the message. At second glance she recognized the code. *Top Dog's private code. I heard about it in management school, but I never expected to receive a message in it. This one's addressed to me personally. Most curious. Top Dog is a silent owner. He seldom participates in management. Why would he contact me, an assistant station manager, directly?* Her curiosity mounted. She kept the decoder in her purse because of her concern that The Weasel might have obtained the combination to the safe. She searched her purse and retrieved it. The message was brief. It gave a phone number with an Illinois area code. She was to phone him from outside the office at 12:00 noon Munich time. His authenticity will be confirmed by his personal secret code name she had received at the close of her management training. She was to tell no one.

This cloak-and-dagger is sort of fun. I wonder if it's really necessary. This is Veritus, not the CIA. Isn't it? Maybe Top Dog is a former CIA agent and he can't break the habit. I guess I'll find out.

There was plenty to keep her busy until noon. The morning passed quickly. At 12:00 noon she located a pay phone inside the department store across the street. She fed one mark coins into the phone until the digital readout showed twenty marks. If the call cost less than that, the instrument would make change at the conclusion. She dialed the number. A short ring suggested that the call was being forwarded. After another ring, a man's voice promptly answered.

"Allison Spencer, my code name for you is Clara Anna. Now listen carefully, please. You have direct access to me. Report to me at 9:00 P.M. Munich time each day at this same number. If I do not answer, you may leave your report on my answering machine by punching in the numbers 5009. If it does not respond, continue following the last instructions I gave you. These are your instructions. Do whatever you think necessary to facilitate the investigation of the monk's death. Add the Baron von Richter to its scope. The Baron likes you. Talk to him. Trust Murdock and Moira, but no one else in our organization. Have Murdock McCabe concentrate on the monk's death to the exclusion of all other files. McCabe is our best investigator. Give him as much room as you can, but you're in charge. Have Moira concentrate on Patti Dale. Perhaps there's a connection. They are our focus, not Richard. It's unfortunate about Richard, but that situation will turn out satisfactorily, I'm sure. I want to know who killed the monk, and why. If Harvey Specter threatens to fire you for not being candid with him, let him. Unknown to him, you will be transferred to a special branch and your pay continued without interruption. The same goes for Murdock and Moira. My instructions have been succinct. You shouldn't have any questions. Do you?"

"No, sir."

"Excellent. Goodbye."

⇥ **17** ⇤

Murdock came to a stop, unfastened his skis, and turned to watch Diana complete the run. She was the essence of grace and trim, confident, extremely skillful, and sexy. She came to a stop next to him.

"Wow," she exclaimed, "that was a challenge."

Murdock took her hand and shook it. "You are a double diamond skier, lady. I do believe that this is one of the toughest slopes in the Alps. Are you an Olympic medalist and hiding it from me?"

Diana smiled coyly. "Would you think more of me if I have Olympic gold?"

Murdock grinned his best boyish grin. "Who said I think of you at all?"

"You're working on it." Diana tossed back her hood and shook out her hair. Sunlight caught the blonde strands and transformed them into burnished gold.

"A woman never tells," she chided. "My mother told me: 'Never blow your mystique.' Besides, a strong, clever, sensitive, and observant man needs to find out for himself. It's part of the mating ritual that propagates the species. After all, the fun is in the hunt, they say."

Murdock smiled. "I haven't given any thought to propagating the species. Are you in a propagating mood, lovely lady? Is that what's making you so playful this morning? You want to propagate?"

"Settle for the hunt now," she admonished.

"I'm not sure that I remember how to hunt. I met Karen my first semester in college and haven't hunted since."

"Have you hunted deer?"

"Yes."

"Then you know the art of stalking. You do it quietly and patiently and with determination."

"Yeah. And remain upwind and don't step in the droppings."

Diana laughed. "You're impossible. But, in any event, yonder approaches a couple of hunters who look far too serious for such a beautiful morning. I suspect our fun is over for a while." She pointed downhill. Rudi and Georg were approaching.

Murdock regretted the intrusion. He waved. Rudi waved back. He and Diana walked to meet them.

"Good morning Rudi, Georg. It is good to see you." *But not right this minute, he thought.* "I'd like you to meet Diana Crenshaw. Diana, this is Rudi Benzinger and Georg Brüner. They're with the Bavarian State Police.

Diana extended her hand. Rudi took it in his and kissed the back of it. He bowed slightly. "Good morning, Murdock, Ms. Crenshaw. We regret the intrusion on such a beautiful morning. Unfortunately, we must speak briefly with Ms. Crenshaw. We can conduct the interview at the Zugspitze Hof, if we may use your room, Murdock. I shall have my own room this afternoon, but we do not wish to wait. Will that by acceptable?"

"Yes. Of course," Murdock said. "I'll have coffee sent up. Anyone want anything else?"

Georg bowed slightly. "I haven't had breakfast, Herr McCabe. I would appreciate if you could arrange croissants and ham?"

"My pleasure," Murdock replied.

*   *   *

The fireplace in Murdock's room was crackling and popping. Georg had inserted fresh logs. Hot embers darted up the chimney. Diana, Murdock, and Rudi warmed their hands. Georg sat at a small table, surgically sliced croissants, inserted thin slices of ham, and consumed them using knife and fork.

Diana turned to face Rudi. "How can I help you?" she inquired.

Rudi, appearing solemn, took out his notebook and casually glanced at its pages for several seconds. No one spoke. He motioned for Diana to be seated. She deposited herself in an armchair next to an end table. Rudi sat in the armchair across from it.

"Ms. Crenshaw," Rudi began, "we are investigating the murder of a monk by the name of Brother Stephen. He apparently had something that somebody thought was valuable. We believe that he was murdered for it. Señor Perez-Krieger arrived here the day before the murder. He came as your guest. Please, how long have you known him?"

"About three months. I'd talked to him on the phone several times, but I met him face to face only three days ago . . . Sunday . . . here at Zugspitze Hof."

"What can you tell me about his background?"

Diana hesitated for several seconds. No one spoke. Murdock

watched her. She appeared composed and unruffled by police interroga-
tion — comfortable with herself. Rudi avoided direct eye contact so as not
to appear confrontational.

"I have a duty of confidentiality because he is a potential client, but
he's a public figure. My staff prepared a biographical sketch of him,
which I have studied. Most of the information came from sources available to you, especially an article about him and his family history, which
appeared in the *New Yorker* magazine last year."

Rudi smiled kindly. "I have not read it. Please, would you share the
information with me?"

"His family in Chile," she began, "exudes wealth. Señor Perez-
Krieger's grandfather, who had emigrated from Saxony in 1899, had
entered the nitrate business. He accumulated fabulous wealth. His grandfather diversified into copper and agriculture. His agricultural invest-
ments included vineyards and a winery, plus market gardening near
Valparaíso. Thus, when the nitrate market disintegrated during World
War I, his grandfather was insulated from a hard fall."

Murdock interrupted. "What happened to the nitrate market?"

"Cut off from Chilean nitrate during WWI, Germany developed a
process that produced synthetic nitrates from the atmosphere."

Rudi nodded in agreement. "Go on, please."

"Next his grandfather expanded into steel production. He bought
the mines and built the mills. Between the two world wars, he made millions by exporting scrap iron to Japan. Enrique's father was even more
successful and became one of the wealthiest men in Chile, if not all of
South America. Enrique was born in Santiago de Chile in 1946. He graduated from the University of Concepción, where he majored in economics and business administration. He completed graduate work at the
University of Wisconsin and received a master's degree in finance. Enrique, his brother, Miguel, and his sister, Estrelita, now own the family
businesses. Although Enrique has acquired the majority share, the sib-
lings are inseparable. Miguel oversees the managers of production units.
Estrelita supervises the bookkeepers and accountants worldwide. She
also does feasibility studies. Recently, they branched into hotels and acquired properties in the lake country of Chile and on Grand Cayman."

Rudi interrupted. "Does he have some connection with a college in
the Caymans?"

"Yes. Enrique founded the College of the Caymans."

"By *he*, do you mean Señor Perez-Krieger personally?

"Yes. I understand that he used private funds."

Rudi's eyes met hers. "Can you tell me why he would do that?"

Diana sat silently for several seconds. Rudi made notations in his notebook. Murdock searched her facial expression. He could read nothing.

"No," she said finally. "I'm uncertain about his motives. He claims that its purpose is to provide an opportunity for deserving young Latin Americans to become educated in the ways of capitalism."

Rudi interrupted. "I am curious, Miss Crenshaw. Do these *deserving* young people come from the oligarchical families? I understand that the average young person in Latin American can afford neither college tuition nor the cost of living in a foreign country. Is that not true?"

Diana nodded. "Oh, I think very much so. Enrique finances most of the students," she replied sarcastically.

Rudi's eyes met hers. "That sounds like a noble endeavor. Do you question his motives?"

"Yes."

"Why, as you Americans say, do you look the gift horse in the mouth?"

"Because it seems *too* noble. It's unnatural. Capitalists, like the Perez-Krieger family, are into making money. Making risky loans to students is not their bag. It smacks of charity. He's not into charity for individuals. He thinks it pauperizes their spirit. He must have some angle. I haven't figured it out, but I question whether he's the paragon of virtue that he holds himself out to be."

"I see. Too good to be true." Rudi smiled. *The woman scorned. Her job was to recruit him for Seneca, but she has not succeeded.* "What else can you tell us?"

Diana was silent again for several seconds. Again Murdock observed her, and again he read nothing in her face. "It's probably not important," she said. "He's into drag racing in the United States. I understand that he's having a car built, and that he'll enter the competition circuit next season. He's probably the wealthiest prospect I've had. And there's something else. He seems to have a private agenda to which a chunk of that wealth is diverted. I don't know what that is. He's secretive. I can't say it's illegal, but secrets make me suspicious. I just don't know. Other than financial matters that I can't discuss, that's about the limit of my knowledge."

Rudi looked up from his notebook and their eyes met again. "How do you know all this? Did the private agenda, as you put it, appear in the magazine article?"

Diana met his eyes with a frosty stare. "No, but it's my job to know everything there is to know about a prospective client. I'm good at it."

"What is it that you can *do* for such a man?"

"We—Seneca Financial—can relieve him of some of the burden of investment decisions, at least as to that part of his portfolio that he has not set aside for capital asset injections. His forte is business development. He needs to concentrate on that. We have an excellent track record. He needs to consider us. We need investors like him. The combination is synergistic."

"Where is he now?"

"Right now he's probably somewhere between Cyprus and here. He flew there yesterday for an overnight meeting. I know nothing more about it."

Rudi smiled politely. "Thank you. You met with the Baron von Richter Monday evening. What can you tell me about him?"

Diana frowned. "Ah, yes. The man who would be king. Now there's a package. He drops names of powerful people in your state and federal government as if they were applying for positions in his cabinet. He was one potential client that I recommended we not pursue."

"So, you no longer consider him a client. Do you know why he is here at Zugspitze Hof?"

"Not for certain. Herr Bayer is one of his admirers. Bayer gives him and his politicos room discounts. I suppose Bayer hopes to be chosen for his cabinet. Frau Bayer would like to boot the Baron in the tailbone. If Herr Baron becomes Herr King, she thinks he'll need a cabinet of five hundred or more, if he keeps his royal promises."

"So Frau Bayer is not one of his admirers?"

"No, and she makes that clear to anyone who asks."

Rudi closed his notebook and clipped his pen into his pocket. "Do you think the Baron is capable of murder?"

Diana met his stare. "I don't see where what I think could be important."

"It is to me."

"But it's not a fact that would assist your investigation. If it's merely your personal curiosity, then it's not an official question and, I need not answer it. Isn't that true?"

"That may be. But it would please me if you did — off the record."

Diana was silent for a moment. Georg had finished his croissants and had taken out his notebook and was writing something.

"Georg," Rudi said. "We need not make a record of her answer. This is merely a friendly question because I respect her intuition."

Georg frowned, closed his notebook, and inserted it into his inside coat pocket. Murdock observed her eyes of steel.

"Yes. I think he would kill."

Does she actually believe that? Murdock wondered. Or is this re-
venge of a woman who couldn't land the fish after giving it too much

play? She's tough. She can handle herself as well as Karen could. But Karen's toughness masked a compassionate interior. Whatever makes this gal tick seems less forgiving.

Rudi thanked her, made an arrangement with Murdock to meet for a few beers later in the afternoon, and then he and Georg left. Diana got up to leave.

"Can you stay a few minutes?" Murdock asked. "We can finish the croissants and ham, and there's plenty of coffee."

"Should a girl feel safe alone in the room of a man who apparently hasn't had sex for two years?" she asked coyly.

"Would you be offended if I said 'yes'?"

"Not so long as I thought you wanted to say 'no'."

"I do, but yes. You will be safe from unbridled passion."

"And the bridled type too?"

"If that's what you want."

"I'll stay."

*   *   *

Enrique's aircraft was cruising at 25,000 feet above the Adriatic Sea. At that altitude the sky was clear. Far below a flock of stratocumulus fair weather clouds were casting shadows on the water. The Alps could be seen to the north. He and Linda were in the middle cabin. He poured coffee for both of them. After he reviewed with her the events at Boris's villa, she began her daily briefing.

"We shall arrive at Garmisch-Partenkirchen very close to our scheduled arrival time. There is a low pressure area just north of Ireland with its cold front trailing offshore and nearing the coasts of Spain and Portugal. Moderate snow is falling as much as four hundred miles in advance of the front. Visibility should still be good at our E.T.A. Garmisch-Partenkirchen is presently experiencing mostly sunny skies with widely scattered snow showers. Dinner arrangements are completed for tonight. Professor Klugman, Murdock McCabe, and that woman will attend."

"Again, her name is Diana Crenshaw."

"Yes. You asked me to investigate the death of Mr. McCabe's wife. She was kidnapped, ostensibly because Mr. McCabe was to testify against some powerful crime figures, and they wanted him to shade his testimony. She was taken from their apartment. The kidnappers demanded that he not tell the FBI she was missing. Apparently he didn't, but they found out anyway."

"Is there something about that story that bothers you, Linda?"

"Yes. The kidnappers were second-story men. They hadn't kidnapped before. I figure they were going through McCabe's apartment when Karen came home and interrupted them. Maybe they panicked and took her. I doubt that it was a random burglary. I think they were looking for something specific because only Karen's computer room was disturbed. There was no attempt to search for valuables in the bedroom. Common burglars would have gone there first. I think whoever controlled them concocted the testimony story to mask the purpose of the break-in."

"Why do you assume they were controlled? Maybe they *were* common burglars working on their own."

Linda poured cream in her coffee and added artificial sweetener. "Police records suggest they weren't smart enough to concoct the story. My guess is that someone wanted something from Karen's files and hired the thieves to get it. Inexperienced at kidnapping, they let the situation get out of control. Then the FBI did their Ruby Ridge routine — went in shooting."

"Who was their controller, and what did he want?"

"Our sources don't know. They lived modestly. Mrs. McCabe owned only costume jewelry. They didn't keep cash in the house. My guess is that it had something to do with her expertise in cryptography."

Both heard the engines spooling down. The aircraft had begun its descent.

Enrique sipped his coffee. "What about the dead monk?"

"Nothing. The police have nothing either. Perhaps at dinner you can find out what McCabe has learned."

"What about our friend, Boris. Is he really descended from Czar Alexander I?"

"Possibly. Russia is awash with information available for a price. I can buy anything you want to hear — maybe even the truth — but we have no way of recognizing it. As for Boris himself, I think he can do what he says he can. He has innumerable contacts everywhere in Russia. If anyone can arrange what you want, he can, but don't let his slime stick to you. My advice is — if you feel you must do business with the likes of Boris Romanovsky, never be completely candid with him, and *never* let him see your soul."

"Thank you, Linda. Your advice is always appreciated." He pointed out the window. "Look. There is the peak of the Zugspitze. You can see the cable car just starting a descent. That's fun. You should ride it and have lunch at the restaurant on top." A grin crossed his face. "I think our copilot has taken a shine to you. Perhaps he would accompany you."

Linda smiled. "Don't even joke about that. He'll be much too busy analyzing the pictures in his girlie magazines. I can take myself."

⇥ **18** ⇤

Murdock checked at the desk. Enrique had arrived from the airport. Impressed by the biography Diana had given to Rudi, Murdock felt that his first impression of Enrique had been confirmed. He looked forward to their meeting. *Even if he isn't entirely what he appears to be, who is? He's certainly not the run-of-the-mill South American millionaire. He's interesting, more so because he's involved in drag racing. Not only involved, but he's having a car built and acquiring a crew—things that I've dreamed about but could never afford. I don't see any connection between Enrique's presence at the Zugspitze Hof and the death of Brother Stephen, so the meeting should be social. At least I'll carry that assumption into Enrique's room. But at this stage of the investigation, all such assumptions are refutable. I hope I'm right on this guy.*

At 3:00 P.M. Murdock knocked on Enrique's door. It opened. Enrique greeted him warmly, and with a graceful sweep of his arm, invited him in. Murdock accepted a glass of white wine and a cigar. They both took seats near the picture window.

Murdock sloshed the wine about in the glass and sniffed. "Delightful bouquet," he exclaimed.

"Thank you."

He sipped the wine. "Ah. A sturdy full-flavored wine, not bitter. I'm not a connoisseur, but this is superb."

"Good," Enrique demurred. "I am delighted that you like it. It comes from our vineyards in Chile. I shall have Linda ship a case to you."

"No, please. That's too much."

"That is nothing. Please don't give it a second thought. You have made me very happy because you enjoy it. It is my favorite vintage. Someday you must visit my country and see our vineyards, and our wine presses, and acres of storage sheds with thousands of barrels. The original grapes emigrated to Chile from the Rhine Valley. It seems that they have been happy in my country."

Murdock laughed. "If they are sad, it isn't reflected in the wine."

Enrique put down his glass and leaned toward Murdock with an appearance of confidentiality.

"I know, Murdock, that we planned to talk about drag racing. I want to do that, but not just now. There are more important matters. I presume that you know I am here as the guest of Seneca Financial through Diana Crenshaw."

"Yes. Seneca goes first class."

"It was not she who chose this location. I chose it for two reasons — and you were one of them. I wanted to meet you. I planned to contact you by phone in Munich and invite you to join me here."

"Me? Why would a man in your position want to meet me?"

"I understand your skepticism. Nevertheless, it's true. Because it's important to me, at the outset of our conversation, that you believe it's true, I'll drop a name. Jerrard Blair. He is your close friend, yes?"

Murdock's mouth dropped open. "Yes, but how do you know Jerr?"

"We both belong to an organization called Plato. You've never heard of it, I'm certain. Few except its members have. Although its membership list is kept confidential, it's not a secret society in the strict sense. Plato is a nonpublic mutual fund. Its shareholders are some of the wealthiest men in the world. I organized it for the purpose of bringing about social change."

"But FBI agents don't . . ."

"If, by being a member, your friend endangers his job with the FBI, you know him well enough to understand that he did not make the decision lightly. He made it for the same reason that all of us did — out of frustration with the direction that the politicians of our civilized world are taking us."

"What direction?"

"Please, let us hold that question for a moment. Let us first begin with me. Do you know anything of the history of my family and myself?"

"Well, a fair amount, I'd say."

"Many people in your country condemn me as an archconservative because I believe that constantly taxing the people who work, and handing their money to generations of people who don't ever work, nor want to, is destructive. It diminishes the purchasing power of workers and creates a disincentive to work. It keeps workers and nonworkers poor and dependent on the politicians who spend money someone else has earned — the taxpayer — to buy their fealty. Aristocrats in my country condemn me as a liberal because I search out motivated poor people who are not members of our social class and loan them money to get the education they need to rise into our class. My family firmly believes in the work ethic of our German grandfather. I founded the College of the Caymans as a business college. It takes students from all over the Americas who are willing to work and study and teaches them the information and skills necessary to succeed in a capitalist society, not the least of which are networking skills. I encourage each to return to his or her home country and work there to produce capital and invest it in job-producing ventures for those less fortunate than they. That's the personal project of myself and my family. Plato goes beyond that. It is probably best described as a mutual fund with highly selective membership. Plato's purpose is to accumulate huge sums of venture capital — huge enough so that, when its assets are strategically injected into a country's economy, it will help unleash the spirit of entrepreneurship, stabilize that economy, and produce jobs that will raise the standard of living of its people. As more of its people rise into the middle class, the less attractive socialism becomes. They realize that socialism is the thief that keeps them poor."

"But isn't that the kind of handout you said you were against?" Murdock injected.

"I am not talking about a handout. We don't invest unless we think that our investment will make money, and that the working person will also benefit by drawing a better wage than he is accustomed to. Thus far our fund has made a profit each year. Members may take that profit out or reinvest it. Most reinvest. They don't need the income. You would realize that if you saw our list of names."

Murdock laughed. "Is this a sales pitch to get me to invest Karen's insurance money into your mutual fund? Pardon me, Enrique, old buddy, I didn't have you figured as a hustler."

"But I am."

Murdock shifted his weight uncomfortably, took a big drag on his cigar, and blew a huge cloud of blue-gray smoke. He suddenly remembered when he and Karen had been tricked into a sales presentation by a friend. He didn't like the feeling then and he didn't like it now.

An enigmatic grin crossed Enrique's face. "You're indeed being hustled, but, no offense, your money would be an infinitesimally small drop in our fund. Most of our members invest millions of dollars."

"Don't you have a problem with the Securities and Exchange Commission?"

"Plato is a Cayman corporation. We never solicit in the United States. The fund is not open to the general public. Each investor must be approved by our board of directors, which is more interested in an investor's commitment to our moral high ground."

"So, you are looking only for highly moral investors."

"It matters not whether a man is diddling his secretary and her administrative assistant so long as he is committed to the moral purposes of

Plato. We're not a religious organization. Our goals are economic — never political, or religious, or personal. Wielding of great economic power necessarily has a political effect, but we never directly support any party or politician. If our injection of assets helps to re-elect a government, that is merely an incidental result — oftentimes a serendipity. If the people of the country we try to help make foolish choices on election day, and a government becomes unfriendly to privatization and free enterprise, and if our investment is threatened, we withdraw swiftly and prudently to minimize losses. Even though our assets are huge and growing daily, they are finite, and we must place them where they can do the most good. We are unabashed idealists, but not foolish ones."

"I know this is repetitive, but why me?"

"Ah, Murdock, you cut to the crux. I admire that. The answer is quite simple. We need people like you and Jerr because we are an army of idealists, like yourselves. We don't need your money so much as we need information. For example, a few years ago we had moved millions of U.S. dollars into Mexican pesos in anticipation of closing the purchase of a major company in Mexico. Two days before the devaluation our mole in the Mexican presidential palace sounded the alarm. We pulled our assets out of Mexico overnight. We would have taken a major hit, and that would have diminished our ability to help people. After several weeks we returned to Mexico and bought the same company. In the last two years that company has added almost one thousand new employees."

Murdock was impressed, but he remembered Diana's skepticism. *She was correct. It sounds too good to be true, but it'll be easy to check out.* "Who makes up the board of directors?" he inquired.

"We have five. I'm a director for life. The others are elected by the shareholders — two from among the group who has invested in excess of the median investment, and two who have invested at the median or below — like Jerr. He's just been elected to the board for a two-year term."

"The FBI will fire him if they find out."

"If they learn about it. They won't unless you tell them, and I know you won't. We want you to be a member. You would need to invest enough money that its loss would mean something to you. That makes your financial interest common to ours. Most of our shareholders could lose several million dollars and not be hurt. We figure that a loss of twenty thousand dollars would hurt you, so we offer you membership for that amount. You can invest more any time. Remember, you're not spending it. You're investing it. You can take out your profits or reinvest them. Your responsibility would be to occasionally feed us information confidentially. But I shall say no more about that. Next you must talk to Jerr."

Murdock grinned and unsuccessfully attempted a smoke ring. "You've made me quite anxious to do that, I assure you."

"Tell me, Mr. McCabe, do you believe there are entities such as good and evil in this world?"

"You are the second person to ask me that today."

"The first was Brother Martin?"

"Yes."

"That's a curious coincidence. I'm anxious to meet him. If I may have your answer, you will see the reason for the question presently."

Murdock pondered the question and considered how to frame the answer. "My answer is 'Certainly,' but that's a cosmetic answer. What one person thinks is good, another may think evil."

"And vice versa, of course," Enrique chimed in. "But that's not the point. Do you believe that absolute good and absolute evil exist?"

Murdock shifted uncomfortably. The chair was straight-backed with unpadded wooden arms. "Exist? Do you mean like an entity unto themselves?"

"Exactly."

"Are you asking whether I believe in God and Satan?"

There was a long silence. Enrique held his cigar firmly between his teeth and casually blew huge puffs of smoke, turning his head slightly away from Murdock. He impressed Murdock as a man accustomed to being totally in control. Not a single facial muscle twitched, other than his cheeks casually sucking in and blowing out the smoke. Removing the cork from the wine bottle, he refilled Murdock's glass, prudently turning the bottle so as to avoid spilling a drop.

"Can one buy this wine locally?" Murdock asked.

"No. I don't believe you can. I brought it from my aircraft." He smiled pleasantly. "But you've not answered my question."

There was another long silence. Murdock swished the wine around in the glass, sniffing the bouquet again. *Where is this conversation going. What's this guy up to?* "I suppose," he began, "that all reasonable people would agree, for example, that the senseless mass murder of children is evil."

"Do you suppose they really do—all those reasonable people? I wonder when I read about central Africa. I believe there is such a thing as evil—an almost palpable presence."

"Does this *evil* have a name?" Murdock inquired.

"It takes many names. One is 'Traction.' "

Murdock looked puzzled. "Traction?"

"A few months ago we gleaned information that suggests the existence of an organization counter to Plato. Like Plato, it's based upon accumulating capital and focusing it so as to influence events. Apparently, however, their motives are radically political. Our information indicates that they want to buy the politicians, which is nothing new, but on a grand scale — grander than we have ever seen before. Their purpose is to destabilize. Their forte is the selling of weapons on a massive scale. Drug profits may provide part of their capital. They're quite secretive and thoroughly evil. We believe they were responsible for the aircraft 'accident' that caused the death of the president of Rwanda several years ago. Then, through paid local operatives, instigated the Hutus to go on the rampage and kill over a half million Tutsis, thus triggering a civil war that spread into the Congo. Through companies they control, we believe they sold weapons to both sides at immense profit. Unfortunately, we've been able to prove none of this."

"You might be jousting at windmills."

"Indeed, we might."

Murdock was uncomfortable with the direction this conversation was taking. He would have given Enrique less credence if Jerr were not involved at so critical a level. He was concerned for Jerr. Murdock was surprised that he would join an organization where he might be expected to feed information, the dissemination of which could adversely affect his career, and could possibly be illegal. And Jerr must have invested. He wondered how much. *I'll play it like I'm interested—at least until I talk to Jerr.* "How can I help?"

"Can you imagine how important information about Traction, if it exists, would be to us and to the future of mankind? What precisely is their strategy?"

"I still don't see how I can help."

"The same rumor that indicated the existence of Traction also indicated that they have a female operative in Munich. When you return to Munich, you could investigate her. See if you can discover what she's up to. In so doing, you may be able to confirm the existence of Traction."

"Do you know her name?"

"Dale. Patti Dale. She's not rumor. She's real. I'm informed that, when she's in town, she hangs out at the Mädchenhaus Café."

Murdock recalled the name. Moira was investigating her. "Is she lesbian?"

"If she isn't, why does she hang out there? The answers to both questions would be helpful. If Traction exists, we need to know how much they know about us, and how we're vulnerable."

"If I were Traction," Murdock began, "my first priority would be to infiltrate your board of directors — get one sour grape on it who could manipulatively politicize it. Idealist organizations, like Plato's philosopher kings, have a limited shelf life. At some point human nature always over-comes idealism. That's why Plato's Republic could never have suc-ceeded. I imagine your board members are competitive folks. Eventually that competitive drive will drive a wedge into your board. It'll lose its idealistic focus. The only question is how soon."

Enrique smiled paternally. "Not until, I hope, we have generated an irresistible momentum. When I set up Plato with myself as trustee of the mutual fund, I put a disaster clause in our contract. I, and any number of others that I may choose, have a right to buy out any member for the fair market value of his or her shares, and pay in either cash or securities of my choice from the portfolio. Fair market value is determined by a for-mula weighted by profit history over the previous five years. If we buy out a board member, he or she is automatically removed from the board."

Murdock cringed. "That doesn't seem fair. You could use securities whose values have a dismal future."

"It may not be fair, but every member knows about it before they buy in. Now you know about it. They know me and trust my judgment."

"That makes you the king of the philosopher kings."

"You could put it that way."

Murdock shook his head. "I suppose that's the only way that an or-ganization like Plato could maintain its focus."

Enrique's frame visibly relaxed. Murdock had not noticed his stiff-ness until he observed the change. Enrique squashed the butt of his cigar into an ashtray and took a sip of wine. He slipped off his shoes, carefully placing them neatly, side by side, next to his chair. Refilling his wine glass, he smiled, and then leaned across the distance between them and offered the bottle to Murdock. Murdock took it and filled his glass.

Murdock decided to take a posture mildly confrontational. "En-rique, my friend, the FBI requires that their agents inform them of the or-ganizations they join. I've known Jerr for many years. He has always been truthful and loyal. Will he tell the FBI the truth about his member-ship in Plato?"

Enrique arose and walked over to the picture window. With his back toward Murdock, he asked, "Truth? What is truth? Whatever it is, I won-der if it matters. Error believed in is truth in effect. People make deci-sions based upon what they believe to be true. They look at the surface of what passes for truth. It takes time and effort to get facts. Ferreting out facts interferes with playtime. Folks rely on politicians' rhetoric and media sound bites, believing whatever they want to believe. When they hear what they want to hear, they reach a comfort level. The skillful politician or used car salesman—they're both cut from the same bolt—determines what people want to believe and feeds it to them, adding whatever spin that's to their advantage."

"Isn't that rather cynical?" Murdock inquired.

"Cynicism is one of the lanes on the highway to truth." Enrique smiled warmly. "Let's talk about aspirin."

"Aspirin?"

"Yes. In your country there is a brand-name aspirin that sells for at least five times the price of several of its competitors. There is no chemical difference between them. They confer exactly the same benefit. Why do people pay five times more for that brand name? Because advertising has convinced them that there is some additional benefit — because there must be, or why would the brand name cost so much more? The manufacturer counts on people making decisions based upon their perception of truth — not truth itself. Politicians are keenly aware of this. That's why truth is unimportant to them. The politician feeds dreams. He or she tells each constituency what it most wants to hear."

Murdock smiled, kicked off his shoes, and loosened his tie. "Is that," he chortled, "why the world seems so illogical? I've often wondered."

Enrique joined in the laughter. "That's putting it mildly. We live in a world in which France was denounced when it openly provided information about its nuclear testing, but China was handled discreetly when it conducted tests in secret. It seems illogical until you understand who is wooing whom and why. The truth of the matter is that it has little to do with the bomb's fallout, but much to do with the political fallout. Do you agree?"

"Absolutely," Murdock replied, the wine adding some gusto to the reply.

Enrique stared out the window. The sun disappeared — hidden by a dark cloud. He sipped his wine and flashed an erudite smile. "Your friend Jerr will tell the truth to anyone, if he's confident that person will tell the truth to him. Presently that doesn't include his superior in the FBI."

"Joe Carlyle?"

"Yes. Murdock, I'm very cautious when I choose new friends. I want *us* to be friends. There are mutually good reasons. I know a great deal about you. You need to know a great deal about me. Talk to Jerrard Blair about me. He now routinely checks his home phone for bugs, so it should be safe. If it isn't, he will tell you in the code that your wife developed."

Murdock sat upright. A look of startled incredulity crossed his face. "You know about that? That was kids' stuff."

"Good. Then it'll work. Those who would hurt us probably can break sophisticated encryptions, but kids' stuff is likely beyond them."

Murdock felt uneasy. "Beyond whom? Traction?"

"Let's just say the FBI for now."

"Do you think the FBI is bugging Jerr's phone? Do they know about Plato?"

Enrique shrugged. "I don't think so. I think they may have another reason. However, our conversation should end now until you talk to Jerr. I sincerely hope that we shall become great friends."

Murdock put on his shoes, his head swimming with questions. Enrique's firmness suggested that the time was not ripe for answers. They walked together to the door, both silent. Enrique opened it. "Goodbye, my friend," he said. "I look forward to your joining us for dinner tonight. But one last thing. I suspect you are on very tender ground when you investigate the death of that monk. It may place you in great personal danger. Be circumspect. Adios, until later."

The door closed behind him. Murdock was alone. He walked to the large picture window at the end of the hallway. Dark snow clouds had captured the peak of the Zugspitze. Light shown from under the door of Baron von Richter's suite. *Rudi and Georg are in there now. I look forward to hearing about that interview. But Rudi will want to know what Enrique and I discussed. That would mean exposing Plato. Enrique didn't swear me to secrecy, but discretion was implicit. Big boys don't need to be sworn. I'll tell Rudi that Enrique pitched a mutual fund in which he wanted me to invest Karen's insurance money. Basically, that's true.* He laughed at his use of the word. *Except for Jerr's part, there's really nothing I can't tell him. He'll have no reason to ask about Jerr.* Walking toward his room, he chuckled to himself. *What is truth? It seems to me that's the same question Pontius Pilate put to Jesus just before he sentenced him to death.*

*   *   *

All morning the professor had been consumed by Brother Stephen's memoirs. The deluge of calculations was daunting, but at times, narratives gave relief. He felt that the narratives had a common strand — Stephen had had a deep and abiding fear that his work might fall into the wrong hands. A third break-in at the factory in Oregon during the second week of October reinforced that fear. Mac had doubled security, coded all the floppy disks pertaining to the super chip project, and run complete background checks on all employees. No internal treachery had been uncovered. Both Stephen and Mac had been puzzled that no attempts had been made to break into the monastery in Bavaria. *Perhaps the secret work on the chip was still secret, and the break-ins in Oregon had nothing to do with it, the professor thought.* That seemed logical, but it didn't make him feel more comfortable. The murder of Brother Stephen a month later, six thousand miles from Oregon, argued against it. But Brother Martin had still insisted that the secret was secure, and that there had to be another motive.

After four hours the professor's head was swimming in a sea of numbers salted with suspicions, and all had begun to lose themselves in the surf. It was time for lunch—time to de-program his brain and relax over a few beers. He shut down the computer, extracted the floppy disk, picked up the second disk from the table, and placed both in the pocket of his flannel shirt. As he walked down the hall toward the restaurant, he felt vaguely uneasy. He looked over his shoulder. There was no one behind him.

⇥ 19 ⇤

Rudi Benzinger relaxed in his room at the Zugspitze Hof. He was comfortable with the thought that he was a Bavarian first and a German second. For at least twenty centuries his family's roots had clung to Bavarian soil. He prided himself as a man conscious of his people's history and of his place and time in it. Bavaria had been held together for almost seven hundred years by the royal Wittelsbach family. Many modern Bavarians have a romantic fascination with the former royalty. Rudi had once opined to Murdock that, if one scratched below the skin of most Bavarians, one would find a monarchist.

Over most of those seven hundred years Bavaria had been a grand duchy within the Holy Roman Empire, which Rudi had suggested to Murdock was neither holy, nor Roman, nor an empire. It was a loose federation of German-speaking states, each ruled by a sovereign duke. In the early nineteenth century, in return for military assistance given to Napoleon, the French emperor crowned the then-reigning duke as Bavaria's first king, Ludwig I.

King Ludwig had transformed Munich—the city that Rudi loved. Begun as a Benedictine monastery, the city preserved tradition in its name. The German name for the city, *München*, means the place of the monks. It had been the capital since the Wittelsbach family settled there in the thirteenth century. Under King Ludwig I the city was transformed into a modern center of trade. He built most of its fine museums.

Rudi was proud that, when Lutheranism spread over the northern German states in the sixteenth century, Bavaria remained largely Catholic. Protestants were not permitted to be citizens until a proclamation by Ludwig I. At the end of World War I, the last king, Ludwig III, abdicated, and Bavaria became a republic.

Rudi was not proud that the Nazi Party had been founded there. When Hitler came to power in Germany in 1933, Bavaria was assimilated into the Third Reich.

After World War II, Bavaria became a republic again. In 1955 it joined the present German federation as its largest state, retaining its own courts, health programs, and school system. The Baron von Richter's idea of restoring the monarchy, and of Bavaria becoming a separate sovereign state within a European Union, was not unattractive to Rudi; but then, he had not thought hard about it. In his heart of hearts he was a professional policeman. But if the monarchy were restored, he did not want the Baron von Richter as his king. He was satisfied that such decisions are not for policemen to make. Now, as he prepared himself mentally to interview von Richter, he didn't look forward to it. The Baron was a wily old goat with some habits that Rudi considered disgusting.

There was a knock on the door. Rudi opened it. It was Georg. "Are you ready, Herr Benzinger?" he asked. "I have confirmed by telephone that the Baron is in his room and that he expects us."

"Ja, ja," Rudi said. He walked over to the bed where his suit coat was lying, put it on, and joined Georg in the hall. "This way," Rudi said, pointing toward the west end, "His is the last room on the left."

Von Richter's suite was the largest at the Zugspitze Hof Lodge. Rudi and Georg were received into its great room by a manservant. He invited them to sit and offered coffee. Both accepted. Rudi noticed a thick photo album on the end table next to his chair. The manservant, observing his interest, quietly removed it and placed it inside a credenza. That made Rudi *want* to examine it, but he had no probable cause that could justify such an intrusion on the Baron's privacy. The manservant went into the bedroom. Presently the bedroom door opened, and the Baron appeared, dressed in casual slacks, a smoking jacket, and slippers. Rudi judged him to be quite at ease. Obviously the police didn't frighten him.

"Perhaps I should be flattered," the Baron began, "that I'm being questioned by such an exalted official as you, Herr Benzinger. Have I been underimpressed by the importance of this murdered monk? What was there about this religious scientist that motivated your superiors to send you? Why are these monks so special? Most of them aren't even Catholic."

Rudi smiled. "I'm here because I'm here," he replied gently but firmly. "Please tell me why you are here."

The Baron frowned. Extracting a silver cigarette case from his smoking jacket, he leisurely opened it, removed a cigarette, tapped it against the case, lit it, and took several puffs, each time exhaling nearly perfect smoke rings. He coughed and answered: "For the same reason."

Georg took out his notebook and observed the Baron impatiently. He planned to remain silent unless he saw the necessity of playing 'good cop.'

Rudi smiled. "Touché, Herr Baron. Unfortunately, in our present roles, it is required that you furnish details, while I am not compelled to reciprocate. Please, you must understand that we would not violate your privacy unless a serious matter confronted us. Murder is serious. Is it true that you arrived at Zugspitze Hof Lodge on Monday of this week?"

Von Richter lowered himself into a lounge chair, kicked off his slippers, crossed his legs, puffed again on his cigarette, arranged the lapels of his smoking jacket, stared out the picture window for a full minute, and then spoke. "I arrived here Monday — the day this monk was murdered."

His eyes met Georg's and then turned away scornfully. Georg wrote something in order to look important. Rudi decided to equalize the aggravation caused by the Baron's slow-motion response. He would take as long to come up with a question as it took von Richter to come up with an answer. He got up, walked over to the window, and watched snow descending through the gloom. Withdrawing a notebook from his inside coat pocket, Rudi pretended to study his notes. After two full minutes of silence, he asked: "Please, tell me why you came here?"

Von Richter sensed that the change of pace was a reaction to his performance. He decided not to continue the game. It was better to be done with these policemen. "I came here for several reasons," he began. "I wished to visit my friend, Herr Bayer, of course, who owns this lodge. I also hoped to do business with these extraordinary monks."

"How is that?" Rudi asked.

"I have the burden and the responsibility of being wealthy, as you are aware."

"The crown weighs heavily," Georg injected, smirking.

The Baron glanced at Georg.

"Please go on," Rudi suggested calmly.

"My family for centuries found financial success by riding leading edge opportunities. But I'm confident that you know my family's history. In the fourteenth century the manufacture of gunpowder got us started. When the twentieth century thrust the electronic age upon us, we exploited opportunities in avionics — the instruments that help airplane pilots determine their geographic position. What opportunities shall we exploit in the twenty-first century? Who can say. We are the creatures of rumors. Rumors have been our lifeblood. Our ears are always to the ground. We seek leading edge technologies. We meticulously check those we deem plausible." The Baron sat upright on the edge of the lounge, his legs crossed, his hands folded in his lap. He leaned forward toward Rudi, lowered his voice, and spoke as if it were in confidence. "Herr Benzinger, you are not a common policeman. You and I are men of the world. We shall not speak of romantic adornments of monarchy. We shall speak of cold, hard facts — industrial secrets. A man in your position certainly must realize that industrial secrets can be immensely valuable. You have a duty to ask questions pertinent to the monks, and I have a duty to answer — within reason. I wish to cooperate. I do not need enemies among the police. I realize that my present title carries little weight in a republic, so I ask for no privilege. But I do ask a consideration — that you do not disclose what I am about to tell you unless you, Herr Benzinger, in your sound judgment and good conscience, decide that I am a legitimate suspect, and that the information is reasonably necessary to the investigation. I shall give you the information because it should convince you that I had every reason to want the monk alive."

"Herr Baron, you must know that I cannot make such a promise."

"But you are a gentleman. There is no need. A promise is unspoken between gentlemen. I wish to speak with you privately."

Rudi nodded toward Georg. "Please wait for me in the coffee shop."

Georg hesitated, frowned, reluctantly put his notebook away, arose, and left the room. When they were alone, von Richter reclined again on the lounge. "Cognac, Herr Benzinger?"

"No. But thank you for your kind offer."

"Herr Benzinger, it was my intention to use what aura my archaic title and my wealth provide to encourage the monks to confirm a rumor. My operatives have heard that the deceased, Brother Stephen, with help from the Spanish monk, Antonio, are — were on to something big. Speculation among my sources is that they were on the verge of a significant advance in systems-on-a-chip, which would dramatically simplify and speed computing. They may have, or were close to, developing one chip that could replace many chips in a computer and forever change the methods used in the design of electronic systems. My sources have heard — and I emphasize this is rumor — that one phase of their work might, for example, make it possible for blind people, whose optic nerve has been destroyed, to see by directly focusing electronic impulses in the three basic color frequencies directly upon the area of the brain that would normally receive such impulses. I would invest in the development of such technology. Many unfortunate people would benefit. Of course, it would make me even wealthier — a synergism that could recommend itself to one in my position. Is it so wrong that both I and the blind would be winners?"

"I am sure that it suggests much to commend it, Herr Baron."

"Herr Benzinger, are you familiar with the term 'gates,' the basic components of every computer?"

"Yes, Herr von Richter. My daughter Rosalinde has explained many computer terms to me."

The Baron smiled. "Good. I had understood that Brother Stephen, aided by this elusive Michael character, was on the verge of putting over ten million gates on a single silicon chip about the size of a thumbnail. What this means, I can barely imagine. My scientists tell me its implications are mind-boggling. The monks sell their technology, giving part of the proceeds to the poor, and using the remainder to do more science. I am interested in helping the poor, and the blind, and myself too. Surely it is fortunate when we can do both at the same time. I had planned to meet Brother Stephen yesterday, but that was rendered impossible by the killer. Did I not have every reason to want the monk alive? If he finished his project aided by my investment, I would stand to make another great fortune. I remain here because I now wish to discuss this project with the Abbot, or Brother Antonio, or Michael, but no one will talk to me until after the funeral of Brother Stephen tomorrow, and no one can find Michael. On my honor as a gentleman, Herr Benzinger, I have no idea who killed the monk. Perhaps it was a competitor. I have no idea who, if anyone, is competing with me, unless it is Señor Jose Enrique Perez-Krieger. Perhaps the rumors were false. Perhaps Brother Stephen's death had nothing to do with the technology about which I speculate. I simply don't know."

"Baron, are you aware that a package was stolen from Brother Stephen when he was killed?"

The Baron's face turned hard as cold steel. He was silent.

"Did you understand my question, Herr Baron?"

"I didn't know anything was stolen. But if it were the plans for the chip, and, assuming that he had finished his work, that would be a great tragedy. It could have fallen into evil hands — hands willing to kill. It would put them in a position of great economic power. If the rumor about the chip is true, of course."

"If you should ever learn what was in the package or who killed Brother Stephen, you understand that it would be your duty to tell me."

"Yes. Of course. Please. The news of the theft is very disturbing. Is there anything else for now? Could you excuse me? I shall remain here a few more days, and I shall make myself available to you."

"No, Herr Baron. There is nothing else for now. Please do not leave without informing me."

The interview ended with pleasantries. In the hallway Rudi stood looking out the picture window where Murdock had stood shortly before. Snow was still falling. The new powder would enhance the slopes by morning. He regretted that he was there as an investigator rather than as a vacationer. He envied Murdock. He could mix the two quite nicely.

The interview had sanded his image of the Baron von Richter. He had found him articulate and, Rudi decided, reasonably forthright. *If his story checks out, von Richter can be removed from my suspect list. Unless these Protestant monks are mixed up with him in some political intrigue that he hasn't revealed. They are unusual. All monks should be Catholic.*

Georg awaited him in the coffee shop.

"Have you had enough coffee, Georg?"

"More than enough, Herr Benzinger. Soon I shall float."

"Georg, it is not necessary for you to remain longer. My travel bag is in the trunk of the car."

"Ja, ja, Herr Benzinger. I shall have a porter take it to your room. Shall I pick you up in the morning, sir?"

"Please meet me here in the coffee shop at 7:30. I will want to know whether there is further information from the airport, and also what the Liechtenstein police have found out about the registration of the biz-jet. Please also bring the forensic report on the gun, if it is available. And I want to know Michael's last name. In the morning I would like you to share with me the present state of your thinking about the case."

Georg, flattered, excused himself.

⇥ 20 ⇤

Far from the great room where the skiers were mingling, Murdock's room was quiet. He kicked off his shoes, sat back, took out his date book, and opened it to the phone number section. Jerr's phone number was first. Gripped by memories, he paused. He and Jerrard Blair had been friends and confidants since both were ten. Not only had they lived next door to one another in Cheektowaga, New York, but they had also attended the same schools. In Boy Scouts, Jerr was patrol leader of the

Hawk Patrol, and Murdock was his assistant patrol leader. In high school they played varsity football together — Jerr at wide receiver and Murdock at safety. On the track team both were distance runners — Jerr ran the half-mile — Murdock the mile. In their senior year of high school they both took flying lessons, and both became multi-engine and instrument rated private pilots before they were twenty. In college they majored in history and government at the State University of New York at Buffalo. Jerr had met Allison there, and Allison had introduced Murdock to her roommate, Karen. They double-dated through four years of college. After graduation, they married in a double ceremony. Murdock and Jerr applied for and were admitted to the University of Michigan law school. Allison enrolled in the criminal justice program at Michigan State. Remaining in Ann Arbor with Murdock, Karen obtained a graduate degree in communications. She studied cryptography on her own. Neither Jerr nor Murdock had planned to practice law, to the chagrin of Murdock's father who wanted him to come into his firm. They were looking for adventure. Together they had applied to the FBI for appointment as special agents. Entering the Bureau with high ideals, patriotic fervor, and dedication, the two young men thought it would be their lifetime career. *It'd be impossible to have a closer friend than Jerr.* He dialed.

Jerr answered the phone drowsily.

"Hell, man, what time is it there in Omaha?" Murdock demanded. "I figure it's 11:30, right? On a Wednesday night? You sound like you're already in bed. What happened to the guy who used to sit up in the dorm and drink beer and tell nasty stories until 2:00? Has all that easy living feeding off the taxpayers made you go soft?"

The voice at the other end sprang to life. "Murdock, you old polecat," Jerr said laughing, "you suckled on the taxpayers' tits yourself. Don't go high and mighty on me. I knew you when you thought that federal milk tasted good. God, it's good to hear your voice. Especially when you're paying for the call. What are you up to?"

"Is your line clear?"

"Yes, I checked it."

"I'm investigating the murder of a monk."

There was a long silence. "The murder of a monk?" Jerr asked. "Incredible. Isn't murder a little out of your line?"

"Not really. You might recall that I investigated three murders perpetrated on federal facilities when I was with the Bureau. I've done two since I've been with Veritus, both involving purported life insurance fraud. But that's ancient history. I've called to tell you that I've met with Jose Enrique Perez-Krieger. If what he tells me is true, you could get fired."

A moment of pregnant silence followed. Murdock recognized the signal. The silence always preceded something heavy — something very serious in Jerr's mind. He remembered the extra long moment of silence just before Jerr had told him that he and Allison were divorcing. When he saw it coming, he never interrupted. After the better part of a minute, Jerr said: "I'm a member of Plato."

"So I'm told," Murdock replied. "Does the Bureau know, or are you the Bureau's mole inside Plato?"

"If I'm a mole, I'd be compelled to deny it. Mole or no mole, as you well know, we work in an environment where truth tends to be fluid. Let's hypothesize that I'm not a mole for the FBI. Let's establish a hypothesis and assume I've been a genuine member of Plato for over a year, and that I genuinely believe in Enrique's goals — to the point where I'm willing to jeopardize my position with the Bureau. Let's assume that I believe it's better for my country that I support Plato and not be completely candid with the Bureau. That gives us a workable hypothesis. I've recently been nominated for the board of directors. I know what you're going to say — if our hypothesis is true, and the Director finds out, not only will there be hell to pay, but there'll be a team here overnight to grab my keys and my code books."

"And," Murdock suggested, "if the hypothesis isn't valid, that makes you a very dangerous mole in the heart of Plato."

"Yes. Indeed it would. But let's stick to our frame of reference. If the FBI finds out and cans me, Allison is confident I can get into Veritus. I can't assess whether her confidence is misplaced. She has little influence with top brass. Enrique would take care of me. So, if the hypothesis is correct, I have a parachute. But tell me. What is your impression of Enrique?"

"This guy," Murdock suggested, testing, "is making himself into a little Hitler. He wants you to follow him simply because he's your leader. Remember the Nazis? They played follow the leader straight into damnation. Anyone who got in their way was eliminated. Over six million people died, Jerr!"

"Yeah. Stalin killed over twenty-five million, but Hitler gets all the press. Hopefully, both are roasting in hell with Jewish and Ukrainian gatekeepers. But this isn't the same, old buddy."

"What's different?"

"Enrique seeks economic power, not political, and he's seeking it for positive, unselfish purposes."

"Excuse me, Jerr, but that's a big chunk to swallow. Which is the tail and which the dog? Let's hypothesize instead that you're a mole for Plato in the FBI."

"Right," Jerr exclaimed. "Or a two-headed mole working for both and spying on both for both. In any event, old friend, regardless of whether any of these hypotheses are correct, I'd never sandbag you. You know that. We've been friends for too long. And I recommend that you invest in Plato. Be vigilant, as always. You're not as vulnerable as I am. You've little to lose by investing for the short term. You'll be able to judge early in the game whether you want to play or turn in your equipment. In the meantime you'll make some money. What do you say, Murdock?"

"I say — What else is new?"

"Okay. But think about it. By the way, I think you know that Joe Carlyle is now in charge of the violent crimes unit. Apparently, he is a confirmed believer in the Paperwork Reduction Act. Carl Sutherland, my informant in D.C., reports that since Joe's promotion, all copies of the after-action critique in the shoot-out that took Karen's life are missing. Even the computer database has been deleted. It's as if these records never existed. Carl doesn't dare ask — with the wrong questions, Joe can downgrade his security clearance."

Murdock chuckled knowledgeably. "I can believe that. I can also believe your home phone is bugged."

"I've checked it."

"Today?"

"Just before your call. It's secure."

"Anything else I need to know, Jerr?"

"Yeah. Joe Carlyle claims he pulled the strings that got my promotion to agent-in-charge in Omaha. I'm inclined to believe him. You know what that means."

"Yeah. Your career is in his hands. You'll be asked to pay a price. What's the up-front price? Do you know?"

"He wants Karen's cryptography notebooks. He wants me to sucker you out of them in such a way that you won't make copies before you give them to me."

"That's pretty candid, old buddy. Do you know why?"

"Not yet, Murdock. Carl is working on it. You still have them, don't you?"

"Yes."

"Have you shown them to anyone?"

"No, but I've met someone special. She dabbles in cryptography and says she may be able to figure out what Karen was dabbling in. But this new information makes me hesitate."

"Anyone I know?"

"Diana Crenshaw. She's here on business. Her employer is Seneca Financial. She's bird-dogging your friend, Enrique."

"That name doesn't ring a bell. Mind if I do a little checking?"

"No. Please do. While you're about it, try to get her sexual preferences too. She hasn't given me a clue. Maybe she's a virgin."

Jerr laughed. "How old is she?"

"Early thirties, I'd guess."

Jerr laughed again. "Yeah. I suppose it could be she's a virgin. Could be that bears don't shit in the woods, either."

Murdock grumbled. "Anything else?"

"Yeah. Big stuff. Rumor has it that Joe Carlyle is up for promotion to deputy director after only six months in his present position, and that the political skids are greased—a shoo-in if he doesn't shoot too many citizens in the meantime. He's popular with somebody, certainly not the street agents."

"Popular, hell," Murdock exclaimed. "He owns somebody's ass. Joe will go far. He understands how to acquire power and how to effectively use it. He goes to church every Sunday and probably prays that God will protect him from the curse of scruples."

"Yeah. But hang on, Murdock. He may get his ass bagged yet. Carl says Joe has one."

"One what?"

"A *mademoiselle d'amour*—an enchantress with big bucks instead of big tits. When Joe chooses between the two, he always takes the bucks. If it's true, the information is tightly held. Carl hasn't a clue whether he's running her or she's running him. Wouldn't that be poetic justice if she's holding the gonads of the guy who specializes in crushing them?"

"What *does* Carl know about her?"

"She's known as Patti Dale. He thinks that Joe and Patti have a hard-on for Enrique. He doesn't have a clue why. Carl says she spends most of her time in Europe. If this Mata Hari exists and she's controlling Joe, then who's controlling her, I wonder?"

"Jerr, one of our operatives is involved in an investigation of a target named Patti Dale. It was authorized by Harvey Specter, our regional director. He knows Joe Carlyle. It doesn't sound like a coincidence. What do you think?"

After a long silence, Jerr responded. "I can't figure it. If your man Harvey has ordered an investigation of Joe's *dame d'amour*, it suggests he's trying to get something on her."

Murdock laughed. "With Joe, that's normal. He builds a file on his friends just in case he decides to make one his enemy."

"What's with the dead monk?"

"Coincidentally, I was a guest at Zugspitze Hof when this monk disappeared. Someone engaged us to find him. Now that same someone wants us to find the monk's killer. Also, do you remember Moira?"

"Yes, you've mentioned her several times. She's the lesbian chick who works with you at the Veritus office in Munich. You think she's a competent investigator. What about her?"

"Moira was assigned to investigate the Mädchenhaus Café, which is a palace for lesbian society in Munich. Her investigation is focused on Patti. Moira's not sure what she's looking for. Neither of us knows who our clients are. These are the first investigations since we've been with Veritus where we weren't given all the facts."

"Murdock, is it possible that everything is interconnected — the murder of the monk, the lesbian society in Munich, Patti Dale, and maybe even Joe?"

"Man, I don't know enough even to suppose yet. I haven't seen any connection, but when you stir in Joe Carlyle and Karen's notebooks, I can fantasize lots of scenarios. Can you think of a reason Joe would want the notebooks? They're history. Hasn't the FBI changed all their codes since her death?"

"Yeah, the codes were changed. I can't guess why Joe wants Karen's notebooks. Look through them. See if she had anything on Joe."

"She would have told me."

"Look anyway. See if you can give me something to give to Joe. He won't know whether he got it all. If he decides he hasn't, he'll have to come back to me for another favor. Meanwhile, find out whether your virgin queen has an ulterior motive for wanting them."

"Will do, Jerr. Got to go now. Meeting Rudi for a few brews. Take care."

"Wish I could be with you guys. Give my best to Rudi. Good night."

*   *   *

A determined blizzard swept over Omaha. The night was bitterly cold. Jerr, glad to be inside in a warm bed, felt uneasy. He hadn't been entirely forthright with Murdock, not as forthright as a best friend should be, or as he had been with Allison who had called earlier. He had told Allison what Carl Sutherland really thought. Allison would decide whether Carl's theory should be shared with Murdock. If so, she would share it face-to-face. Carl was convinced that the kidnapping of Karen was staged to cover the real motive for her murder. According to Carl's theory, the kidnappers were dupes. They had to die in the shoot-out to protect the guilty. Joe Carlyle personally commanded the agents in the shoot-out. Carl thinks that Joe wanted her dead. *But Carl can't find a motive. The theory doesn't jell without a motive. But Carl's intuitive and not known for incautious guesses.* Jerr considered him a foursquare straight arrow. He would see Carl at the Michigan game on Saturday. *We'll put our heads together after the game and see if there's a common thread that could possibly hold together a murdered wife, a murdered monk, a lesbian café in Munich, and Joe. No mean task.* He hoped the thread didn't exist. It was a frightening thought if it did—more so if Joe had Karen killed in order to further some government policy. Jerr was deeply distraught. *If Karen's death wasn't an accidental shooting but cold-blooded murder by agents of her own government, as Carl suspects, then this Ruby Ridge Two may be more sinister than the first. Where would the shock waves reach if the media gets hold of it? What national security interests would be invented to mislead the media and simonize it? And above all, how would Murdock react if it turns out that Carl's theory is correct? What if Joe is connected with Traction? And if Traction's cold hand reaches into the FBI and even into a lesbian café in Munich, who's safe? Obviously not some obscure monk in Bavaria.*

⇥ 21 ⇤

The lounge at Zugspitze Hof was jammed. Murdock found Rudi sitting at the bar with one stein of beer in front of him and another in front of a vacant chair next to him. Rudi had been expecting him. Diana was curled up on a couch reading. Deciding not to disturb her, Murdock made his way to the bar. Greeting him, Murdock climbed onto the bar stool, took the stein of beer firmly in hand, and drank a fair sampling. Rudi appeared excited—a stretch for this superbly poised man.

"Okay, what is it, Rudi?"

A broad grin crossed Rudi's face. "I just spoke to Angelika's nurse, as I do every day. But today she had news! She saw Angelika's eyes follow her. Just once. But she's sure they followed her. Hope, Murdock! There is hope."

"That's wonderful, Rudi, especially after two years of discouragement."

Rudi turned his head away from Murdock, to hide tears, and stared down the bar. Murdock knew that the two years have been difficult for

Rudi. He loved her deeply. She was his angel. There had been no sign that she could ever become cognitive until today. Rudi had never given up praying and hoping. He had remained faithful to her. Murdock believed it would take a miracle for her to regain consciousness — assuming that God exists and that miracles aren't mere happenstance.

"Truthfully, Rudi, I don't know whether to be happy or sad. Don't get your hopes too high. If the nurse thought she saw just one movement, she may have imagined it."

Rudi beamed. "It's prayer, Murdock, not hope. Hope is a state of mind. It does nothing. Prayer does all things. Every day I have asked the Blessed Virgin to intercede with our Lord and ask him to restore her to me. Now I have a sign that my prayers are heard. That's all I can expect. The decision is God's, and I'm resigned to His wisdom. But, I think he will give her back to me."

Murdock decided not to dampen Rudi's enthusiasm. *If it helps to believe there's really a god out there who gives a damn, so be it.* "I don't know," he said. "Maybe you're right, Rudi. In the words of Alfred Lord Tennyson, 'More things are wrought by prayer than this world dreams of.'"

"Ja, you are right, Murdock. I must not dwell on it. Now, let us mix some work with our pleasure. Please, what did you learn from the abbot, Brother Martin?"

Murdock shrugged. "Have you heard of the Sinaiticus Codex?"

"Yes," Rudi replied, "and I have heard of Professor Tischendorf who stole it from the monks at Saint Catherine's monastery on Mount Sinai. But what can this possibly have to do with the murder of Brother Stephen?"

"Martin indicated that Brothers Stephen and Gustav were preparing a web site that would provide the original Greek text of the Codex. He speculates that some group wanted to prevent that."

"So," Rudi injected, "he has had not been forthright with you either."

"I didn't say that. Maybe he believes that preventing the web site was important enough to someone. There are religious fanatics. Men have been killed for less. What did *you* learn from von Richter?"

Rudi drank from his stein and savored the taste of the beer. He moved his chair closer to Murdock's and spoke in a subdued voice. "The Baron, as you know, is heavily invested in electronics. He heard a rumor that Stephen may have invented something that he, the Baron, would want to buy. He came here to check it out. He will meet with the abbot in a day or two. He has assured me that he will furnish me with any information that comes to his attention that might assist in our investigation."

Murdock sensed that Rudi was exhibiting a more amenable attitude toward the Baron. "Have you learned the identity of the owner of the biz-jet that's made so many flights to Cyprus?"

"The police in Liechtenstein have not responded, and I don't expect them to for a few days."

Murdock squirmed. "Do you remember Joe Carlyle."

"Yes," Rudi replied. "I still do not have a high opinion of your former boss. Why do you ask?"

"You've heard me talk of my friend Jerr."

"Yes. He is the agent in charge of the FBI office in Omaha. Carlyle led the raiding party that attacked Karen's kidnappers."

"Joe has asked Jerr to obtain Karen's notebooks."

"That is curious," Rudi replied, leaning still closer to Murdock. "There is some confidential police information that I feel I must tell you. We are gentlemen, Murdock. I know I can trust you. Besides, the minister of justice has authorized us to be open with you. Have you met her?"

"The minister of justice? No."

"She seems to trust you. Anyway, our intelligence section keeps a watch list — a highly confidential list of people in other police agencies who are not to be trusted with the most highly confidential information. Joe Carlyle's name has just appeared on that list."

Murdock glanced over his shoulder toward the couch where Diana had been reading. She wasn't there. Had she overheard any of their conversation? He turned back toward Rudi. Murdock shook his head. "That sounds like an appropriate move," he said. Do you know why his name popped up?"

"No. I've just seen the new list. I shall talk to my friends in the intelligence unit. Now please tell me, why did Señor Perez-Krieger wish to see you?"

Murdock decided not to mention Plato unless directly asked. It still didn't appear to have the remotest connection with the murder of the monk. "He wants to sell me some shares in his private mutual fund. He knew about Karen's life insurance money. But I'm a white knuckle investor. Right now it's in a money market account back in the States — what's left after I bought the BMW."

"What is your impression of him?"

"He seems like a good sort. He certainly comes from a reputable family. Family honor is important to aristocratic Chileans. If you're nervous about him, why don't you run a criminal check on him?"

"We have. Nothing has been turned up in Europe or in Chile. By tomorrow we should have a worldwide check. However, as we inquire outside of North America and Europe, information becomes more elastic. Unfortunately, there are still many countries where a criminal record can be erased by an infusion of American dollars. Señor Perez-Krieger has many dollars, and he is a world traveler, so one can never be certain about such men. So, our progress is slow. Everyone here is still a suspect except you, Murdock."

"Thank you, old buddy. That's a relief."

"Tell me why Señor Perez-Krieger is here."

"He chose Zugspitze Hof because it's close to St. Luke's. He hopes to invest in one or more of the scientific projects that these unusual monks are working on."

Flipping through his pocket notebook, Rudi stopped at a page where he had folded the corner. His eyes met Murdock's. "Who is your client?"

"I still don't know."

"Is that not unusual?"

"Yes. Most unusual."

"You have asked Allison?"

"Yes. She doesn't know."

"Maybe she is holding back from you?"

"No. If she were holding back, it would be because she had been ordered to, and she would tell me that. And I would respect her duty to follow orders."

Murdock couldn't blame Rudi for disbelieving him, and that was frustrating. Neither had had cause to disbelieve the other before. Murdock was concerned that it might affect their friendship, and friendship was important to him.

Rudi wrote something in his date book. Without looking up he said: "I believe you, Murdock, but I would not like to think that Veritus is investigating on its own account. It is not licensed in Bavaria to do that. Questions of motive would come to mind, suggesting political implications. It is not good for a detective agency to have its own agenda. In fact it is unheard-of. Veritus could lose its license. I must insist that you find out who your client is and tell me. And find out how your client knew this monk was missing so soon after his disappearance." Rudi looked up from his notes, his eyes met Murdock's. "You understand that it is my duty to discover the answers to these questions and, with Richard missing, it is Allison's duty as your top person in Bavaria to furnish them to me. You will remind her of that so that I needn't. Right?"

"She knows her responsibility to the police, Rudi. She's as concerned about our relationship with you as I am. Our orders are to keep Harvey out of the loop. I agree that's unusual too. It closes our normal channel to headquarters in Chicago. I'm sure the folks in Chicago understand our duty to the police and, hopefully, they're working on the problem. Can you give us a few days to sort this out?"

"Oh, yes. The state minister of justice is not as concerned as I am, but then she is not a policeman. I, being a policeman, feel compelled to ask — do you know why this politician would order us to give you and Allison free reign?"

"No. I didn't know she had."

Rudi smiled. "If Doctor Watson were telling this story about Sherlock Holmes, he might entitle it, 'The Most Curious Case of Curiosities.' I think we could use Mr. Holmes right now. It is not so good that we founder much longer. We need progress."

"It's been only two days since the body was found."

"Ja, Murdock, but we are drawing a complete blank. Any suggestions, my friend?"

"A few. First, I want to talk to Professor Klugman before dinner. I suspect he knows why Brother Martin has not been forthright with us. Maybe he can give me a clue as to how I might unlock that door. Second, I think I can find out whether Enrique — Señor Perez-Krieger — knows anything about the second biz-jet that practically followed him to Cyprus yesterday. Third, you need to take that Spanish monk — Brother Anthony — into the police station and jerk him around until he tells you what was in the package that Brother Stephen was taking to the post office. Fourth, I think you guys need to find out whether that mystery plane with the Austrian registry was at the Munich airport early yesterday morning when Richard disappeared. If it was, when did it leave? What was its manifest? What was its flight-planned destination? Did it get there?"

"Those are good suggestions, Murdock. We have been working on the fourth. The third will require the commander's permission before we drag Brother Anthony from the monastery. That will be sensitive. Our government does not like to disturb monks in monasteries — at least not without explicit probable cause. Besides, Brother Anthony has been missing from the monastery for two days, and it had not been reported to the police. They didn't tell you that?"

"No."

"So," Rudi exclaimed, "it is like old times when we worked together when you were in the FBI."

"Yes, old friend. Those were good times. But for now if you can find the Spanish monk, hold him in protective custody, if you can."

Rudi grinned. "Yes. I agree. I have already applied for authority."

"Doesn't a man in your position already have such authority, Rudi?"

Rudi shook his head sadly. "Ordinarily yes. But this is not ordinary."

"What's extraordinary about it?"

"The state minister of justice has taken an interest. That suggests political implications, does it not?"

"I suppose," Murdock replied. "You might also check out this atheist professor. He seems incredibly close to these monks for a nonbeliever, don't you think?"

"Agreed. But remember, Murdock, the other person in an incredible position is the private investigator with an illusory client. That mystery may also confuse the killer. Ambiguity may increase the danger to you. Be on guard with everyone. You may be a target. One murder is quite enough. Another suggestion: Deliver Karen's notebooks to me for safekeeping and don't let anyone see them."

"Why, Rudi?"

"I don't know why. It's my policeman's intuition."

"If I give you Karen's notebooks, what does Jerr tell Joe Carlyle?"

Rudi emptied his stein. He stared at the mirror behind the bar. Murdock emptied his stein and ordered another round. Rudi began humming. *Ah, Murdock thought, he's concocting something.* The bartender slammed two fresh steins onto the bar, suds running down their sides. Rudi took a sip, wiped the suds from under his nose, and turning toward Murdock, said: "Have Jerr tell Joe that the Bavarian State Police seized Karen's cryptography notebooks without explanation and that you are trying to get them back. Then we sit back, watch Joe wiggle, and we see who else wiggles too. What do you think?"

"Marvelous."

⤙ 22 ⤚

Sorrow, a medicine of the mind, is a softening agent. It ameliorates the brittle remembrance of tragedy. But Murdock knew that, like many drugs, if abused and overused, sorrow can become addictive and softness can obliterate some of what is human in us. For two years he had lived alone. Sorrow went to bed with him like a cold sheet that never warmed. His loneliness had a bite. Since he arrived at Zugspitze Hof, where he had spent contented days with Karen, the bite was beginning to hurt. Its pain contrived a sense of urgency—an urgency to shake off sorrow and make space in his life for a woman again. *Perhaps Diana is the right woman*. His wristwatch indicated that it was time to join her and the professor at Enrique's table. As he closed the door of his room behind him, he noticed light under the professor's door. He knocked. The professor opened it and invited him in.

"Ah, Murdock, I'm glad you stopped. I know it's just about time for dinner," the professor said, "but I'm anxious to hear about your meeting with Martin. Did he explain Stephen's project to you?"

"He explained that Stephen and Brother Gustav were working on setting up a web site for the Sinaiticus Codex, but I'd never heard of it. Have you?"

"Yes."

"While it sounds like an interesting project, professor, I'm not convinced that people would kill for it."

A wry smile crossed the professor's face. "It wouldn't seem so. I wonder, though, whether things are always as innocuous as they first appear. Come, we'll be late. We can talk while we're walking toward the dining room." They exited the professor's room and walked down the hallway. "Did Martin mention any other of Stephen's projects?"

"No."

"It's possible he doesn't trust you yet. I consider myself a good judge of people and I trust you completely. The policeman, Rudi Benzinger, trusts you too. Talk to Martin again tomorrow. I'll speak to him beforehand. Be a close listener and sparse interrogator. I assume that you're not a Christian — or at least you don't work at it." Murdock shrugged. "I recommend that you let him think he might convert you. Genuinely open your mind. Don't fake it. He can spot a fake a mile away. Let yourself go, but at the same time be careful. He *might* convert you. He's made me weaken several times, but, alas, I'm an incorrigible atheist. I wallow in the delight of knowing that there is no intellect higher than man's. I'm convinced that we can understand and explain everything in nature without resorting to a god. But be on guard. He's no ordinary preacher. He can dazzle you with disarming truths. You may remember what a reprobate sinner St. Augustine of Hippo was until he took the cure and became a bishop. He was able to write authoritatively about sin and evil because he was an expert on both. When Martin speaks about sin and evil, believe me, he's experienced it. He believes his Jesus came to minister to sinners, not saints. If that were true, Martin and I would be near the top of Jesus' list of problem kids. We're a bad lot — us atheists and quondam atheists."

As they entered the dining room, they found Enrique and Diana already seated. Enrique welcomed them warmly, invited them to be seated, and offered a red wine from his vineyards. The table was square, imitation rustic, nicely prepared with a forest green linen tablecloth, white linen napkins, fine Bavarian china, Czech crystal wine glasses, Frau Bayer's sterling candlesticks, and sterling silver flatware reserved for special customers. Two candles, a lighter shade of green, offered a pleasant contrast. The flickering flames of the candles in the dimly lighted corner induced dancing shadows on the walls. Complimented by the gift of warmth from the wine, they encouraged conviviality.

"In my family," Enrique announced, "we play a little game. When an unacquainted group such as ours comes together, we ask each person to turn to the person on the left and ask a question. That party must give the first answer that comes to mind." He turned to Murdock. "For example, tell me without hesitating, one thing you don't like."

"Darkness," Murdock responded.

Enrique smiled. "Now you may give us a very brief explanation, or you may choose to say nothing at all. Either way we learn something."

Murdock chuckled. "I shall share my deep, dark secret. I love mornings — especially first light — what the Spaniards call 'La mañanita.' If I sleep past sunrise, I feel that I've missed the best part of the day. Dawn is my *pièce de résistance*. In the early dawn, I see flowers escape from the darkness and come alive with color. At sunrise I'm thrilled by aquamarine lakes reflecting puffs of stratocumulus clouds punctuating a clear blue sky, or the severe clear of frosty air as a bright winter morning dissolves the night. Darkness is a blindfold that prevents us from seeing the beauty of creation."

Enrique smiled. "I think you have the heart of a poet, Murdock. Now it is your turn to ask a question of the professor."

Murdock pondered thoughtfully, and then, grinning, turned to Professor Klugman. "Professor, have you ever been passionately in love with a woman?"

The professor threw up his hands and laughed. "How unsporting a question to put to an old bachelor like me. Yes. Desperately. Her name was Clarissa Gallagher. She taught English poetry at Oregon State, and she liked to read philosophy. We spent innumerable enchanted hours discussing Shelley and Keats. Did you know that Percy Shelley's wife, Mary, wrote the Frankenstein stories? She did. She was pretty keen on me too — Clarissa, not Mary — but not keen enough to leave her husband and children. She had two girls — one I was particularly fond of — Amy. Intelligent little tike. By age seven she could recite *Annabelle Lee* from memory and with such passion that, if there were a heaven, and if her recitation could have drifted up there, it would have delighted the soul of Edgar Allen Poe — assuming, of course, that heaven was his venue. Now she's a young astrophysicist in Oregon. I helped coax her into that choice. But, enough of me." He turned toward Diana. "It is my turn to put a question to this delightful lady. If I were forty years younger, I would plead with you, beautiful Diana, to bear my children."

They all laughed.

"Thank you, kind but naughty sir," Diana replied. "That is indeed a compliment from so famous and distinguished a scholar. I shall not ask how many women have been fed that line. I trust they were all suitably titillated."

The professor's eyes engaged hers. "I am undaunted by your flattery. My modesty prevents me from admitting I deserve it. The answer to the question I put to you shall be held in reserve just in case these young, handsome men ignore you."

"Oh, my," Diana replied coyly, sporting a broad grin.

The professor continued. "Lovely lady, I wish to know whether you like Shelly and Keats?"

Diana grinned coquettishly. "I'm afraid I detest them both, professor. I'm sorry."

The professor chuckled. "Please don't be sorry. I detest them both too. You see, it was Clarissa whom I enjoyed." A roar of laughter circled the table again. "Can you imagine what I went through all those years pretending that I adored them? I'm a man of dogged perseverance. Perhaps it came from having a scant supply of women interested in me." He looked around the table. "You are too polite to ask whether our relationship was prosaic. Let me put it this way. Her husband was interested in the work of a lady anthropologist who studied the mating habits of apes. It was rumored from reliable mongers that he aided her in some of her experiments, but I understand that the apes watched with only mild curiosity."

Diana roared. "Naughty, naughty, professor. Surely you're making that up."

"You give me credit for more imagination than I can take credit for, lovely lady. In any event, he seemed happy cavorting with his ape woman, and I was sublimely happy making poetry with Clarissa."

"You wrote poetry?" Diana asked.

"Please," the professor replied. "Our poetry could never be put down in mere words."

Diana turned toward Enrique. Their eyes met. "And now it is your turn to answer," she said. "My question is a simple one. What one word in English would best describe what you feel is most important in life?"

"Honor," he replied without hesitation.

Her eyes widened. "Will you explain?" she chided, "Or shall we be left to speculate?"

Enrique observed, one by one, each person around the table. He straightened his back. His face assumed a look of mock propriety. He grinned. "Your speculations may be much more absorbing than my answer, so I shall not deprive you of them."

There was a murmur of surprise and a general nodding of heads as Enrique's meaning sank in. He continued jovially.

"Your answers make me want to get to know all of you better. I want to discover what is really behind Murdock's dislike of darkness. It is none of my business, but it is one challenge that will make getting to know him more interesting. And in getting to know you, Diana, I would like to learn what poets you *do* like, and why you, like the professor, detest Shelley and Keats, both of whom I enjoy. And you, professor. I should like to know more about Amy."

"You mean Clarissa."

"I mean Amy."

The professor chuckled, but gave no response.

"Oh, more naughty, naughty," Diana gasped mockingly. "Did something happen in between Shelley and Keats? I imagine Clarissa as the aggressor — armed with an ode. Did the husband find out? Don't answer. You are right, Enrique. The unanswered questions are the more fun. They ignite the imagination. Professor, you and I must talk more."

Enrique's eyes met Murdock's.

"You may be disappointed," the professor injected. "A gentleman may spike the imagination, but he never tells. However, I shall be pleased to have a drink with you if Murdock doesn't object."

Enrique frowned.

Murdock cocked his head and smiled. "Just keep your hands on top of the table, professor, unless you have a strong heart."

They all laughed.

"My heart is strong," the professor insisted, "but I shall cling to the stein with both hands."

Diana tittered. "An interesting man allows the woman the opportunity of saying 'no.' That way the woman will not feel that *she* is uninteresting to the man."

Enrique chortled. "Oh, the delightful games we must play to make one another feel secure. They make life interesting." He turned toward Diana. "I must tell you, Diana, that you look most radiant tonight. Something has changed. I can't put my finger on it. It is — I think — your smile. It has a new luster. What secret are you hiding from us?"

"Well actually," she said, pleased, "I've had a bit of good news. Just before dinner I was informed that I've been promoted to senior vice president of Seneca Financial. It is a grand opportunity. I'll not be bird-dogging prospective clients any longer. You, Enrique, have the honor of being my last. Brace yourself. That means I must make a special effort to land you."

"Wonderful news," Murdock injected. "Congratulations."

Enrique stood, leaned over the table, took her hand, and kissed it. "Yes. Congratulations. And perhaps you *shall* land me. That is marvelous news. We must celebrate." He caught the waiter. "Champagne," he ordered as he released Diana's hand. "We must talk business tomorrow. Are you available for lunch?"

"That depends upon when the professor planned to buy my drink and clutch his stein. I wouldn't want to miss a stein-clutching."

Laughter again circled the table.

The professor took her hand. "This is such good news, and you, pretty lady, are much too much for a foolish old man's withered charms. Certainly you must have lunch with our host."

Diana squeezed his hand. "Professor, I look forward to having a drink with you. Some of the most charming men I've met were older than you. Years of experience teach some men the art of utterly enchanting a younger woman to the point where she would plead to be their Lolita. I must confess, though, that I'm not Lolita material. I have an ulterior motive. I want to learn more about your secret love."

The professor squeezed her hands. "Oh," he said, "I didn't say it was secret. Her husband never asked Clarissa questions that might be embarrassing, and Clarissa never inquired about the experiments with the ape lady — I mean the ape lady's experiments."

Diana laughed. "I think you said what you meant."

"Truly, ignorance *is* bliss," he continued. "I thought it was admirably congenial. We were, after all, adults."

Diana shook her head. "I'd never have guessed how delightfully naughty you can be, professor. That is a tad more adult than I would care to be, but I *do* look forward to having a drink with you. Tomorrow, however, I shall lunch with my client."

Murdock felt a tinge of jealousy. *Enrique is handsome, and at least ten thousand times wealthier than I. And it sounds like she's just gone into six figures. The professor is a renowned philosopher and author, and he's probably a dirty old man who really knows how to use his hands artfully under the table. Right now he's holding her hand above the table. I'd like to look under it and see where his knee is. If I want her, I'd better act quickly. As the old Korean proverb says, 'Man no win charming lady by courting too slow.'*

*   *   *

Meanwhile, over 1,500 miles to the south and east, a man sat cross-legged in the moonlight on the Cypriot shore of the warm Mediterranean Sea. He was short — about five-six — but powerfully built. His beard was unkempt. He was filthy — not because he explicitly chose to be — but because he chose not to wash. A scabbard hung on his belt. Sitting there, he slowly and deliberately sharpened the twelve-inch knife that the scabbard housed. Back and forth and back and forth across a stone. An evil grin exposed his few remaining but neglected teeth. His name was Sascha. If he ever had a last name, he had long forgotten it. Angrily he spit on the stone. Then back and forth and back and forth again, sharpening ever finer. The whore, whom his friend Theo had brought all the way from Limassol, had refused him. He had offered twice the money she had charged Theo.

"Maybe you're a nice man," she had said, "but you need a bath and clean clothing. Call me when you don't smell like a pig farm."

He spit on the stone again. *The Greek bitch, he thought.* Back and forth and back and forth. He considered cutting off her breasts and watching her slowly die. But she was Theo's favorite whore. Sascha was proud of his deep sense of honor. *Honorable men don't kill their best friend's favorite whore. Soon Theo will tire of her. Then I'll present him with two toys. He will like them and thank me. We'll drink and laugh together.* He spat into the sand. *And then we will find two new whores, and if mine won't take my money, my knife will convince her. Or maybe the boss will let me have a woman who is not a whore. That would be fun. She will make love to both me and my knife—in either order—whichever she chooses.* He snickered. *Either way, I will be her last. That would really be fun.*

He arose, unzipped his fly and urinated into the sea. Finished, he turned without zipping his fly and ascended the path that led to the top of the bluff. On top he could make out the single bare lightbulb burning in the guardhouse above the dungeon. Sascha walked toward it. He lived there alone among the uncleared refuse. Unlatching the door, he stepped inside. The stone walls were decorated with magazine cutouts of nude women. Theo bought the magazines in town for him. Sascha didn't care to go to town. Townspeople stared at him and talked behind his back. He didn't like them. *Someday soon I will set fire to the town. But I must be careful. The boss will not like that. He must never know who did it.*

He chose one of his favorite nude pictures — one of the most explicit — and did what he did every night before he went to bed.

It had been a full day. Murdock was relieved to see Wednesday come to a close. Two days ago he had set out for a vacation at Zugspitze Lodge, and by the next morning he was embroiled in a murder investigation. And that was only yesterday. His room was warm. Herr Bayer had arranged for a roaring fire in his fireplace. Excited embers swirled about in the pit and danced up the chimney. He hadn't yet turned on the lamps. The glow of the fire cast a soft light that soothed his nerves. Dressed in a robe and slippers, a scotch in his right hand, Murdock looked at his watch. It showed eleven. He dialed Allison's number. She answered on the second ring.

"Murdock?"

"Yes. Good to hear your voice, Allison. How are you?"

"Fine. Just came in. Picked up Moira at the train station. She just returned from Regensburg. We stopped at the coffee shop."

"What's new with her?"

"She made the final client contact to wrap up the Herzog Insurance investigation. They're happy. Our relationship with them is solid. How was your day?"

"I met with Brother Martin briefly this morning. He indicated that the dead monk was working on several projects. The one he mentioned was a web site for the Sinaiticus Codex. Have you heard of it?"

"Yes. That's the Greek Bible that Professor Tischendorf stole from the monks at St. Catherine's on Mount Sinai. It's on display at the British Museum. How could that be important?"

Murdock was silent for several seconds, amazed that she'd heard of it. He leaned over and threw another log on the fire. "I guess it's important because he mentioned it. It doesn't make much sense that anyone would kill to stop a web site. It isn't that difficult to create one. And who'd be threatened by the codex anyway?"

Allison hesitated. "Do you think he's blowing smoke?"

"Yes. What else can it be? But you'd think that an intelligent man could do a better job of it. A Bible web site. Really."

"Well, join the crowd. Patti Dale is misleading Moira. Dale told Moira that she worked as an English librarian at BMW. I checked with Karl Kunkel. She doesn't work there. Moira is not convinced that Patti is a dyke. Tell me about Señor Perez-Krieger. Is he a suspect?"

"The Chilean businessman is a fascinating character. I don't see any connection between him and the dead monk. He jetted off to Cyprus yesterday afternoon and returned today. Tonight he hosted a dinner for Diana, the professor, and myself. If he's up to no good, he's the best con man I've met."

"His full name's Jose Enrique Perez-Krieger, is it not?"

"Yes. Why?"

"He's the major shareholder in Siegfried Insurance. Has he mentioned that?"

"No. He mentioned that he's heard of Veritus, and that he's impressed by our reputation."

"Good. What did you learn about Diana tonight? Can you talk? Is she in your room now?"

"No. Of course not. I did make a halfhearted pass, but she put me off. I think Enrique likes her too. I can't compete with Enrique; he's one of the wealthiest men in the world."

"If it's money she's after."

"What do you mean?"

"I'm not sure. Did the professor turn out to be what he professes to be?"

"So far, Allison. He's concerned about what the computer age is doing to science — or rather, what it's doing to scientists. He feels that the virtual inundation of information is trivializing the moral responsibility of individual scientists."

Allison groaned. "This morning it took me two hours to review the daily printouts that landed on Richard's desk." There was a moment of silence. "Are you romantically interested in Diana?"

"Yes, but I don't think she'll let it go anywhere. If she's fishing, Enrique is by far the better catch. But there's always hope. She announced tonight that she is being promoted to senior vice president. She won't be recruiting clients anymore."

"Hustling clients."

"That's not fair, Allison."

"Hasn't she been a procuress for the rich and powerful? Or do you see it differently?"

"Only incidental to her recruiting job."

"Murdock, a large part of my job is recruiting clients. I don't arrange sex for them."

"You're different, Allison."

"Really? What have I got that she hasn't — besides a conscience? Thank God for that. But if you two get serious, remember that your marriage to Karen worked because she was a writer and cryptographer, and she could work out of her living room anywhere. Karen followed you without compromising her career. You *know* how hard Jerr and I tried to make our marriage work with divergent careers. If Diana is going to be just a good friend or a casual romance or even a one-nighter, that's one thing. But if you're more serious — and I think you're toying with the idea because of the kind of man you are — ask yourself whether she's willing to give up her promotion and her career to be with you. She must be making much more money than you are. Are you willing to give up your career to play *hausfrau* for her? Romance *can* cloud one's thinking."

"There hasn't been any *real* romance yet."

"By *real* I suppose you mean sex."

"Well, yes. She isn't the kind of woman you just fall into bed with for a one-nighter."

"Murdock, you're an old-fashioned man. Have you ever fallen into bed with any woman for a one-nighter in your entire life?"

"Well, no."

"You'd be too polite to ask. I'm not being critical. I love you for it. Karen was my best friend, but you and I both have to put her to rest. I'm glad that you're beginning to fish." She didn't sound convincing. There was silence at the other end of the phone. Murdock decided that Allison needed support.

"Allison, there's no woman in the world that I admire more than you."

"How romantic."

"You know I'm not just saying that. We go back too far. Remember the late evening debates in college — you and Jerr and Karen and I? I mean, we solved the problems of the world over a case of beer. Of course, the next morning we couldn't remember what the solutions were."

"Murdock, don't worry yourself about me. It's just a little late evening funk . . ."

"From a young woman who needs some romance in *her* life."

"From a woman who is pressing precariously close to forty without romance in her life."

"Thirty-eight isn't all that precariously close."

"Maybe not when you're a man. I'd guess that your Diana is younger, isn't she?"

"I'd put her at about thirty-two."

"*That* is not precariously close to forty."

"I've known a number of men who seemed to be interested in you, Allison. You've turned them away."

"Because, frankly, not one of them was a Jerr . . . or a Murdock."

Murdock fell silent. Allison had never said anything like that to him. He felt honored that she would measure other men by him — Jerr he expected, because he presumed that she was still in love with him. But why the compliment now? *Is she worried that I'm going to do something foolish? Good question. Am I?* He searched his mind and didn't find a quick answer.

"How is Rudi's wife?" Allison asked. "Any news?"

"I'm glad you asked. I forgot to tell you. One of her nurses thinks that Angelika followed her briefly with her eyes. That's the first genuinely encouraging sign since the accident. By the way, I wasn't suggesting that Rudi was romantically interested in you, Al. I just meant . . ."

"I know what you meant, Murdock. And you're right to a point. Rudi challenges me intellectually. We have a common interest in Bavarian history. But romantically, he's confused. He wants to believe that Angelika will pull out of it, but deep down he doubts it. And if Angelika dies, I think that he would eventually come calling. If I'm still in Germany."

"And Rudi needs a woman to talk to. You've been a great friend to him. I think we're natural groupies, Allison — you and I. Remember the little discussion groups in the dormitory rooms in Buffalo? Now it's you and Rudi and Richard and I in the beer halls of Munich. And speaking of Richard, is there any word?"

There was a long silence. "No *word*," Allison began. "The police are working on it. But I have an extremely uncomfortable intuition."

"Your intuition is often right on, so let's hear it."

"You recall my conversation with Top Dog?"

"Yes."

"Did something strike you as odd?"

"He certainly de-prioritized the search for Richard."

"Exactly. He made that clear. But from the tone of his voice, his assessment of Richard's situation was totally dispassionate."

"Heartless?"

"No. It sounded more like the unconcern of a man who knew there was no need for concern. He said that Richard's disappearance was 'unfortunate' but he was certain that it would turn out 'satisfactorily.' I thought that it was simply a bromide."

"What does your intuition tell you now, Allison? That Richard's gone under?"

"Yes, Murdock. Do you feel the same way?"

"We need to consider that possibility. He spent a lot of years with the Swiss military intelligence. He's certainly been trained to slip under-cover. Do you believe he was taken by kidnappers who ask for no ransom?"

"Not hardly."

"And," Murdock added, "we have now solved the mystery with pure speculative reasoning and without being burdened by an ounce of hard evidence."

Allison laughed. "I agree. We've solved nothing, but we have found a plausible theory. And we *do* know some other facts. We know that Top Dog is Veritus's only shareholder, but he doesn't operate it. He leaves that to management. So, my intuition takes a giant leap and tells me that, in the case of the unfortunate monk, Top Dog is our client."

Murdock sighed. "Whoever Top Dog is. Shall we cling to that as-sumption for lack of a better one?"

"Let's."

"But if your intuition is correct, why is Top Dog interested in Moira's investigation of Patti Dale and the Mädchenhaus Café? That was instigated by Harvey."

"He may be interested in why Harvey instigated it."

"Allison, could you come down here after the office closes on Fri-day? I'll get you a room."

"Do you want me to meet Diana? I don't want to play the wise-counseling big sister routine."

"I'd like you to be close by. *My* intuition tells me that something is going to pop in this case by the weekend. And I suspect you'll be safer here than where you are. I think we're amidst a nest of scorpions."

"Do you think I'm unsafe in Munich?"

"I think that nothing may be what it appears to be. The only people I'm certain of are you and Rudi, and maybe Diana. But I'd like you here where we can protect each other's tails."

"In more ways than one."

"Will you come?"

"Yes. I'll send Moira too, if she doesn't mind working the week-end."

"Good move," Murdock said. "She'll bring her skis and mix in a little fun, I'm sure. By the way, Rudi is investigating a business jet that has made several round-trip flights between Cyprus and here and be-tween Cyprus and Munich. One of those flights into Munich was yester-day morning, arriving shortly before Richard disappeared. That could blow your theory, or be a mere coincidence. It had Austrian registry. The owner is a Liechtenstein corporation. Rudi doesn't know yet who owns the corporation."

"There's millions of deutsche marks flowing between banks in Munich and Cyprus every day. Not all of it is legal, Murdock."

"Yeah. But I don't think these monks are gunrunners or dope runners. They don't need money. The professor thinks they're the genuine item, and that's something, considering that he's an atheist."

Allison yawned.

"I heard that," Murdock said. "It's time to turn in. Get some sleep. I'll call you again tomorrow night, boss."

"Fair enough. I'm very interested in that biz-jet. Let me know what Rudi finds out. Good night."

"Good night, Allison."

He hung up the phone and poured another scotch. Morning will bring the funeral. He didn't like funerals, but he'd be there. He and Rudi. *It'll be a memorial service. The police are still holding the body, and when it's released, it will be flown to America for burial. I wonder whether Michael will be there.* He drifted off into sleep, seated in the chair, his feet on a stool, his hand wrapped around the glass of scotch resting on an end table, and his head drooped over his chest. He snored.

*   *   *

After lunch and after taking a long walk down a trail that led to the Liederbach Meadow, the professor returned to his room and to the memoirs of Brother Stephen. By late afternoon he encountered a text that digressed from the super chip data to a discourse on elementary particles and the nature of matter. The latter dealt with particles that exist on the borderline between physical science and philosophy. He had spent a career within that discipline and felt at home. He dived into it avariciously, feasting on every word.

In his younger years the professor had often debated determinism with his colleagues, taking the position that everything, including one's choice of action, is the unavoidable result of a sequence of events. But Stephen's text speculated in the field of nonlinear dynamics or *chaos*, a field that suggests that the *real world* may not be as *real* as we once thought. Wading through deep pools of arguments and counterarguments punctuated occasionally with insight, the professor began to consider the possibility that he'd been wrong. *Is the universe, after all nothing more than nearly empty space parsimoniously populated by material animated by a quantum of coincidences?* He began to wonder what this deliciously esoteric stuff had to do with a super chip used as a central processing unit in a computer, and if nothing, then why had Stephen been so fascinated by it?

Over the last several hours the professor had noticed no references to further break-ins at the processing lab in Oregon. He supposed there had been no more. He sat back, gazed out the picture window at the sun retreating over the crest of the Zugspitze, and mulled over the occurrences of the past few days. He wasn't sure of Brother Martin — it seemed to him there was more to Martin than met the eye. Jose Enrique Perez-Krieger would be immensely interested in the profit potential of a super fast computer chip. He had seen but not met the Baron von Richter, who would recognize the wealth produced by the chip as a stepping-stone to power. But would someone kill for it? He and Stephen had shared the fear of the almost limitless power that wealth brings when it has no moral counterweight.

As he was about to shut down the computer and rest his mind, he came upon a personal notation.

Dear Professor Klugman.

I'm afraid that much of what I have written is rather esoteric and outside your fields of expertise. At the expense of appearing didactic, let me briefly summarize the basic science involved in my research. As you know, silicon has been the favored element used to produce the myriads of semiconductors used in a computer's integrated circuits. We are all aware of its limitations. My goal was to develop extremely tiny nanocomputers designed for specific predetermined tasks. Instead of silicon, I worked with carbon — essentially soot. When carbon is vaporized in an inert gas such as helium and permitted to cool slowly, it forms what we call buckyballs. These are chemically inert and extremely strong. They may have electrical properties. I was fascinated and experimented with them for over a year, but got nowhere.

Last year I switched my interest to buckytubes. We often call them nanotubes. I made them by adding millions of carbon atoms to the buckyball molecules and stretching them out to form a tubular fiber. I discovered that these nanotubes were, at certain points, conductors of electrical currents and at other points resistors — thus they could function as semiconductor devices. The junctions between the two, within the space of ten atoms, function as Schottky barriers — the barriers that make transistors work. Amazingly, these nanotubes are almost impossible to break. I have been working with multiwalled nanotubes — several tubes within one another, and I have succeeded in making what I believe is the first reliable carbon nanotube semiconductor device. Over the last several months I have integrated these devices into a computer central processing chip, which functions at incredible speeds. This, I think, is more than leading edge technology. It's over the edge. The next hundred or so pages will explain how I accomplished it. I have inserted a plethora of footnotes to help you understand. Lastly, I shall explain my purpose for pursuing this knowledge.

The professor pushed his chair back from the computer and shook his head. *Now I've found something that men might be willing to kill for.*

Thursday
November 20

⊰ **24** ⊱

Wednesday dawned cold and dreary. A brief memorial service had been held for Brother Stephen in the chapel at the monastery. Brother Martin had agreed to see Enrique and Linda shortly afterward. Martin felt no sorrow. Brother Stephen was in heaven, and that was a good thing.

No roads led to the monastery—only trails accessible by snowmobile or ski in winter. Enrique didn't like snowmobiles. Linda had arranged for a chopper to deliver him. When the American military had controlled the Zugspitze Hof, a helicopter pad had been constructed in a clearing only a thousand yards from the lodge. Linda had boarded the chopper at the airport. As it slowly settled onto the pad, she saw Enrique waiting with his briefcase in hand. She tapped the pilot on the shoulder.

"You don't need to shut down the engine," she shouted. "He's climbed into many choppers with blades rotating."

As the vehicle came to rest, she opened the door. Enrique was already running toward them. He settled himself into the copilot seat in front of her and shut the door. Linda tapped the pilot on the shoulder and gave him a thumbs-up. She and Enrique donned earphones with microphones attached so they could converse over the noise of the engine.

"What do I need to know?" Enrique asked.

"I have nothing to add to the written briefing I gave you last night, but I suggest that you let me carry that briefcase. It will seem less intimidating. Brother Martin knows that you're one of the wealthiest men in the world. He'll be expecting arrogance and intimidation. You need to show him humility and profound concern. If you succeed, I think he'll respond favorably. It comes naturally to you. You don't need to work at it."

"Thank you, Linda. You are very kind. How did things go with Erik Müller yesterday?"

"Fine. You made a good choice in him. Siegfried Insurance will show a respectable profit this year, and, unless there's a major downturn in the economy, it should really blossom next year. I gave him the proposal on the reinsurance company."

"What did he think?"

"He didn't respond. He'll study the proposal and get back to us on Monday. You know Erik. He's cautious."

"But not too cautious, or Siegfried wouldn't have turned the corner this year."

"You're right." She tapped the pilot on the shoulder. "Can you put down in the courtyard?"

"No, Fräulein. I'd rather put down outside the wall. You will be close to the entrance gate, I promise you."

"That'll be fine," she said.

As the monastery came into view, Enrique noticed a large brown patch between the monastery walls and the tree line. "What's that?" he asked, turning toward the pilot.

The pilot slowed the aircraft to a hover, extracted field glasses from his flight bag, and focused on the spot. "Ha," he said. "Amazing. Look for yourself."

Enrique took the glasses. "It appears to be about four dozen monks close together in the snow. What are they doing?"

"Stomping," the pilot answered. "They're stomping snow so that our prop wash won't cause a whiteout when we attempt to land. A whiteout would prevent us. Your visit must be welcome."

They hovered until the monks dispersed.

*   *   *

The conference room was appointed comfortably. Upholstered chairs in light brown and cream tones gave one a sense of warmth. A picture window faced the downslope. Brother Martin drew the drapes to reveal a breathtaking view. Enrique could make out the Eibsee, a picturesque lake in the mountain valley below, and a train running on the tracks of the narrow gauge Bavarian State Railway, which carries passengers the short distance from Garmisch-Partenkirchen through the village of Grainau and to the cable car station at the foot of Zugspitze Mountain. Near the northern horizon he could identify the valley in which Oberammergau was located—famous for its wood carving and its passion play.

"Do you enjoy our view?" Brother Martin asked, pouring coffee. "It must be as beautiful in its own way as the Andes in your native Chile. Please help yourselves to the cakes."

Enrique arose and took the tray of cakes over to Linda who was seated across the room. Brother Martin delivered a cup of coffee to her. She thanked them both.

"I believe," Enrique began, "that the Chilean Andes and the Bavarian Alps are the two most beautiful places on Earth. We are both fortunate, are we not, that God has given us such beauty and the ability to appreciate it?"

Brother Martin seated himself between Enrique and Linda. "We are indeed," he said. "Señor Perez-Krieger, I know that you are an assiduous man. I'm sure that your time is more valuable than mine. It is very kind of you to visit us. Perhaps we should come to the purpose of your visit. We don't often have such distinguished guests. While we enjoy having you here, and many of my brothers would like to meet you, we don't want to impinge upon your time. I am quite interested to know what brings you here."

Enrique's eyes met Linda's. She nodded in the affirmative. An enigmatic smile crossed Enrique's face. "You know of my family's business interests?"

Brother Martin nodded. "I know that they are *your* business interests and that your brother and sister merely participate. You have a reputation for fair dealing and honesty. I know that your great-grandfather emigrated from Bavaria — Oberammergau I believe — to Chile, one hundred years ago. I know that your family is Catholic — as one would anticipate considering your Bavarian origin. I can't imagine why you're interested in a group of polyglot monks — only a few of whom are Catholic. I presume that your interest is not religious."

"Can we speak in confidence, Brother Martin?"

"I may need to share what you say with my brothers. They are men who can be trusted. You must leave that judgment to me."

"The purpose justifies the risk. May Miss DiStefano make notes?"

"Of course, if that is important to you."

"It may become important if we progress beyond the preliminaries. Have you heard of an organization called *Plato*?"

"I have not."

"That's good. We don't publicize it. Plato is a mutual fund with highly selective membership. It accumulates venture capital from its investors — sums sufficient that, when strategically inserted into a country, there will be a significant impact on its economy, stabilizing it by producing jobs that will raise the standard of living of its people. As more people ascend into the middle class, the falseness of the promises of socialism become more apparent."

Brother Martin raised an eyebrow. Linda made a note of it. Enrique continued unfazed.

"With our help, people will realize that socialism was the thief that kept them poor."

"Do they also realize that unchecked capitalism can stomp them into the dust?"

"Of course. They need to see that extremes at both ends of the economic pendulum are destructive."

"But, excuse me. Don't your handouts simply make people dependent on Plato instead of on the government?"

"I am not talking about handouts. Our beneficiaries work for their wages, and we don't invest unless we think that our investment will make money. The working person benefits by having a job and drawing a better wage. We have the managerial horsepower to make a business work. Our fund realizes a comfortable profit annually. Each member may withdraw that profit or reinvest it. Most reinvest it; they don't need income. You would realize that if you saw our investor list."

Brother Martin chuckled. "Do you see my monks as potential investors?"

"In other words, am I hustling you for money? Yes. I'm hustling that and more. Perhaps some of your people would see the financial wisdom in participating in the Plato Fund. We can talk about that some other time. Today, I'm more interested in an alliance. Your monks have some of the best minds in the scientific world. They haven't prostituted themselves to government largesse. They work on leading edge technologies. At some point products that result from these advanced technologies can be produced and marketed. What we in Plato say is, 'Let's produce those products in regions where it will do the most social good.' "

"Are you saying that they should be produced in the third world as opposed to the already industrialized nations like Germany and America?"

"I wouldn't draw that line. We have just constructed a plant in the American state of New Mexico — near the Mexican border. We employ several hundred formerly jobless poor — many of them Indians — at decent, even generous wages. Our plant produces boxes that are purchased by companies just across the border in Mexico, companies that assemble clothing, box it, and ship it to the United States and Canada. There are many unfortunate people in the United States, and other developed countries, who also need an opportunity to improve their lot in life. We are more interested in people than we are in geopolitical boundaries."

Brother Martin appeared nervous. "When you infuse significant capital into a nation's economy, it has political implications. Are you suggesting that we become involved in politics?"

"Nothing is further from our purpose. The *sine qua non* of our existence is the desire to increase the membership of the middle class throughout the world. None of us has personal political ambitions."

Brother Martin frowned. "Are you saying, Señor Perez-Krieger, that your organization — this Plato — has no political implications?"

"I can't say that. Economic progress, we believe, goes hand in hand with political freedom. If a country's economy is going to prosper, its citizens must be free to work and to keep most of what they earn. Individuals and companies must be free to trade with whomever they desire. A comfortable middle class will resist socialism and totalitarianism, so there certainly is an incidental political implication to what we do. We believe that the prudent use of economic power can create a climate in which larger numbers of entrepreneurs will demand more political freedom, and that those demands will overpower the selfish interests of the old guard politicians and bureaucrats to the point that they become marginalized. There are many poor people in the world who desperately need decent jobs. We don't invest in a country because we are gamblers — except in the sense that all investors are gamblers. We try to win; sometimes we lose. Our goal is profit, but we want our associates, and our employees in that country, to benefit as much as we do. Our goal is capitalism with a friendly face. We think of ourselves more as St. Francis of Assisi without the halo."

Brother Martin frowned. He'd heard grand economic ideals preached before. He wondered whether he had become too callous to ever recognize genuine integrity if he saw it. "Perhaps *you* deserve the halo," he said, sarcastically.

Enrique smiled. "I understand your skepticism. You wonder what my real motive is — my deep-down purpose hidden in with and under the virtuous words. There may be nothing I can say that will convince you that my heart is pure. You already believe in things you have never seen. Consider believing in Plato. There's a lot at stake. Working together — your organization and ours — on certain projects may generate a synergism that could produce worthy results, but we can accomplish nothing together unless we are able to trust each other."

Brother Martin turned toward Linda. "You impress me as an honest woman, Miss DiStefano. If you were in my shoes, would you take Plato at face value?"

"No," she said without hesitation. "But I would consider the fact that it *could* be what he claims it to be, and that, if it *were*, there would be tremendous potential if we worked together."

"Thank you for your candor, Miss DiStefano." Brother Martin turned toward Enrique. "I assume this would not have to be a total commitment?"

"If you mean exclusivity, or a merging of our organizations, I think not. We can cooperate strategically on a case-by-case basis. Some of your people may want to invest in the mutual fund. I don't see investment as critical to our arrangement, but obviously, the more economic power we have, the more potential for results."

Brother Martin looked puzzled. He shook his head. "Why now? What brings you here *now*?"

"We received information that you are on to something really big, something having to do with the speed and sophistication of computer central processing chips, something with tremendous implications, something that will revolutionize computing. Our information barely rises above rumor, but a rumor with such implications must be verified. It occurred to me that, even if the rumor weren't true, you and I should still meet. Because of the broad scope of your research projects, an association between our two organizations would still be worthwhile. To a great extent, I believe we share a commonality of purpose. We're both concerned with the moral implications of what we do — moral from the Christian point of view."

Brother Martin appeared guarded. Enrique and Linda glanced at one another, their eyes asking whether he was being cautious or whether he had some other agenda. Martin stared out the picture window. He understood fully the economic and political impact of what was being proposed. He felt uncomfortable with the political aspect. *But, in a sense, the work that our monks are doing has political implications too, he thought. Whenever we stake out a moral high ground, there are politicians who latch on, and use it to promote their causes, and other politicians who put a spin on it that makes St. Luke's look like a bunch of crazy religious extremists with dangerous ideas.*

Enrique glanced at Linda. She moved her hand subtly, palm down, advising him to wait for Martin to speak. He nodded in agreement. After several minutes, Martin's eyes met Enrique's.

"Señor Perez-Krieger, we are both aware that for every force there is an opposing force. We would need to know exactly what we are getting into. I understand that this conversation is merely exploratory, but I must know. Is there a force in opposition to Plato?"

Enrique leaned forward in his chair and lowered his voice. "There are, of course, many powerful people who disagree with our purposes — people who profit from discontent. We have learned only recently of a particular group. They call themselves *Traction*. We have only a modicum of information about them. We believe they profit from destabilizing economies. They may be gunrunners or worse. We have no hard evidence, but we believe they may be responsible for the murder of Brother Stephen."

Brother Martin's eyes widened. "If you are correct, there is one of them among us!"

"Yes. We have a contact who claims to be a mole in Traction. He's selling us information. His motive appears to be profit, but Traction may be inserting him to mislead us. Tentatively, we're inclined to believe him. In our first and only contact so far, he indicated that Traction is interested in your work here at St. Luke's."

"What work?" Martin asked casually.

"Work on an advanced central processing chip. Such a chip would have tremendous military applications. The potential for profit is immense—enough to kill for. Was Brother Stephen working on such a project?"

Brother Martin frowned. "The development of computer chips was Stephen's specialty. That's how he made his fortune in America, but you must already know that so I assume your question was rhetorical."

Enrique shrugged. "If such a chip exists," he said, "perhaps a combination of your organization and ours can get out in front with it. Once the new technology becomes known, Stephen's work may become obsolete quickly. The big profits will be made within six months or a year, and we'd like to see them in our hands—not theirs."

"Excuse me," Martin said. He picked up a pad from an end table and began to write, occasionally stopping to think, tapping his pencil in frustration. Enrique and Linda watched silently. After several minutes without looking up from his pad Martin exclaimed: "I don't believe that Stephen's work would be appropriate for commercial exploitation in its present form." He appeared to be speaking more to himself rather than them.

Enrique and Linda glanced at one another. They heard the sounds of a chopper engine outside, hovering nearby, on the side opposite to where theirs had landed.

Martin looked up. "At first blush, I see synergism in what you propose, but . . .

An explosion sent shards of window glass into the room, narrowly missing them, and a bullet smashed a table lamp between Enrique and Brother Martin. "Hit the floor!" Enrique shouted as he thrust himself on Linda, knocking her out of her chair, both landing on the carpet next to Brother Martin who lay flat on his stomach. Without another word, in a crouched position, Enrique sprinted through the door and into the hallway, past three startled monks, out the main door into the cold and snow, and across the courtyard toward the heavy oak door in the outer wall. It was open. Just outside, his pilot crouched close to the wall. "Did you see what happened?" Enrique shouted.

"Not all of it. I saw a chopper approach from the east, coming in low. Suddenly it climbed directly overhead. A burst of fire from an automatic weapon sprayed the area with bullets, and then the chopper, as fast as it had appeared, disappeared downslope. At first I thought he was shooting at my chopper because the bullets struck here first, but he sprayed the general area. I couldn't get a registration number."

"Can we follow it?"

"The engines are cold, and I need to check for damage. By the time we could be airborne, it'll be out of sight."

Enrique returned to Linda and Brother Martin. They were standing in the hallway, just outside the conference room door. He pushed his way through a crowd of monks. "Are you hurt?" Enrique inquired. Both assured him that they were not. Enrique explained what had happened.

"Who were they shooting at?" Brother Martin asked.

"My guess is that it was a warning to me, or perhaps you, that we are playing with fire." Enrique's eyes fixed on Brother Martin's. "What's going on here?" he demanded. "What fire are we playing with?"

Brother Martin shrugged. "We are engaged in many scientific research projects. Who can say what they want."

"Well," Enrique suggested, "they're determined to scare someone into giving it to them, whatever it is. We must go now. May we call on Monday?"

"Yes, of course," Brother Martin replied. "God go with you."

"*Vaya con Dios,*" Enrique replied.

*   *   *

The pilot reported no damage to the chopper. As they lifted off, Enrique and Linda connected the mike and earphones.

"He wants to believe you," she said, "but he's not convinced."

Enrique looked over his shoulder at her. "I concur. Did you get the feeling that we might have hold of something quite different from what we thought?"

Linda nodded. "Yes. He suggested that Brother Stephen's invention may not be marketable in its present form. If it's a super-fast CPU chip, it would certainly be marketable. I can't imagine what it is."

"Nor can I. I'm drawing a blank. But I think we need to make it our business to find out what the hell's going on in that monastery."

Linda stared out the window. The ski slopes passed beneath them. They were crowded. People looked like hundreds of ants. *They're enjoying themselves, she thought, while we may be playing with their future. Which of us is happier? Probably them. They don't know what they need to be afraid of. Do we?* She turned toward Enrique. "Maybe our imaginations are running at Mach two," she said, "but I don't think so."

"I don't either."

⊰ **25** ⊱

Murdock looked at his watch. It was 11:30. *It's a delightful day—cold, but clear. The slopes are ideal. The investigation is going nowhere. I need a break.* He recalled how attractive Diana had looked in her sheer white blouse in the candlelight. *Maybe I'll see whether she's free for skiing and dinner and whatever.*

After three days at the Zugspitze Hof, he hadn't found time to socialize with the Bayers. He decided to call on them. They were more than merely landlords to him. He and Karen had known them well. Before his rheumatism dissuaded him, Herr Bayer had often skied with them. Frau Bayer would prepare apple strudel in the Bavarian fashion that Karen enjoyed. Many evenings had been spent in the Bayers' chalet drinking and singing beer hall songs. On his way to the office he met Enrique.

"Good morning, Enrique. Did your meeting with Brother Martin go poorly?"

"Good morning Murdock, if it is still morning. Is it written on my face?"

"You don't look pleased."

"Please forgive me. "We merely had a preliminary discussion. Actually, it went as well we could expect. Did you hear the gunfire?"

"What gunfire?"

"Someone in a chopper with a high-powered rifle fired a round into our meeting room. Fortunately, no one was hurt. I think you need to know who the perpetrator was as much as I do. I just talked to Martin on the phone. The police are checking the airport, but the chopper could have crossed the Alps from Austria or Switzerland. Let's talk later. Right now I must make some phone calls." He bowed slightly, and with a flourish set off for his suite.

Murdock poked his head in the office, but Herr Bayer wasn't there. He found Frau Bayer in the kitchen. Without a hello-how-are-you, she placed her hands on her hips and demanded: "Do you know this so-called Baron, this Rupert von Richter?"

Murdock took a step back. "I know who he is," he replied defensively.

"He is a fool and a leader of fools," she exclaimed loudly. "I would not be so annoyed, but one of his fools is my husband." She was kneading a roll of dough as she spoke. Her motions became more vigorous. "Herr Bayer discounts the room for von Richter and his cronies. Von Richter is wealthy and we are poor. Well, poor compared to him. But my husband gives *him* discounts on rooms and restaurant. Maybe Herr Bayer has been promised a cabinet post when the Baron becomes king — which will happen when hell freezes over. I suspect that our *king* would need a very large cabinet in order to keep all his promises."

"But . . ."

"Each fool finds his own paradise."

"You don't like von Richter?" Murdock suggested with a wry smile.

She stopped kneading. Their eyes met. "I just wish he'd leave. I don't trust him. I don't want Herr Bayer associating with him."

Murdock smiled. She often referred to her husband formally when she was angry.

"Why should Herr Bayer associate with rakes? Von Richter is no good. That's the truth." She began kneading again with renewed vengeance. "You, please, could talk to my husband. Ja? He may listen to a friend. Tell him, maybe, that he is being what you Americans call a jerk."

"I doubt that it'll help."

"Good. But you will try. Perhaps the king will make Herr Bayer the minister in charge of gooses."

"Geese?"

"Yes, gooses. Now I must supervise the preparation of the sausages. We can talk more tonight. Stop by our chalet tonight, please. Bring Rudi and this Diana friend of yours. Please excuse me now."

Murdock joined Rudi in the dining room. After small talk and ordering lunch, Murdock turned to business.

"I talked to Jerr yesterday. His mole at FBI headquarters believes that Patti Dale is connected with Joe Carlyle. The mole doesn't know which is the tail and which is the dog."

"Could she be an undercover agent for the FBI?"

"She could. But I didn't get that impression."

"A paramour?"

"I think that's the impression that Jerr had. What have you learned?"

"A great deal," Rudi replied. "Several reports were waiting for me when I returned from the memorial service. Brother Antonio, it seems, is descended from Spanish royalty, although his family has dropped all titles. He is a not-too-distant relative of the present king of Spain. Antonio's family lost its lands under Franco. Twenty years ago they were poor. Today they own several profitable businesses. The family's money is sufficient to buy political legitimacy with both the socialists and the conservatives. Although Antonio lives here, he assists the family with computer programming. I wonder if they profited from work done by our deceased monk too."

"Diana knows the family quite well. They're clients of Seneca Financial. She's close to Antonio's sister, Maria Rosita. Diana often entertains clients at Zugspitze Hof. Whenever she's here on Thursday, she attends matins at the monastery so that she can visit Antonio."

"Is she religious?" Rudi inquired.

"No. I think not. No more than I am. She's curious, I think, and a friend of Brother Antonio."

"You are more religious than you think you are," Rudi suggested. "You learned from your father that it's macho not to appear to be. But, I think deep down you have your mother's faith."

"Perhaps," Murdock replied.

Rudi studied his notes. "I worry about von Richter," he said. "We have information that he will meet with Brother Martin today or tomorrow. We don't know whether they've met before, or whether Antonio will participate. Antonio and von Richter both have royal connections. My concern is that the monks may unwisely align themselves with von Richter to their discredit."

Their food was served. Rudi had ordered a sausage; Murdock an open-faced sandwich. Rudi eagerly sliced his sausage. Murdock seemed not to notice his food.

"They are not a Roman Catholic order," Murdock pointed out. "Why are you concerned about them?"

"The public is not as perceptive as you, Murdock. They prefer to have the media reduce information to its most simplistic form, so that they'll not have to work hard to decide what they are supposed to think. If the monks appear to align themselves with von Richter, and his sexual pleasures become known, the media will give it a spin that will tar all the monks. Then — the damage done — the media will move on to something else, totally unconcerned with the damage they do to innocents. Journalism is devoid of ethics. They invoke morality only for profit."

"I wouldn't be quite that cynical," Murdock protested.

"Then you have been away from police work too long. I'm seeking permission from Commander Weiss to disclose to Brother Martin the voyeurism practiced by von Richter and his sybaritic cohorts. You know of Bavaria's confidentiality laws, so that permission is unlikely. I doubt that even the justice minister can grant it. You *do* understand, don't you?"

"Yes, old pal. Because you have been given discretion to share information with me, and because I'm not a policeman, you want me to spill the beans."

"Can I stop you?"

They both laughed.

Rudi became serious. "Allison has met von Richter. She told me that he took a shine to her. She could be helpful."

"She will be joining us here tomorrow night."

"Murdock, please phone her. See if she will make contact with von Richter while she is here and try to charm some information from him."

"I'm sure she'll be glad to help. Do you think he's mixed up in the murder?"

"Possibly. Murdock, have you ever heard of someone called Der Fuchs?"

Murdock laughed. "Sure. El Zorro. In California two hundred years ago."

Rudi looked up from his sausage, bewildered.

"Sorry," Murdock said. "Bad joke. The German *Der Fuchs* and the Spanish *El Zorro* both translate into English as *The Fox*. El Zorro is a character in a classical Hollywood movie made in the 1930s or 1940s, starring Tyrone Power. Why do you ask?"

"The federal justice ministry has provided some information that is troubling. You are familiar with the Stasi?"

"Yes. The former communist East German secret police."

"The federal ministry is searching the Stasi files that came into their possession when East Germany fell. Der Fuchs is a code name for a secret agent. Parts of his file are missing—probably stolen or destroyed shortly before the end. This agent was sent into deep cover in West Germany thirty years ago. His original assignment was to study at a seminary, become a pastor, and infiltrate the Evangelical Church—what you Americans call the Lutheran Church. Churches influence the minds of millions. Followers can be manipulated to either stabilize or destabilize a society."

"If I remember correctly," Murdock injected, "the Evangelical Church opposed godless communism, did it not?"

"As a general rule," Rudi replied. "In East Germany, the church was not exactly an ethical touchstone. It played a morally ambiguous role. By doing so, it helped neutralize objections to the communist government. Most pastors straddled the line between their moral persuasions and pragmatically dealing with the Stasi, so the Stasi wouldn't deal with them. When choosing between God and the Stasi perhaps the Stasi seemed closer at hand."

Murdock nodded in agreement. "I'm aware of how churches can be used to manipulate. History is full of it. Early in the Fourth Century, the Roman Emperor Constantine stopped the persecution of the Christians and legalized Christianity so that he could use the organization of the Church to cement his empire, even though Christians at that time numbered only ten percent of the population."

"Ja, ja," Rudi replied. "As many kings and emperors have done since. As Franco did in Spain."

"Murdock looked puzzled. "This man — Der Fuchs — could no longer pose a danger, could he?"

"In 1988, shortly before the Berlin Wall came down, over five million U.S. dollars were transferred to his account in Zürich, Switzerland. The Swiss will not disclose information. Our federal justice ministry feels that the money — if it still exists — should be distributed to the five states that were formed from East Germany."

"What was the purpose of the transfer to Der Fuchs?"

"We don't know. When Der Fuchs was given the money, he also received an additional agenda. The record indicates that a secret file with higher security was opened. The entries end there. The file with the higher security can't be found. We know that the decision came from the president himself, Erich Honecker. But we can't ask him. As you know, he died in exile in Chile. I understand that, before his death, he became acquainted with Miguel Perez-Krieger, the brother of your new friend, Enrique."

"And so?"

"And so nothing," Rudi replied.

Murdock sat in silence for several minutes, eating his sandwich. He washed it down with a stein of dark beer. Presently he looked up at Rudi. "Has it crossed your mind that Brother Martin might be Der Fuchs? Is that why you're telling me all this?"

Rudi smiled. "It has crossed my mind."

"Any evidence to connect?"

"No."

"Do the Feds suspect anything?"

"Yes. They suspect."

"Do the Feds have some idea of what happened to the five million?"

"No. Or if they do, they're not sharing it with state authorities, just like your FBI doesn't share everything with state and local police."

"Rudi. Have you ever heard of the Plato Mutual Fund?"

"No. I'm not interested in investing."

Murdock was tempted to say more but decided against it. *No need unless I find out that Enrique is mixed up in the murder somehow. There's a plethora of information muddying the waters already.*

"By the way," Murdock said, "do the Feds have a warrant for Der Fuchs arrest?"

"No. Or if there is one, they haven't told us."

"Do they usually tell you?"

"Yes."

"So, maybe they're being cute. Like we used to be in the FBI."

"I'll be flying to Cyprus tomorrow night," Rudi announced, changing the subject. "I'm using the new biz-jet that we confiscated from the gunrunners a few months ago. The state has finally appropriated the money for its maintenance and operation. I should only be gone overnight. If it stretches into more, we need to keep in touch. I'll phone you here and let you know where I'm staying. It's good working with you again, Murdock. Like the old days when you were FBI."

"Old days? Less than two years ago."

"But good, nevertheless. It's not just friendship. I respect your ability as an investigator, Murdock. And you're someone I can trust implicitly."

"Likewise."

"Thank you."

"Rudi, you've heard Allison and me talk about Top Dog, haven't you?"

"Yes. It's what you American's call a nickname. You've given this one to the owner of Veritus International — a man who has taken enigma lessons from the late Howard Hughes. We have too many enigmas in this case."

"He takes no part in the management of the business. I believe you know that."

"Yes. I believe that. So?"

"Allison thinks he may be our client on this case."

Rudi looked startled. He shook his head. "That would be legitimate," he said. "Veritus should not be working on its own account. But I know of no law that would prohibit a person from engaging a company in which he owns all the shares. Does Allison know why he is interested in Brother Stephen?"

"I don't think so. We can ask her tomorrow night."

"I shall be on my way to Cyprus. Will she still be here Sunday?"

"I expect so. Remember, she doesn't know for certain that Top Dog *is* our client. Call it female intuition. If he is, maybe he knew Brother Stephen from America. Stephen was one of the giants of the Silicon Valley. At the time of his death, he still had a fab in Oregon."

"A fab? What is this?"

"Sorry, that's computer industry talk — a fabricating plant. He owned a plant that fabricates computer chips."

"Ach. You Americans like these nicknames, ja?"

Murdock laughed. "Ja, Rudi. Maybe Top Dog was an associate of his, or a shareholder in one of his businesses. I don't think we can help you by investigating our own owner. You'd better try the police in Oregon."

"I'll do that, if it becomes necessary. This is a most unusual case. Usually, as we learn more, our path narrows, the case becomes less complicated, and we follow the narrowing path to a solution. But in this case, everything we learn makes it more complicated, and the path widens. As Georg so artfully put it, the whole world is still suspect — except, of course, you and me."

Murdock laughed. "Have you learned more about the biz-jet?"

"No, but these mysterious flights suggest that the key to our investigation may be found in Cyprus. The police there are not forthcoming. Money often buys the little soldiers and the record clerks, as well as top brass. I shall go there and speak to my counterpart. I am curious whether this Boris Romanovsky has invested enough to own him."

They laughed and finished their lunch. Rudi excused himself. Murdock remained at the table and ordered dessert. He stared out the window at the people enjoying themselves on the slopes. *What if Brother Martin was a Stasi secret agent? So what? The government he served no longer exists. Unless he were working for the Russians. If the Feds have a warrant, they would arrest him. They haven't—so far. Does von Richter know Martin was a Stasi secret agent? Does Enrique? How about the other monks? Do they know? Martin couldn't have killed Stephen. All the monks told the police that he never left the monastery on Monday. He could have hired it out. But why would he? If he is Der Fuchs, did he begin as an infiltrator in the Church and then experience a miracle conversion? Do horses grow wings? But assuming this horse did, was it before or after the Stasi gave him five million? If it's Martin, and if he's still got five million, why is he screwing around with this monastery? Why not disappear into Brazil or Argentina and enjoy the money? Could it be that the Russians are controlling him. If he doesn't have the money, how did he spend it? Whoa, wait a minute. My imagination is overcoming my common sense. It's bad investigative form to assume that Brother Martin is Der Fuchs. I'll explore the possibility and keep my mind open. If the Feds were certain, they would have done something. It would be too good to leave alone. But then, the Feds could have slipped Rudi a red herring, just like the FBI does to local police on occasion.*

He looked at his watch. *Diana should be back from the village by 1:30. If she's willing, I'll spend the rest of today with her. After all, Richard did send me here for a vacation. Diana's responsibility to entertain Enrique ended this morning. She's on her own time now. Tomorrow, she flies to Frankfurt for a conference regarding her new position with Seneca Financial. She'll be back Saturday night when she begins a week's vacation. If we crack this case, I'll join her.* He felt lighthearted. *Why am I enjoying myself so much? Maybe it's because I've got my teeth into a fascinating case and working with Rudi again. Maybe I'm anticipating the lovely Diana. I'm going to have some fun—with my eyes and ears open.*

Friday
November 21

⤝ **26** ⤞

Terry had arrived at the office at 7:30 A.M., and by 8:00 he had reviewed all the communications received overnight. He yawned. There were some days when he wondered whether Harvey Specter was really an ally. This was one of them. He sat back in his chair and turned their relationship over in his mind, looking for leverage. Terry knew many of the call girls that Harvey liked in Frankfurt and Munich. Harvey liked the youngest ones. Experience was wasted on him. Terry preferred experience, but he couldn't afford much of it, except when Harvey was treating. If old Harv charged these amorous affairs to the company, that information would be priceless. Terry knew that Harvey's bookkeeper in Frankfurt was cheating on her husband. He decided to get in on the cheat. *She doesn't seem too fond of Harvey, and she's playful when she talks to me. She'd know if the company's paying for his screwing. I need bargaining chips. Besides, it'll be great fun if I can get a little right under Harvey's nose.*

In her office, Allison read Terry's report on Siegfried Insurance and decided it was inconclusive. *If Erik Müller hasn't phoned by eleven, I'll phone him.* She clicked her mouse. Thursday, November 20 appeared on the display. Ten o'clock. An appointment with Linda DiStefano. She had never heard of her. It was almost ten. She buzzed her secretary. "Hilda, who is Linda DiStefano?"

"A new business prospect. She mentioned the name of Erik Müller. She didn't say whom she represents. Ah . . . that could be her walking in the front door now."

"If it is, have her sit down. My private line is ringing."

It was Erik. "Good morning, Allison."

"Good morning, Erik. It's good to hear from you. I regret that I couldn't make our presentation in person yesterday. I hope Terry Crawford was able to answer all of your questions."

"He was a bit nervous, but he did fine. I had pretty much made up my mind before he arrived, but I had hoped to meet you. I prefer to do business with a face rather than just a phone. I will engage your firm to handle our investigations throughout Europe under the terms of the agreement that you proposed. But I'd like you to personally deliver the contract for my signature. You must have lunch with my wife and me."

"I can work that out. I look forward to meeting you."

"How would next week Tuesday morning be . . . at eleven? You could catch the mid-morning train."

Allison was pleased. "That'll work fine."

"Good. You will join us at my club for lunch. I shall include my department heads with whom you will be dealing."

"I look forward to that."

"There is another reason that I wish you had been here yesterday. There was someone who wanted to meet you."

"Someone on your staff?" Allison inquired.

"No. Her name is Linda DiStefano. When you couldn't be here, she arranged an appointment to see you this morning at your office in Munich. Unless I'm mistaken, she should be there about now. Miss DiStefano is extremely punctual."

"Who is she?"

"No doubt you have heard of Señor Jose Enrique Perez-Krieger, ja?"

"Yes. He's at the Zugspitze Hof Lodge right now, I believe."

"Ja, ja. Señor Perez-Krieger owns a controlling interest in Siegfried Insurance. Ms. DiStefano is his administrative assistant. She's a *very* capable lady. She recommended me for my present position. Talking to her is the next best thing to talking to Señor Perez-Krieger himself. She didn't share with me the purpose of her meeting with you, but she asked me to phone you and confirm our contract before she arrived. But I must leave you now. I look forward to Tuesday. *Auf wiedersehen.*"

"*Wiedersehen.*"

Linda entered the office, walked across the room with the quick pace of assurance, offered her hand, and seated herself .

"Please call me Linda," she said with authority. "May I call you Allison? I feel like I already know you."

"Of course," Allison replied.

"Have you talked with Erik Müller this morning?" Linda inquired.

Hilda brought in a tray with coffee and cakes. Allison nodded. Hilda poured two cups, distributed them, and departed quietly.

"I spoke to him just before you came in."

"Good. Then you're curious why I'm here. Our conversation can be confidential. Yes?"

"Absolutely."

"Señor Perez-Krieger owns insurance companies in Canada, Chile, and Germany. A major acquisition is pending in the United States. He'll also form a reinsurance company, which will probably be incorporated in the Caymans. As you may know, there are dozens of other businesses in his stable. Enrique — he prefers first names — will employ Veritus, if the terms are right, as the worldwide investigating agency for all of our operations. This would be a major piece of business for Veritus. I presume your company is interested."

"Certainly. We are pleased to be given an opportunity to bid."

"He will not bid. He knows the reputation of your company. He will employ your services after you and I work out the financial details."

Allison sat silent for several seconds. Linda waited.

"Why me?" Allison asked warily.

"Why do I bring by far the largest single account your company has ever had to an assistant station chief at a backwater Bavarian office six thousand miles from company headquarters?"

Allison took a yellow legal pad from a desk drawer. "That puts it accurately."

"Señor Perez-Krieger — Enrique — desires that you and Murdock McCabe receive credit for the acquisition."

"But why?" Allison asked incredulously.

"Enrique prides himself on being a good judge of character. I can assure you that it is pride well-placed. Like most wise businesspersons, he does business with people, not companies. If he likes you, he makes things happen for you. Enrique has been successful *because* he has bonded with the McCabes of the world. He calls them *Las Joyas* — The Jewels."

I smell a rat, Allison thought. Does he expect to own me? Or is he trying to buy Murdock through me?

"But again," Allison injected. "Why *me*?"

Linda thought for several seconds, staring out the window. "Because Enrique has concluded from McCabe's comments about you that you are *una joya* too. Mister McCabe thinks very highly of you. Jerrard Blair concurs."

Allison made a few notes on the pad. Without looking up, she said, "You talk as if you know Jerr."

"We do. He's another *Joya*."

Allison exhaled noticeably. "You've done your homework."

"Homework is my craft."

Neither spoke for the better part of a minute.

"You're thinking that when something appears too good to be true, it usually is," Linda offered.

Allison nodded. "You've read me accurately."

"It's wise to doubt my credentials. You may phone Erik Müller, or have McCabe check me out with Señor Perez-Krieger. But you've already talked to Erik. So you must consider that maybe the gift horse is really a gift horse."

"I think you're genuine," Allison said.

Linda arose. "I think that you are someone I'd like to know better. We shall be friends, but I must go now. We'll get together next week and work out details. I am very pleased to have met you, Allison."

They shook hands. Linda exited swiftly without another word. Allison sat back in her chair and caught her breath. *That was a whirlwind meeting. It looks like I've effortlessly landed the biggest contract of my career. It shows what patience, hard work, and determination can accomplish when supplemented by a dose of dumb luck. This spells promotion for sure. Even Harvey won't be able to hold me back.* She called Hilda, instructed her to prepare a proposal, and then summoned Terry. He arrived in minutes, walking in his usual slouch over to the desk, and seated himself. Allison arose, leaned across the desk, and offered her hand.

"Congratulations," she said. "You won the Siegfried contract."

An initial appearance of surprise was quickly replaced by a wry smile. "Thank you," Terry replied. "I had no idea which way they were going when I left Regensburg yesterday."

"You did well. Erik has asked me to handle the actual signing next week. But in my report I'll mention the part you played. Herr Müller was pleased with your presentation. He said you were a bit nervous, but that's understandable. You've never been out there on the firing line before. If you're going to get ahead in the company, you'll need more experience like that. I'll mention that to Richard when he gets back. That's all. Thank you for coming up."

"Thank *you*," he replied.

As he rose to leave, she reached into a desk drawer for her shoulder bag, but it slipped out of her hand and dropped to the floor with a thud. He bent over to retrieve it. "It's heavy," he exclaimed. "You got a gun in it?"

"As a matter of fact, yes," Allison replied. "A Smith and Wesson .38 caliber revolver. Does that surprise you?"

"Yes. Sort of. I know women like to protect themselves, but you shouldn't carry a gun, especially a .38, unless you know how to use it. You can hurt yourself."

"I *do* know how to use it," she replied firmly. "But thank you for your concern. I know you look into personnel records, so you must be aware that I'm a graduate of the law enforcement administration program at Michigan State University. On the pistol team I won dozens of sharpshooter medals. I'm still a marksman. I hit what I aim at."

"I'm impressed," Terry said sincerely. "I have a .22. I've done some target shooting."

"Wonderful," she responded, delighted that she had found something she liked in The Weasel. "Rudi Benzinger has given me access to the state police range. Would you care to shoot with me some day?"

Terry's face brightened. "I'd love to," he replied, genuinely grateful. "I've thought of moving up to a .38."

"It gives you more recoil, but you can reload your own ammunition, if you have a black powder license. Rudi helped me obtain one, so I retrieve my brass and reload it. I'll help you get one. Bullets aren't cheap—not when you're firing fifty or a hundred rounds in an evening. Please do come along. You'll meet some of the best marksmen in the state police. I'm sure they'd like to meet you. Most of them have great respect for our company."

"Do the local police shoot there too?"

"There are no local police in Bavaria. They were abolished about thirty years ago. Just local offices of the state police."

"I didn't realize that," Terry exclaimed. "I guess I never thought about it. The uniforms are the same everywhere. I guess that should have been a clue."

"No matter," Allison replied. "I'd be pleased to take you as my guest. I'll be out of town this weekend. Maybe some night next week."

Terry hadn't seen this side of Allison before. He left and closed the door behind him and returned to his desk. He checked the computer looking back two days. He found a coded message to Allison from Chicago. After an hour of searching his code books, he couldn't decode it. He was convinced that it concerned an investigation. He checked the time sheet summaries. All investigations were accounted for. This message didn't fit. He concluded that Harvey was right—that there was an investigation being carried on off the books. He phoned his moles at the Bayerisher Hof Hotel and Telecom. Within an hour he had heard from both. There had been daily calls from Zugspitze Hof to Allison at the hotel and at her apartment. He reported his findings and suspicions to Harvey.

Allison's intercom buzzed. Hilda had Harvey on hold. Allison braced herself and activated the speakerphone. "Yes, Mr. Specter," she said. "How can I help you?"

"There's something afoot there that I don't know about—an investigation that isn't showing in the reports. You know that's against company policy. I don't believe Murdock McCabe's on vacation at Zugspitze Hof. Are you people working on an assignment from Chicago that hasn't passed through my office yet?"

Allison grinned—pleased with his exasperation and glad that Harvey couldn't see her. "If we were working on something assigned discreetly from Chicago Headquarters, and if headquarters decided that it was so confidential that the chain of command shouldn't know about it, would you risk censure by compelling me to disclose it?"

"Don't get smart-assed with me. Have you been in direct contact with Chicago?"

"If I have, I would not have instigated it. I wouldn't be anxious to disclose it to you, if I thought disclosure would get you into trouble. But the decision—and hence the risk—is yours. If that *were* the case, however, under such circumstances, I would request that if you order me to breach company security, the order should be in writing. Surely you can understand my caution."

He grumbled something that sounded like bullshit, and hung up.

He backed down, but he knows something's afoot. And he believes Chicago is communicating with me directly. He hasn't guessed that it's Top Dog. He also knows that it gives me more power than he's comfortable with. He'll sic The Weasel on me in spades now. Those bastards will try to find ways to discredit me.

She noticed her shoulder bag lying where Terry had placed it. Last night, when she got home from work, she had been too tired to check her mail. This morning, as she had rushed to the garage, she had opened the lockbox and stuffed the mail into her shoulder bag. She unzipped the bag and retrieved it. A picture postcard fell onto the desk. She recognized the famous old church clock tower in Zürich. The card had a Swiss stamp and postmark. The greeting was typed: "The fox has a long tale, but it's claws are benign." *A homophone—tale for tail—and no signature. Another little mystery I must think about when I have time.*

*   *   *

Meanwhile, far away in Cyprus, Sascha was angry. He reclined in a filthy stuffed chair in the guardhouse above the old dungeon, the light of a single bare bulb cutting the darkness. The rancid odor of the chair, repugnant to Theo, didn't bother him. Theo didn't have to live there. Yesterday, Theo had brought him two new girlie magazines, and Sascha had cut out the pictures of the nude women and pasted them on his walls. He was still angry because the whore from Limassol had rejected him last night.

The whores from Alexikas, the nearest village, refused to attend him since Theo had brought him Jeanette, a nineteen-year-old French girl with small breasts. Theo had *known* that Sascha liked large breasts. In a fit of anger, Sascha had tried to remove both with his teeth. Her screams had carried all the way to the villa, and Theo had come running to rescue the girl. For several weeks Jeanette had suffered great pain, but, when the news circulated that her breasts were extremely tender, it had made her the most popular prostitute. Men in Alexikas enjoyed inflicting pain on their whores. If they wanted to be gentle, they had their wives. But the popularity of a whore can be fleeting, and the other women of ephemeral pleasures were unwilling to pay *that* price to achieve uncommon popularity. Sascha was off-limits.

Alone in his filthy chamber, the features of his face twisted into a flagitious parody of something human, Sascha closed his eyes, unzipped his fly, and reached inside. He conjured a vision of Patti Dale. He had wanted her since he had first seen her three months ago, but even Theo couldn't have *her*. The mere vision of her excited him, and that excitement was swiftly rewarded. Relieved, Sascha sat back, spat on the floor through his missing front teeth, and grinned. After the whore from Limassol had recoiled from Sascha, Theo had promised him that he could have the next attractive woman they captured, after his betters were through with her. He decided that he would lock her in the deepest cell in the dungeon and keep her alive until she lost her allure.

⤳ 27 ⤶

The alarm had gone off at six. It was Friday morning. At eight Murdock would have his second meeting with Brother Martin. Propped up in bed by pillows folded behind his back, feather bed pulled up to his chin, his feet sticking out from under at the far end, Murdock was thinking. Confused, he shook his head. The confusion came, not from the investigation, but from the women in his life. Yesterday, he had spent a glorious afternoon skiing with Diana. She seemed more alluring than when he first met her. But the romantic evening he had planned hadn't happened. Upon returning from the slopes, Diana had received a message. Her meeting in Frankfurt had been moved up to Friday morning. A company plane collected her at six. Adios intimate evening.

Then Allison had called. She had put a hypothetical to him. A man and woman are in love but they hesitate to marry because she has a better job. Would a man, she wondered, sacrifice his career to follow where his wife's career took them? He had replied that Jerr hadn't. After a long pause, she had changed the subject. She had received a postcard with a curious message. Murdock had received one too. He was convinced the cards were from Richard. She agreed. Richard — if it were Richard — had not identified himself. If he had, they would have had to notify the police. He had been missing for three days. Allison had seen no significance in the sentence, "The fox has a long tale, but its claws are benign." Murdock shared with her the information Rudi had given him about Der Fuchs. He interpreted the *fox* to be Brother Martin, and the *tale* to be a story he might tell. Allison agreed that he should pursue that possibility.

Murdock dressed and joined Rudi for breakfast. Rudi was distressed.

"What's bothering you?" Murdock inquired.

"The state justice minister seldom inserts herself into an ongoing criminal investigation, but she has twice in this case. First, she authorized us to share information with you. The second occurred late yesterday afternoon. Now we must not unduly disturb the monks. Their scientific work may be of critical importance. She is convinced that Martin had nothing to do with the murder of Brother Stephen. We must not respond to the information the Feds passed on about Der Fuchs. She would like me to impose upon my friendship with you and ask you to pursue that part of the investigation through your *unofficial* channels."

"In other words," Murdock said, "she wants Martin investigated, but she wants the government to have a low profile. That way, if she draws flack about persecuting monks, she can blame it on Veritus. Is that how you read it?"

Rudi's eyes met his. "Of course. But I don't know what flack she expects. Will you do it?"

"I would do it anyway. It's a logical part of my investigation." Murdock shook his head. "The only difference between your investigation and mine is that I understand the reason for yours. I don't know the reason for mine."

"Perhaps we should meet at my room at 1:30 to review your meeting with Brother Martin."

"Can do."

*　　*　　*

The morning was bitterly cold. Upon meeting Murdock at the gate, Brother Martin guided him to the same conference room where he and Enrique had met the day before. After the chilling ride up the trail, its warmth felt good to Murdock. He peered through the picture window. Searching far down the slope, he could make out the snow-covered meadow and the Liederbach Creek. He couldn't precisely identify the location where the body had been found.

"Can you imagine," Brother Martin said cheerfully, "what this big barn of a place was like during medieval times, before central heating and thermostats?"

"I don't want to think about it," Murdock replied, somewhat less cheerfully. "I'm just beginning to warm up."

Martin poured a steaming cup of coffee and offered a tray of small cakes. Murdock took one to be polite. He sipped the coffee.

"Now, how can I help you?" Brother Martin asked.

"Have you ever lived behind the Iron Curtain?"

Brother Martin frowned. "So. The rumor rears its ugly head again. Does this question have anything to do with the investigation of Brother Stephen's murder?"

"Yes."

"Am I a suspect?"

"Unfortunately, everyone is a suspect. We've not narrowed the field. Do you mind answering the question?"

"I was born and brought up behind the Iron Curtain — in Leipzig."

"I take it that you escaped. Is that correct?"

"Yes. You could say that I escaped."

"How old were you?"

"Twenty-two."

"About thirty years ago."

Brother Martin smiled. "Is that when Der Fuchs was sent over?"

Their eyes met. "I'm afraid," Murdock said, "that it is my job to ask the questions. Will that be okay?"

"It must be."

"How did you escape? Did you scale the wall?"

"I agreed to work for them."

"For whom?"

"The Stasi — the East German spy service. The Stasi wanted me to go into deep cover — to study religion at a seminary in West Germany, become a pastor, infiltrate the Evangelical Church, build my influence among its pastors and people, and await the Stasi's orders. Is that what Der Fuchs is supposed to have done?"

Murdock ignored the question. "Why did they choose you?"

"Both my parents were clandestinely Christians. The Stasi knew that. My parents condemned atheistic communism. They could have been arrested. That threat of arrest would give the Stasi a hold over me while I was in the West."

"But if you were going into deep cover, it could take decades for your influence to mature. How would they control you after your parents died? I mean, you being a Christian and . . ."

Brother Martin interrupted. "Oh, but *I* wasn't a Christian. My parents were. I was a totally dedicated atheistic communist, loyal to my party, and tolerant of my parents only because they were *my* parents."

"Let me be more direct," Murdock said firmly. "Are you Der Fuchs?"

"I understand that is the cover name the Stasi put on my file."

Having expected cunning repartees, Murdock was taken back by his candor. Before Murdock could ask, Brother Martin avowed: "The five million U.S. dollars were never under my control. They were spent by other agents using Swiss banks as transfer agents. Several businesses were purchased in the United States and in the United Kingdom. Their shares were registered in my name. I don't know why they chose me. Perhaps they were certain that they controlled me."

"Why were these businesses bought?"

"They didn't tell me. Perhaps they could be used to help destabilize the American and British economies when the order was given. Maybe they were a bulwark of protection against the fall of communism so that the leaders could escape, like the Nazis did to Argentina and Paraguay, and receive income from the businesses."

"Did you hear from Erik Honecker after he escaped to Chile?"

"No. I expected to, but I didn't."

"Why did you expect to?"

Brother Martin shook his head. "I thought that the escape scenario was the more rational, and that any day he would contact me and ask for money."

"What are the names of these businesses?"

"They could not possibly have anything to do with the murder of Brother Stephen. If you can show me that they do, I shall answer."

"Let's go back to your being injected into the Evangelical Church as an operative — a spy — thirty years ago. What exactly were you programmed to do?"

"At some time, the Stasi would make a move to destabilize West Germany. Because the pastors would trust me, I could inject misinformation into the church — misinformation that, when disseminated by the pastors to their flocks, would cause people to doubt their political leaders and lose faith in their capitalist economic system. Sermons can bite."

"Would you have done it?"

"When my parents were alive? Well — let's just say that your question is not relevant. The order never came."

"What if your monks find out?"

"They know."

"How could you fake being a Christian all these years?"

Brother Martin poured himself another coffee. Murdock observed that he was utterly cool. So cool, that it was difficult to disbelieve him. *And, Murdock wondered, why should I disbelieve him. He's just confessed.*

"I became a Christian twenty-five years ago. The Stasi never guessed. They thought it was part of my act. In fact, they complemented me for the thoroughness of my ruse."

So now let's see if he can explain how the horse grew wings. If the wings are fake, then my intuition tells me, this guy had something to do with Stephen's death. Murdock shifted his weight to his left side and crossed his right leg over his left. He felt uncomfortable. The shifting hadn't helped.

Martin waited. He smiled. "I regret if I make you uncomfortable. You wonder if my conversion was sincere, yes?"

Murdock nodded.

Brother Martin refilled Murdock's cup and thought for a moment. "When I was a young parish pastor, people told me that they struggled to believe. Others confessed that they struggled to not believe because believing in something you can't see is irrational. I asked both groups the same question. What is it exactly that you're trying to believe or not to believe? Most gave a woolly answer. Some yearned for a religion that I would describe as a vague, phantasmagorical colored light show. What they sought, I decided, was entertainment. They danced a fool's dance. Eventually I caught myself believing, but trying not to believe. What exactly was it that I was resisting, I asked myself. The answer was simple. I didn't want to get suckered into believing that Jesus was the son of God, or that he offered eternal life. That was absurd. I searched for logical explanations, not superficial platitudes. I carefully reasoned it through. I came to the conclusion that there was no logical reason to believe in the Jesus myth."

Brother Martin remained silent while Murdock pondered his words. Murdock heard the ticking of a small clock on the corner table. He wondered why, with all the latest electronic equipment easily available in the monastery, these monks would still use a windup clock. The ticking captured him and gave him a sense of time passing. Presently he asked, "Are you telling me that, if I reason logically, I can conclusively find that God doesn't exist?"

"Or . . .?"

"Or that he does?"

"Good! Every coin has two sides," Martin declared. "I believe you can find an equal number of logical arguments to prove whichever premise you *want* to prove. Proofs of God's existence or nonexistence are equally compelling."

"So, if I contemplate, I can find God?"

"No, I don't think so."

"What exactly are you telling me?" Murdock inquired with some frustration.

"I'm telling you that you can't believe in something unless you know what that something is. That's a rather obvious aphorism, but it needs to be said. There is pleasure in definition. I took pleasure in the definition that God was a fake — an opiate of the people, as Karl Marx would say. I found pleasure, but no joy. I've learned that pleasure is always within our power, but joy never is. The surest way of spoiling a pleasure, is to start examining your satisfaction in it. When I examined mine, it dissolved. Atheistic communism, the antigod, lost its luster, but nothing filled the gap. I had no joy at all."

Murdock remembered the professor's cynical advice. Let Martin think you may wish to be converted, and he will bond with you. *That shouldn't be difficult. I'll crack the door.* "No one has ever tried to convert me. Who converted you?"

"Who was the catalyst who set it in motion? My Stasi controller."

Murdock's eyes widened. "He was a Christian?"

"No. He didn't intend it. When I was a child, my parents had taught me the Jesus story. One day my controller referred to Jesus as a two-bit prophet who might have amounted to something if he hadn't claimed to be God. That struck a nerve. As a child, I'd enjoyed the stories about Jesus. As I grew older, I read scientific journals too. I found nothing that conclusively precluded a spiritual element in humans as my communist brethren had taught. In fact my introduction to quantum physics suggested just the opposite. Quantum physics holds the promise of opening our view of the universe to include shadow worlds dramatically different from ours. Some eminent physicists have speculated that these different worlds might very well approximate the afterlife described in many religions. From that point on, when I listened to those who argue that there is no proof of angels or afterlife — men like our friend, the professor — I say to them that there is also no proof that such things *don't* exist. Any reasonable person would at least keep an open mind. I decided personally, that the principal reason that I rejected mysticism of any breed was because I had never experienced it. I don't suppose I was different from most people in that regard."

Murdock stood up, walked over to the picture window, and looked out. "The professor thinks it's all bunk," he said. He decided to open the metaphorical door further. "My mother was a Christian. I often wish I had her faith, but I can't argue against the professor's position."

Brother Martin smiled. "How old were you when she died?"

"Twelve."

"Were you close to her?"

"Yes." Murdock felt uncomfortable again.

"Was your father antichurch?

"Yes."

"Did you respect him?"

"Yes."

"Did your father believe that a person can be upright and ethical without having to carry religious baggage?"

"Yes." Murdock was unconcerned that he had lost the initiative. His goal was to learn what made this man tick, and whether the ticks were in sync.

"From all I have learned about you," Martin continued, "I believe that you are an upright and ethical man. Both parents brought you up that way. Oh, so your father was as firm in his disbelief as your mother was in her faith. Neither was lukewarm. Nothing is more destructive to the human spirit than being lukewarm. You must choose for yourself."

Murdock turned his head away from Brother Martin and stared out the window again. "The professor," he said, "has searched for God all his life, and he's convinced of God's nonexistence. If searching can result in either conclusion, is it worth the trouble?"

"Ask the professor his opinion about the superstring theory."

Murdock searched his memory. He turned away from the window and faced Brother Martin. "I've read something about superstrings recently. I can't remember what."

Brother Martin joined him at the window. They both gazed down toward the Liederbach Meadow. "When I was a child," Martin said, "I was taught that the smallest particles of matter were atoms. That was false, but most scientists believed it — on faith, even though they couldn't actually see atoms. Later I was taught that atoms are made up of elementary particles called protons, neutrons, and electrons. Again, scientists couldn't see them, but their experiments suggested their existence. Later I learned that protons and neutrons were not elementary particles either. Protons are made up of still smaller particles called quarks. Still later they discovered that quarks come in six *flavors* and each flavor comes in three *colors*: red, green, or blue. Then I heard that electrons were not elementary particles either. They're made up of leptons, and maybe spin and charge too, or maybe electrons *are* a kind of lepton. I'm not sure. I don't know what to believe. Some scientists believe — and I emphasize *believe* — that all these things may be controlled by something called *strings*.

Strings vibrate at various frequencies. We'll never see them — not just because they're so small — but because, the theory says, they exist in either tenth or twenty-sixth dimensional space. We're not able to see or otherwise sense anything outside three-dimensional space — four-dimensional if you count time."

Murdock interrupted impatiently. "What do strings have to do with our conversion?"

"If these *strings* can exist in the tenth or twenty-sixth dimension, it's a very small leap to believe that God and angels can exist in the tenth or twenty-sixth . . . or whatever dimension."

If this guy's faking, Murdock thought, he's really slick. If this is a diversion, what's he hiding by this religious camouflage? "Is that what convinced you?" he asked.

"No. I hadn't heard of strings twenty-five years ago. I was a skeptic, like your father. God would have to talk to me directly before I would believe. Then it struck me. If Shakespeare were to talk to Hamlet, it would have to be Shakespeare's doing. So why couldn't God write himself into the human scene? In his script of the universe, why *couldn't* an all-powerful god be born of a virgin and become a man living in our three-dimensional space — a man whose humanity we could understand? I found no logical reason that he couldn't. This is an argument that troubles the professor. And this was the argument that opened the door for me. God will never enter our hearts unless we open the door, and whenever we open the door, God will enter."

"At that point did you think that he chose you?"

"At that point I became certain that it really happened — that the Jesus myth was true. At that point he chose me."

"Would he choose a person like me?" Murdock tested, playing the game.

"He will choose anyone who opens his heart to him. I'm certain, because he chose a fool like me."

Murdock turned toward him. They stood facing each other next to the icy picture window. Neither moved. Neither spoke. Finally Murdock broke the silence.

"Are you equally certain that Brother Stephen was murdered because he was preparing a web site for the Sinaiticus Codex? Does that idea work for you?"

"No," Martin replied, engaging his eyes. "I'm not certain at all. It may have nothing to do with it. Have you heard of 'Q'?"

"Obviously you mean something other than the letter."

"Yes. It's a school of theological thought, which originated in Germany in the nineteenth century, and infiltrated to America in the twentieth. It comes from the German word *Quelle* which, as you may know, means *source* in English. This school of thought, now led by some American theologians, seeks to destroy the Christian religion by reducing Jesus to the status of a dusty wandering philosopher. They employ circular reasoning."

"Like what?"

"The four canonical gospels were written at least twenty or thirty years after Jesus' death. All except St. John's are quite similar. The theologians compared the verses in Matthew, Mark, and Luke that agree with one another. They argue that their authors must have read the same source. So, they reason, that there must be an earlier document — a lost document — written when Jesus was alive, that was the original source, and hence of greater authority. No one has found such a document. But having reached the conclusion that it must have existed, these professors took the verses common to Matthew, Mark, and Luke, and from them, by inverted reasoning, reconstructed the supposed lost document. It contains no resurrection story. By circular reasoning, they used this document that they had created to prove that Jesus was nothing more than a sage wandering the dusty roads of ancient Palestine. Jesus would have remained an obscure sage, if the gospel writers hadn't embellished the story and grossly inflated his importance. These theologians feel safe in their conclusions because those who knew the facts are all dead and can't contradict them. They assert that their hypothetical source exposes the weak underbelly of Christianity. With Moslem hordes at the door, can you imagine the political implications of debunking Christianity? Do you see how the work of these people can be used by opportunistic politicians — forgive the redundancy — to help destabilize the western world?"

"Yes, but I think such a threat is overstated. Many people today pay only lip service to Christianity. Besides, how would the murder of Brother Stephen help them? It's not that difficult to build a web site."

"It's difficult to find men like Stephen and Gustav who are willing to spend endless hours to enrich its content. They intended it as a powerful tool to debunk 'Q'. I'm convinced Stephen's death had something to do with his work. This was his best known project. Who would kill a kind, gentle, brilliant, humble man like our Stephen just for the hell of it?"

That question resonated in Murdock's head all the way back to the Zugspitze Hof Lodge. It took his mind off the cold. He was vexed because he wanted to believe that Brother Martin's conversion story was genuine, but he couldn't. His opinion of Brother Martin had changed for the worse. He knew how shrewd the Stasi had been and how well they had trained their operatives. He wondered whether Enrique had gotten close to something, and Martin had orchestrated the rifle shot to scare him away.

* * *

It was Friday morning. For three days the professor had reveled in Stephen's memoirs. The work was daunting because he felt a tension between the cold discipline that commanded him to read and the emotion that said he was intruding on the work of a man so brutally murdered. He placed the second floppy disk in the drawer and brought the file up on the screen.

The flow of the text had changed, shifting from scientific notations to private thoughts. There had been no more break-ins at Stephen's computer chip fabricating plant in Oregon. The perpetrators had become less subtle. Mac Townsend, his manager, had received a note that threatened the kidnap and torture of his wife and children, unless he turned over to the writer the design of Stephen's new computer chip — and he was to tell no one. The note had been signed *Traction*. Mac had immediately hidden his family in Alberta and notified Stephen.

The name *Traction* had meant nothing to either of them, but the note compelled Stephen to change course. Stephen wrote:

> I fear that continued secrecy imperils my friends. I must accelerate my work to the point where secrecy is no longer necessary before it becomes impossible. At that point, the danger won't be specific to my friends — it will be common to all men.

⇥ 28 ⇤

After breakfast with Murdock, Rudi had returned to his room. He looked forward to Murdock's report on his meeting with Brother Martin. Georg, who was waiting for him at the door of his room, presented him with the overnight dispatches. Georg hadn't eaten, so Rudi sent him to the restaurant for breakfast at state expense. Alone, inside, he reviewed the documents. He extracted his journal from his briefcase.

Friday, November 21st

> We have no new information regarding either Michael or the man in the green nylon ski jacket who observed us at the crime scene.

Boris Romanovsky, who has been a frequent passenger on the mysterious biz-jet, is known on the streets in Munich. Reliable sources report that he has a villa on Cyprus. He is a facilitator. When a man in one business needs a man in another, he brings them together. On occasion, our sources believe, he may deal on his own account. Last week he negotiated the sale and purchase of a considerable amount of zirconium. While the deal was made here, the zirconium probably will be shipped illegally from the United States to a destination in Chile where it will be used in the manufacture of cluster bombs. We do not know whether Romanovsky acted as principal or agent. In either event, the negotiating of such a deal is not illegal here, because the zirconium is not located here and will never pass through Germany.

The Liechtenstein police report that the corporation, which owns the Austrian registered aircraft, is itself owned by a Cypriot corporation. We are checking with authorities in Nicosia.

We received a "no warrant but watch" advisory from the American FBI in regard to Jose Enrique Perez-Krieger. We are warned of possible fraud in the Caymans and possible personal illegal sexual involvement with girls twelve and under in Thailand and the Philippines. One of the girls allegedly was handled so roughly that she died. However, there are no warrants anywhere. The FBI promises that detailed information will follow later today.

Von Richter has made an appointment to meet with Brother Martin tomorrow, Saturday morning. Their agenda is unknown.

It appears that Patti Dale is connected with the FBI's Joe Carlyle. It seems unlikely that Joe would be interested in a lesbian. Maybe she's bisexual, or maybe she's an American agent undercover. Is she CIA? If she *is* a spy, who is she spying on? Us? Not likely. I know of no one in our governments, state or federal, who is operating in the Mädchenhaus Café.

Our informant who furnished the Romanovsky zirconium information is a patron of the Mädchenhaus Café, which is where Patti Dale hangs out. This informant has given us reliable information before. She claims to know nothing about Patti Dale, other than that she is a free spender.

I have arranged to meet my counterpart in the Cypriot police at 8:00 A.M. tomorrow. I shall spend tonight at the Olympian Hotel in Nicosia. Tomorrow afternoon I shall drive to Limassol.

Rudi closed his journal. He was looking forward to the trip, not only because he expected to find some answers to an investigation that offered precious few, but because the Mediterranean climate should be a pleasant diversion.

*   *   *

A brilliant Friday morning had dawned in Munich — clear but biting cold. Outside the coffeehouse, people bundled in heavy coats, warm hats, and scarves paraded by, leaning into a bitter northwest wind, their breath showing. Inside, over a steaming cup of hot coffee, Allison looked puzzled.

"What do you mean?" she asked.

"I mean," Moira said while buttering her croissant, "that I think she's either an elective lesbian or a counterfeit."

Staring out the window, Allison sipped her coffee. She regretted the personal remarks she'd made to Murdock last night. She hoped they hadn't muddled their friendship. Across the street, lights shown in the lobby of Veritus, but Gustav would not have unlocked the doors yet. Turning toward Moira, she spoke hesitantly. "I respect your privacy. Perhaps you don't like to talk about your sexual orientation." She paused.

"Go on."

"When you use the term 'elective lesbian' you lose me."

"I don't mind talking about it at all. Please don't feel uncomfortable, Allison. I am what I am, and I'm a *primary* lesbian. That means I had no choice. I was born that way. By the time I started kindergarten I knew I was different from other girls. I wasn't sure why. I didn't have a label to put on myself. By the time I was twelve, my girlfriends were giggling over boys. Again, I couldn't understand why. I was emotionally and physically attracted to girls and young women."

"I don't mean to pry, but did you ever date boys?"

"I had a few dates with boys. It was the thing to do to be cool. But I never had any emotional bond. I felt intensely close to my girlfriends. That intensity was not reciprocated. I remember having an awesome crush on Jody Summerfield. Whenever she wore a dress or skirt, I fantasized that she wasn't wearing panties. I desperately wanted to explore her, but I was afraid of losing her friendship. She was the absolute frustration of my high school years — my unrequited love. I thought it was immaturity on my part."

The waiter brought another pot of coffee. Allison filled both cups. "It must have been extremely frustrating. What did you do?"

Moira added cream and sugar, stirred, and tested. She added a bit more sugar. "I'm beginning to like things sweet. Maybe I'm becoming Bavarian."

Allison smiled, waiting.

"In college I met other lesbians. It was only then that I learned to savor my feelings. I felt more comfortable with myself."

"What makes Patti different?"

"*I* had no choice. Elective lesbians do. I think most bisexual women are electives. They're lesbians because they choose to be. That's not to say that all elective lesbians are bisexual. In my experience, elective lesbians often don't become lesbians until later in life, sometimes after or during marriage or some other significant relationship with men. Some continue to live with their husbands while having an emotionally satisfying relationship with a woman lover. Some tell me that their feelings are neither heterosexual nor homosexual — just sexual. They make love with whomever makes them feel good — man or woman."

Allison looked troubled. "So, you think Patti Dale is an elective lesbian?"

Moira frowned. She buttered another croissant and added raspberry jam. "Like I said, I'm not certain that she *is* lesbian."

"If she were not," Allison injected, "why would she hang out at the Mädchenhaus Café? Do many nonlesbians frequent the place?"

"No. You'd feel uncomfortable there. But if you'd like to visit, come as my guest. I have to warn you, though, you'd be fresh meat for the predators."

"That's kind of you, Moira, but no thank you. My interest is merely in Patti Dale. If I were there with you, that might complicate your situation."

"Are you afraid people would think you were one of us? Or that *he* would hear about it?" She pointed across the street.

Terry was entering the Veritus office. *Later than usual, Allison thought. He's slipping.*

"The Weasel is not your friend," Moira said.

"I've guessed that, but why do you mention it?"

"Are you aware that my brother works the communications desk at the Veritus office in Boston?"

"I wasn't."

"I asked him to spook Terry — to ask Terry how it was to work under a woman assistant station chief. Terry doesn't know he's my brother. Terry told him yesterday that the word is that you are trying to bed Harvey so that he'll appoint you to replace Richard. There's even a rumor, according to Terry, that you may have had something to do with Richard's disappearance, although Terry gallantly avows disbelief. He knows how to plant seeds effectively. Terry suggested that you were trying to come on to him because you need screwing real bad, and because he can help you lay Harvey. He doesn't come right out and say these things. He hints broadly."

"Has he passed this on to others?"

"He doesn't know my brother well. He's not Terry's confidant, so I'd guess he's telling anyone who'll listen."

"Do you think many believe him?"

"No. Most know him for what he is. But there's always someone. My brother calls him Fantasy Dick because Terry thinks he's God's gift to every damsel that he imagines to be in heat."

A petulant smile crossed Allison's face. "I don't mean to be spiteful, but I need to neutralize that son of a bitch."

Moira raised her coffee cup in a salute. "*Neuter* might be a better term."

Allison laughed. "In the meantime, why does Patti Dale spend so freely at the Mädchenhaus? Where does she get her money? And who is she?"

"There's a coven of about a dozen patrons who network information. If their employers have secrets, they'd better not share them with these gals. Patti is a buyer. She pays cash. Sometimes handsomely. Rumor has it that she's connected with someone high in the American government. The seemingly unlimited cash she flaunts reinforces that rumor. American taxpayers are such sheep."

"Has the name Joe Carlyle come up?"

"I haven't heard it mentioned, but I know who he is. Is Patti Dale connected with him?"

Allison shrugged. "Unless I'm mistaken, she is. We — Richard, Murdock, and I — believe that Harvey has some pipeline to Carlyle too. The order for your investigation of Patti Dale came from Harvey. We may not have a client. It may be adventurism on Harvey's part — using the company's money."

Moira grinned. "That's against company policy."

"Yes, I know. So we must have a client. Right?"

"So, if he comes after you because you have Murdock investigating the death of the monk without a client, you have a saber for a counterthrust."

"Exactly, *if* Murdock were investigating the death of a monk without a client."

"Come on, Allison. Moira figures things out. I'm not stupid. But if Harvey and Patti are both mixed up with high brass in the FBI, I'd better watch my step. I could get hurt. I need to figure out what Harvey's up to. I know a gal who works at Harvey's favorite escort service when he's in Munich. She may be able to put me on to his favorite girl. Men tell some pretty confidential things to their regular whores."

Allison ordered more coffee.

Moira continued. "Patti sat next to me at the bar in the Mädchenhaus last night. First time. It seemed contrived. She had the choice of several stools — it was a slow night. For the first time she was friendly.

However, none of her network was there, so she could have picked me at random. But I don't think so. I think she'd made a conscious choice to engage me in conversation. We talked for over two hours — small talk. She shrewdly avoided substance. If I approached it, she would subtly turn the conversation away. You know — let's not get serious on the first date. But, she set up another date for tonight. I'll meet her at the bar again."

Allison grimaced. "Is she after your body?"

Moira thought for a minute. Allison refilled her cup. "Yes and no," Moira replied. "Everything she says suggests that she's making a pass, but she leaves me with the impression that she's an accomplished actress. So, Boss, do you still want me to accompany you to the Zugspitze Hof tonight, or shall I keep the date with Patti Dale?"

Allison pondered the question. Staring across the street, she saw an elderly man exit a taxicab and try the door at Veritus. It was not yet opening time. He turned up his collar and waited in the door bay.

"Keep the date. Drive down to Zugspitze Hof tomorrow. But be careful. Jerr suspects that Joe Carlyle's involvement with Karen's death may not have been benign."

A look of shock crossed Moira's face. "You mean that maybe she wasn't accidentally shot when the FBI tried to rescue her from the kidnappers?" Do you mean . . ."

"That the entire kidnapping could have been a deception where the kidnappers and the kidnapped were expendable. More than that. Jerr thinks that the kidnapping was the cover for an execution."

"But why?" Moira asked, aghast.

"Karen did some freelancing for the FBI — code work. Beyond that I can only guess. But be careful. If Patti's interest in you is not sexually inspired, you may be sucked into a most dangerous game. And I have no idea what the game is. Do you want off this assignment?"

Moira paused, thoughtfully. "Thank you, Allison. No. It's become too fascinating to let it go."

Finished with breakfast, they bundled up and stepped out and into the cold. Traffic was heavy. Patches of ice caused them to walk cautiously. Allison glanced at her watch. It was still five minutes until opening time. Dodging traffic, they crossed the street at mid-block. At the Veritus office the large glass doors were still locked. Waiting outside was the elderly gentleman, obviously uncomfortable in the cold. Old Gustav, who was standing in the lobby, saw them approaching and unlocked the door. All three stepped inside.

"I am sorry, sir," Gustav said to the elderly man, "but the office does not open for five minutes."

"It's okay," Allison interjected. "Can someone help you?"

"Yes," the elderly gentleman replied. "I wish to see Allison Spencer."

"I am she. And you are . . ."

"I am Professor Otto P. Klugman — from Oregon — in the United States."

⤐ **29** ⤎

Murdock had arranged to meet with Enrique at 1:00 P.M. It was close to that time. Murdock, alone in his room, stood in front of the picture window, his feet wide apart, his arms behind him, his hands gripping one another, looking outside at the snow-covered mountains, his mind turning over what Allison had told him. She had phoned him minutes earlier and informed him of her meeting with Linda DiStefano. He was puzzled. Enrique had come to Zugspitze Hof as a guest of Seneca Financial. According to his story, Enrique had chosen this location because, in addition to conferring with Diana, he wanted to make a business proposal to Brother Martin, *and* because he wanted to meet Murdock. Murdock was convinced that Jerr had made the suggestion to Enrique. Jerr would also have suggested that Enrique throw a little business Allison's way. This all made sense, but the timing disturbed Murdock. Enrique was a suspect. Was the offer that Linda had communicated to Allison an attempt to divert Murdock? This was a major account, not just a little business. He decided that he would not mention Allison's phone call — he'd play dumb.

His watch read 1:00 o'clock. He exited his room, walked down the hallway, and knocked on Enrique's door. Enrique opened it and invited him in. After pleasantries, they were seated, and Murdock came to the point. "I must ask you a few more questions," he said, and without waiting for a response said, "Have you ever done business with the former communist government of East Germany or with any company owned by that government?"

"No."

"Have you ever heard of an East German secret agent called 'Der Fuchs'?"

"Never."

"Is it possible that a large sum of money — say five million dollars — could be invested in Plato without your knowing the source of the funds."

Enrique arose and walked over to the window. He gazed outside for several seconds, his back to Murdock. Presently he turned around to face him. "I can't imagine that happening. I personally know each of our investors. Do these questions have something to do with the murder of Brother Stephen?"

"Perhaps. Tell me more about Plato. I'm not well-versed in economics. Why would Plato be needed today when economic fundamentals seem so positive?"

Enrique reseated himself. "Poor people can't eat positive fundamentals. Poor, hopeless people are easily led. To the ears of desperate, hungry men, the rhetoric of revolutionaries is music. During a transition from a socialistic to a capitalistic system, gaps widen between haves and have-nots. The *percentage* of people in poverty worldwide has been reduced, but enormous population growth has caused the *actual* number of people living in poverty to soar. Real unemployment is high. Real wages are low. Capital — money — is our response."

"Money is power," Murdock remarked offhandedly.

"Money can buy the power of intrigue," Enrique responded, "but not the power of command. However, neither are objects of Plato."

"Money can buy many things," Murdock said, watching Enrique's face for a response. He saw none. "How long do you plan to remain here?"

"Until the police say I can leave. They've permitted me to fly to Cyprus this weekend, however, for a couple days. I'll return here on Monday."

"Whom are you meeting on Cyprus?"

Enrique shrugged. "I can't imagine that this question has anything to do with your investigation, but then, I am not an investigator. I shall meet a man by the name of Boris Romanovsky. I may engage him to assist Plato in establishing businesses in Russia. I'd rather not go into private business matters. Is that all for now?"

"Yes," Murdock said. "I'm sorry that I must pry . . ."

"But that's your job," Enrique interrupted. They rose. Enrique, his face a blank, escorted Murdock to the door.

*   *   *

Murdock checked his messages. A note from the professor indicated that he had taken the train to Munich. He would be back by 3:00 P.M. He was anxious to speak with Murdock. Allison had called and awaited a return call. He went to his room and phoned her. She indicated that she would call back in ten minutes from a phone in the café across the street. She did.

After the pleasantries, she paused. Murdock waited. "What is it?" he asked.

"I've been in direct contact with Top Dog again. *He* contacted *me*."

"Why?" he asked incredulously.

"To give me much more authority in regard to your investigation. Harvey and The Weasel are not to know."

"Wow," Murdock exclaimed. "Is it authentic? It could be a fake. Has he ever made management decisions for the company before? Harvey might be tricking you and setting you up for a fall."

"I believe it's authentic. He used a discrete code that I received in management training—a term that was personal to me."

"Do all management people have such a code from Top Dog?"

Allison was silent for several seconds. "I assume so. Before I get there tonight, I want you to take off the gloves with this professor. He visited me this morning. He said you and he had become friends and asked me to keep a sealed envelope for him in my safe. If I should hear of his death, you or I are to open it. He assured me there was nothing illegal in it."

"Did you take it?"

"Yes. But I'll decide how long to keep it after you and I meet tonight. Is Rudi still there?"

"Yes, but he's flying to Nicosia tonight to confer with his Cypriot counterpart. Tomorrow afternoon he'll drive to Limassol. He's convinced that some of the missing pieces of our puzzle are to be found there. Should I join him?"

She was silent again for several seconds. "No. It's vital that you and I meet tonight. Will he phone you from Cyprus?"

"Yes. After he talks to the police in the morning, and again tomorrow evening from Limassol."

"We can decide at that time whether you need to go to Cyprus."

*   *   *

The professor had phoned Murdock asking to be picked up at the train station at 3:06 P.M. It would be neither late nor early. Murdock knew he could set his watch by German trains. Engineers considered it a personal disgrace if their trains didn't arrive exactly on time.

The professor stepped off the train at 3:07. When he noticed Murdock, he threw his arms in the air and exclaimed, "Glad to see you. I suppose you've already heard about my adventure. Yes. Of course. Miss Spencer has told you."

Murdock laughed easily. "I know you met with Allison. But there are other things we need to discuss."

The BMW 528i was standing alone in a far corner of the parking lot. The surface was icy, and Murdock didn't want someone sliding into it. The professor opened the passenger door and scrunched down into the passenger seat. Murdock slipped into the driver's seat, started the engine, and engaged the heater. It was still warm. Murdock pulled out of the parking lot and into the city traffic. "Please forgive me. I don't like to pry, professor, but murder is a nasty business. Is there anything belonging to or pertaining to Brother Stephen in the envelope that you gave to Allison?"

The professor folded his hands in his lap. He looked straight ahead. "Allison is a delightful lady," he said. "Just as you described her. I instantly felt that I could trust her. If you let her get away, you are a fool. But I disfavor prying too, so I shall say no more on that subject. The documents in the envelope are my personal papers. They have nothing to do with the murder. I felt they would be safer away from Zugspitze Hof because the killer may wrongly think they are important. If the police investigation should foolishly focus upon me, and if you or Allison feel uncomfortable about the envelope, either of you may open it and satisfy yourselves that it is benign. But I'd rather you didn't, except in that instance, or in the instance of my death. I fear the killer too."

"What do you know that would interest the killer?"

"I'm not certain. It's more what the killer may *think* that I know. It's common knowledge that I'm an astrophysicist and a philosopher. That rare combination alone makes me an odd duck. People feel uncomfortable with and threatened by odd ducks. There's authentic science going on in the monastery. They don't broadcast what they do, but most of it isn't secret either. Scientist-monks are odd ducks too. I suppose I fit in."

Murdock stopped at the Q8 station to fill his tank. The professor remained inside, out of the wind. Murdock wished he'd brought his scarf. When he closed the car door and restarted the engine, he was grateful for the warmth. The professor waited for him to speak. Folding back into traffic, Murdock proceeded down the road that parallels the tracks of the narrow gauge railway that runs from Garmisch-Partenkirchen to the cable car station at the foot of the Zugspitze Mountain. Murdock glanced at him. "You used the term *authentic* science. What did you mean?"

The professor shrugged. "As I mentioned before, back home much of our science is corrupted by bureaucrats and the political process. Scientists frequently make results of research fit political realities. A goodly amount of expensive research is junk science. Conclusions are politically predictable. Bureaucracy proliferates. Our university had a department dedicated to studying grant sources. Another department specialized in obtaining grants — schmoozing the federal bureaucrats and the politicos. Still another department specialized in administering grants. A branch of our finance department made certain that we received all of the grant money to which we were entitled and justified — often imaginatively — the expenses charged to the grant. As our French brethren say, these are the *folies de grandeur*. And that brings up another reason that I commiserate with these monks. Like myself, they detest junk science and the misinformation it perpetuates. I planned to work with Brother Stephen to develop a second web site dedicated to informing people how their tax money is being wasted on false science and how they are being misled into false security — particularly about products they eat and the pharmaceuticals they use."

"It's dangerous to be right when the government is wrong," Murdock injected, "even in America. Big money generates enormous incentives to protect itself. It keeps politicians in power. That often means keeping the taxpayers ignorant. They might be surprised to learn who all are suckling on the federal tit."

The professor laughed. It wasn't a happy laugh. "Too many taxpayers don't want to know. I believe it was Socrates who wrote, 'Ignorance aware of itself is the only true knowledge.'"

"But," Murdock injected, "I don't see how killing Brother Stephen would prevent the creation of this dangerous web site." A thought struck him. He asked himself why he hadn't seen it before. "Unless it was to scare you fellows off."

"Yes," the professor acknowledged. "That is a possibility, isn't it? Do you believe in Evil? An entity of absolute evil?"

"A devil? I'm not sure that I do," Murdock replied.

"I don't. Brother Martin does. Do you believe there are things that we humans should not know — that our science should forever avoid?"

Murdock shrugged. "I can't think of any. Why do you ask?"

The professor stared out the front window. They had entered the forest of tall pines. Traffic was light. He turned to face Murdock. "Brother Martin put that question to me. I don't have a suitable answer. Do there exist facts, the knowledge of which, by their very nature, would unleash profound evil? Or, as the monks put it, knowledge forbidden by God? Is it possible that we are on the threshold of opening a Pandora's box that could place so much power in the hands of the possessor that he or she could rule and destroy at will?"

As they turned up the curving road that led to Zugspitze Hof Lodge,

Murdock shook his head. "I confess I've never thought about it."

The professor turned and looked directly at Murdock. "It reminds one of the fruit of the forbidden tree in the myth of the Garden of Eden."

Murdock didn't respond.

"I'm rambling on," the professor admitted. "Perhaps I digress."

As they crossed the bridge over the Liederbach Creek and rounded the sharp curve, the professor suggested they pull off the road at the same spot Murdock had chosen on Monday. "The view from here is magnificent," he explained.

"I agree. You've been dancing around something, professor. What is it?"

"There's one thing I haven't told you about Brother Stephen and myself."

"I presume there's more than one."

"Perhaps. We shall see. Brother Stephen was a student of mine."

"At which university?"

"At no university. By correspondence. I assigned reading and essays."

"When was this?"

"It started earlier this year and continued until his death. Stephen had many interests. He had an undergraduate degree in physics. He was studying advanced astrophysics and philosophy with me, both at the same time."

"Isn't that an unconventional combination?"

"Thank you. Those are my fields."

Murdock's face flushed. "I'm sorry. Please go on."

"There isn't much to go on about. That's it. Except he was helping me with a paper I'm writing for a scientific journal, if that's of any importance. We were using the Socratic method, and . . ."

"Excuse me," Murdock interrupted, "but it might be helpful to know the subject of this paper."

The professor shook his head. "I was definitely coming to that. My paper is about the Goldilocks Zone."

"The Goldilocks Zone?"

"I'm reticent to offer too much information. I often bore people."

Murdock caught himself at the threshold of a sigh. "I'll not be bored," he assured him. "Please tell me about the Goldilocks Zone."

"I shall keep it simple. Have you heard the term *exoplanet*?"

"No."

"An exoplanet is a planet that revolves around a star other than our Sun. The first confirmed exoplanet was just discovered in 1995. Since then many others have been found. In the universe, I believe, there must be billions and billions of them. The newly discovered planets, of course, are all relatively close by — in the Milky Way Galaxy."

"I've forgotten. How far away is the Milky Way Galaxy?"

"It's right here. You and I — the stuff that makes up our bodies — are part of the Milky Way Galaxy. Our Earth, our sun, our solar system — all are part of it. The newly found planets are not farther away than twenty times the distance light travels in one year — in other words — within twenty light years. Perhaps, as I'm telling you this, someone is finding a planet revolving around a star thirty light-years away. Having said that, we come to the ultimate question. Does life exist on any exoplanets? It is inconceivable to me that it doesn't. The odds favor it. I believe intelligent life exists on millions of them. But life may exist only on exoplanets of the right size and on those that orbit their star at the right distance so that they are neither too hot nor too cold. Huge planets, like our Jupiter, Saturn, Uranus, and Neptune are usually made of gases and are very far from their star, and very cold. Smaller, rocky planets like our Mercury, Venus, Earth, and Mars are solid enough, and some are the right distance. Exoplanets that might otherwise be too cold may have sufficient carbon dioxide in their atmosphere to sufficiently warm them by the greenhouse effect."

You were going to tell me about the Goldilocks Zone."

"I am. The area between the inner and outer orbital limits within which life can occur is referred to as the Goldilocks Zone — a habitable zone. A planet closer to its star would be too hot for life; a planet farther out would be too cold. One could also call it the habitable zone."

"Why was Brother Stephen interested in the subject?"

"He too was fascinated by the probability of extraterrestrial life. He believed that there must be billions of exoplanets within their respective Goldilocks Zones that have some form of intelligent life. The odds favor it. Aren't you interested?"

Murdock hesitated. He didn't want to trigger a long, esoteric lecture. "Yes," he replied. "I'd enjoy discussing it with you sometime." Murdock remembered Brother Martin's suggestion that he prod the professor about superstrings. *It would at least shift the subject, he decided.* "I'm also fascinated by the superstring theory, although I don't know much about it. Could you explain it briefly in laymen's terms?"

A wry smile crossed the professor's face. "Martin has put you up to this one. Okay. I shall be succinct. Some scientists believe . . ."

"*Believe*? Like some people *believe* in God?"

"Touché. Some scientists have found evidence to support the proposition that all the infinitely small particles that make up everything and everyone in the universe is constructed from waves called superstrings.

The theory has its curiosities. These superstrings, if they exist, are the basic stuff of the universe — the real indivisible *a-toms* as Democritus called them when he predicted their existence 2,300 years ago. They are quite peculiar. Their size is postulated to be a mere 10 to the minus 35th power centimeters — that would be a decimal followed by thirty-four zeros and a one. That means very, very small. It's predicted that we'll never see them, even if we could build a microscope capable of capturing such a small thing, because these superstrings exist in ten dimensional space — or, some theorize, in twenty-six-dimensional space. We humans understand only four dimensions — the three dimensions of space plus Einstein's fourth dimension of time. The superstring theory suggests that these four dimensions may be an illusion. There may exist a shadow world that contains entities in other dimensions that do not interact with the world we perceive except by way of gravitation."

"What does all of this mean?"

"Astronomers have calculated the known mass of the observed universe. Given the Big Bang, which started it all, they have found insufficient mass to have created the universe as we see it. There is missing mass — some thing or things that were present at the Big Bang but can't be found anymore. Perhaps 90 percent of the mass necessary to do the job can't be found. Superstrings may contain the hidden mass of the universe."

A long silence followed. Murdock broke it. "Where did these superstrings come from?"

"Many scientists have reached a tentative conclusion that all matter, as we know it, was created out of a vacuum state."

"Out of nothing? Have they given a name to the creator?"

The professor laughed uneasily. "No."

"Do you believe that this superstring theory is on the right track?"

"I wouldn't preclude it. The architecture of the universe is still open to reasonable explanation."

"Do you think that Stephen's interest in your paper has something to do with his death?"

"I wouldn't reject the idea out of hand, but I see no link, though the paper was to be published soon in a scientific journal."

The engine of the BMW was still running. Murdock pulled back onto the road. "Have you heard of 'Q'?" he inquired.

The professor's demeanor relaxed. His face brightened. "Oh, yes. It's a rather interesting effort to bring reason to the Christian myth."

"Can I bring you and Brother Martin together to talk about these things sometime? That could make for an interesting conversation."

The professor tensed. For several seconds he stared out the right window. Murdock wasn't certain the professor had heard him, but before he could repeat the question, the professor spoke. "I'll arrange it for tomorrow morning, if that's okay with you."

Murdock hadn't anticipated that response. "It is," he replied, somewhat startled. "It's for my personal pleasure," Murdock offered apologetically.

The professor turned his head toward him. "I doubt that we have time for personal pleasure. I fear there'll be another killing. Martin is holding something back."

"Withholding pertinent information from the police in a criminal investigation is a crime itself. I'm not the police, but if he didn't tell Rudi . . ."

"Martin wouldn't willfully commit a crime. In his mind the information he's holding back could have nothing to do with the investigation. Only three knew of it. One was Stephen. The others are Martin and I. Antonio worked on parts of it, but he doesn't know its purpose. He certainly doesn't know the part that makes the information so valuable that someone would kill for it. I disagree with Martin. I think he needs to share with you. He trusts you. He doesn't trust the police or their governments."

"Can you give me some idea?"

"I'd like to, but I've given my word. Martin feels that, if it leaked, and if it has something to do with Stephen's death, giving it to you may put your life in danger also."

The professor appeared deeply troubled.

"I appreciate his concern," Murdock said, "but that doesn't cut it. He's got to tell me."

The professor nodded in agreement.

The parking lot at the Zugspitze Hof Lodge was nearly filled. Murdock found a spot near the path to the helicopter pad. Picking up the professor had been profitable.

⊰ *30* ⊱

Rudi closed the zippers on his travel bag. Reaching into the inside pocket of his suit coat, he reassured himself that his passport was there. Georg had offered to drive, but instead he had accepted Murdock's offer. Murdock had requested a heart-to-heart talk fast, and they could have it on the way to the airport. There was a knock on the door. Grabbing his travel bag, Rudi opened the door and joined Murdock in the hallway. Behind him, forgotten, lying on the bed, was his journal. They headed down the narrow hallway, through the crowded lobby, out the main door, and into the parking lot. The BMW was still warm from the trip to the train station, so the heater relieved the chill almost immediately. As they descended the serpentine road, Rudi was pleased with the stability of the 528i. "It lives up to its reputation," he said. "It has a fluid ride. Are you satisfied with it?"

Murdock smiled proudly. "So far. I've only had it for a week, but I've no complaints."

"When do we start the heart-to-heart?" Rudi inquired.

"Now. I want you to put on two hats. I need to talk to you both as policeman and friend."

"I'll try," he said, with trepidation. "You know that's not easy."

"I know. First, Brother Martin or the professor could be the killer, or they could have acted in concert. They may have concocted some puzzle to snare me in a net of red herrings. But let's assume that neither is the killer. We must test your Frau Justice Minister. Martin is holding something back. I suspect there's some proprietary secret on which he and the professor have a difference of opinion. The professor thinks he should tell us, but Martin feels it's not relevant. I may learn that secret, *if*, and I emphasize *if*, I promise not to reveal it to the world — and the world includes the police. I'll attempt to negotiate a condition — that I must reveal it if it's necessary to convict the killer. Now my problem. If I succeed in obtaining this information, my withholding it would give me an edge over you guys. It would also be a crime for me to withhold information pertinent to your investigation. Before the meeting tomorrow, I want a fax from your justice minister granting me immunity from prosecution for failing to disclose, except under the condition I mentioned. The fax needs to be generalized — not focused on Brother Martin because Herr Bayer will read it when it comes off the fax. Not that I mistrust him; I just don't want to have to. If Frau Justice Minister wants my help bad enough, she'll grant it."

"Ja, ja. She may. I'll phone Herr Weiss as soon as we reach the airport. He has access to her."

"Here's my cellular. Call now."

By the time they reached the airport, Herr Weiss had assured them that Murdock would have his fax. *Amazing, Murdock thought. It's hard to believe. What the hell is going on here?*

As they entered the airport drive, a biz-jet was taxiing for takeoff. As it turned onto the departure end of the runway, they passed near enough to read its registration. Murdock nudged Rudi and pointed. "Austrian," Murdock said. Rudi picked up the cell phone and called the tower. The tower reported that the aircraft had arrived from Munich only a few minutes ago, picked up a passenger at the private aircraft terminal, and was departing for Limassol. The state's biz-jet was awaiting Rudi at the same terminal.

Murdock parked next to the general aviation terminal. As they were about to exit the car, Rudi caught Murdock's arm. "Wait," he ordered. "There are several things you need to know. Señor Perez-Krieger has a private jet. On Tuesday it flew to Limassol and returned on Wednesday. During the last week, the jet that we just observed has made five round trips between Limassol and Munich or Limassol and Garmisch-Partenkirchen. Sometimes it files flight plans for other destinations such as Vienna or Palermo. But it's a ruse. They're intermediate stops. It always terminates at Limassol. I can understand Munich if it's arms or drug traders, but I don't understand Garmisch-Partenkirchen. We've had no evidence of gun or drug trading here. The aircraft is owned by a Liechtenstein corporation, which is in turn owned by a Cypriot corporation. Cyprus has become a Russian banking center and a mecca for the Russian Mafia. A frequent passenger on that jet is one Boris Romanovsky. Have you heard of him?"

"Yes," Murdock assured him. "Is he Russian Mafia?"

"We have no direct evidence to link him. He is former KGB, an enigmatic figure. Our information indicates that he's no longer connected with the Russian government. He carries a Ukrainian passport, which I find strange. I don't like enigmas. I'll see if the Cypriots have some answers. This Romanovsky fellow holds himself out to be a facilitator for investors interested in opportunities in the Russian economy. He has an account with a substantial balance at a major bank in Munich. Within the last month, some rather large amounts of money have been transferred to that account from Syria, enough to create a smell, but we can't identify the odor. I don't like coincidences, either. That aircraft was parked here last Monday — the day that Brother Stephen was murdered. The Russian

Mafia employs some of the most ruthless killers in the world. I know you are friendly with Perez-Krieger. Be careful. The Cypriot police report that he spent Tuesday night at the villa of Boris Romanovsky. One other thing, Murdock. Remember that we have a report from the FBI that Perez-Krieger may have committed brutal sexual crimes on prepubescent girls in Thailand and the Philippines, resulting in the death of one. It's a 'no warrant warning' so we haven't yet determined how reliable it is. More information should be available tomorrow. I have instructed Georg to provide it to you. When will Diana return?"

"By noon tomorrow."

"Good. I don't relish requesting this because I know you two are attracted to each other, but please talk to her, Murdock. Frankly, we need information and she's been in a position to know his sexual peccadilloes." Rudi paused and sighed. "She is quite a different woman from Karen, Murdock."

"Do you plan to arrest Enrique?"

Rudi was silent for several seconds. "No. His crimes—if he committed them—were not committed in our jurisdiction. As you know, we can't act without a warrant from Thailand or the Philippines."

"It's difficult to imagine Enrique doing that," Murdock insisted. "It's difficult to imagine *anyone* doing that. Do we live in an age where passion is totally divorced from morality? Today, it seems, instead of God being the judge, men have made God the accused. Without any sense of shame, we'll drift back into the jungle. If there is a god, how could he let such monstrous things happen to little girls? There. Now I've done it."

"Done what?" Rudi asked, bewildered.

"I've accused God, and I'm not even sure I believe in him."

Rudi shrugged. "We can't have it both ways. God gave us a gift that angels don't share—free will. We're free to do good or evil. When we do evil, we misuse the gift. But that's *our* choice. Inside our psyches are many dark corners. If, in one of them, it's possible to find pleasure in brutalizing and raping young girls, the stubborn, irreducible fact of life is —someone will."

"And," Murdock injected, opening his car door, "while you're in Cyprus, remember, my friend, that in some countries the cost of buying a cop is less than in others."

Rudi shook his head. "Another stubborn, irreducible fact."

Exiting the vehicle, Murdock retrieved Rudi's travel bag from the trunk.

Their collars turned up against the wind, they made their way to the waiting aircraft. Its engines were already running. Murdock handed Rudi's travel bag up to the copilot. "One moment," Rudi said. He turned to Murdock. Over the noise of the engines, he shouted, "I just remembered. I left my journal lying on my bed. I don't want the chambermaid reading it. Would you mind putting it in a safe place? Here's my room key." He stepped into the plane saying, "See you tomorrow," and he was gone.

Murdock waited until the plane disappeared into a high overcast. Night was falling and the city lights had come on. Re-entering the highway, he noticed that water from melted snow was beginning to freeze on the road. Proceeding cautiously, his headlights barely penetrating the gloom, Murdock realized that his mood matched the weather. He was in a funk. The investigation was not going well, Diana was gone, the professor had unloaded teasing information but no answers, and Brother Martin had not been forthright. Pulling into the parking lot of a restaurant, he stopped, reached into his coat, and pulled out the telephone directory for the monastery, which Georg had provided. Each monk had his own phone. *Another improvement over the Middle Ages, he decided.* He dialed Brother Gustav's number. After pleasantries, he asked, "Have you ever heard of anyone called Der Fuchs?"

"Yes," Gustav replied without hesitation. "That was Brother Martin's code name when he worked for the Stasi."

Murdock was startled by the directness of the answer. "How many monks know that?"

"All of us. He told us up front. We purchased the monastery shortly after the fall of the East German government he had represented."

"Thank you. Have a good evening."

Well, Martin didn't kill Stephen because Stephen might disclose his secret. I'm beginning to trust Martin. I think he, too, is beginning to trust me. But why should he? I've made him do most of the talking. Rush hour traffic was moving slowly through the city center. *How does one know whom to trust. Karen and I knew instantly that we could trust each other. Why would Martin trust me? What have I said? I've told him almost nothing. Some people I instinctively trust—like Rudi, Jerr, and Allison— but I'm not sure of Martin yet.* Now the city traffic was behind him. Except for a small village, only open road separated him from the Lodge. *With some people, trust comes slowly, like my confidence in Enrique before today. Sometimes it takes weeks or months for confidence to grow.* A crosswind of the mind tilted his thoughts. *It's Friday night. Allison will be there. We'll have supper together.* His funk disappeared.

By the time Murdock arrived at Zugspitze Hof Lodge, it was totally dark except for thousands of stars and a rising last quarter moon. The parking lot was full. He drove the BMW around to the back of the snowmobile shed and parked it where he knew it would be safe. Bayer wouldn't mind. Entering the main door to the lodge, he felt cold, tired, and hungry. He checked the desk. Allison had left a message. The lodge was sold-out for the weekend, but the Bayers had put her in the extra bedroom at their chalet. Before supper, though, he had a job to do. He walked down the hallway to Rudi's room and upon entering noticed the journal on the bed. As he leaned over to pick it up, the phone rang. He answered.

"Herr Benzinger?"

"No. He's out just now. This is Murdock McCabe. May I help you?"

"Ach. Good. I am Doctor Kurt Kohl. We have met."

"Yes," Murdock replied. "You are Angelika's doctor. It's good to speak with you again. I'm afraid Herr Benzinger is on his way to Cyprus, but I'll be talking to him later this evening. Please, is there something I can tell him?"

"Yes, by all means. I know that you are like family to Herr Benzinger, so I shall tell you that I confirmed this morning that Frau Benzinger is moving her eyes and that the movement is controlled."

"Wonderful. Rudi will be elated. This means that she may regain consciousness, doesn't it?"

"Possibly so. One cannot say. But it is certainly not a bad omen. As I entered the room, I noticed her eyes followed a departing gentleman visitor. A nurse suspected controlled eye motion yesterday, but she wasn't certain. I think Frau Benzinger has improved since yesterday."

"Excellent. Wonderful. Marvelous. Rudi should be back by Monday. I'm certain he will visit her then, and the two of you can talk. You said she had a gentleman visitor?"

"Yes. A rather abrupt man. I caught only his first name. Michael. Do you know him?"

Murdock ignored the question. "Please describe him."

"He was taller than you, Mr. McCabe, muscular, light-skinned, blond hair, and startling blue eyes."

"Doctor, Frau Benzinger may be in mortal danger. I'm going to phone Commander Weiss at the state police and ask him to give her protection. Please post her room for no visitors, and do whatever else you can to protect her without putting your staff in danger. Hopefully, the police will arrive soon. Goodbye."

⤙ 31 ⤚

It was Friday night. The slopes were deserted, and by 6:00 P.M. the crowd had moved into the restaurant at the Zugspitze Hof Lodge. Voices and laughter filled the air. The lights were dimmed, and a warm, red glow emanated from the fireplace. Hundreds of embers danced up the flue. Allison sat across the table from Murdock. To her it seemed like an evening designed for camaraderie and romance instead of a practical working dinner. She was anxious to be brought up-to-date. He was interested in Allison's contact with Top Dog. They knew service would be slow, even though Frau Bayer, standing just outside the kitchen double doors, her abundant arms folded, was frantically encouraging the waiters to hurry. With the babble all around them, they could talk freely.

"How do *you* feel about Enrique?" Allison asked. "Have you formed an opinion?"

"I'm dubious. But Jerr's completely convinced that he's a knight in shining armor. Have you ever known Jerr to be *that* wrong about someone?"

Allison thought. "No, but he may not have the information you have."

"Rudi gave me a copy of an FBI report. I've faxed it to Jerr at home.

It's seven hours earlier in Omaha, so he won't be home until later. I'll call him at the office after we finish dinner."

Allison nodded. "I agree. Have you met Linda DiStefano?"

Murdock held up their empty wine glasses and caught a waiter's eye. "No. I'm supposed to meet her early next week. She's preparing the documents necessary for me to join Plato. I'm not sure now. I think I'll pass."

"What exactly is Plato?"

He repeated Enrique's explanation. Allison listened without interrupting. When he had concluded, she observed: "It's a sad commentary on our society. People who are apparently upright in their public lives, and are philanthropic and outwardly quite noble, sometimes have secret, repulsive lives."

Murdock cringed. "But sex with little girls? That's sick."

Allison shrugged. "Sick or not, there are countries where families sell prepubescent daughters into prostitution. There is no shame — only necessity. They aren't burdened by our Christian morality."

"Yeah, Al. There are people in America who don't share our Christian morality; some in high places."

Allison shook her head. "I know. But how can you judge people who live in a culture where child prostitution is condoned?"

"Allison, are you saying 'When in Rome, do as the Romans do'?"

"Not at all. I'm disgusted with cultures that accept these practices. I guess what I'm saying is that Enrique could be guilty of these outrageous crimes, and Plato could still be genuine. In history there is a profusion of characters with disgusting habits. On his way to free the Holy Land from the Saracens, King Richard the Lionhearted of England took his young boys with him on the First Crusade. I don't mean his sons. His sexual preference was inconsistent with having children."

"I can't argue with you. I just don't like it. I know you don't either, Al. To change the subject, what was your impression of Linda DiStefano?"

"She's extremely competent. Siegfried Insurance, and all the other Perez-Krieger family businesses, have commendable reputations. Linda's okay. She may not know about Enrique's darker side, although she impresses me as a woman who doesn't miss much. I like her."

"And I like Enrique. Have we both been attracted to a couple of con artists?"

Allison shrugged. "On occasion I've misjudged people. But I don't get *any* negative vibes with Linda. What's your feeling about the abbot, Brother Martin?"

Murdock considered his reply. The waiter arrived with a bottle of Riesling, opened it, and poured. Murdock sampled the wine. He nodded in appreciation. The waiter half-filled both glasses and took their dinner order.

"You know, Al, I consider myself a good judge of character, but over the last few days, I've met several characters that I'm at a loss to judge. I'm not certain what to make of Brother Martin. Sometimes I'm inclined to think he's trustworthy, but I formed a rather firm prejudice against Stasi agents during my FBI days. Is it logical that they would send him just to infiltrate the Evangelical Church? I suppose that, under extreme political uncertainty, the strategic injection of misinformation from the pulpit could be disastrous. But he claims that he changed, that he actually became a Christian long before the Berlin Wall came down. I'm not sure I believe that. We change, but we don't leave everything behind. Whatever we were, in some form, we still are."

"He can't be Stasi anymore," Allison injected. "Neither the Stasi nor the government that created it exist."

"Yes, but I think he's impeding the investigation. Tomorrow morning I'll find out. He and the professor know something they aren't telling. Brother Stephen wasn't killed over some religious web site. That holds water like a sieve."

"I'm not so sure. There are many millions of people who define themselves in terms of their Christianity. If 'Q' helps to undermine people's faith, where do they turn? One thing's for sure. Restless masses don't all turn in the same direction. Turmoil means profit for whomever controls Traction, and it's the birthing bed of totalitarianism."

"Al, do *you* buy the web site as the motive for murder?"

"No, but I'm saying that we can't completely discount it. People who wish to debunk religion can be as zealous as evangelists."

"What do you think of Martin's alleged conversion?"

"It's possible. From the way you described it, I'd say it's likely. But let's put our heads together tomorrow, after your meeting with him and the professor. By the way, how do you figure this Professor Klugman?"

"If Klugman's on the wrong side in this, I'll hang up my jockstrap."

Allison laughed. "Do you have one?"

"I'll buy one. I don't see where he has any agenda . . ."

"Unless he stole Stephen's invention," Allison injected, "whatever it is."

"If Stephen *had* an invention. He and Martin have been cagey on that subject. But you're right. No one can be counted out completely."

The waiter reappeared with their salads and refilled their wine glasses. A lone candle flickered in the center of the table. Allison held her wine glass in front of it and studied the flame dancing through it. Murdock interrupted her reverie. "Did you do a background check on the professor?"

Allison put the wine glass down. "The professor is what he says he is," she replied. I bypassed Terry and phoned a friend at our Portland office. She confirmed the professor's biography. She also talked to a John Hanley, a friend of the professor at Cannon Beach, Oregon. This friend is also a retired professor. Interestingly, he says that Klugman has been a sort of a Don Quixote — frequently attacking academic windmills, taking his lumps, but resilient. Professor Hanley commented that in universities, dissenters from current orthodoxy are often treated like dinosaurs — they're shunned. Apparently our Professor Klugman shares a little of Admiral Farragut's recklessness; you know, 'damn the torpedoes and full speed ahead.'"

Murdock chuckled. "Yeah. I get the impression that, if he stakes out a position, you aren't going to move him easily. He and Martin have locked horns over something. Whatever it is, I think they're trying to resolve it before I meet with them tomorrow."

Allison smiled. "I hope so. You need a break in this case."

The waiter delivered the main course. They ate silently for several minutes. Murdock watched Allison out of the corner of his eye. *She's almost as attractive as Diana. Diana's a little younger. Although Allison's been around, Diana is more a woman of the world. Diana's vivacious. Allison has a more modest charm. They're both competent at their jobs. Diana probably makes twice as much as Allison. How would I feel if my wife were making three times as much as I am? What would that do to my self-image?* Murdock broke the silence.

"Will you meet with von Richter tomorrow, as Rudi asked?"

Allison shrugged and groaned. "I might as well let him hit on me one more time. He enjoys gamesmanship. I wonder if he's the type who enjoys the game more than the victory."

"Be careful, Allison. He's at least twenty years older than you, but he's handsome, suave, and incredibly wealthy. He might drown you in charm."

"Would it matter to you?"

Murdock turned his head and stared out the window. "Of course," he replied.

By the time they finished dinner, the hundreds of voices had diminished. There were many empty tables. Both Bayers were seated at one of them. They looked exhausted. A waiter delivered apple strudel to Allison and Murdock. "Two coffees, please," Murdock ordered.

Allison took her fork and cut a piece of her strudel. Deciding to wait for the coffee, she put the fork down. She glanced at Murdock. "Have you learned anything about this Michael character that you think poses a danger to Angelika?

"Nothing. We still have no last name. The police have run up a blind alley. The professor claims he's a brilliant man, and that's high praise coming from him. Martin claims to know squat about him. I'll press him tomorrow."

The coffee arrived. They both attacked Frau Bayer's famous strudel. Allison wondered just how concerned Murdock really was about the possibility of von Richter making advances toward her. She was tempted to tease out an answer, but Murdock was in too serious a mood. "Are you convinced," she asked, "that the Michael of the abbey is also the Michael of the nursing home?"

"No! Dr. Kohl gave a description very close to the professor's. If it's the Michael of the abbey, why in God's creation would *he* visit Angelika? How would he even know her? If he's involved in the murder, and if Rudi's on to something that I don't know about, is Michael planning to kidnap Angelika in order to manipulate Rudi?"

"Like Karen all over again?"

Murdock lowered his head. His thoughts turned inward. "Just a thought," he said, without lifting his head.

Is this the time to tell him that Jerr's friend, Carl, is convinced that Karen's death was not an accident? No. The time isn't ripe. "Was Brother Stephen shot at close range?" she asked.

"Yes. No signs of a struggle. Possibly someone he knew and trusted."

"He knew and trusted Michael. Right?"

"Yes. And Martin, and Antonio, and Gustav, and the Bayers, and the professor, and a few dozen monks, and hundreds of colleagues, and other folks. Oh, well," he sighed. "By the way, where's Moira?"

"She has a date tonight with Patti Dale."

"I don't know much about Patti. Jerr's friend, Carl Sutherland, thinks that Joe Carlyle has a darling by that name."

"Moira doesn't know much either. She's been edging closer to her at the Mädchenhaus Café. Patti's taken the bait. She made the date for tonight."

Murdock hesitated. "It's none of my business, but doesn't Moira have a lover?"

"Yes. She doesn't talk about her. I never ask."

"How does her lover feel about this date?"

"I don't know," Allison shrugged. "I don't mean to sound unsympathetic, but that's Moira's problem. When she took the assignment, she must have foreseen that this woman could come on to her. She's made of stern stuff. She'll handle it."

"I hope so," Murdock replied. "I worry about her sometimes."

Murdock refilled their coffee cups from a pot left on the table. Allison stirred in some rich Bavarian cream and added sugar. Murdock took his black. Allison finished her strudel. "Worry about Moira? Why?"

"Well," Murdock said, his head half-cocked, "I don't think she's happy in her love life. There's some complication. It's none of my business. She's a delightful person. She's the first — you know . . ."

"Lesbian?"

"Yeah. The first lesbian I've gotten to know well."

Allison looked at him directly. "Was it difficult for you to use the word?"

"Yeah, sort of. I like to think I'm broad-minded. Moira and I have worked well on cases together. But it's hard for me to get used to the idea of women doing — you know — to other women."

"But it's okay for men to — you know — to women?"

"Come on, Allison. I can't imagine someone as nice as Moira . . ."

Allison interrupted. "What's *nice* got to do with it?"

Murdock hesitated. He shook his head. "You're right, of course. A few years ago, I would never have imagined that you would defend homosexuality."

Allison's eyes met his. "I'm not defending it. I'm merely challenging your logic. But it does seem ironic that homosexuality is becoming 'accepted' in our culture, and yet we can criticize child prostitution in another's culture. We draw ever finer lines."

He finished his strudel without speaking. The waiter replaced the coffee pot and refilled their cups. Allison's held hers with both hands. Looking over the top of it, through the steam, she asked, "Shall we have a dark crème de cacao on the rocks?"

"But that was Karen's favorite after dinner drink," Murdock protested.

"Karen's dead," she said softly but firmly. She ordered the drinks. He offered no further protest.

*   *   *

Later, back in his room, Murdock picked up the phone and dialed the number for Rudi's hotel in Nicosia. The man who answered spoke serviceable English, and they were quickly connected. Murdock began to repeat Dr. Kohl's message, but Rudi interrupted. "Thank you for taking prompt action, Murdock. I just got off the phone with Commander Weiss. A guard is posted. Tomorrow, Angelika will be moved. Commander Weiss visited her an hour ago and thought she recognized him. She tried to smile. Murdock, is it possible? So many lonely nights. So many prayers. How wonderful if we could all be together again at the Zugspitze, skiing, and . . . Oh! I'm sorry. Karen . . ."

Murdock interrupted. "Karen will be with us in spirit. I believe that." He heard a sigh of relief.

"Then she will be," Rudi insisted. "After I meet with Colonel Constantine tomorrow morning at national police headquarters, I shall fly, rather than drive, to Limassol. That will save time getting home after I've finished. Needless to say, I'm anxious to see Angelika."

"Don't get your hopes too high, Rudi. Dr. Kohl didn't promise anything. Do you think you'll make it back by tomorrow night?"

"Probably Sunday morning."

They bid each other good night. Murdock looked up the phone number of Jerr's private line at the office and punched in the numbers. Jerr answered. "Good to hear from you, Murdock. What's happening?"

"Serious stuff, Jerr. I'll come directly to the point. There'll be a fax waiting for you when you get home. It's a copy of a document that Rudi received from the FBI in Washington."

"What is it?"

"It's an alert with more information to follow. It suggests that Enrique has been involved in unlawful sex with prepubescent girls in Thailand and the Philippines. It indicates that one girl's dead and infers that he was at fault."

"Are there warrants?"

"No warrants. In some parts of the world, anything can be bought. Did you know about this alert?"

There was a long silence. "Hold on. I'm tapping his name into my computer," Jerr said unemotionally. "No . . . I wasn't aware of it . . . It's coming up . . . Here it is . . . I'm still not . . . Nothing here I haven't seen before . . . Did you see the source code?"

"Yes. It's not from regular channels, Jerr. Higher level. Curious. Either someone in top management feels that Enrique is extremely dangerous, or . . ."

Jerr interrupted. "Or it comes from someone high enough to be authorized to furnish misinformation to a foreign police agency. I'm inclined to believe the latter. In either event, we need to know. I'll get on the phone to Carl as soon as we hang up. If it *is* the latter, it came from someone with a lot of power. You better believe they know you're working with Rudi, and that you've interviewed Enrique. We can assume there's some mighty big fish they're wanting to fry. Be careful. Make sure you're not one of them."

"I know," Murdock replied. "If I am, perhaps I should feel honored. It *does* make it interesting, doesn't it."

Jerr laughed. "You and I have always thrived on this crap. So, here we go again. Let's shake the frying pan, and the devil be damned. Can any two guys have more fun than we do?"

Murdock roared. "It beats sleeping in front of the television."

"After talking to you last time, I decided to find out who owns Veritus. I couldn't. It's closely held, so the stock record isn't available to the SEC. I called Veritus's headquarters in Chicago. They won't disclose the names of shareholders without a subpoena."

"And," Murdock interrupted, "you can't justify the subpoena because there's no ongoing investigation. Right?"

"Right. But I found out that there has been only one previous owner —a Howard G. Gregory. He lives in Des Moines. I called him, but he won't discuss anything over the phone. He wants to see my ID. I'm going to drive over there tomorrow. I've met somebody—a widow with a little boy. She's a nurse. I'll take them along for the ride."

Murdock laughed merrily. "So, you've finally met a woman with a portable career. Good for you. Does Allison know?"

"Not yet. I'll tell her if it gets more serious. I'd appreciate if you didn't mention it just yet."

"No problem, Jerr."

"Murdock, Allison and I will never get together again. We'll stay good friends. Don't turn your back on her for my sake. Everybody needs somebody to love. Karen's dead."

"You're the second person to remind me of that today. Believe me, there's no woman in the world that I admire more than Allison. I'm trying not to fall in love with her. She and I would have the same career problems that you and she did. It wouldn't work. The last thing in the world I would want to do is hurt her."

"What about Diana?"

"We're compatible. I expect to be seeing her much of next week, or at least that's the plan, unless the investigation takes an unexpected turn. She hosted Enrique for several days. She may have some insights that you don't have. In any event, she'll be back tomorrow. I'll talk to her."

"Is she pretty well-built, old buddy?"

"Like a sleek sailing ship. The cut of her jib is enchanting, especially by candlelight. But this call is costing me a fortune. I'll call you tomorrow, after I talk to her."

"Wait, Murdock. Could the FBI report have come from Joe Carlyle's office?"

"Yes, unless they've changed the source codes since I left."

"Carl thinks that Karen's death wasn't accidental. He hasn't been able to nail anything down, but he thinks that Joe may not have clean hands."

"That's not a reach, Jerr. I'll call you tomorrow, after you get back from Des Moines. Good night."

"Good night, Murdock. Be careful."

* * *

It was Friday afternoon. The professor had spent most of the last three days closeted in his room, his eyes glued to the computer display. Astonished by what he had seen, he had come to the conclusion that Martin had been mistaken, and that, as Murdock had suspected, the murder of Stephen had nothing to do with a codex or a web site, but with Stephen's new computer chip. However, the professor doubted that the perpetrator had fathomed the enormity of what Stephen had done. One thing became certain in the professor's mind: Martin must release him from his vow of secrecy before common sense compelled him to violate it. Murdock McCabe had to be told before anyone else had to die.

⌨ **32** ⌨

Friday night had cleared the streets of downtown Munich of most of the crowd. Moira looked out the window of her apartment. She had lived in Munich for three years, and had become accustomed to the nuances of Bavaria's capital. Bavaria was the most conservative state in Germany and the most Roman Catholic. Homosexuality was frowned upon by the vast majority of the population and by the government. Her apartment near the Gärtnerplatz, the center of what few gay bars there were in the city, was within walking distance of the Mädchenhaus Café. Shortly after she arrived in Munich, she had discovered the *Frauenzentrum*, the Women's Center, on the Güllstrasse. Lesbians gathered there on Friday evenings, but tonight she wouldn't be among them. She has a date with Patti Dale at the Mädchenhaus Café.

Moira lifted the phone and punched in a number. A woman's voice answered. "Ah, Kitten, I'm glad I caught you," Moira said. "How have you been?"

"Unhappy," the voice protested. I've not seen you, my love, for a week. I miss you terribly. Can you tell? Does the urgency in my voice give me away? Yes, of course it does. You always know. I'm empty without you. My husband is in Rotterdam. Are you free tonight? Is that why you called? Please say yes."

"I miss you too, Kitten. I've been in Stuttgart and Regensburg most of the week."

"Do you have friends there?"

"You are my only lover, Kitten."

"You're not free tonight, are you? I can tell by the tone of your voice."

"No, and tomorrow I must go to Zugspitze Hof Lodge, probably for several days."

"Does it have something to do with the monk who was murdered there? It's been in all the newspapers."

"Yes, but the lodge is full. I'll be staying in Garmisch. When will your husband be back? Could you meet me halfway tomorrow night?"

"You know I want to, my love, but it's politically dangerous. Are you working again tonight?"

"I'm working undercover in the Mädchenhaus Café. That's what I called to tell you."

"You've been on that assignment for several weeks. Who's your target?"

"I'm sorry, Kitten. I really can't say. It's confidential."

"Is it that woman Patti Dale?"

"I really can't say. I'm a professional. You know that."

"If it is, *do* be careful. She's well-connected in Washington, and she could be very dangerous."

"If I meet her, I'll be careful."

"She hangs out at the Mädchenhaus."

"Kitten, have you ever been in the Mädchenhaus?"

"No, dear. You know I can't. This person . . . This target . . . Will you have to make love to her? Is that part of your job?"

"No," Moira replied abruptly. "It's not part of my job. Do you take me for a whore?"

"I'm sorry. Please don't be angry, my love. It could happen anyway. You could be forced into it to avoid blowing your cover. I'm jealous of your time. I *need* some of it. Badly."

"Hasn't your husband been . . ."

"I don't need him. I need you. When will you be back? I know. When the killer of the monk is found. Okay. Foolish me. I'm a big girl. Work hard, dear. Get back as soon as you can. I ache for you."

"I shall, Kitten. Got to get dressed now. Love you. Bye."

"Bye."

At nine o'clock, when Moira entered the Mädchenhaus Café, there was standing room only. As she wormed her way toward the bar, the crowd pressed around her.

"Hi, Moira," one of the women said. "Want to dance?"

"Not now," she replied, giving the woman a friendly pat on the buns. "Maybe later."

The room was filled with cigarette smoke. Her eyes burned. She hated cigarette smoke. She and Patti were to meet at the bar. Her five-foot-four height didn't permit her to see the length of it. *There's too many people and too much smoke*. Then she saw her. Patti Dale was standing next to two empty stools with drinks in front of them, waving to her. Moira squeezed through the crowd and joined her. Patti was a tall woman, 5'10", with a slim figure, dark brown hair, fullish lips that gleamed red, and bluish hazel eyes. Her nails were long and painted purple to match her lipstick.

"Sit down," Patti invited cheerfully, as if she'd known her forever. "I bought the drink to hold the stool. You're right on time. I like that. Let me help you with your coat." She held Moira's coat as she slipped out of it. Patti hung it over the back of the bar stool. "Very nice. Expensive leather. Best to keep it here. That way you'll be sure it'll leave with you. How really nice of you to come. The drink is scotch and soda; if you want something else, just push it aside. I'm anxious to get to know you. How have you been?"

Moira seated herself and reached for the drink. *She comes on a little too strongly.* "I like scotch and soda." Moira took a sip. As she put the drink down, she felt Patti's hand on her thigh, moving confidently upward under her miniskirt. Moira grabbed her wrist. "Please. That feels good, but . . . maybe later." Patti, accepting the rules of engagement, withdrew her hand. Her sweet smile was totally unaffected.

"Good," Patti said. "You've passed the test. I don't like easy women. Do you?"

"Not hardly," Moira replied.

"Do you have a regular lover that I need to worry about?" Patti asked.

"Why should *you* worry? But, no. You have a right to know before you invest your time. She's gone back to her husband. You know — one of those recreational *femmes* who wants a taste of honey but doesn't like the buzzing in the hive."

"Yeah. One of those," Patti said, trying to sound sincere. "You're better off without her. So you're free. So am I. Good." Patti turned her head. "Bartender, a bit more nectar please."

"What are you drinking?" Moira asked.

"Club and soda."

Moira decided to test the theory that she'd discussed with Allison. "Do you have a regular, Patti?"

"No."

"Have you ever had one?"

"No. Not really."

"Have you ever had a woman?"

Moira noticed a subtle knee-jerk reaction, but pretended not to have. The answer was obvious. *Will she lie? Moira wondered.* Patti picked up her drink and took a long swallow. She studied the glass before she put it down. "Does it show?" Patti asked without looking at Moira.

"We needn't talk about that. We just need to find out whether you're ready now. But you're not sure, are you? Not certain that you like girls?"

She's faking. I'm almost certain of it. But why? Patti waited for

Moira to speak. Moira decided to push. "Do you have a husband or a boyfriend?"

Patti stared at the liquor bottles neatly arranged on a shelf in front of the mirror behind the bar. "No. Not anymore. I divorced two years ago," she said wanly. Since then, I haven't found a man that I'd want to be intimate with."

"Or a woman either?"

Patti half turned her head away from Moira. "No."

This is all bullshit, Moira thought, but she's a damn good actress. "It seems to me you need to make a decision," she said. "Do you prefer men or women? Of course, some women enjoy both. They enjoy sex, period. But two years without any sex is *not* healthy for anyone your age. I put you in your early thirties. Right?"

"Right. I'm sorry. I'm a little complicated, Moira. I'll understand if you want to sit with someone else."

Shrewd move. I'll play to it. "Not at all. I've watched you over the last few weeks. You were trolling like an overripe virgin waiting to be picked. There are dozens here tonight that would like the pick. Why me?" *The confrontation will make it look less like I'm on to her game.*

"That's a fair question. Most of the women in here have the sensitivity of vultures. I'm not looking for birds of prey. I've watched you. You're unassuming, patient, sensitive. You keep popping up in my fantasies. I've lived with nothing but fantasies for two years, but you excite the parts of me that need to be excited."

It sounded sincere. *She's had dramatic training.* "So, you've decided I'm the honeybee that may lead you to the hive?"

"I've decided to get to know you better," Patti replied.

Moira turned her head away and scanned the crowd. *She seems to be skillfully putting the make on me. Why lure me? Does she know I'm investigating her? She's a remarkably cool liar.* Patti tried to get the attention of the barmaid. *I'd better get to work, Moira decided.* "What do you do for a living, Patti?"

"I'm a librarian."

"Where?"

"In the English library at BMW."

We already know that's a lie. "How long have you worked there?"

"I get into heat when I sit next to you."

"Thank you. But let's not rush it. It may not happen. How long have your worked there?"

"I've worked there eighteen months. Why?"

"Just curious."

"Where do you work?"

"Veritus Investigations International."

"Really? That sounds exciting. What do you investigate?"

"Mostly insurance fraud. Have you heard of us?"

"I've heard the name. Is it a German company?"

As if she didn't know. "No, American. But we have offices world-wide. Our Munich office covers all of Bavaria and part of Baden-Württemberg."

A sterile grin crossed Patti's face. "It sounds fascinating. Please tell me all about it." Her folded hands were placed firmly on the bar. Moira thought that strange.

"I really can't say much," Moira replied. "My work is confidential. It's just ordinary gumshoe detective work. Nothing really special. Not very exciting, I'm afraid."

"It sounds exciting," Patti said, attempting to sound enthusiastic but not quite succeeding. "Very exciting," she added flatly. "Do you like sports?"

"Some."

"What's your favorite, Moira?"

Moira flashed a coquettish grin. "Need you ask? Why do you think I hang out here?" They both laughed awkwardly — Moira's awkwardness skillfully contrived. *She's not as good an actress as I first thought, or she doesn't consider me important enough to put on her best performance.*

The barmaid finally responded to Patti's signal. "May I buy you another drink?" Patti asked, reaching out her right hand and taking Moira's left in hers.

Moira decided to accelerate the pace. "Are you hitting on me?" she asked calmly. The same sterile grin crossed Patti's face. She caught herself. She curled her lips into a most engaging smile. Moira noticed the change. *She's just upgraded the performance.*

"Yes," Patti replied. "Is that okay? Like you said — I'd be like a virgin girl. You could bring me up the way you want me."

Moira pulled her hand from underneath Patti's. "Yeah," she said. "I'll have that other drink."

The bar was U-shaped. They were seated in the outside belly of the U. All the bar stools were occupied. A four-piece, all-woman band, showing off the power of its amplifiers, made conversation difficult. Diagonally across the U, on Moira's left, she noticed two women, both with green hair, engaging in animated conversation, their handbags next to each other on the bar. Suddenly one left.

"Did you see that?" Moira asked.

"What?"

"The two with the green hair. One left and took the other's hand-bag."

Patti grasped Moira's upper arm, gently. "It's best not to notice such things here."

"I can guess several scenarios. My curiosity would like to know which is correct. Do you know?"

"They're all correct. Leave it there."

Moira raised her glass. Out of the corner of her eye she saw an older woman subtly slip a note to Patti without stopping to speak. Patti made no effort to look at it. It disappeared into a pocket of her dress.

"Please excuse me," Patti said. "I need the rest room. Unless you'd like to come with me."

"Thank you, but no," Moira replied. "I use it as little as possible. I hate to disturb people. I'll hold our seats."

"Personally, I've learned a lot in *that* rest room. Most of the girls aren't disturbed. They hardly notice you're there." Patti slipped off the bar stool and edged her way through the crowd. The barmaid returned with two more drinks. She leaned over toward Moira. "I hope you know what you're doing, honey," she said. "Word's out . . . don't touch . . . she's straight . . . might be a cop. Be careful. Dump the bitch and circu-late."

"Thanks," Moira replied. "I appreciate your warning. I'll play it carefully and try to find out for you."

"Your funeral, honey."

Moira locked her heels in the rungs of the bar stool and raised her-self so she could see over the crowd. Patti wasn't in the rest room. She was in a telephone booth.

*   *   *

Earlier in the day Terry had received a call from Patti Dale. Now he was sitting in his apartment waiting for her to call again. His instructions from Harvey had been twofold — to assist her and to inform him. At 8:00 P.M. an envelope had been slipped under the door of his apartment. In-structions on the outside directed him not to open it until Patti called again. It was nearly 9:30. The phone rang. It was Patti Dale. Without pleasantries, she came directly to the point.

"Have you received an envelope?" she asked.

"Yes."

"There are five hundred German marks in it. If you answer some questions for me, you can keep it. Do you understand?"

"Yes. What questions?"

"Is Moira Zawadska investigating me?"

Terry hesitated. *How do I know this is Patti Dale's voice?* He opened the envelope. Inside was a crisp, new five hundred mark note. *This is the real thing. Does it make any difference whose voice it is?* "I'm familiar with all of our investigation files. I haven't seen one with your name on it. Do you go by some other name?"

"Don't get cute with me you little prick, or I'll send someone over there to retrieve the money and crush your balls. Could there be a hidden file? One you wouldn't know about? Do they ever do that?"

"Well . . ."

"Well bullshit. Give me a damn answer."

There was an incisiveness in her voice that made his vocal cords knot. *She's dangerous.* He stammered, "I've never been aware of one, but I suppose it's not impossible."

"So it's probable. Don't be condescending with me. Who ordered it? And don't tell me you don't know. Jerks like you poke their dirty little noses into everything. Lie to me and I'll have your balls cut off. Do you understand me? Answer yes or no."

"Yes, I understand you." *Big talk, but I'd better not take chances. Besides, I can use five hundred marks.* "If there *is* such an investigation, and I'm not saying that there is, I imagine that it would have been ordered by Harvey Specter."

"Why is he interested in me?"

"I don't know that he is."

"I know that you're acting stupid," Patti declared angrily. "Bozos like you always know. There's more money where that came from."

"At least I didn't know until this afternoon. I think that, if Moira is investigating you . . ."

"Cut the *if* shit."

"Harvey has a friend who is a high echelon administrator in the FBI in Washington."

"Come on. Don't be cute. This bigwig has a name, doesn't he?"

"Harvey mentioned the name Joe."

"That son of a bitch," she said. "Keep the money." Click.

*   *   *

Near midnight Moira and Patti left the Mädchenhaus. The cold, clear air was a relief from cigarette smoke augmented by noxious cigars. No other pedestrians were in sight. Walking arm in arm without speaking, they turned onto the Oberanger Strasse, strolled past the city museum, and turned up the narrow Wiederstrasse, which led to Moira's apartment. Bitterly cold, a light, dry snow was falling. There was no traffic. The only light, a lonely street lamp, shown far ahead at the next corner. The only sound was the squeaking of the new snow under their boots. Intermittent gusts of wind swirled down the S-curves of the lonely street and prompted them to increase their pace. Three-story apartment buildings stood on either side of the narrow street. When they reached Moira's building, Patti turned into the doorway without Moira identifying it. Moira's apartment was on the top floor of a three-floor walk-up. The stairway and the halls were cold and barely lighted. Patti walked directly to Moira's door, as if she had been there before. Moira fumbled for the key. She had preferred coming to her apartment rather than Patti's because she felt she would have more control. Once inside the room, the powdered snow on their coats began to melt. They draped them over the backs of chairs to dry. Two stuffed chairs and an end table formed a semi-circle around a fireplace.

"Would you like a drink?" Moira asked.

"You know what I want," Patti answered, her eyes like narrow slits.

"Be patient. There's time for that — if things work out." Moira reached for matches on top the mantel, kneeled in front of the gas logs, lit them, and carefully adjusted the flame. The additional heat was welcome. "I'm going to have hot cocoa," she said. "Would you like some?" As she arose and turned toward the kitchen, out of the corner of her eye she noticed Patti's panty hose in a heap on the floor. Moira decided to ignore it, but Patti wouldn't be ignored. She grabbed Moira's left arm, pulled her off balance. Moira fell toward her, landing hard on her knees. "This isn't the way it's done," Moira protested, getting back onto her feet. Patti grabbed Moira's dress with both hands, pulling her off balance again.

"Don't tear," Moira protested. "Be patient. It's more fun. Dresses are expensive. Let me help." She loosened her belt, unbuttoned the top, and allowed the dress to drop to the floor. Patti grabbed the hem of Moira's slip, lifted it over her head, and yanked it as Moira withdrew out of it.

"Take the rest off," Patti commanded.

"Not so fast. Let me teach you how it's done. There's fun in the anticipation."

Patti snatched her brassiere and yanked. It stretched but didn't tear. "Wait," Moira pleaded. She reached behind, fumbled for the clasp, and unhooked as Patti violently pulled it off. *I'm going to have to go farther than I wanted.* Patti pointed to her panties. Moira dropped them and stepped out. Patti lifted her dress up to her navel, and sat down on the edge of a chair.

"Please," she said. "I've waited for a long time. I can't wait anymore.

"Why me? Why did you wait for me?"

"Not now. Love me first. Orally. Please. I've dreamed about it. Please, for God's sake, I've got to have it."

"I'm not into it," Moira responded. "It won't be much fun for me."

"Do it. I'll make it up to you. You can show me how."

Moira reluctantly knelt before Patti. Patti took Moira by the hair and drew her between her knees. *Everything's happening too fast. It's getting out of control.* "Stop that," she protested, but Patti grabbed her head firmly with both hands, and pulled her off balance. Patti was strong. Before Moira could recover her balance, her face was between Patti's thighs and Patti's legs were wrapped around her head. They were powerful legs. Moira grasped Patti's thighs with all her strength, but she couldn't pull them apart. *She's strong as a man. Maybe she's a man in drag*, but that thought melted into oblivion as her face was forced into the evidence to the contrary. She couldn't breathe. Struggling for air, she fought to pull Patti's legs apart, dug her nails into Patti's calves, then frantically, desperately grasped both of Patti's wrists. They were cupped around the back of Moira's head, locking her in. Patti was too strong — her grip like a vice. She mustered all her strength, attempted to break Patti's grip, but the effort used the oxygen her brain needed. Her body fell limp. Patti released her, and Moira slumped onto the floor unconscious.

When Moira awoke, she half rose and sat on her heels, still dazed, her disheveled hair dangling in front of her eyes. She vomited. Across the room, in the full-length mirror, she saw her naked body with vomit running down her chin and her belly. She felt utterly vulnerable. Her eyes began to focus through the black dots that swam in front of them. Rage gripped her. Patti was standing near the dresser, fully clothed, her feet wide apart. As Moira's sense of balance returned, she eased herself to her feet, staggered for a few steps, and then lunged at Patti. With the butt end of an automatic pistol, Patti struck a brutal blow across the side of Moira's head. Again Moira fell to her hands and knees. The black dots returned with a dizzying vengeance. Patti calmly walked over to the closet, opened the double doors, extracted a robe, and threw it to Moira. It fell in front of her. Still dazed from the blow, she struggled to focus her eyes. Sitting on the floor, she picked up the robe, held it in front of herself, and then threw it down in disgust. She had nothing left to hide. "You bitch," she screamed. "You could have killed me. What the hell's the matter with you? Are you some sort of sadomasochist?"

A pernicious smile crept across Patti's face. "I, or my organization, can *still* kill you . . . any time we want. By now you should have learned that your life means no more than a piece of dirt to me, you little pussy-loving queer. Don't you forget that. Ever. You're alive because I let you live. I can use you. You needn't report what happened here tonight to the Bavarian police. They don't like little pussy-loving queers. They'll figure you got what you deserved."

Moira moved to get on her feet."

"Stay there, naked little bitch. Sit in your slop."

Moira moved to get up.

Patti pointed the gun. "I enjoy using this pistol. Come at me again and I'll prove it. Is that clear?"

Moira nodded.

"Your investigation of me is finished — I repeat, finished. In this envelope is the final report you will present to Harvey Specter. Sign it."

Patti threw the envelope at her. It fell close to Moira's knees. A ball-point pen was clipped to the envelope. Moira extracted the document and began to read it.

Patti snarled, "I didn't tell you to read it; sign it, damn it."

Moira signed and tossed it to Patti's feet. Patti picked it up and sealed the envelope. "I'll see that Terry processes this through to Harvey Specter. I'm leaving this copy on your bed. But you and I aren't finished. There are a few things you need to understand if you want to stay alive."

Moira, still sitting on the carpet, took a handkerchief from the pocket of the robe and cleaned her chin. The investigator in her reawakened. "You spoke of your organization. Does it have a name?"

Patti smiled sardonically. "Traction. Have you heard of it?"

"No. What's it got to do with me?"

"All you need to know now is what *I've* got to do with you. I'm going to talk, and you're going to listen carefully, you little bitch queer. In the envelope on your dresser, there are one thousand American dollars in cash. It's yours."

"I'm not a whore," Moira protested. "Keep your money."

"I said *listen*. Keep your mouth shut. I don't pay for sex. I pay for information. There are three bits of information I want you to acquire for me. For each of them, you will receive another five hundred American dollars. If you acquire the information and decide not to give it to me, your life won't be worth shit. There's nowhere in the world you can hide. You don't know what terror is until Traction decides to teach you. You just had a taste of it. Did you enjoy it?"

Moira glared at her.

"No? I'm so sorry. I've heard that some women like hard sex. Too bad. One other thing you need to remember — we're protected by people in high places. Our association with you probably won't last long. I hear that you're a practical bitch. Just do what you have to and you'll have money to spend. After this assignment, you may never hear from us again. But do not — and I repeat — do not *ever* tell anyone about us or about what happened tonight. Am I making myself clear?"

"Abundantly. What do you want?"

"I understand that you are going to be involved in an investigation at the Zugspitze Hof Lodge. It involves the death of a monk. One of your people, Murdock McCabe, is working closely with the state police. He's in their confidence. He knows what they know. There's a monk named Brother Antonio. I want to know where he is. That's number one. The second is this: When the investigation focuses on one person, I want to know immediately who that person is. Both assignments are simple. Do you understand them?"

"Yes. What's the third?"

"For this one you will receive five thousand American dollars. Karen McCabe had several notebooks, which she used in her cryptography. I don't know whether they're hard copy or on disk. I want them. Is that clear?"

"Why do you want them?"

Patti walked over to her and struck her again across the face, knocking her sideways onto the floor, and kicked her hard in the right breast. "My question was 'Is that clear?' "

Moira grabbed herself, rolled over onto her stomach, and writhed in pain.

Patti tried to kick her in the crotch, but Moira rolled and took the force in the buttocks.

"I haven't heard the answer yet," Patti said calmly.

"Yes. It's clear. How will I contact you?"

Patti squatted down next to Moira, the gun pointed at Moira's head. "Remember two more things. First, don't ever call me bitch again. Second, *you're* the pussy-licking bitch." She put the barrel of the gun against Moira's skull. "Can you remember those?"

"Yes."

"I'll give you credit, little bitch. You don't cry. When you obtain the information I want, you will leave a message with Terry at Veritus."

Moira turned her head toward Patti. Patti pulled the gun away. "Is Terry a member of your organization?"

Patti laughed. "No, he's just a jerk who's been ordered to assist me. In his dirty mind he'll figure you and I are lovers. Give him a telephone number where you can be reached at 6:00 A.M. each day. You be at that number. Is that clear?"

"Yes."

"In a short time this'll all be over. Let me summarize." Patti spoke in a clipped manner. "Do what you're told. You'll make a few bucks.

Cross us and you're dead. Remember tonight. It's not that difficult to kill you whenever we want to. That's all you need to know. You're smart. Figure out how to get all of this done."

Moira's eyes met Patti's. "May I ask one question?"

"What?"

"If you're paying me thousands of dollars, why was all this brutality necessary?"

"For money alone, you wouldn't betray your friends." Patti put the pistol in her shoulder bag, turned, and walked out of the apartment, leaving the door open behind her. Moira picked herself up off the floor, ran over and closed the door, double locking it. The clock indicated that Friday had slipped into Saturday. She was shivering. The thermostat read 76°. Resetting it to 80°, she walked over to the dresser, picked up the envelope, and opened it. It contained the promised report, and ten crisp, new, American one hundred dollar bills.

Saturday
November 22

⊰ 33 ⊱

The trip to the monastery had been bone-chilling, but inside the conference room, the coffee was steaming hot, and the cakes irresistible. Murdock chose two as Brother Martin poured.

"Black?" Martin asked.

"Yes," Murdock responded.

Martin turned toward the professor. "And you prefer to mix your own, so please help yourself."

"Thank you," the professor replied.

The conference room was chilly. Martin adjusted the thermostat. For several minutes no one spoke. They ate their cakes and savored the rich Colombian coffee. Then, turning to Murdock, Brother Martin broke the silence.

"Today, we must be candid." He looked toward the professor, who nodded in agreement. "First, do you have any questions from our last conversation?"

"Yes," Murdock replied. "You criticized the 'Q' theologians for their circular reasoning. What exactly did you mean?"

Martin extracted a pipe from the drawer of the side table, casually filled it with tobacco, and lit it. Murdock hadn't seen him smoke before. Martin settled back into his chair. A pleasant vanilla aroma drifted across the room. "Imagine," Martin began, "a nine-year-old girl who has no recollection of having been sexually abused by her parents. To some psychologists, that fact suggests that the abuse was so horrible that she's suffering from suppressed memory. So, because she was obviously abused, the psychologists force her to remember, to implant the memory that may never have been there, and in turn prosecute the 'guilty' parents on the basis of her now anguished testimony. That's circular reasoning — the same type of reasoning by which 'Q' is justified. Because Matthew, Mark, and Luke are similar, the 'Q' theologians deduce that they must have been drawn from a common document now lost. By comparing their similarities, they reconstructed the so-called missing source document. Having done so, they used the deduced document as the authority by which they discovered the 'true' Jesus."

"I understand," Murdock replied. "Let's move on. I'm not convinced that either 'Q' or the web site had anything to do with Stephen's murder."

Martin deposited his pipe in an ashtray. "The professor and I come from different poles — I am a man of God — he professes to be an atheist."

The professor corrected him. "I *am* an atheist. And my being an atheist does not detract from a concern that Martin and I share." The professor turned toward Brother Martin who was relighting his pipe. Martin and the professor again exchanged glances. Martin began.

"We propose, under certain conditions, to share with you information about a highly confidential project, which engaged Brother Stephen at the time of his death — the project that prompted Stephen to join our monastic order in the first place. We did not share this information with you earlier in the week for two reasons. First, I didn't believe it could be a motive for Stephen's murder because it was known to so few people. Secondly, disclosure of Stephen's results would be no less than earthshaking. We think you are a man with an open mind and a pure heart who can serve as an honest broker between us and the authorities. We want Stephen's killer caught. If Stephen's work *does* turn out to be the motive for the crime, then the secret is out. *If* it's out, we need your help to discover whether what's out is accurate. Are you willing to be our intermediary, and our fact finder?"

"But you barely know me," Murdock protested. "Why do you gamble so much on a five-day acquaintance?"

The professor arose, resolutely walked over to the coffee urn and refilled his cup. "I confess that Martin knows more about you than I do," he said. "We both know that you have the absolute confidence of Rudi Benzinger, who is close to the top of the Bavarian State Police. We know that the state justice minister has granted you immunity which, under certain circumstances, permits you to hold back information from the police. We are prepared to disclose certain information to you if you agree not to disclose it to anyone — including the authorities — unless it is absolutely necessary for the administration of justice. And, if you decide that it is, you will warn us one hour prior to disclosure."

"May I discuss this information with my supervisor, Allison Spencer?"

Martin and the professor again exchanged glances. The professor spoke. "We trust her, but for her safety I would suggest that you don't."

The professor walked to the picture window and glanced out. Below him lay the Liederbach meadow where the body of Brother Stephen had been found only five days earlier. He shuddered to think of the immense burden they were prepared to place on Murdock McCabe. He sighed. "I shall try not to be esoteric. When you and I spoke over a few beers, I complained about junk science. The monks here at St. Luke's are true scientists. Their work is not eclipsed by someone's political agenda. Individually, over the last few days, Martin and I have discussed with you some rather basic stuff, like, for example, the question of whether God exists. We disagree about the answer. But Martin is not ignorant of science nor am I ignorant of religion. We do have common ground. We both agree, for example, that the superstring theory is plausible. Let's postulate that superstrings, which we talked about yesterday, exist in the tenth or twenty-sixth dimension. Humans can only see things that have two or three dimensions. It's logical that unseen things could exist in many dimensions. But, if they do, what exactly are they? We can barely comprehend the possibilities. Are there *things* that transport intelligence from place to place in the universe faster than the speed of light? Are these *things* the elusive communicators between the quarks and leptons that give them mass? And if they are, where did the intelligence they communicate come from? Is the source of this intelligence some mysterious eternal essence? Some god?"

Murdock shifted his weight so that he sat upright. He had recently read a magazine article that speculated that angels existed in the twenty-sixth dimension. He had thought the idea as being rather ridiculous. It seemed to him that these men were telling him nothing that might bring him closer to solving the murder of Brother Stephen. *What's their game?*

Martin, who had stood up and was pacing back and forth, interrupted. "Some of the superstring theorists postulate the existence of a shadow world and come close to acknowledging a form of life after death, where the fifth dimension is spirit-like, and where one's spirit continues to exist in some nonmaterial form. Personally, I don't believe in death."

Murdock interrupted. "Just a minute." He arose from the chair and walked slowly to the window as the other two men waited in silence. Murdock, deep in thought, looked outside at the mountain. He turned and faced them. "Brother Martin," he said. "Does the word *death* mean *nothing* to you?"

"Depending upon how you define it, there remains a whole prairie of ideas the word can express."

"How would you define it?"

Martin smiled. "Death is the step beyond bewilderment."

For what seemed several minutes to Murdock, no one spoke. He felt uncomfortable. These subjects were interesting, but he was an investigator, and this conversation, although interesting, seemed to be taking him nowhere.

The professor broke the silence. "We are talking about eternal paradoxes: Where did the universe come from? What caused the Big Bang? What, if anything, existed before the Big Bang and how can we know it? What, if anything, is matter? Answers to these questions have eluded scholars since antiquity. The easiest way to obtain answers is to ask someone who already knows."

Murdock shook his head. "If these answers have eluded everyone, whom can you ask?"

The professor squirmed in his chair. His eyes met Brother Martin's. Martin gave an affirmative nod. "When I was a boy, I read Flash Gordon comic books, which contained stories about men and women orbiting the Earth and going to the Moon. They were considered science fiction. Now men and women have done both. Today's science fiction becomes tomorrow's cliché. It would've been more accurate for me to have said, 'Ask a person from another planet who knows.' "

Murdock starred at him blankly, his mouth slightly open.

The professor continued. "There are billions of galaxies. Our Milky Way is just one of them. It alone contains over 100 billion stars. A few hundred of them are within 100 light years, close enough to the Earth that they are within range of our present technology's detection. Since 1995 astronomers have identified several planets, each revolving around stars other than our Sun. In addition to looking through optical telescopes, we've been listening. Since the 1960s, radio astronomers have directed antennas toward space, trying to detect some intelligent signal. All they've heard is interstellar chaos."

Murdock, his feet wide apart and his eyes locked on the professor's, confronted him. Pointing out the window and toward the heavens, Murdock demanded: "Come to the point, man. Who's out there. Who have you talked to?"

The professor stared out the picture window, pensively. Avoiding Murdock's glance, he answered, "*I* have talked to no one." The professor turned to face Murdock directly. "Look," he said, "there must be billions upon billions of exoplanets — planets revolving around other stars. Intelligent beings must exist on millions of them, and some of them must be more advanced than we are. If we could ask them about superstrings and life in other dimensions, they might be shocked that we don't know the answers to such simple questions." The professor shrugged. "I believe that nature obscures truth. It hides simplicity in a thicket of complicating circumstances. Out there," he said pointing out the window toward the sky, "beings may exist who have learned conclusively that God is nothing more than wishful thinking." He looked toward Brother Martin and smiled. "I'd like to think I was right about that."

Brother Martin interrupted. "Or they may have learned that God created the superstrings. And if, on planets in other solar systems, they had a Jesus, was he the Christ of the gospels or the wandering sage of 'Q'? You see, Murdock, the professor and I both search for truth, but we begin with a different bias. I firmly believe that intelligent beings exist in other dimensions, perhaps even in the dimension we call *death*."

Murdock arose and joined the professor at the window. A light snow was falling. "But," he said, "whether or not God or superstrings exist, Brother Stephen is still dead." He turned and glanced at Brother Martin. "At least the police consider him dead, even though you don't believe in death. And, we're looking for a killer who made him dead. Are you telling me that this computer chip will make it possible to communicate with the dead — that Brother Stephen will tell us who killed him?"

Brother Martin shook his head and frowned. "No," he said. "I don't believe it will ever be possible to speak with those that you regard as dead. What we're telling you is that Brother Stephen found a way to communicate with people on planets in other solar systems."

Murdock glanced at the professor. He nodded in agreement. Murdock fell silent. He had read several magazine articles about SETI — the search for extraterrestrial intelligence. He was aware that, for years, scientists have used huge radio telescopes at Arecibo, Puerto Rico, and others, to search the heavens at every conceivable frequency, trying to find some evidence of intelligent life elsewhere in the universe. They had found chaotic noise. As a young boy, like many young boys, he had read stories about fictional people who lived on planets outside our solar system. He had dreamed of contacting them and becoming their friend. Ironically, when fiction turns into fact, naiveté often is replaced by alarm. Murdock squirmed. "If you're telling me that Brother Stephen succeeded where hundreds of scientists have failed, please tell me what he did that was different."

The professor and Brother Martin exchanged glances again. The professor responded. "A few years ago, while using the Arecibo radio telescope on Puerto Rico, Stephen detected what he believed was something other than the usual chaotic static. But this vague lack of randomness was not detected by his colleagues. They heard only the incessant crackling of static — essentially noise. Stephen's project took off on pure intuition — the fallopian tube in which most true science is conceived. Stephen recorded several hours of what his colleagues concluded was chaos. Here, at the monastery, he listened to those sounds daily for over a year. He told me that, from the beginning, he had been haunted by a hint of pattern." The professor glanced at Brother Martin, who again nodded his head. The professor continued. "He was listening for the same thing all

SETI scientists listen for—cosmos, something orderly, some distinguishable harmony, some sign that somebody out there was trying to communicate, something other than chaos. Please understand that the technical part of this is over Martin's head and mine. I can't give you an erudite exposition, so I'll put it simply."

"Thank you."

"One day it struck Stephen that these 'other than random sounds' might be some sort of digital bonks. Maybe they were communicating using a very sophisticated method so that their message could only be received by dedicated equipment. He speculated that their transmissions might be rapidly shifting frequencies over a wide spectrum, perhaps every three or four nanoseconds, in a predetermined pattern. Or Stephen thought they might use nonlinear dynamics, or possibly a quantum pattern, if that term is not self-contradicting."

"I'm sorry," Murdock interrupted. "You've lost me. I know that a nanosecond is one billionth of a second, but what do you mean by dedicated receiver, nonlinear dynamics, and a quantum pattern?"

"A dedicated receiver would be one built to receive only a particular sequence of frequencies. By nonlinear dynamics, Stephen referred to frequency sequences that are illogical or complex yet capable of conveying meaning. Quantum pattern suggests that the transmitted signals are not radiated continuously or predictably. He reasoned that they may be discontinuous in multiples of definite, indivisible units, which he called quanta. Stephen favored the first. He believed that extraterrestrials were sending messages using a predetermined sequence of frequencies. His friend, Michael, favored the second—the quantum solution. But, either way, Stephen reasoned that intelligence encased in rapidly fluctuating frequencies would he heard as noise unless it could be decoded."

Murdock raised an eyebrow. "If extraterrestrials are searching for life and want to communicate with us, why would they make it nearly impossible to recognize their transmissions? Does that seem logical?"

The professor turned and leaned his back against the windowsill. "Possibly they're communicating among themselves, and they have not intended their transmissions for our ears."

Murdock knew enough about computers to realize that sorting out such transmissions would be a daunting task. He had heard of no computer capable of speeds fast enough to search all of the possible trillions of frequency fluctuation combinations and complete it in our lifetime. What these men were telling him was incredible. Murdock shook his head without speaking. If someone with political experience knew the purpose of Stephen's chip, murder would be a mere stepping stone. He had arrested men who had killed for much less. He needed to assess the probability of this being the motive for Stephen's murder. "I know precious little about such things," he said, "but wouldn't it be a super hassle to build a receiver that could decode random fluctuations of frequency? Wouldn't it require a super computer? I read recently that it would take today's best computer five years to factorize the number 15. In my humble understanding of mathematics, that simply means finding the number that you can divide into fifteen and come up with a whole number. If that would take five years, it seems to me that it would take more than one lifetime to find the right frequency sequences in the billions upon billions of probabilities, and, if they use quantum fluctuations, it would seem impossible." Murdock paused and shrugged. "I could use one of your cigars, professor." The professor removed another from his inside pocket, unwrapped it, and gave it to Murdock who put it in his mouth without lighting it.

The professor began pacing. "To appreciate what we're talking about," the professor began, "you need to have some appreciation of the problems of building a quantum computer."

Murdock assumed that another lecture was imminent, so he lit the cigar, sat back and relaxed, and attempted a smoke ring. It fractured. "By *quantum* do you mean one that can deal with nonlinear dynamics, as you put it?"

"That's close."

"Fire away," Murdock said.

"Stephen knew that a quantum computer would totally revolutionize computing. From the day he arrived at St. Luke's three years ago, he dedicated part of his day, along with his wealth, to the development of a super computer central processing chip. The present digital computers process one bit of information at a time. Granted, they do it very quickly. A quantum computer would perform parallel functions — do several things simultaneously. When you get down to the basics, a computer is just a bunch of switches. At any given nanosecond, each switch is either on or off — either it has about five volts on it or it doesn't. We call the voltage *one* and the lack of voltage *zero*. So, the most complicated computer in existence today uses only two numbers — one and zero. Every switch — or we could say each bit — is set at one or zero at any given beat of the internal clock. Each bit in a quantum computer, as I understand it, would not be set at one or zero, but floating at changing combinations of ones and zeros. That is a rather dynamic environment. It'd be like information floating across erratic waves rather than traveling cleanly across a hard, smooth surface. Such a computer might factorize fifteen in hours rather than five years."

"What prevents the building of such a computer?" Murdock asked.

The professor seated himself next to Murdock and deposited his cigar in an empty water glass sitting on the side table. He leaned toward him, his elbow on the arm of the chair. He spoke in a slow, firm voice. "Two things that I know of, and there is much I don't know of. This isn't my specialty. First, computers make mistakes. Sometimes a switch doesn't set correctly. That could screw up everything, so every computer has an error-correcting code. Each bit is copied twice. 0 becomes 00 and 000. If one of these disagrees with the others, it is immediately and automatically corrected. But correcting in a quantum environment is daunting. The circuits needed would be extremely complex. From my limited knowledge, it seems to me that there would need to be thousands of comparisons for each bit, and I'm not even certain that there would be a *right* answer — maybe only a *probably right* answer. And that's only the first of the two problems. The second is the question of what material can be used that would inflect its voltage fast enough? The speed by which present technology can change from one to zero, or vice versa, is too slow. Physicists are considering beryllium ions. They can change states at a speed almost too fast to measure. When cooled to -273° C, which is one degree above absolute zero, that ion has only the two energy levels that a computer needs. Ions are atoms with one or more missing electrons."

Murdock turned again and peered out the window. The man of God and the atheist were seated behind him. The scattered light snow showers were increasing in intensity. Downslope the deep woods devoured their whiteness into the mysterious cavity of its darkness. A steel gray sky roofed the visible world for as far as the eye could see. A chill ran down his spine. His world had just become infinitely smaller. "Are you telling me," Murdock asked, "that Brother Stephen had developed a quantum computer?"

"He developed a truly remarkable central processing chip," Brother Martin replied, "that included integrated parallel memory units. This chip processes information one thousand times faster than any other. I don't understand how. From what Stephen told me, I believe that it will lead to the greatest acceleration of scientific discovery since the beginning of the world."

"So," Murdock interrupted, "Stephen's chip cut through the chaos and decoded a frequency fluctuation pattern, and he communicated with extraterrestrials. Why are you keeping that a secret?"

The professor shook his head. "I'm not convinced that it's accurate to say that he *communicated with them*. He believed that he did. I am studying Stephen's journals. They are eclectic and difficult, but from what I've read thus far, I'm convinced that he had intercepted an intelligent signal that was not transmitted from Earth. Nor was it a message directed *to* Earth, but a communication among themselves. Using what

Stephen called 'their frequency base variants,' Stephen directed a signal to them. The result was portentous."

The professor paused. Murdock studied the faces of both men. Brother Martin, his face a closed book, looking out the window, his stare focused on the downslope toward the Liederbach Meadow where Brother Stephen's body had been discovered. The professor stood by the fireplace, his hands folded behind him, his expression froze. Murdock decided not to interrupt the flow. The professor broke the silence.

"Have you ever observed a circle of people chatting at a party, only to have the conversation abruptly stop when you joined them?"

"Is that what happened?" Murdock asked.

The professor unfolded his hands, reached into the pocket of his sport coat, extracted another cigar, and lit it. "Stephen records that he did not hear the signals again. He was murdered five days later." The professor seated himself and blew several smoke rings. A wan smile crossed his face, and he shrugged. "You must understand the implications of their silence. Assume *their* planet orbits Proxima Centauri, which is the nearest star to us other than our Sun. It's about four light-years away. That's about 23 million-million miles. If Stephen transmitted a 'good morning' to them on radio waves traveling at the speed of light, it would take four years to arrive at their receiver and another four years for their response to reach our receiver. And, so far, we haven't found planets that close."

Murdock walked over to the window and stood there, his feet wide apart, his back to the other men. The professor arose and joined him. A golden eagle soared on an updraft, which lifted its elegant body toward the summit of the Zugspitze. Their eyes followed it as Murdock spoke. "Can we look through a telescope and see the surface of an exoplanet, like we can Mars and Jupiter?"

The professor smiled. "No. It'd be too far away. We couldn't build a telescope large enough. The only way we'll see the surface of an exoplanet would be to establish radio communication with one that has intelligent life, and have them fax us a picture."

Brother Martin's eyes brightened. "But think of it," he said. "If our radio telescopes can reach far enough into space, we may detect the beguiling echo of Creation."

That thought fascinated Murdock, but a more sinister idea occurred to him. "So," he said, "if Stephen's message had already been received by extraterrestrials, they would be close, maybe traveling toward Earth, perhaps within the boundary of our solar system. If their conversation stopped when they learned they had been discovered, it could mean . . ."

"That they are not scientists," the professor interrupted, "but military, and a threat . . ."

"Or," Murdock suggested, "they had to report the contact to some higher authority before acknowledging."

The professor laid his hand on Murdock's shoulder. "I'm merely postulating. Stephen didn't know why the signals stopped. Several questions are raised. Have they developed some form of propulsion — maybe gravity/antigravity — that permits them to travel at a speed near or even beyond the speed of light? *If* space is truly curved, have they found a way to cut the curves and alter distances — do they perceive space in contours totally unimagined by us?"

A thought struck Murdock. "How could Stephen communicate if he didn't know their language?"

"He could transmit mathematical equations that they would recognize."

Murdock pressed. "The time required for Stephen's message to get to them and their answer to get back — would that tell us how far away they are?"

"Not necessarily. We'd have no way of knowing whether they responded immediately. It would only tell us how far away they aren't."

"Did Michael give Stephen the frequency sequences?"

The professor frowned. "How could he know them if they're dynamic?"

Murdock watched the professor's expression. "Detective Georg Brüner asked you whether you thought Michael was an extraterrestrial. You thought not. So you told him. What do you honestly think?"

The professor's expression turned to one of extreme irritation. "I don't give dishonest answers," he said curtly.

"Forgive me. I put it poorly. Have you changed your mind?"

"No. I don't believe he's a being from another planet."

"Are both of you convinced," Murdock repeated, "that Stephen has communicated with extraterrestrials?"

Brother Martin appeared mildly irritated. "Yes," he insisted, "but even if Stephen were wrong, error believed in is truth in effect. I'm fully aware that if someone believes that Stephen had priceless information, that belief alone could be sufficient reason to kill, but I'm *not* convinced that the veil of secrecy has been broken. I can't imagine who would have broken it. I acknowledge that rumors abound in regard to our work at St. Luke's, but, I reiterate, the outside world only knew that Stephen was working on the web site, and I assume someone wanted to stop that."

"That seems very unlikely," Murdock said. He felt a sudden chill. He walked across the room to the fireplace. "Why keep it a secret? Shouldn't you tell the whole world, now?" Murdock asked.

Brother Martin arose and joined Murdock at the fireplace. They stood side by side, facing the professor who was pouring himself another cup of hot coffee. Martin broke the silence. "Before we broadcast the news of Stephen's work, we need to learn to deal with the extraterrestrials so that we may prepare our world."

Murdock studied both men. "You're both fearful. What is it that you fear?"

The professor shrugged.

Brother Martin began to pace, nervously dragging on his pipe, smoke trailing behind him. He took the pipe out of his mouth and laid it in an ashtray on an end table. "Let's think aloud," he began. "What is myth in one world might be fact in another. What is religion in one world might be sham in another. What if contact with an advanced civilization proved beyond doubt that only one of the religions of our world was true?"

"Or none of them," the professor injected.

"Think about the political impact," Martin continued. "There are politicians who use religion to control people, or to divide them, and even to justify killing them. Look at the Middle East or Northern Ireland. Think about ordinary people who deal with the traumas of life by looking to religion to make some sense of it all . . . often for some reason to continue living. What if they suddenly lost that comfort? Or suppose Christ has revealed Himself on several planets."

The professor interrupted. "Suppose they have confirmed the super-string theory, or found the elusive top quark that our science has not been able to find. Suppose the shadow world of which we spoke exists, but the extraterrestrials have learned beyond doubt that it contains neither spirits, nor angels, nor gods. Suppose they possess answers to other scientific dilemmas. What if they know things that we don't want to know because humankind is incapable of handling such knowledge? Think of the shock waves! Think of who might kill to get control of the chaos chip first!" He banged his fist on the table. "Damn it," he exclaimed, "I think Martin's wrong. I think a rumor has found wings that Stephen developed a super computer chip, and I think it floated out of Brother Antonio's family in Spain. They helped develop the software, even though they didn't know Stephen's intended use. Even without the chaos factor, you can imagine the value of a CPU chip one thousand times faster than any available on the market today."

"In any event," Brother Martin injected, "we don't want word of extraterrestrials to vent until we've decided how to manage it. As soon as any government or politician learns of it, it'll be politicized. In the meantime, one of our monks is a xenobiologist and . . ."

Murdock interrupted. "Excuse me. What is a xenobiologist?"

Brother Martin chuckled. "I asked the same question. They study the possible biological configurations of foreign beings — aliens, and we . . ."

Murdock interrupted. "I don't think you can assume that it's possible to withhold the information for long. I believe one man has already died because of the secrecy, and I suspect he will not be the last if you continue to stonewall the world." Murdock turned to Brother Martin and loudly and firmly asked, "As the abbot of the monastery, what action do you plan to take?"

Brother Martin frowned. "As soon as the professor completes his reading of Stephen's memoirs and studying their intricate calculations, he will give me his advice. He and I then shall meet with the congregation of brothers and decide upon our response."

Murdock shook his head in disbelief. "I suggest that you read rather quickly, professor. Does Madam justice minister have any idea of what you are withholding?"

"We think she has no specifics," the professor replied. "I feel certain that she suspects something momentous is going on here, and that she doesn't want her government left in the dark. The German federal government would like to know too."

Murdock searched the faces of the two men. "I read recently," he said, "that the United Nations has a committee dedicated to the peaceful uses of outer space. I understand that the General Assembly has adopted a resolution that calls upon nations to report all contacts with extraterrestrial beings to the secretary-general."

"Fortunately, we aren't a nation," Martin suggested. "We're just a bunch of monks."

"*Just* is the understatement of the year!" Murdock exclaimed. His investigator's skepticism reminded him that the professor and Brother Martin might have concocted this entire plot to deflect attention from them and embroil the investigation in a colossal cock-and-bull story. It occurred to him that, if the story were true, Stephen's friend Michael could have been the leak. He turned to the professor. "How much did Michael know about the chaos chip?"

"I believe Michael gave Stephen some assistance. I'm better than halfway through the memoirs and as yet, Stephen hasn't mentioned Michael's part. But the last time Stephen and I met, he told me that Michael was a catalyst. I'm absolutely convinced Michael had nothing to do with his death. He had no motive. You and the police are wasting your time on Michael."

Murdock sat down. "Possibly. However, the mystery in this investigation becomes deeper at every turn. You say that only the two of you

and Stephen knew about the chaos chip. You suggest that Brother Antonio might have guessed. But you both ignore Michael. He knew."

Brother Martin leaned over toward Murdock. "Why does the mystery become deeper?" he asked. "Because you don't know whom to believe? You think that the professor and I may have contrived this whole
story. Right?"

"Right. It's possible."

"You assume we're protecting Michael and you wonder why.
Right?"

Murdock smiled. "Right on."

"You wonder if Brother Antonio's family is involved. Could they
have killed Stephen in order to gain advantage for their software business? After all, Antonio and his family business helped develop the software that drives the new chip."

"That was my next line of inquiry."

"But to what avail?" Brother Martin asked. "Would you believe our
answers?" Brother Martin shook his head. "Would you believe me if I assured you that Brother Antonio's family is above suspicion? Of course
not; you can't afford to."

"Not before I confirm it through outside sources."

"You and the police have limited resources. Meanwhile the killer's
trail becomes colder. Perhaps once you decide to believe in someone or
something, the riddle will seem less complicated."

Murdock shook his head skeptically. "Do you think then I'll find
God-given revelation?"

"Perhaps. Pray for guidance."

"But prayer . . ."

"Is simply talking to God. Try it."

Murdock frowned. "I tried it once. I prayed that my wife would survive a kidnapping. She didn't."

The professor changed the subject. "I'll concentrate on Stephen's
memoirs. Hopefully, I'll know better by the first of the week why
Stephen was convinced that he made contact."

Brother Martin arose and walked over to the window. He stared outside, his heels together, his arms folded. "Pray for our world too. How
will humankind react if we meet beings who have an entirely different
sense of right and wrong? How quickly will we make practical distinc-
tions between their values and ours so that we don't lose our equilibrium?
We'd best consider such possibilities before they become compelling."

"I agree completely," the professor injected.

Murdock's expression turned gravely serious. He decided to test
their openness. "What did the package contain that Brother Stephen was

carrying when he was killed?"

Brother Martin's mouth opened as if to speak but before he could, the professor snapped back, "Schematic drawings of the chaos chip."

"Then both of you *knew* the motive for the crime."

"No, indeed." Martin said loudly. "As I've repeatedly said, the work on the chip was so secret, we . . . I couldn't believe that anyone had gotten wind of it. Besides, Stephen was an extremely wealthy man. His computer chip businesses had been immensely successful. He was into many things including the web site. Don't ignore the potential destabilizing effect of 'Q'. Who knows what the *killer* thought was in the package."

Murdock shook his head. "So, someone has the secret of the chaos chip."

There followed a long silence. Brother Martin and the professor exchanged glances. Martin nodded toward the professor.

"They probably don't know what they have," the professor said. Besides, the schematics that Stephen carried were fundamentally flawed. An immense expenditure of effort would be required to discover that. Stephen wasn't taking any chances. The corrections are in a separate document. Neither document alone had much value. If the killer knew about the chaos chip and was after it, he wouldn't have known about the dual documents."

Murdock pushed. "Where is the separate document?"

Martin and the professor again exchanged glances. The professor responded. "I shipped them yesterday morning from Munich."

"To where?"

"To Stephen's laboratory in Oregon—not too far from where I live. Mac Townsend, his trusted manager, will place the unopened package in his vault. Stephen's instructions limit access to the vault to Martin, myself, or our designee."

Murdock sat back, dragged on the cigar for several minutes, then suddenly appeared to lose interest in it. He crushed it in an ashtray. No one spoke. Finally, Murdock broke the silence. "So, *if* someone obtains *both* documents, they could make contact with the extraterrestrials. Is that correct?"

The professor shook his head negatively. "If they guessed their purpose, but not without a lot of work by someone as intuitive as Stephen or Michael. One could build the chip, but the schematics don't include the frequency variant that starts the quantum process. But a separate document, which contains the frequency variant, has been placed in a sealed envelope, along with my last will, and deposited in the wall safe in Richard Laplatenier's office by Allison Spencer, who isn't aware of its contents. Brother Martin and I have photocopies." The professor seated himself and smiled at Murdock. "Well," he said, "you've acquired a great deal of scientific information today."

"The more I learn," Murdock complained, "the more questions I have."

"That's science," the professor replied. "Essentially, what we learn is how to ask more provocative questions."

⊰ **34** ⊱

A man in a sullied policeman's uniform that gave evidence of breakfast coffee ushered Rudi into a third floor office in downtown Nicosia. The windows were open, and a ceiling fan moved the air and gently discouraged the flies. *The office is comfortable but the cleaning contractor wouldn't last long in Munich.*

Behind an oversized desk sat a very small man. His uniform was impeccable. He arose and offered his hand. "I not speak German and you not speak Greek, so we speak English," he said cheerfully. "I am Colonel Constantine, second deputy commander of National Police. Welcome to our country. Be seated, please. I have strong Greek coffee for you. You will enjoy. Later we share ouzo."

"Thank you," Rudi responded, sitting down. "It is good to be here and to meet you, colonel. I have heard good things about you. I have also heard of ouzo, but I have never tasted it."

"Ah. Then you must taste it while you are here. It is colorless Greek liquor flavored with aniseed. Very powerful. More powerful than your German beer. Tonight we celebrate. We go to restaurant with best belly dancers — most beautiful Greek women. Some owe us favors. You are a policeman. You know. We have fine time. Are you married? Bad question. Makes no difference. I married too." He roared with laughter. "You like my desk? Big desk for little man, eh? But I plenty big enough for job. You will see. How can I help?"

"We requested that your people meet an aircraft, which departed Garmisch-Partenkirchen late yesterday afternoon for Limassol. Did your officers identify the occupants and contents?"

A saccharine smile crossed the colonel's face. "Most unfortunate, but our men arrived too late. Aircraft parked. No one near it."

"Did its crew and passengers pass through customs?"

The saccharine smile returned. "I am very sorry. Our customs officer at home having dinner with family. Airplane arrived at unfortunate time."

Rudi attempted to meet his eyes, but the Deputy Commander's were focused on a side wall. *He's a devious gentleman, Rudi thought. Perhaps that is a prime requirement for promotion here.* "What time did our request arrive?"

"7:30."

"Please forgive my curiosity, but shouldn't that have been at least an hour before the plane touched down?"

"Herr Benzinger, you and I, we are men of world. We know how things *should* work, and how they *do* work. Either our people arrived too late, or their money arrived too early. I cannot say. Problem is endemic. Surely you understand. Is not same everywhere?"

"It's not endemic in my country," Rudi said coolly. Risking offense, he pushed. "Perhaps your government should study the problem. I'm sure there are solutions."

"Ah, my friend, perhaps proper study of shepherds is sheep, not other shepherds. You understand?"

"Perhaps. I'm interested in one of your sheep. Are you familiar with a person in Limassol who calls himself Romanovsky?"

"Yes. Boris. I have met him. He owns villa near Limassol. Quite elegant. I visited there. Boris has Ukrainian passport, but he is Russian. Former KGB. Solid man. Very astute. One of most successful Russian émigrés who act as middlemen between emerging Russian businesses and the more organized world. Recently, he become part owner of Russian bank with branch in Limassol. Has he darker side? I cannot say. Our records show nothing, but money purges records. You understand. Having dark side often is necessary for to do business within Russia. You understand."

"Are you suggesting that he's clean?"

"I'm suggesting that our records do not indicate contrary. If you want rumor . . . well . . . many Russian businesses sell guns stolen from Russian army, or sold by officers who are not paid. One rumor says Boris is called 'K' for Kalishnakov. But this is rumor. You understand. Maybe rumor floated by enemies. Who can say? In Limassol you can buy almost any rumor you like. Most informants are liars. We hear Romanovsky is connected with many legitimate Russian businesses, but legitimacy in Russia may mean something different from in Germany. I hear he even represents monks on lower Volga who sell allegedly ancient manuscripts for big money. Are the monks honest? Who knows? Does Romanovsky know whether manuscripts genuine? Who knows? Do museums buy? Yes. Do their directors know they may be fake? Who can say? If they get kickback, who cares? Do bad things happen in Cyprus? Why not? Are illegal weapons traded in Munich? Why not? You're a policeman. You understand."

"Please, will you give me a letter of introduction to the local police so that I may question people in Limassol?"

"Of course. Tomorrow. After party tonight. Yes?"

"Thank you, Colonel. I would enjoy your company, but I would like to fly to Limassol after I leave here. I am anxious to complete my work. My wife is ill."

"I am so sorry to hear that. The letter is already prepared. Here." He slid a document across the desk. Rudi picked it up and reviewed it.

"This is quite adequate," Rudi said. "Thank you."

Colonel Constantine also gave Rudi an envelope. It wasn't sealed. Rudi opened it and examined the contents. "Thank you," he exclaimed, pleased. "It is the information on the Cypriot corporation, the owner of the Liechtenstein corporation that owns the aircraft in question. Thank you again. You are most efficient. May we move on to another subject?"

"But certainly," Constantine responded, tipping his chair back and folding his hands in his lap. "You want to know what we know about Señor Jose Enrique Perez-Krieger, who apparently does business with Romanovsky. Yes?"

"Why, yes," Rudi exclaimed, surprised.

"We find no criminal record. He is, as they say in America, squeaky clean. You already know about his family and businesses."

"Have you checked with the American FBI?"

"Should we have a reason? Can they be trusted?"

"We've received some disturbing information. No warrants. Usually they can be trusted."

"But not always. Eh? Sometimes all of us float misinformation. Eh? Nothing pure this side of heaven. Eh? Must we believe what the Americans want us to believe? Eh?"

"Have you met Señor Perez-Krieger?"

The Colonel straightened his chair and rested his folded hands on his desk. "Not yet."

"Do you plan to?"

"If he seeks me out."

"Are there customs records that indicate what the aircraft has carried in the past?"

"Yes. It has carried only passengers. Nothing has passed through customs."

"Are most of its flights to Germany?"

"It frequently flies to Russia, Ukraine, and Lebanon. Romanovsky has class. He's not so foolish as to carry contraband."

"Thank you, Colonel. I have taken too much of your time. Could you have someone drop me off at the airport? I have a private plane."

"Yes, I know. I shall drive you personally. That way we may become better acquainted. Someday soon I shall be in Munich, and you show me famous beer halls. And someday you will come back here, and we drink ouzo and enjoy nightlife. Yes?"

"I'd like that," Rudi said politely.

"The letter I gave you, it does not authorize you to carry a weapon. You are not carrying a weapon, are you?"

"No."

But, one hour later, when Rudi had landed at Limassol, Theo was. Rudi noticed the shoulder holster under his impeccably clean teal blue sport coat. Theo was a tall man, broad shouldered, bearded, and with large friendly brown eyes. The flight from Nicosia to Limassol had taken less than a half hour. Colonel Constantine had promised a driver. Theo had met him at the gate. Together, they walked to the short-term parking lot. Theo was cordial, but had not offered to carry Rudi's travel bag. As they approached a Volvo parked alone in a far end of the parking lot, Rudi observed no police markings on the vehicle. A man exited the front passenger side, opened the right rear door, and held it open for Rudi. He was short, powerfully built, with an unkempt beard. Rudi noticed, as he approached him, that the man was filthy. A scabbard hung on his belt, the handle of a knife exposed. The man grinned, exposing his few remaining teeth. Rudi stopped. He looked over his shoulder. Theo was close behind. He played a hunch.

"Where are the police officers who were to meet me?" he asked.

Theo's face was expressionless. "They had a flat tire. They asked us to drive you."

"I'm sorry," Rudi said. "You must excuse me. I forgot to phone my office." He turned toward the terminal. "I'll be back in a few minutes."

"But Sascha is holding the door for you. Get in. I'll drive you to the terminal. It is a long walk, no?"

"I don't mind. I need the exercise."

Rudi started toward the terminal. Someone grabbed his right arm from behind. It was Sascha. "Please don't make me hurt you," Sascha pleaded. "I don't want to hurt you. You understand that I must hurt you if you do not come quietly."

Sascha's grip was firm. Theo came up on the other side. Together they cuffed Rudi's hands behind him, dragged him to the car, and pushed him into the back seat. Sascha jumped in, blindfolded him, and forced him down between the seats. "Please do not attract attention. I have killed many men. I try not to, but sometimes they die anyway."

Rudi remained silent. They drove. After a half hour, they turned off the highway onto an uneven road — dirt, Rudi thought as the vehicle bounced along. When they stopped and exited the Volvo, Rudi heard waves rolling against a shore and smelled a sea breeze. He felt the warm sun on him but not for long. As they walked, Sascha held him firmly by his left arm, leading him down an oval staircase. Rudi sensed darkness and dankness. The steps were unevenly spaced, smooth and hard. *Probably stone, he guessed.* They stopped. He heard a metal door squeak open. One of them pushed him. Then nothing, except a cold, deathly stillness, and the sound of three men breathing. Water dripped. *Subterranean. Maybe a cave. No. A cave wouldn't have a spiral staircase.* He remembered there were crusaders' dungeons on Cyprus. *That's it.* He recognized the loathsome odor of Sascha standing behind him. The blindfold fell. A single candle, stabilized in its own wax, stood erect in the center of the floor. They were inside a circular cell. The metal door was iron — thick iron — and very ancient, but still strong. *I'll hunt for rust and weak spots later.* Theo stood on the other side of the candle. Rudi could read his face. It was a hard face, entirely devoid of mercy. *In the flickering half-light, it looks like the face of a fallen angel.*

"Why am I here?" Rudi demanded, his own voice sounding as if it came from a tomb.

Sascha slapped him hard across the face, knocking him to the floor. "Theo will ask the questions, not you. Do not make me hurt you again."

Rudi, on his hands and knees, shook his head. Sascha helped him to his feet. Theo spoke softly but firmly.

"You are investigating the death of a monk by the name of Stephen. He was developing a computer chip. Tell me about this chip."

"I know nothing about a chip."

Sascha came around from behind him. In the faint light Rudi made out a crowbar, held in both hands. He swung it with full force. He was a strong man. The blow broke Rudi's right arm above the elbow, knocking him off balance. Again he fell to the floor. Screaming in pain and anguish, he grabbed his right arm with his left hand and held it tightly against his body. Sascha grabbed his left arm and forced him to his feet. Rudi screamed again in pain.

"You see, you really must tell me," Theo said placidly.

"My God, man, I really don't know."

Sascha's closed fist smashed into his face. He passed out, falling flattened, onto the stone-cold floor.

*   *   *

When he awoke, Rudi sensed that considerable time had passed. He was alone, shivering. His warm clothing was in his travel bag, abandoned in the airport parking lot. The candle's life was ebbing. In the shadows near the circular wall, two small, beady eyes shined in the gloom. *A rat.* Rudi hated rats. He groaned. The pain was excruciating. For the next half hour, he drifted in and out of consciousness. When he regained awareness, the eyes were gone. *I've never been bitten by a rat. But what can I do to protect myself? Nothing.* The candle flickered its finale. The cell fell into the darkest dark he ever remembered experiencing and made more dreadful by the total silence. *I've got to fight off numbing fear, or I'm lost. This could be my tomb.* He felt a large insect crawling across his face. His reflex was to brush it off, but when he moved his right arm, the agony of pain robbed him of consciousness again. When he awoke, his bladder was full. He got to his feet. Putting his left foot gingerly forward, he dragged it around the gritty floor, searching the perimeter for some facility. Nothing. He smelled his sleeve — the elbow where it had landed on the floor. There would be no facility. The odor was that of decomposed human feces mixed with urine. He moved the fingers on his right hand. *The damage can't be too bad. I've still got my grip. The key is . . . do somethin . . . don't just sit here and whimper.* He found the bars on the narrow iron door. *Strong.* Gripping one tightly by his right hand, with all the force he could muster, he jerked his body backward. Above his scream, he heard a loud snap. *Thank you God. It worked.* He felt his right arm. The broken bone was in place. The pain diminished, but not by much. He fashioned his undershirt into a sling. He urinated between the bars of the door into the passageway. Kneeling in the filth of the cold stone floor, he crossed himself with his left hand. Raising his eyes in the empty blackness toward the heavens he couldn't see, he pleaded loudly, "Holy Mary, Mother of God, pray for me now, and in the hour of my death." His voice echoed up and down the spiral stairway.

They can't afford to release me, so they are keeping me alive because they think I know something. I must buy time. Every hour that I survive increases the chances someone will find me. I'll make up a story. He knew he was a poor liar, and he detested people who lied, but in this instance, lying seemed desperately practical. *It can't be very wrong to misinform sinister people. Besides, I'll live so long as they think I have more to tell.* Sitting with his back against the wall, he tried to recall all that his daughter, Roselinde, had taught him about computers. *I need a story. I can feign repetitive unconsciousness and string out the story—and my life—for a while.*

For several hours he grasped islands of consciousness interspersed upon a sea of pain-induced anesthesia. In his mind's eye — or was it a dream? — he saw undulating water, gurgling and splashing over rocks in a fast-falling stream in the foothills of the Alps. He heard voices of water nymphs happily chanting. Their sisters, the nymphs of the deep woods, answered brightly with wispy voices, which sounded like wind in the pines. He saw a lake. Its still, cold water reflected the peaks of snow-capped Alps scraping against a clear blue sky. He sat in the soft shadows of the deep woodlands of his Bavaria, that place he had known in another lifetime. He saw Angelika's face, helpless, in an endless coma.

*   *   *

In that far-off place, in those Alpine foothills of Bavaria, in a nursing home in Oberammergau, Angelika was seated in a chair, talking to Commander Weiss as if it were only yesterday since they had last spoken. He reminded her that it had been two years.

⇥ 35 ⇤

Georg slid a document across the lunch table. Most of the skiers were on the slopes, so Murdock and he could talk freely without being overheard. Murdock picked up the document and read it.

"Odin has found the wolf, and its name is Hecate."

"Mysterious," Murdock exclaimed. "Rudi showed this to me. I understand that Brother Stephen wrote this sentence in his date book on the page assigned for the date of his death. What do you make of it?"

Georg felt uncomfortable discussing confidential police information with a private detective. His face assumed an appearance of official disdain. "I interviewed Brother Gustav a second time," he said. "Under close questioning, he told me that Stephen often sent him riddles based on the classical myths and legends."

"That's understandable," Murdock said, "Gustav being a classicist. Do you have a clue to its meaning, Georg?"

"Maybe. Are you familiar with the Germanic and Nordic myths and legends?"

"Not very well," Murdock confessed, grossly understating the truth. *Making Georg feel important will get me more information than showing off my knowledge of classics, Murdock thought.* Georg puffed up a bit, pleased that he knew something that this ex-FBI college boy didn't.

"Our ancient legends describe Odin as the one-eyed king of the gods, like Zeus and Jupiter in Greek and Roman mythology. He was the god of war and was sometimes called Woden. Woden's day was the middle of the week—in English the word changed from Wodensday to Wednesday."

"I've often wondered about that," Murdock said with as much sincerity as he could muster.

Georg ignored the remark.

"Odin created the world out of mist. Have you heard of Valhalla?"

"I've heard of it."

"Odin held court in Valhalla—a place perhaps similar to the Christian idea of heaven."

Murdock was becoming impatient. "What's the connection?" he asked.

Georg ignored the question. "A different legend," he continued, "describes a storm giantess who destroys ships at sea. She always appears riding upon a wolf, but the name of the giantess was not Hecate. I believe it was Angerboda."

"Hecate sounds Greek," Murdock injected. "Perhaps Brother Gustav can help us."

"Yes. Perhaps. But there is a more fearsome legend in which a wolf plays a part. It predicts the last day of the world. Odin will engage in mortal combat with a ravenous wolf named Fenrer—an avenging monster that has broken free of its chains. Fenrer's immense jaws gape from heaven to earth. Odin will fight him with a spear. Artists have painted visions of the battle that depict fire spewing from the wolf's nose and eyes. A prophesy predicts that Odin will fearlessly face his hour of doom engaged in horrifying combat, but he can't prevail. On the last day the wolf will kill Odin and devour him."

Murdock searched his memory. He had taken a course in ancient literature at the University of Buffalo, but that was a long time ago. "I think," he speculated, "that Hecate was the Greek goddess of the moon. But why did Brother Stephen mix German and Greek mythology? We must ask Brother Gustav. Shall we go together?"

"Yes," Georg said firmly. "I am willing to take you along—tomorrow. My staff shall make the arrangements. There are other matters I have been directed to share with you. Last night we received an additional report from the FBI on Señor Perez-Krieger. It shows a conviction three years ago for fraud in Venezuela. He paid a minor fine. Last year he purchased an eleven-year-old girl from a stable of virgins in Manila — a girl who was later found dead from strangulation. The autopsy indicated that she had had oral sex just prior to death. Also, in the search of the area where the monk's body was discovered, we have found a Russian automatic pistol about 500 meters from the Liederbach Creek."

Murdock was deeply disturbed by the information about Enrique. He tried not to show it. That would be unprofessional. "Was the pistol found in the area where we saw the man in the green ski jacket?" he asked.

"No. In the opposite direction. I shall personally deliver the gun to the state forensic center in Munich later this afternoon. We shall soon know whether it is the murder weapon. Herr Benzinger also ordered me to check on your friend, Diana Crenshaw."

Murdock raised an eyebrow. "Does he suspect her?"

"She's a name on the list."

"What have you learned?"

"Not much. She was born in a declining coal mining town in central Pennsylvania. The family was middle class. Her father owned a pharmacy. He was not particularly successful, but they lived in reasonable comfort. She graduated from Penn State University. The lady is a friend of Brother Antonio's family and is often a companion of his sister, Maria Rosita. Antonio's parents have a large villa west of Marbella on the Andalusian Sun Coast. Miss Crenshaw was vacationing there when she first met Maria Rosita. She has been with Seneca Financial for five years." He paused. "You like her, don't you?"

"Yes. Is there more?"

"No," George replied.

"Have you considered the possibility that Brother Stephen used some of his fortune to invest in gunrunning, and that he was tied in with the people on the mysterious biz-jet from Cyprus?"

"Yes, but we have no evidence."

Murdock frowned. "That's our problem. We've no evidence connecting anybody with anything, except it appears that Enrique is a creep."

"Perhaps," Georg replied. He arose and stood formally erect, his heels close together and planted firmly. Murdock resisted the temptation to leap to his feet and salute. "You must excuse me now," Georg said officiously. "I must drive to Munich. I shall have my assistant inform you of the time of the meeting with Brother Gustav. *Auf wiedersehen.*"

"*Wiedersehen,*" Murdock replied, offering his hand, but Georg had already turned away. *Oh, well, the man is chagrined that he has to confide in me, and I think he's pissed because Rudi took charge of the investigation.*

He heard footsteps approaching from behind him.

"May I join you?" Allison inquired cheerfully. "I haven't had lunch, and I'm famished."

Murdock arose and positioned a chair for her. "Thank you," she said. "That isn't necessary unless you're afraid the Europeans, of which few are present, would think you're uncouth."

"I become more European by the day," he replied, grinning. "Especially when the courtesy honors you." She let the remark pass, sat down, and placed the strap of her shoulder bag over the back of her chair. He reseated himself and gave her a report on his meeting with Brother Martin and the professor. She glanced about nervously.

"There's no one near us," Murdock said. "It's safer here. Our rooms could be bugged."

Allison listened intently. When he finished, she asked, "Do you think Brother Stephen was in contact with extraterrestrials?"

"I'm open-minded. I suspect he was capable of it. If Martin or the professor know for certain, they're being extremely cautious about admitting it, but I think they're still skeptical. The professor is reviewing Stephen's memoirs. He'll talk to me again Monday."

Allison's eyes met his. "It's mindboggling," she said. She toyed with her coffee cup and subconsciously rearranged the salt and pepper shakers so that they were more symmetrically aligned with the sugar bowl. "Even if he didn't talk to extraterrestrials," she postulated, "an advanced quantum computer would be enough to kill for. Last week I was talking to a friend who teaches computer science at the University of Innsbruck. You know that computers consist of millions of electronic switches, each of which must be in either of two states—on or off. My friend is enthused about the possibility that quantum computers will be developed in which a switch could be both on and off at the same time. Each switch could do two calculations at once. A quantum computer might quickly solve problems that would take the fastest present-day computer from now until the end of the world. That's fast. I'm anxious to know what you learn from the professor."

She ordered lunch and poured a cup of coffee. Their eyes met again.

"Allison, have you considered the possibility that the information that Rudi obtained from the FBI was misinformation?"

She nodded. "We don't *know* that it's misinformation, but it could be a smoke screen to divert everyone from the truth about what they stole from Brother Stephen."

"Exactly, Al. Whoever *they* are."

Allison took a mirror from her shoulder bag and looked at herself. She needed to run a comb through her windblown hair, but the dinner table was not the appropriate place, so she rationalized that it made her look daring. She noticed that the cuff of her left sleeve was unbuttoned and buttoned it. "Do you think our government could have been involved?"

"From my experience working for our government, I know it's not impossible."

Allison frowned. "We need to explore that possibility. See what Jerr can learn. If he's forced to divide his loyalty between the Bureau and us, I think he'll choose us, at least so long as his butt isn't on the line."

"And maybe even if it is, Al."

A waiter brought Murdock a message. "Urgent phone call in my room," he said. He excused himself and departed before she could respond. After several minutes he returned, his face ashen. He slumped into the chair.

She put her fork down. "For heaven's sake, what is it?"

"That was Angelika."

"Angelika!" Allison shrieked. "She came out of the coma?"

"Yes. Last night."

"That's wonderful. Why do you look so glum?"

"Commander Weiss is with her. While he was talking to her, he received a phone call informing him that Rudi has been kidnapped. He tried to hide it from her, but couldn't."

"My God! Kidnapped? In Cyprus? Poor Angelika. What do the Cypriot police say?"

"Commander Weiss doesn't trust the Cypriot police. Angelika wants our help."

Their eyes met and locked. Neither had to tell the other that Rudi was in mortal danger. Neither believed the danger was motivated by the Sinaiticus Codex.

Allison was silent for several minutes. Murdock's confidence in her judgment deterred interruption. When she spoke, it was with resolve. "Top Dog gave me free reign," she said. "Are you convinced that his kidnapping is connected with our investigation here?"

"Yes."

"So am I," she said. "I'm going to hire a biz-jet to take us to Cyprus. You find a phone and wake up Jerr. Better warn him that he may be vulnerable. I smell Joe Carlyle in this somewhere. Because Carlyle knows Jerr's a friend of yours, he may be looking for a reason to turn a flamethrower on Jerr's arse. Warn him about Perez-Krieger and ask him to confirm the FBI report. It'll take several hours to get a biz-jet from

Munich. I'll go ahead with my planned meeting with von Richter. Do your date with Diana and see what she knows about Perez-Krieger. It's eight hours earlier in Omaha, so wake up Jerr now before he gets away for the day. But be cautious. We don't know how far Perez-Krieger has turned his head."

Allison arose to leave. Murdock grabbed her arm. "Wait. Did Moira reach you?" he asked.

"No. She may have called when I was in the kitchen talking to Frau Bayer. Now there's a woman who has nothing good to say about von Richter. She thinks her husband is a fool to . . ."

"Allison," Murdock interrupted, "time is short. I'm sorry."

"Go on."

"Al, Moira phoned me when she couldn't reach you. She told me that during her date last night with Patti Dale, Patti nearly killed her. She'll give you details. Patti gave Moira money to spy on us and threatened to kill her if she didn't, or if she warned us. Dale wants Brother Antonio's location. She also wants to know who killed Brother Stephen as soon as we know. Now here's the amazing part. She also wants Karen's cryptology notebooks. Moira believes Patti's threat is genuine. Patti bragged about friends in high places in the American government. Moira suspects that Patti controls Joe Carlyle rather than the other way around."

Allison sat down again. A man seated himself at the next table. She leaned across the table and spoke in a low voice. "Moira is fearless and honest to a fault. I know she can take care of herself, but I won't be comfortable until we learn more about this Patti Dale character."

Murdock motioned with his head. They both arose and walked toward the lobby. "Patti referred to an organization called *Traction*. Have you heard of it, Allison?"

"Not that I can recall. Have you?"

"Only from Jose Enrique Perez-Krieger."

*   *   *

It was mid-afternoon when Murdock arrived at Rudi's temporary office at the police station in Garmisch-Partenkirchen. He had decided to use Rudi's secure phone rather than call from the lodge. It would be 7:00 A.M. in Omaha. Jerr liked to sleep late on Saturday mornings. Murdock woke him up.

"It's still night here, Murdock. What the hell's happening?"

"Things are jumping. My friend Rudi has been kidnapped in Cyprus."

"My God. Any idea who got him?"

"I could jump to some conclusions, but that would be counterproductive. Allison is hiring a jet and we're off to Cyprus later today. The state police received another fax from the FBI. It shows Enrique has a conviction for fraud in Venezuela and confirms the child sex stuff. What have you learned?"

"Not much. I phoned Carl Sutherland again late Friday — yesterday afternoon. I couldn't reach him. His secretary was mysterious. You know how FBI headquarters effortlessly immerses itself in mystery, so that doesn't mean much. He's my main man there, so I haven't learned anything. I'm leaving for Des Moines at 8:30 A.M. I'll try to reach him on the cell phone en route. Last time I talked to him, he said there was compelling evidence that Joe Carlyle was in bed — literally *and* figuratively — with Patti Dale. Carl had no idea where she popped up from. Word is that she's a trim brunette in her early to mid-thirties, and very intelligent. So it appears old Joe has a première tryst-master."

"She may be more than that. Last night she nearly killed one of our agents in Munich. She's paid her to spy on me. Money or death. Some choice."

"And your agent told you?"

"Yes. She's quite a gal. She had a date with Patti; they got acquainted at the Mädchenhaus Café, which is a local lesbian hangout. Maybe Joe's got himself a bisexual. If she's Joe's girl though, why is Joe spying on me?"

"Hey, Murdock, I had no idea he was. I'll see what Carl knows."

"What's your feel for Enrique, Jerr?"

"I can't believe I've misjudged him that much. My guess is that Joe trashed him. I have no idea why."

"Would you bet your life on it?"

"Yes."

"You've always enjoyed living more dangerously than I."

"Keep an open mind, Murdock. If it's misinformation, it wasn't disseminated for light and transient reasons. I'm also concerned that Joe may not be the top of the ladder. It could reach higher in the government than the FBI."

"Or," Murdock suggested, "the ladder could reach someone outside our government. Joe and Patti — I'd like to know which is master and which slave."

"In bed?"

Murdock laughed. "There too."

"Murdock, Enrique could not have killed anyone — especially not a young girl. It's too incredible."

"I hope for your sake you're right, Jerr. In the meantime, I'll keep my mind open, but I won't turn my back to him. You watch out. If Enrique goes down in flames, and Plato is exposed, you've got a heap of personal problems. I'll let you go pick up your nurse and her son, and cross the rolling hills to Des Moines. If you discover the owner of Veritus, please let me know."

"Will do, Murdock. Adios."

"*Auf wiedersehen.*"

⧻ 36 ⧼

Murdock checked at the desk. Diana had just returned from Frankfort. *I'll give her a chance to unpack.* He sat in the lobby by the picture window that faced up-slope. A mixture of emotions assailed him. His delight over Angelika's coming out of the coma was mixed with concern for Rudi. *It was a cruel fate for Commander Weiss to receive the message while he was visiting her. She came out of a two-year coma to learn that Rudi had been kidnapped.* He shook his head. *How could God permit such a cruel thing to happen?* Rudi's comment came back to him — we can't have it both ways — both free will and a Garden of Eden. *It's human nature. If folks were handed a Garden of Eden, they probably wouldn't tolerate it. They'd want something slick and more common—which can be anything they don't have.*

He recalled his years with Karen. *To say that we were happy would be to understate. We found true joy in each other. Just being together was our Garden of Eden. Karen was a special person. I always knew where she stood. She believed in things firmly, like God, and the rule of law, and in people who had a sense of honor. Her concept of honor wasn't slushy. She disliked plastic people molded by money or words.* He felt vaguely uncomfortable. *I need to deal with the thought that Joe Carlyle might have murdered Karen. If he did, was he operating on his own? Did someone higher in the government order her death? Or did someone outside the government control him—like maybe Patti Dale? Why would anyone want to kill Karen? I'd never heard of Patti until Moira got the assignment to investigate her. Besides, Karen never told me about anything she was working on that could have been dangerous.*

He looked at his watch. *Diana's had enough time to unpack.* He walked toward her room and knocked. When she let him in, her face was radiant. He couldn't resist giving her a bear hug. Her body felt good against his. Murdock had forgotten how good a woman's body felt. Diana returned the hug, and then backed away.

"You've missed me," she teased. "Has it been dull around here without me?"

"Something's been lacking."

"And you don't know what?"

"Are you fishing for a compliment?"

"Maybe. Is that okay?"

"Yes. It was *you*, Diana. My life has been empty without you."

She chuckled. "Okay. Cut the hyperbole. You win."

"You look all aglow," he said. "The trip to Frankfurt must have been stimulating."

"I found a bottle of your favorite Scotch," she said. "It's there on the table next to the ice bucket. Help yourself while I finish unpacking." She turned toward her travel bag, her back toward Murdock. "Yes, it was exciting. At the expense of sounding like a libber, women aren't promoted to senior management every day."

"Come on now, don't give me that self-pity-because-you're-a-woman routine. It doesn't fit your self-sufficient character."

Murdock extracted two ice cubes from the refrigerator and drowned them in Scotch. Diana looked back over her shoulder. "Have you solved the murder of the monk?" she asked.

"Not yet."

"You've got to quit messing around and catch that killer so you'll be free to do some serious skiing next week. I've taken the week off. You're supposed to be on vacation too, aren't you?"

"Yeah. That was the original idea. I think."

Diana stopped in the middle of hanging a skirt and turned toward Murdock. "You sound a mite troubled," she said. She laid the skirt on the bed. "Want to talk about it?" She seated herself in a chair across the table from him.

"I've had two pieces of bad news, Diana. First, it appears that my wife's kidnapping might have been a ruse to mislead us about the real motive for her murder."

Diana gasped. "My God! Why?"

"As I mentioned a few days ago, Karen's specialty was making and breaking secret codes. She may have broken some code that would incriminate someone — possibly someone in the FBI. The answer may be in her notebooks, but I can't make any sense out of them. Cryptography isn't my cup of tea. Recently, my apartment was broken into; nothing was taken, but maybe that's what they were looking for — her notebooks."

Diana searched his face. Leaning across the table, she took his hand and said: "I'd like to help."

"Thank you. Really. But I don't know what you could do."

"I mentioned to you that breaking codes is a hobby of mine. If they're on disks, I could go through her notebooks on my laptop and probably give you a pretty good idea what Karen found. Are they on disks?"

"Yes."

"Do you think any of it is secret government stuff?"

"No."

"So I wouldn't be breaking any law by reviewing it. May I help?"

Murdock didn't answer.

"Murdock, if you'd feel awkward about my going through Karen's things, I'd understand. But I don't think you'll ever put Karen to rest until you learn the truth about her death. Frankly, I'd be happy if you *could* put Karen to rest."

Murdock, his eyes lowered, was silent for several seconds. When he looked up, her eyes were searching for his. He withdrew his hand from under hers. "You're right, of course," he said decisively.

Her eyes held his. "Would Karen want you to fall in love again?"

He hesitated. *She's asking for a commitment that I'm not prepared to give.* "She would want me to be happy," he replied."

"Do you think a woman would want to fall in love with a man who's still hopelessly in love with his dead wife?"

Murdock was silent. He stared out the window. Hundreds of people were enjoying the slopes — the same slopes he and Karen had enjoyed together. The thought of her voice . . . *Oh, my God. I can't remember the sound of her voice.* Diana arose quietly, retrieved the skirt from the bed, and hung it in the closet. Then, sitting on the edge of the bed, her hands folded on her lap, she waited. Murdock's stare had become unfocused. A single tear meandered down his cheek. *This is stupid. I tell Diana not to wallow in self-pity, and I'm doing it myself. Fate's dealt me a straight flush with this woman and an opportunity for closure.* He turned toward Diana. "I'm sorry," he said. "I've been a sot, haven't I? I'd be very pleased if you'd help. I suspect we're getting close to the truth about Karen."

"Good," she said. "When can you give me the disks?"

"Hopefully by Tuesday. They're in a bank vault in Munich. We've got to fly to Cyprus today."

"Cyprus? Why Cyprus?"

"I told you there were two items of bad news. The second is that my friend Rudi, the policeman you've met, has been kidnapped in Cyprus."

"We?"

"Allison, my supervisor, has hired a biz-jet, and she's going with me. She's a friend of Rudi and Angelika too."

Diana arose from the bed, slid a chair over close to him, and sat down. "I'm glad there is something I can do. I was hoping we could spend the evening together tonight, but I understand. You wouldn't be much fun worrying about your friend." She leaned over and gently kissed the tear on his cheek. "A man who can love a woman that much is not easy to find."

Murdock was embarrassed. He had shown a sign of weakness. Getting hold of himself, he remembered Enrique. Rising from the chair, he retrieved the bottle of Scotch and recharged his drink. "What is your assessment of Enrique?" he asked.

Diana frowned. "In what respect?"

"Do you know anything about his sex life?"

She looked away.

"What is it?" Murdock asked.

"There's something you need to know, but I'm not sure I can tell you."

"I'm a big boy."

"It's not that. It's client confidentiality . . . my professionalism."

"In that case, don't . . ."

"I just don't want you to make a serious mistake. You've treated him as a friend. Technically, Enrique isn't my client. He's merely a prospect. As yet, I probably don't have a duty of confidentiality, so, to answer your question, I think his sexual activities are pretty disgusting."

"Why?"

"He asked me to obtain virgin girls — the younger the better. That's easy in the Far East where many families are desperately poor and fathers sell eight-year-olds into sexual slavery."

"Eight-year-olds?"

"Yes. If you're wondering whether there's a market — believe me, there is. The rich and powerful, as well as ordinary businessmen, from all over the world, including America, use them. They do things with these children they would never think of doing with children back home."

Murdock winced. "I've heard about such things, but it's still hard to believe. Karen and I wanted children, but she was unable to have any."

Diana engaged his eyes. "More than one million children each year are added to the appalling total of children used as prostitutes. Ninety percent of them are little girls. Child prostitutes are engaged by nearly twelve million men each week. One-third of those children are HIV positive. They'll die young. Sometimes it's necessary to murder the girl or boy in order to mask a powerful face. Wherever children live in abject poverty, they face that potential."

"Don't their countries have laws against it?"

Diana lit a cigarette. He hadn't seen her smoke before. "Yes, they have laws, but they don't enforce them. Brazil, Sri Lanka, Thailand, and the Philippines are cracking down, but usually the children are arrested instead of their customers. Child sex adds billions in hard currency to national economies. Some poor countries can't afford to discourage it. Inexpensive international air travel has ballooned the problem by increasing demand. But my bottom line is that *I* wouldn't procure such children for Enrique or anyone else. I've told clients where they could find a procurer, even travel guides do that, but not for kids. But what really ticked me off was, when I refused to procure, he immediately changed his tack and tried to buy *me*. Women are toys to him. His first offer to me was $1,000. He's up to $15,000 now, and he's a patient man. I confess that I'm curious to see how high he'll bid, so I'm toying with him. Besides, I wonder about myself—do I have a breaking point? And what I would think of myself if I went beyond it?"

"Everyone has a breaking point. It's not a toy to play with."

"You care?"

Murdock hesitated. "Yes. Of course."

"Thank you," she said. "That's touching."

"What are you going to do?"

"He's an insensitive predator who needs to be shot down. I'm playing with his mind. I'll run up the price to the breaking point, pull the rug out from under him, and point out how much he can save by playing with himself."

Murdock was stunned. *The FBI information might have been massaged, but Diana confirms that he's interested in virgin girls. Enrique's a creep.* His eyes met Diana's. "He seemed like a decent guy," he said.

A contemptuous grin crossed Diana's face. "Fallen angels have friendly faces," she offered.

Murdock shook his head in disbelief. He was profoundly disappointed with himself. He'd let Enrique fool him. *But why should I believe Diana? I've only known her a few days. Why would she lie? Maybe she's the woman scorned—she hasn't been able to land the fish. Maybe Enrique rejected Seneca, and she's losing a big commission. Could her child sex story and the FBI's be mere coincidence? If this child sex stuff is true, Jerr couldn't know and still consider Enrique his friend. Jerr needs to know.* He glanced at Diana. She appeared remarkably composed. He shook his head and remarked: "No one could accuse him of having vapid sexual desires."

"True," she responded. "I could find a more descriptive adjective, but I'll spare you."

Murdock rose to leave. Together they walked to the door. He leaned toward her and kissed her cheek. She didn't pull back. "Diana, I really appreciate your sharing that information with me and offering to help with Karen's notebooks. It means a lot." He searched her eyes. They met his instantly.

"Let's just say that friends help friends."

* * *

Across the parking lot, in the Bayers' chalet, Allison was packing a travel bag. The biz-jet was arranged. She'd left a message at the desk for von Richter to phone when he returned from his meeting with Brother Martin. The phone rang. It was Terry.

"What can I do for you, Terry?" she asked somewhat impatiently.

"Nothing. I just wanted to tell you that your plane has been canceled."

"What?"

"The air taxi phoned to confirm that you had authority to spend fifty thousand marks. Early this morning you received a fax from Harvey directing you not to authorize any extraordinary expenditures unless I agreed."

"If you have to agree, then I am being demoted. Harvey can't do that. Company policy requires a written performance review before a management employee can be demoted."

"This is a temporary order until he can give you a performance review on Monday."

"And you don't agree, do you?"

"No, I don't. We have no file that requires a trip to Cyprus. I phoned Harvey at home. He's supporting me. He wants to see you in Richard's office at 8:00 A.M. sharp Monday morning."

"Do you know Harvey's home phone number?"

"I can't give it out. He'll put me in charge Monday."

Allison laughed. "That should impress the home office. Am I going to be your assistant?"

Terry snickered. "I hardly think so. Richard had the combination of his wall safe changed without authority. Harvey's ordered you to give me the new combination. I need to look in it."

"I'm so sorry," Allison said with mock sadness, "but it's written in a code book I've left in my apartment. I'll bring it Monday." She hung up and immediately dialed her travel agent. There were no seats on a flight to Athens until Tuesday. Nor was there another route available. She booked two seats for Tuesday. *Three days is like three months in a kidnapping.* But she didn't know what else to do. *Maybe Murdock can pull some strings through Madam Justice Minister, but he's never met her, and he doesn't understand why she's given him so much slack.* She would talk to Murdock after her meeting with Baron von Richter.

⇥ 37 ⇤

Baron Rupert Karl Hermann Otto von Richter was an ambitious man, keenly focused, and persistent. As he dressed for his meeting with Brother Martin, he looked into the mirror. He saw himself as the political reincarnation of King Ludwig II of Bavaria. *Ludwig was right, he thought to himself.* Ludwig had opposed his government's desire to meld Bavaria with Prussia into a strong German Empire. It meant war with France, and Ludwig was a Francophile. An urbane grin crossed his face. *The king depleted the royal treasury by castle building so that Bavaria would be too poor to raise an army against France.* One hundred fifty years ago the politicians had neutralized Ludwig by spreading the rumor that he was crazy, weakening the king's position to the point where they felt safe in arranging his "accidental" drowning. *With Ludwig II gone Germany was united and became the premier economic and political power in Western Europe. That, combined with the natural megalomania of Germans, led to destabilization of the natural European alliances and three major wars.* He brushed dandruff from the shoulder of his dark gray pinstripe suit coat. *If Ludwig had succeeded in preventing the grand German unification, we could have avoided the Franco-Prussian War and two World Wars.* He was convinced that today Europe is moving in dangerous directions again. The Baron stopped in the middle of tying his tie. *I've been on the pulpit again, preaching to myself.* After his meeting with Brother Martin, he would meet with Allison Spencer. *Now there's a woman fit to be a queen. And she's writing a book about my ancestor. Meeting her again will indeed be a pleasure. She is quite pleasant to the eye, and clever. Maybe she will pay attention to me if I agree to underwrite the publication of her book. I think she shares my point of view. I wonder what she thinks of me? I antagonize many people, but, as Shake-speare wrote, "I shall so offend as to make offense a skill, redeeming time when men think least I will."*

The floor-length mirror reflected a man flawlessly groomed, shoulders back, standing erect like an officer of some palace guards, heels together — all as he imagined King Ludwig would have — much like a monolith waiting to be photographed. Satisfied, he procured his Spanish leather briefcase, and set off. A snow vehicle with a heated cabin transported him up the trail to St. Luke's. The morning was cloudy. *It will snow by evening.* Brother Martin had invited him to lunch. He was hungry.

Upon arrival, Brother Martin ushered him into his private room. Braunschweiger, pumpernickel bread, an onion, fresh creamery butter, a wedge of French Brie, and a tumbler of goat's milk graced the table. Von Richter smiled. "You know my favorites, I see."

"Yes," Martin replied, "and I share your delight. A repast fit for a king, yes?"

The Baron chuckled good-naturedly as they seated themselves. Brother Martin reached into a drawer and extracted a bottle of Chambord liquor. "And this may delight us after our midday feast."

Von Richter tucked his napkin into the neck of his shirt. "Truly a delightful blending of German and French, like our modern politics."

With an ironic laugh, Brother Martin injected: "My good Baron, I suspect you are not here to talk of politics."

"But Reverend Abbot, I always talk of politics."

"But we are apolitical, Herr Baron."

"That is why your advice would be helpful. Neither of us has lived a cloistered life. We are not naive. Neither of us totally approves of the other, but that is unimportant. You have devoted your life to God — or so it appears. I try to make Europe safer, politically. Both are noble devotions. I believe you are sincere. I ask you to assume, at least for the sake of this conversation, that I too am sincere." Von Richter waited for a response.

"Please continue, Herr Baron."

Von Richter cut off a slice of pumpernickel, buttered it, covered it liberally with braunschweiger, sliced a thick shard of onion and placed it on top, took his knife and fork, and proceeded to slice and eat. Brother Martin waited. The room was silent. The Baron broke the silence.

"Reverend Abbot, I need advice on a moral problem — a question of what is proper under certain circumstances."

Brother Martin's eyes met his. "Are you not a Catholic?" he asked.

Von Richter smiled. "I consider your opinion more valuable than that of a naive priest."

"Why is that, Herr Baron?"

"It may become obvious if I may pose the problem to you as a hypothetical."

"Please do."

"I have a friend."

A supercilious grin crossed Brother Martin's face.

"Let us suppose," von Richter continued, "that he, unknown to the public, owns some assets that make him uncomfortable because he would rather that the public not know. Ridding himself of them would expose that my friend owns them in the first place. Exposure would embarrass him and leave him vulnerable to vicious attack by certain political parties. Let us also assume that disclosure would raise a question as to how he obtained the purchase money. Eyebrows would be raised in certain centers of power, including the government of the United States, the governments of the Federal Republic of Germany, and the State of Bavaria. Let's assume that I know why, if the assets were sold, the money can never be returned to those who furnished it. Assume that the large amount of money generated by a sale would be difficult to hide. Assume that my friend would — in his mind because he is a moral person — feel unjustly enriched. He wants the proceeds of any such sale to be diverted from him to some appropriate causes. Assume that I want to purchase some or all of the assets. Am I under a moral duty to insist that the proceeds be put to some specific use that I feel would be legitimate, or at least appear to the public to be legitimate in the event my purchase was disclosed?"

Brother Martin cut a slice of Brie from the wedge and a chunk of pumpernickel from the loaf. "That's a rather convoluted question, if not a riddle. Is your concern moral or political?" he inquired.

Their eyes met. Von Richter's face was devoid of expression. "Surely you do not test me, Reverend Abbot. You know full well that any solution that appears to hold the moral high ground is also politically prudent."

"Under the circumstances, for the sake of your conscience, you have a duty to propose a disposition that seems morally appropriate to you."

"Thank you, Reverend Abbot. You have been most helpful. I shall take your advice. My staff shall prepare a proposal next week." Von Richter stood and offered his hand. Martin arose. They shook.

"Herr Baron, I'm certain your friend will be pleased to receive your proposal. I hope you will let me know the outcome."

Von Richter grinned. "You shall be the first to know."

* * *

Light snow showers dusted the Zugspitze. Back in his room, von Richter brushed the flakes from his overcoat and hung it in the closet. A fire popped and crackled in the fireplace. He added a log, walked to the table by the window and, as he picked up the phone, he saw Allison walking across the parking lot. He cradled the phone. *She is not beautiful in the cute sense. Her beauty has strength.* The wind caught her scarf and it danced in front of her. She tucked it into her jacket. *Her mannerisms indicate refinement and grace. Ach, to have such a woman. We must talk about her book. More casual is appropriate.* He changed quickly into a sport coat and slacks. She knocked. Von Richter waited several seconds before responding. "Ach, Fräulein Spencer. It is good to see you again. Please come in."

"It is good to see you too, Herr Baron," she replied with a brave smile.

He took her coat and they were seated. Conversation was animated. Both assumed the pretense of old friends becoming reacquainted. They had danced last summer at a ball in Munich given by the Bavarian Minister of Justice. Dependable Moira had obtained Allison's invitation. Allison had learned that evening that the Baron was a womanizer of enchanting delicacy and culture. But this afternoon they talked mostly about her book, a book with only three completed pages as she pointed out.

"I think you have a genuine fondness for the subject — a sensitivity to the plight of my unfortunate ancestor. Why do you hesitate to write?"

"Time constraint. Especially now that my boss is missing. I'm doing my job and his too."

"You must take a vacation. In January I am taking a group of friends to Costa Rica for two weeks. You must come. You shall have a private suite with only one key. Do you need a laptop?"

She didn't respond. He waited. The torture evident in her eyes had not been triggered by his offer. "I am truly sorry," he said gently. You are upset. Is it your friend?"

Their eyes met.

"The policeman?" he prodded.

"Yes."

"I heard he has been kidnapped. I am sorry. I should have been more sensitive." Allison attempted a smile but only managed a distorted grin. "You must let me help," he insisted. "Please, what can I do?"

She didn't answer. Her head was lowered, her shoulders slouched, her hands folded and planted in the bay of her skirt — atypical of Allison.

"Please, what can I do?" he repeated.

"Really nothing," she insisted, "unless you have a handy airplane that could fly us to Cyprus today."

Von Richter stood and walked over to the wet bar. He poured a VO on the rocks, and handed it to her. "Drink this," he commanded, "and please excuse me for a few minutes." He disappeared into the bedroom, closing the door behind him. Allison sipped the liquor. Recovering her composure, she determined to question von Richter, as Rudi had requested. Before she could formulate a plan, he returned.

"We must locate a pilot. It is already late Saturday afternoon. But I guarantee that one of my company planes will be here no later than 3:00 A.M."

Her eyes widened. "But, but . . . we can't just take *your* plane?"

"But you shall not *take* my plane. *I* am flying to Cyprus. I'm inviting you and Mr. McCabe to accompany me. We three shall find your friend."

Allison was shocked. "Why should you do this?"

"I have many reasons. I have never been in Cyprus. It is warmer than here. I want to be your friend. Besides, it is a political coup. The murder of the monk has been mentioned in the media all over the world. The kidnapping of your friend while investigating it will generate a journalistic feeding frenzy and consume tomorrow's headlines. Monday's headlines will report that his two best friends, with the help of the Baron, Rupert Karl Hermann Otto von Richter, have flown to Cyprus in the Baron's private jet to rescue him. By Monday evening my staff will have television news services interviewing me to learn what I think. The next day they will interview the kidnappers to expose the deprived childhood that drove them to such madness. The next day they will have me explaining how we can alleviate the conditions that invite deprived childhoods in Europe."

Allison's eyes widened. She was appalled at the simplicity. She knew it was true. "But," she protested . . .

"But nothing, my dear. You must know my reputation as a publicity hound. The Baron von Richter should never be predictable. Nonpredictability serves my purpose. What price can you put on the worldwide publicity I shall receive?"

"Thank you," Allison said. "Thank you very much. What do you expect from me personally?"

A shrewd smile crossed his face. "You Americans are very direct. I will give you a direct answer. I expect you to tell me whether you wish to depart at three o'clock in the morning or later."

"Three," she exclaimed, rising from the chair and hugging him. "I could kiss you."

"Please do."

Allison planted a solid kiss on his cheek.

"Such passion," he offered humorously, "but a fair reward from a woman who could be a queen." He put his arm firmly around her shoulders and walked her to the door. "Now you must inform Mr. McCabe and make your preparations. Get to bed early. My car will be at your door at 2:00 A.M., if that will suit you."

"It most certainly will," Allison exclaimed as she turned down the hall toward Murdock's room. She stopped and looked back. Von Richter was standing in the doorway. "I will arrange for someone from Veritus to pick us up at the airport at Limassol," she said. "What is our estimated time of arrival?"

"About 6:30 A.M. My staff will arrange customs and immigration."

"Thank you again," she said, and turned toward Murdock's door.

*   *   *

Murdock's shoulders drooped when Allison told him of Harvey's cancellation of the biz-jet and of Terry's arrogance. Next to Jerr, Rudi was his closest friend, and he could think of nothing other than dashing to his aid. He was stunned by the Baron's offer and spontaneously gave Allison a firm bear hug, lifting her off her feet. "Astonishing," he exclaimed. "As the Brits say — good show, old girl."

"Were you able to contact Jerr?" she asked, pleased with herself.

"I snagged him on his cellular somewhere in Iowa. He's pretty disturbed by Diana's confirming the FBI report. He phoned Carl Sutherland in Washington. Carl was scheduled to be on weekend duty, but he wasn't there. The scuttlebutt was that he was out on an investigation. That's strange. Carl's a desk jockey. No one would tell Jerr why Carl was involved. When Jerr called me back, he was more upset than earlier. He's continuing on to Des Moines. Something's boiling in Washington, Allison. I can feel it."

"Is there some special significance to Carl's not being there?"

"Those weekend duty schedules are really firm, unless someone gets sick. If they pulled him off at the last minute, that would be an unusual happenstance. Using him as an investigator is unusual. He's not trained for that."

"Why wouldn't they tell Jerr? He's one of their agents-in-charge."

"Why indeed. That's singularly disturbing. Jerr could show up at his office on Monday and find the locks have been changed."

Allison squirmed. She was beginning to share Murdock's apprehension. "We'll find him a position at Veritus."

"Allison, when you don't show up to meet Harvey on Monday morning, and you won't — you'll be in Cyprus, it will create a confrontation that your job or his may not survive."

"Poor Harvey," she insisted.

"I hope for your sake that the voice on the telephone was really Top Dog, and that he's decided to interfere in the management of the Company. Harvey's gotten to where he is by knowing precisely which asses to kiss. He couldn't have gotten there by management skill. It will be difficult for you to rise above Richard's position — station chief. That requires political sophistication, but you'll keep bumping into your ideals."

"That's bad?"

"That's marvelous, Allison. It's one of the attributes I most admire about you. I have the same problem, perhaps to a lesser extent. Those ideals limit us. We're not politicos. Ideals are baggage in politics. We lack the skill of instantly bullshitting our way from the dung heap to the moral high ground. You can rise to station chief by professionalism, but beyond that you'll suck air."

She smiled wanly. "Apparently we've impressed Top Dog."

"Perhaps. If it's Top Dog."

*   *   *

It was late Saturday afternoon. The professor returned from a five mile walk along a trail through the woodlands in the Alpine foothills. Evening shadows had begun to capture the Zugspitze Hof. Dressed in an orange parka, pullover sweater, insulated ski pants, woolen mittens, and trail boots, he seated himself at a table on the veranda. He inhaled deeply. Cold air filled his lungs. He held his breath briefly and slowly exhaled. Several couples were seated at other tables drinking hot coffee from insulated mugs, chattering among themselves. They seemed not to notice him. He envied them. They were young and seemed carefree. *Ah, to share both luxuries*. He caught a waiter's attention and ordered a coffee and a double whiskey. When they arrived, he removed the top from the mug, added the whiskey, replaced the top, and took a drink. The hot liquid delighted him.

Earlier that afternoon, while reading Stephen's memoirs, he had come upon a notation meant chiefly for him. He mulled over what Stephen had written. Stephen hadn't seen Michael for some time, had no idea how to get in touch with him, and didn't even know Michael's last name. The professor had printed the notation and placed it in the inside pocket of his parka. He took another sip of his drink, extracted the printout, unfolded it, and reread it.

> Professor Klugman, I must tell you frankly what I think of Michael. He has played a significant part in the development of the chaos chip. I doubt that I would have discovered the method by which copper could be used to create a chip fast enough to resolve

the quantum probabilities required to decode the chaos we hear from outer space. It seemed that every time I was most confused and discouraged by my inability to penetrate the complexities of the required mathematics, Michael would knock on the door of the monastery. Totally unconscious of social niceties, he would refuse food and drink and insist that I tell him what was tormenting me. After patiently listening to my predicament, he would ask a series of questions that appeared, initially, to have nothing to do with my problem, but ultimately, I would discover that they had everything to do with it. As I calculated answers to *his* questions, the solutions to *mine* became obvious. Most amazing of all: the man's intellectual mastery seems casual and effortless.

Who is this man? I've asked myself that dozens of times.

Where did he acquire such insight? I have no answer. I have only a guess, and you won't believe it. Michael may come from a dimension foreign to us. I think he's an angel. I'm convinced that he has helped me to make contact with extraterrestrial beings, and I'm also convinced that, as you read on, you will agree that I've succeeded.

The professor refolded the paper and placed it inside his parka. *Stephen was correct. I don't believe it.* But deep down a question gnawed. Eminent particle theorists had speculated that a form of life may exist after death in another dimension beyond the four familiar to us. *What can exist in dimensions beyond our comprehension? But for the sake of argument, if angels do exist, why would one help Stephen learn to communicate with people on other planets?*

The professor took another sip from his mug. When he looked to his right, he noticed a man had taken a table once removed from his. The man was smiling at him. It was the Baron von Richter. The professor wondered how long he had been there and what he knew. The professor returned the smile, nodded politely, arose, and returned to his room. The second floppy disk would contain answers. Its lure had become irresistible.

Sunday
November 23

⇥ 38 ⇤

Murdock, Allison, and the Baron were seated on comfortable swivel chairs around a narrow conference table which dominated the aircraft's cabin. Air over the Alps was cold, smooth, and as the pilots say, severe clear. Above the cloud cover, the night sky was cluttered with stars. The aircraft climbed quickly and leveled at a cruise altitude of flight level 320 — approximately 32,000 feet. A boyish smile on the Baron's face suggested an almost childish anticipation of adventure.

When the pilot turned off the seat belt light, the Baron brought out a large thermos of coffee and poured three cups. Murdock discovered a copy of *The Economist* and began reading. Von Richter turned toward Allison. "Please tell me more about your book."

Allison shifted awkwardly. "As I mentioned earlier, I've barely started writing."

"Will you mention me?"

"My work will describe events in the middle of the nineteenth century. How would you suggest that I present you?"

An ironic smile crossed the Baron's face. "I apologize, Fräulein Spencer. I have asked an awkward question while you are trapped here as my guest. I take it that you have checked the descendants of King Ludwig II?"

"And found none," she said. "No offense intended."

"Ach, kind lady, no offense taken. I shall help you. There are other sources — other lines of descent in the shrubs around the family tree. In your country, during the period in which Ludwig II lived, the prominence of a man in New Orleans was judged by the elegance of the mansion in which he kept his mistress and his — what do you say — his second family. Many pillars of the community in modern New Orleans are descended from second families. My title, of course, comes from my lands, not from my royal descent. But such other-than-legitimate royal lines are common in history. The malevolent Italian conqueror, Cesare Borgia, was the illegitimate son of Pope Alexander VI. Your own Alexander Hamilton was born fifteen months after his mother's husband had gone to sea. The story of my great, great, great, etcetera grandmother might add spice to your story. What kind of a presentation do you plan to make?"

Allison appreciated his sharing. *It would indeed add spice to a chapter or two.* "I want my book to be precise, fast moving prose salted with delicious tidbits, not a six hundred page yawn. You've given me an excellent idea. Those who also served."

The Baron laughed. "You have a delightful sense of humor. I could point you to dozens of stories about the ladies who mothered the bastard sons of the aristocracy, and of the descendants of bastards who control grand corporations today."

Murdock put down the magazine. "Forgive my eavesdropping, folks, but I'm getting an entirely different image of you, Herr Baron."

Von Richter turned to him. "We face high adventure. Maybe danger. Please, let us follow the American tradition and call each other by first names. My familiar name is Rupert. I can tell from your face that you did not expect such informality, no doubt because you have heard that I am infatuated with titles, like King, for example. Those rumors are true, but I also enjoy being unpredictable. Note that it does not also mean that I am unreliable. I promised an airplane and here we are. And to you, lovely lady, I promise to help you with your book, as much help as you would like. There are no strings attached, but that does *not* mean that I shall also be unfeeling toward you."

Murdock interceded. "Now that we're first name friends, tell me whether you're serious about becoming King of Bavaria, an event that seems, if you'll forgive me, singularly unlikely."

Von Richter was silent for several seconds. He turned toward the thermostat and adjusted it for a slight increase in the cabin temperature. He folded his hands and placed them firmly on the conference table. "So," he said facing Murdock, "please tell me whether you have been in politics."

"No. But I studied it at the university."

"That is not the same. Let me say that it is important that certain people believe that *I* believe that I shall be king. You and I are big boys. Just between us, let me say that I don't disbelieve it."

Allison edged forward. "What is your purpose?" she asked.

"Before you can bring about political change, you must first catch the attention of people. There are many barons. The title means very little in republics. It didn't mean all that much in the days of kingdoms and empires. My title offers little notoriety. But my claim to be king—that's a whole different story. The media mostly ignore it, but they won't ignore this trip. I have followers, and each month their numbers grow. First they are attracted by the title—King. Scratch a Bavarian and underneath you will find a monarchist. When they hear my concerns, they learn that they share them."

"What are they?" Allison asked.

"We have a grand opportunity to bring unity and peace to Europe. Nation-states stand in the way. With all the talk of European union, have we become Europeans? No. Germans are still Germans. French are still French. And the British are different still."

Murdock and Allison laughed and nodded in agreement.

"Progress in Europe is attenuated by nationalism. The whole idea of European monetary union creates new frictions. France and Germany argue over whether the new European central bank shall be as independent as the Bundesbank. The French prefer some degree of political influence upon its decisions. Germans demand a currency as hard as the D-Mark. The old international stresses are still there. If we are to have peace, we must have a truly united Europe. That can never happen as long as the present nation-states exist. We must break them up. We don't need Belgians, for example. Let them be Walloons or Flemish and each have their own state. Dissolve the German federal government. Divide France into its provinces and abolish its national government. Let each of these smaller units become equal members of a European Confederation. Let Bavarians have a king if they want. History proves that devolution of power to smaller units is the right way."

Murdock frowned. "Are you saying that history creates some moral imperative that requires the dissolution of the nation-states?"

A reluctant smile crossed von Richter's face. "History is a progression of transformations and upheavals almost totally devoid of moral purpose. I'm saying that if peace in Europe is a legitimate goal, and a closer union of European peoples is necessary to achieve it, then devolution into smaller parts is the only way it will work. That's my message. Do I really want to be king? Yes, because I think it would help. Bavaria is not a natural part of the German union. Bavarians have been a distinct people for two millennia or more. So have the Walloons in Belgium, or the Basques in Spain and France."

Murdock folded *his* hands and placed them on the table. He leaned toward von Richter. "Do we substitute a Bavarian megalomania for the German megalomania?"

"Hopefully, we denigrate both and replace them with a concept of European citizenship. I believe that Europe has a geographic destiny in which the ridiculous boundaries that divide us will disappear and will be replaced by political units whose boundaries are more natural and who have little or no nationalist traditions. They will be joined together by a confederation, perhaps like the Canadian or Swiss confederations."

Murdock's eyes met his. "I haven't met a single person who subscribes to your solution."

An ironic smile crossed von Richter's face. "That only suggests that I'm an eccentric. It does not prove I'm wrong. Four hundred years ago, people thought that Leonardo da Vinci was an eccentric when he predicted man would fly. Yet here we are."

"Somehow," Murdock suggested, "the idea of a confederated Europe is both reassuring and terrifying."

Allison agreed. "When, for hundreds of years, Germany *was* made up of many ministates," she reminded him, "there were constant wars."

"Because," von Richter suggested, "they were surrounded by nation-states using them as a battlefield."

*　　*　　*

Rudi estimated the diameter of his cell to be about ten feet. It had to be fairly deep underground, since no surface sounds reached him. The air stank. Cold and dampness were pervasive. He shivered uncontrollably. Hunger tore at him. Several hours had passed since Theo and Sascha had last visited him. He figured it was nighttime. During their two visits, he had feigned semiconsciousness, writhed in pain, and mumbled something about memory chips and duplicate processing — some terms he had heard his daughter, Rosalinde, use. Theo was convinced that Rudi possessed the information they sought. He decided to obtain pain killers and feed him. He wanted Rudi lucid. *The game is working, Rudi thought.* For how long, he had no idea.

He fought fear. Consciousness seized him, released him, and seized him again. He thought — or dreamed, he wasn't certain which — about a Sunday several summers ago. He, Angelika, and Rosalinde had driven to the Chiem Sea. It had been one of those delicious days — clear, sunny and warm, but not humid. The lake was calm. They purchased round-trip tickets on the passenger ships that cruise this largest lake in Bavaria. Snowcapped peaks of the Alps crowned the southern horizon. They picnicked on the larger of two islands, the Herrenchiemsee, and toured the unfinished castle of King Ludwig II. The king had drowned in this lake. Construction had stopped upon his death. After the picnic, they boarded a later boat to continue the round-trip. They had stopped at a smaller island, the Frauenchiemsee. He remembered walking up a shady pathway to a convent church, which had stood there for hundreds of years. In the coolness of the sanctuary the family had knelt at a side altar and raised their eyes to a statue of the Virgin Mother. "Holy Mary, Mother of God, pray for me, now and in the hour of my death," he had prayed. It had been a thoroughly happy day. Rosalinde would have been fifteen, he guessed.

He longed to see them both, and to feel the warmth of the sun again. But it was hopeless. They couldn't make that trip again. Not with Angelika in a coma.

Rudi's arm was swollen and his clothes filthy. He shivered. Someone had stolen his suit coat. Although he felt thoroughly miserable and isolated, the conviction that somehow he was going to get out of there alive died hard. He prayed silently: *Holy Mary, Mother of God, pray for me, now and in the hour of my death.* He reached for his rosary beads. They too had been stolen. A Christmas gift from Rosalinde, they were precious to him. His watch was also missing. He guessed it might be toward morning, and yearned to know the time. A disciplined cadence in life was important to him. *Now time has become meaningless, but I can't shake the habit.*

*   *   *

Allison and von Richter had drifted off to sleep. Murdock changed his watch to Cypriot time. It was nearly 5:00 A.M. Von Richter was more complicated than he had imagined. Monday evening, when he had first seen him with his cronies in the Zugspitze Hof restaurant, he had assessed him as an egocentric plotter with noise but no substance. *Rudi's impression had changed, Murdock recalled, but Rudi was still reluctant to take the Baron at face value. The man's a headline-grabber, but he's not entirely motivated by egomania. He believes in his agenda. It'll never work. Politicians have too much invested in the present system. They'll talk change, as politicians always do, but nothing much will happen, as nothing much ever does. He'll never be king. But if he can grab headlines, he'll make people think. That's okay. His staff has probably already penetrated the media. Americans like eccentrics. They'll like von Richter. Besides, it's not what you actually do that counts, but whether you can manipulate the spin the media puts on it. Von Richter is shrewdly trying to manipulate it. Using his private aircraft to help rescue a kidnapped Bavarian policeman investigating the murder of an innocent monk has positive spin potential. I hope American network news doesn't meet us at the airport this morning. They'd get in the way. Rudi's life is more important than sound bites, but we're getting there in von Richter's airplane. We'll need to make him look good.*

Murdock tipped his chair back and dozed off.

*   *   *

Rudi awakened again. Someone had lit a candle and left some dry bread on a metal plate and water in a metal cup. Also on the plate were some capsules. Painkiller? Or poison? If poison, why the bread? *They have resolved to keep me alive for a while.* Voraciously, he consumed the bread and took one of the capsules. In the faint light at the edge of the gloom, he saw something glitter. He moved the candle. It was his rosary. The subtlety of the message didn't escape him.

*   *   *

Theo and Sascha stood atop the cliff, overlooking the Mediterranean, an onshore breeze at their backs. The predawn air was cool, the sky clear and star-filled. A sliver of moon, past last quarter, hung above the eastern horizon.

"Your problem, Sascha, is that you enjoy hurting people," Theo said. "That is only useful to us when you are able to control it. Your lack of control has made this prisoner incoherent. I didn't want you to do that, but it may turn out to our advantage. The next prisoners will see what you did to Benzinger, and they'll respond to my demands more soberly. But if you wish to remain in our employ, I don't want you breaking people's bones or bouncing their heads off the floor unless I tell you to." He moved away from Sascha with disgust and covered his mouth and nose with a handkerchief. "Don't you ever wash yourself and your clothes? Were you fathered by a yak? I can't stand you."

"But, you see, it is part of my torture technique. Some of our customers talk so they won't have to smell me again." He turned and began walking to the dungeon.

Theo shouted after him. "You always have an excuse."

Sascha stopped and looked back. "Theo. You promised me that someday I would get the woman. When we take the new prisoners, will I get this woman?"

"Maybe. Eventually. But for now, be careful with them, especially the woman."

⇥ 39 ⇤

Von Richter's aircraft began its descent for a landing at Limassol. Yawning, Murdock looked out of a port toward the east. A molten spike of sun pierced the horizon, enflamed the rim of the Mediterranean, and painted orange-red the bases of a few stratocumulus clouds.

"Good weather clouds," Murdock remarked. He had studied meteorology in preparation for the instrument rating on his private pilot's license. The turquoise sea below was empty except for a few fishing boats, their wakes slicing through the almost calm waters. As the pilot lowered the flaps, Murdock saw the shoreline of Cyprus pass beneath them, followed quickly by a cluster of white stone houses with painted light-blue roofs, many with red bougainvillea climbing the walls. People were standing in front of a church door. A donkey was tied to a tree near them. The pilot lowered the landing gears and gradually flared the aircraft into a nose-high attitude to bleed off speed in preparation for touchdown. A squeal of tires announced that they were on the ground. As the pilot applied reverse thrust, Murdock observed the administration building pass by on their left. It was a small, squat building, desperately in need of paint. The aircraft slowed, turned onto a taxiway, and rolled past the administration building toward a Range Rover parked at the far end of the general aviation ramp. Murdock observed an attractive olive-skinned young woman, her short hair tossed by a light wind, exit the Rover and walk toward them. As they disembarked, she met them at the bottom of the stairs.

"I am Yiouli," she said firmly, "from the Limassol office of Veritus. You, I presume, are Allison Spencer and Murdock McCabe." Allison offered her hand. They shook. Murdock offered his, but the young woman's attention was directed to the top of the ladder. The Baron stood there. "And you must be the Baron, Rupert von Richter," she said, bowing slightly. He acknowledged pleasantly. "Please follow me," she said. Not waiting for a response, she began walking. "I have that Range Rover. It is for your use, but first you must take me home. The man standing next to it is from immigration. He will stamp your passports. Please let us move quickly, if you don't mind. Sunday is my day off."

Allison caught her arm. "Please," she said. "We don't know you."

"Oh. Sorry. I have ID but you probably cannot read Greek, can you?"

"No," Allison replied.

The Range Rover was parked in the general aviation parking lot, nearly five hundred feet from the main terminal. When they reached the vehicle, a man exited the main terminal building, stood just outside the door, and watched them. He was too far away to identify. Murdock took Allison's arm and pointed to him.

"He's watching us," she said. "Let's check him out."

Yiouli shrugged. "Words of advice. You Americans have a tendency to take bold action, but you must remember that in a place such as our beautiful island, where Europe, North Africa, and the Near East all come together, when you act boldly, it is not always easy to remain alive."

Allison smiled amiably. "Thank you. I'm sure that was prudent advice. Sometimes we forget where we are. You are kind to remind us. We have come here to search for a missing person. Will you assist us?" she asked.

"As I said — please forgive me — I do not work on Sundays. I pick you up today as a special favor. Tomorrow I will help you."

Allison pushed. "Time may be critical."

"There is no doubt of that," Yiouli replied. "But I must be at my mother's for dinner at one o'clock. I can be free at three. If you will pick me up, I shall help you. Since you can't speak Greek, you obviously need me."

They cleared immigration and loaded their travel bags into the Range Rover. Yiouli drove. "I will leave a map with the location of my mother's house marked. After you pick me up, I will help you check into your hotel."

The Rover started abruptly, tires squealing, and sped out of the parking area onto a dirt road. A huge dust cloud swirled behind them. Shortly after Yiouli turned onto the highway, the vehicle began to lose power. She floored the accelerator, but the engine quit, and the vehicle rolled to a stop on the shoulder. They exited. No traffic could be seen. Murdock looked under the hood but nothing appeared amiss.

"I had the same experience with an FBI car," he said. "Someone had put sugar in the gas tank. If that's what it is, someone had to do it at the airport. Was anyone near that vehicle when you walked out to us?"

"Only the immigration official," Yiouli replied.

Murdock smiled sourly. "Can immigration men be trusted around here?"

Yiouli laughed. "Can they be trusted in America? Half the illegal drugs in the world pour across your border. *Money* can be trusted." She took a cell phone from her shoulder bag. "I shall call the Sunday duty officer at Veritus and obtain another car for you." She punched in several numbers and conversed in Greek. Her tone suggested frustration. Finished, she turned toward Allison. "I regret that our office has received a communication from a Terry Crawford in the Munich office. He says that you have been suspended by your regional manager — a Mister Harvey Specter — and you are not entitled to receive our assistance. Mister Crawford says he is in charge now. I shall phone the airport for a taxi, but often there are none this early on Sunday morning. If I must call one from the city, it will take an hour. I really *am* sorry." Her expression confirmed it.

Murdock looked back toward the airport. A van was fast approaching. Yiouli saw it too. She waved. It slowed and came to a stop a hundred yards past them and backed up. Murdock saw writing in Greek on its side. "What does it say?" he asked.

"Church of St. George," Yiouli replied.

A tall man, avuncular, heavily bearded, heavy dark eyebrows, bare-headed, dressed in a long black cassock, disembarked and walked over to them. "I am Father Theo," he said cheerfully, in English, holding out his hand. "I see car is sick. But you are not. That is good, no? Of course. Things can always be worse. God is kind. He maybe gives me chance to be Good Samaritan, no? Yes. Of course. Do you know what is problem?"

After a conversation in Greek between him and Yiouli, he said: "Please to come with me. I must say liturgy in half hour. You can join congregation, or I take you to rectory. My wife will provide baklava and strong Greek coffee. This young lady will stay with vehicle. She has cell phone. Will call for mechanic. She also has pistol in purse to protect herself. Please, we put your bags in my van." He reached into the Range Rover, picked up two travel bags, and placed them in the rear of his van. Murdock added a third.

Von Richter introduced himself to the priest, and thanked him profusely. He helped Allison into the front seat of the van. He and Murdock arranged themselves on the middle seat.

"I am really so sorry," Yiouli said again. She waved goodbye.

Father Theo pulled the van onto the highway, accelerating rapidly. "If you have never see Greek Orthodox Liturgy, you please join us. Very colorful. Rich tradition. Our church dates back to Apostles. New Testament originally written in Greek. We have very ancient traditions. Look," he said pointing. "There is Mediterranean Sea. Landscape changed little since Saint Paul was here two thousand years ago. You must enjoy beaches before you go back to cold country. You will like my wife's baklava. She very good bakery. I think you prefer baklava and coffee, and go to church some other time. God is patient. He forgives." The van slowed as they passed a man walking alongside the road. "Ah. There is a member of my parish walking to church. Poor man. We pick him up."

As the van came to a stop in front of the pedestrian, Murdock turned to watch him. *An ugly, mangy looking character, if I ever saw one, Murdock thought.* All the upper front teeth between the canines were missing. The man opened the back doors, climbed aboard, and slammed the doors shut. Climbing over the luggage, he sat himself in the third seat. The van accelerated. The new man spoke. "I am Sascha," he said. "I have a Smith and Wesson .38, fully loaded. Don't look back. No need. I pass up blindfolds. You tie over eyes. If you don't know where you go, we can release you alive. You have not seen our real faces — only disguises. Before next sunrise, you will tell us secret of dead monk. Yes? Yes. You will see."

No one spoke. Blindfolds were passed forward. Each obeyed.

Murdock broke the silence. "I take it you're not a real priest, *Father Theo*," he said sarcastically.

The man in the black cassock replied in a mockingly jovial tone. "When I was a boy, I wanted to become priest. Good job, I thought. Never go hungry, I thought. Even poor people give money to support priest. I went to seminary at eighteen. I memorize first prayer in the liturgy of Saint Basil: 'It is you who have deemed me, your humble and unworthy servant, worthy of the service of your Holy Altar. Through the power of your Holy Spirit, make me then able to fulfill this holy office.' Good prayer, I thought. God makes me worthy. I feel important. But, as my studies progress, I grow a little older and much wiser. I realize that feeling important is not profitable. God is poor. Devil has U.S. dollars." He roared with laughter.

Allison fumbled with her blindfold. "What does it profit a man," she asked, "if he gains the whole world and loses his own soul?" She looked over the blindfold and watched his face. A sly grin crept across it.

"St. Mark's gospel?" he asked.

"Yes. And St. Luke's."

"You think maybe I go to hell? Maybe. Maybe I convert back before too late. But, nevertheless, I changed careers. Now I live comfortable on six digit U.S. dollar annual income. More than you, lady. Yes? I contribute money for upkeep of priest. He prays for me. Now I pray for you. You need prayer. You will be in Sascha's dungeon, which he inherit from crusaders." He laughed loudly. "Maybe not directly from crusaders. They long time ago. But one of you must tell me all about secret of dead monk. Is it a computer chip he made? If I'm sure you told all, you and the policeman all go free. If not, Sascha play with you for few days. Sascha like to play. His toy is sharp knife. Very, very sharp. People that Sascha play with always become dead. Sascha . . . he does not believe in hell, so he not afraid for soul. Maybe he's not got soul. Some say his father was a yak." He laughed. "Anyway, if Sascha got soul, he cannot find it, so he doesn't care whether you live or die. You understand problem? Is clear?"

No one replied.

"Is clear?" Sascha shouted.

Each acknowledged that it was.

Over the years of his career, Murdock had seen some excellent disguises, so good that he had been certain they were not masks when in fact they were. He was convinced that these fellows were not wearing masks, and that they had seen their real faces. *The blindfolds are a ploy to convince us that we could save our lives by cooperating. They're going to kill us unless we can stop them. I don't think the jerk in the back is too*

bright. We have to be smarter than he. Maybe Rudi already has a plan.
He hoped they would join him.

*   *   *

When the blindfolds were removed, they were descending a circular
stone staircase — down far as the meager light of the candle shown. Murdock shuddered. *This filthy pit looks like something out of Edgar Allen
Poe. I hope the walls don't move."*

Sascha, holding the candle, and a gun, was behind them. "Walk," he
commanded. As they descended, they passed a solid iron door. "Wait," he
shouted. Taking a key from his pocket, he unlocked and opened the door.
"You," he said, motioning with his hand toward the Baron, "Inside."

"You shall not get away with this," the Baron announced authoritatively. "I am a powerful man."

Sascha's laughter echoed downward into the deep shadows. "You
have made me so afraid," he said sarcastically. He gave the Baron a hard
kick in the buttocks, slammed the door behind him, and locked it. "I see
you again in few minutes," he shouted through the door. My knife will
cut truth from you." His laughter roared again up and down the pit.

They came to a cell with a barred door. Sascha unlocked it. Rudi's
voice came from inside. "My God, Murdock, they've got you. And Allison, too. This is terrible." Sascha pushed them both inside, slammed the
door shut behind them, and locked it.

"I come for you later, nice lady," the filthy man said. "For now you
enjoy seeing friend again, yes? Sascha take good care of you, nice lady.
You not worry. You see." Allison speculated that Sascha's definition of
good care might be different from hers.

The three were silent. The sound of Sascha ascending the stairway
echoed downward, ever deeper into the pit. Murdock wondered how deep
the pit was, and what was at the bottom. They were all professionals.
Each knew the cell might be bugged. Caution was essential. None had to
be told that, if their captors believed they were of no value, they would
die. *Perhaps, Murdock thought, if we appear to be unconcerned, it will
make our captors cautious. They'll need to figure out the reason.*

"You've taken a fall," Murdock said calmly.

Rudi tried to sound upbeat. "Oh, yes. My arm. It will heal."

"That's great," Murdock said brightly, trying to confuse the captors.
The others caught on to the tactic. "We have some very good news."

"Good," Rudi said, picking up a cheerful tone. "It has been rather
dull down here."

Turning to Allison, Murdock said: "Do you want to tell him or shall
I?"

Allison forced a lilt to her voice. "I shall." she said pleasantly. Angelika has come out of the coma."

"Wonderful," Rudi shouted gleefully. "Wonderful. Is she . . .?"

"She's okay," Murdock injected. "I have spoken to her on the phone. There seems to be no permanent damage. Commander Weiss was with her. Of course to her, the last two years haven't happened. The Commander assured her that you never gave up hope, and that you were faithful to that hope."

"Good," Rudi said. "That is important. Is she happy?"

"Unfortunately, the Commander received word of your capture while he was there. Angelika asked us to help. Von Richter furnished the biz-jet or we wouldn't have gotten here until next week."

"Von Richter?"

"Yes. Allison talked him into it."

"It wasn't difficult," she said. "He values the publicity."

"The Baron came with us," Murdock explained. "He was put in a cell above us."

"It is too bad that all of you were drawn into this trap. I am very sorry."

"We will not be trapped for long," Murdock said. "It was a long walk from the van to this pit. I lobbed my emergency locator radio beacon into the vegetation along the path. Veritus knows we're in trouble, and they also know our approximate location."

It was a lie—a calculated risk. The others knew it. But if the walls had ears, their captors would spend fruitless hours searching for it. It would buy time.

* * *

"Well, did he or didn't he?" Theo demanded.

"How can I be sure?" Sascha asked, sneering. He farted.

Although Sascha had always been loyal to him, Theo still respected the fact that he was an inherently dangerous man. Subduing his anger, Theo laughed under his breath. "Perhaps if you had watched them all instead of just the woman's ass, you would have noticed."

"This is the woman I want. When can I have her?"

"Eventually. For now you must keep her unspoiled. Maybe in a few days you can have her. But now you must find the radio beacon. I will monitor their conversations."

"But do you promise that I will get the woman?"

"Yes," Theo laughed. "In a day or two. But first, maybe you should bathe. You like women to fight and scream, but is there much pleasure in pillaging a woman who has passed out from your odor?"

40

Several hours after von Richter's jet departed Garmisch-Partenkirchen, another departed on a flight plan that followed the same route. It achieved cruise altitude with the Adriatic below, its nose pointed southeastward toward Limassol. Linda prepared lunch and poured coffee. She sat back and watched Enrique. He picked up a sandwich without taking his eyes off a document that he was studying. After several seconds, he noticed her staring at him. "I'm sorry," he said. "Thank you. The sandwich is very tasty. But our time is limited. I must work and eat at the same time."

She smiled. "You usually do."

He placed the document on the conference table. "What is your opinion?" he asked.

"Boris Romanovsky is a two-headed monster," she responded without hesitation. "One head may be more benign than the other, which assumes that any part of a monster can be benign. Yours is a perplexing choice. If you wish to find a legitimate business in Russia—assuming that phrase isn't an oxymoron—Romanovsky can assist you. If you're disposed to dealing with bad lots, he may be the best of the bad. It may be difficult for you to preserve the appearance of clean hands. We know the Bavarian police are investigating him. We have no information from Cypriot police. You need clean hands if Plato is to remain pure. I recommend that you don't invest in Russia at all. There is too great a risk to your reputation. The problem with Russia is that it's full of Russians. They have very little concept of Western business propriety. Doing business without bribery of public officials or criminal elements is almost unheard of. So, if you choose to do business there, do not involve any of your U.S. companies, because bribery of foreign officials is a federal crime in the States. I recommend that you do not involve Plato at all. Deal in your private account, if you must deal at all."

"What do you see as the dangers, Linda?"

"Okay. I'll give you some hypothetical scenarios based upon problems other investors have faced. Scenario number one: you invest in a company that will employ people to produce widgets. At the end of the first year, your ledger shows that you've grossed ten times more than you expected. You also have ten times more expenses. You run off to Russia and visit the factory. The little village in which you built it looks as poor as ever. Unemployment is just as high. In the factory you see few people working. Some widgets, however, are ready for shipment. The manager assures you that the gross will double in the coming year."

"Money laundering?"

"Big time. Scenario number two: your company actually produces marketable widgets, but a raw material supplier, run by former communist party bosses, doubles his price in mid-contract. You threaten to sue. They laugh. They know that Russian judges don't know what a contract means. The idea of their enforcing one is foreign. The dispute is resolved by your hoodlums, excuse me, your security personnel, working it out with their, ahem, security."

"That doesn't sound gentlemanly," Enrique exclaimed with a wry smile.

Linda laughed. "It works."

"Is there a third scenario?"

"Yes. You find it difficult to make a profit because 80 percent of your gross is taken in taxes. You fudge your gross. Now you're in massive trouble."

"From all I've read about tax collections in Russia, I thought the government's tax collectors weren't all that efficient."

"It's not the tax police you need to worry about. Someone in your organization will be a pipeline to the Russian Mafia, and they will blackmail you. Your choice will be to pay them or spend part of your life under despicable conditions in a Russian prison."

"That's a totally negative assessment, Linda."

"Okay. Here's the positive side. Romanovsky may come across as loudmouthed and self-confident, but I think he's afraid of you. He's never dealt with anyone whose wealth approaches yours, and he's uncertain what buttons you can push or whom you control. I've let his attorneys know that we are well-connected in Washington. He'll probably deal straighter with you than he would with others. If you determine that Plato money will go into Russia, consider creating a Cypriot shell corporation as an insulator. Bottom line, if you wish to avoid dirty hands, make certain Boris wears gloves when you shake his. Shall I have the pilot turn back?"

"No. What's our next step?"

"His attorney will meet us at the airport. He will provide us with copies of the proposed agreement. I have explained that I'm licensed to practice law in the Caymans. The agreement will contain a provision that the contract will be interpreted under Cayman law—English Common Law. I'll remain with the aircraft and review the document. You will enjoy Romanovsky's hospitality at his villa. I suggest that you review the agreement too. We'll demand changes. They've anticipated that and have inserted provisions that they are willing to cut. We must identify those provisions, demand that they chop them, and then demand that they chop some meat too. We'll look tough. I expect he'll price his services at five times what they are worth and expect to settle for half that. I recommend that we stonewall him, and negotiate down to less than what *we* think it's worth and, if he doesn't buy it, walk away and see if he follows."

A mocking grin crossed Enrique's face. "If he doesn't follow, you'd be happy, wouldn't you?"

Linda's grin matched his. "Yes. If it were my decision, I'd tell the pilot to turn around now."

"Thank you, Linda. Your assessment makes me more cautious. You know that I've determined to accept more risk in Russia, even the risk of appearing to fall from the moral high ground. I think our presence there is important. Besides, it's lonesome on the high ground."

Linda shook her head. She stared outside a port window toward the infinite beyond. With her back to him, she said: "The moral high ground is like toyland in the song—once you have crossed its borders, you can never return again."

Enrique ignored the remark. "Do we have a response yet from Jerrard Blair or Carl Sutherland?"

Linda swiveled around and faced Enrique. "Not since my contacts yesterday. Jerr abandoned his nurse and his car in Des Moines and flew to Washington. They obtained a search warrant for Joe Carlyle's house. I should have details shortly. Today is not a pleasant Sunday for some folks in Washington."

A devilish grin crossed Enrique's face. "No," he said. "It is not indeed. Does Murdock know?"

"Not yet." Linda's eyes caught his. "You're going to do it, aren't you."

"Do what?" he asked coyly.

"You're going to do business with Boris Romanovsky."

"That *is* possible."

Linda's eyes searched his. "Most of the time, Enrique, I think I know you. You're a lintel of stability. But occasionally, I sense deep shadows—a different, puzzling Enrique hidden in with and under them—and then I'm not sure that I know you at all."

Enrique's eyes dropped. "Everyone has a dark side, Linda—a side seldom shared even with our closest confidants. In each human mind hides a deep dark dungeon where, in its cells, we imprison thoughts we're not proud of. It's the strength of the locks on those cells that defines our character. So, if I'm a riddle, I'm normal. Besides, it will be Boris Romanovsky with whom I do business—not the devil."

Linda turned, looked out the port. "I'll take your word on that," she said absently.

*   *   *

The aircraft touched down at Limassol just after noon. Boris's Cessna 310 was parked, awaiting his arrival. The jet rolled to a stop just a short walk away. The lawyer was waiting. Upon the copilot's lowering of the stairs, the lawyer climbed onboard and presented a package containing copies of the proposed agreement to Linda. She extracted one copy and gave it to Enrique. He excused himself. As he started down the steps, he stopped and turned back toward Linda. "Any parting piece of advice?" he asked.

"Yes. Be careful whom you screw tonight."

He smiled. "Do you think that I . . ."

"Yes."

Enrique shook his head and chuckled. Grabbing a handle on the Cessna 310, he stepped onto the wing and lowered himself into the passenger's seat. The pilot started the engines and began to taxi for takeoff. Enrique was disturbed. He had been taught—and air regulations required—that every pilot do a complete preflight check. The pilot had ignored the start-up checklist. Enrique scanned the engine instruments. The fuel tanks hadn't been topped off. He knew that Boris didn't keep fuel at his dirt strip for fear that enemies might contaminate it. The gasoline gauges for the main tanks read a hair over half full—more than sufficient to take them to Boris's villa and back again. The gauges for the auxiliary tanks read empty, but they wouldn't be needed. With some annoyance the pilot took his suggestion that he at least do an engine run-up magneto check. Enrique wondered if Boris was more particular with the jet pilots he hired. *I would never allow this man to work for me.* He recalled that Murdock was checked out on Cessna 310s. *He would never be this careless. He enjoys life too much.*

*   *   *

Boris had been hitting the ouzo before Enrique arrived. He met him dressed in an open chenille robe and a brief bathing suit. "Good to see you, my friend Enrique," he boomed. Boris dropped his huge left arm around Enrique's shoulders and shook hands with the other. "Come," he said. "We go directly to pool. My men take your luggage. Maid will hang your things. I have bathing suits at pool. If you want, a young lady will help you change." Enrique smiled and shook his head. They walked under an arch overgrown with flowering red bougainvillea into the pool area. The pool was Olympic size with three levels of diving boards. Eight racing lanes were marked. With an overweening gesture, Boris's right arm swept across the scene. "Beautiful, eh? You like? Yes, of course you like. Who wouldn't like, yes?"

Enrique smiled pleasantly. "This is glorious, but I really had planned to review your proposed contract so that we could discuss it."

"No contract now. Now you enjoy. While sun is warm. Later you read contract. After dinner. After entertainment. You will like entertainment. You will see. Surprise. I'll not tell you yet." He roared in laughter. "But you will like. Boris promises. Because, if it is not good enough, we will do better. You will be pleased. Besides, in Russia a contract is made with the shaking of hands. Pieces of paper are unimportant."

In a cabana, Enrique changed into a bathing suit without help. After an exhilarating swim, he dried himself and joined Boris at a table sheltered from the hot Mediterranean sun by a large umbrella. A gin and tonic with a slice of lime awaited him. A beautiful woman, in a swimsuit so brief that it was superfluous, brought crackers and caviar.

"From the Caspian Sea," Boris explained. "You like?"

"Delicious," Enrique replied. "It tastes fresh."

"Flown in this morning from Makhachkala in Mother Russia. Maybe you would like to invest in caviar business. The middle class is growing in the Third World. Market for sturgeon caviar will grow with it. You can employ many people in Makhachkala."

"But Boris, I heard that legislation is pending that will reimpose a state monopoly on exports of sturgeon caviar from the Caspian Sea."

Boris roared with laughter. "That would be wonderful, my friend, if it passes. Not much passes in Duma. Too many politicians. Too many political parties. Too many fools. Caviar business will bring more profit for us if government owns it. Everyone is more happy. Employees get jobs, and sometimes even get paid, if government finds money. We pay government's plant manager small fee to let us steal caviar. He is happy because he can buy new Japanese color TV. We acquire caviar very cheap. We mark up 2000 percent plus cost of transportation and sell to willing middlemen who sell to willing consumers, who are happy to pay price. Same as America, yes? We love capitalism in Mother Russia."

"In America and Chile we don't steal the product."

An ironic smiled crossed Boris's face. "Last year," he said, "my favorite mistress had her eyes checked by doctor in New York. He prescribed glasses. The frames cost $149.00. I looked at frames. I can mass produce them for less than $1.00 each. Maybe another dollar or two to package and transport. Is not selling at obscene price the same as stealing?"

"That's not all there is to it. In America frames for glasses . . ."

"In Mother Russia, we are more truthful. We *bribe* plant manager and *steal* from government. In West, how many taxpayers fail to report all income? Is that not stealing from government? We are honest about being thieves. So now you say to me, 'Boris, I want to start business in Russia and employ many people, but I don't want to get my hands dirty.' Yes? That is what you want?" Enrique nodded. "Then you must be undisclosed principal. One of my corporations must act like principal, but in secret be your agent. That way, if tar flies, it sticks on my corporation, not on you. See how Boris protects you?"

"Do you think the methods of doing business will improve any time soon? Why is Russia so infected with the criminal element?"

Boris threw up his hands. "Simple. During Communist period — over seventy years — all private enterprise was illegal, but that didn't stop private enterprise. We had successful capitalists, but they were underground. Does making something a crime stop it? No. Did Prohibition stop alcohol or drugs in America? No. If a law makes selling something illegal, selling it becomes more profitable. Many of our new entrepreneurs have criminal origins. When the Soviet state disintegrated, there was a breakdown of law and order in commercial matters. That failure created a market. Businesses needed protection. The mob moved in and ran protection rackets. Now we call them security services. Is that good? What is better? The police? Which policeman can you trust when you buy him? Which mob controls him? Money is the cause of much blindness. You will see. But it is better that you do *not* see. Let Boris see for you. You need a roof."

Enrique's eyes widened. "A roof?"

"That is what we call the security service. I was KGB. I use roof run by friends from KBG. They charge 25 percent of profit."

"Twenty-five percent!" Enrique exclaimed. "How much danger would my business be exposed to?"

"None. Do not worry. Boris's friends will protect you. My organization is not the mob. We are good guys. If someone tries to hurt you or your business, he only try once. You can forget his name. If you use one of my corporations as your front, mob will stay away because they will think you are us, and they don't want to get hurt so much. Forget contract for now. We enjoy sunshine and water and ouzo. More caviar?"

*　　*　　*

Meanwhile, at the Zugspitze Hof Lodge, Moira had just come off the slopes. She stashed her ski equipment in Allison's bedroom in Bayers' chalet. She was troubled. *When someone with powerful connections in Washington threatens your life, it is not to be taken lightly.* Contrary to Patti Dale's instructions, she had told Allison and Murdock about Friday night. She couldn't play Patti's game because she couldn't imagine herself a modern Janus. *Better to die free than live a slave to fear.* But the argument didn't reassure her. *Better to defang the serpent than to die.* When Allison and Murdock returned from Cyprus, they'd plan a strategy. Today was Sunday. She was free to enjoy herself. She forced a smile and, famished, set off for the restaurant. It was noon hour. The restaurant wasn't crowded. She took a table near the entrance and ordered a draft beer. *The day would be perfect if Kitten could be here.* But she knew that was politically impossible. Besides, Kitten's husband was home. While waiting for the beer, her eyes wandered. At a table near the picture window, a young woman engaged in animated conversation with a much older man. Moira's heart sank. She recognized the woman. It was Patti Dale. She cringed. The old man looked vaguely familiar. She scratched her memory. It struck her. Two days ago on Friday morning at the Veritus office, just after she and Allison had had breakfast, he was the old man waiting for Allison outside the door in the cold. Moira couldn't remember his name, but she recalled that he was a professor from Oregon.

*   *   *

It was a magnificent Sunday afternoon, an ideal day for a long walk, but the professor returned to his room after lunch. On Saturday he had waded through endless pages of Stephen's memoirs filled with incessant speculations by Brother Gustav on the form of language that people alien to this Earth might understand. The professor learned more about Sanskrit than he had ever cared to know. But Stephen had urged that he not jump ahead, so he trudged on. He came upon a narrative, which again contained Stephen's private thoughts.

> On Tuesday, November 11, I became discouraged. Brother Gustav, as you have already concluded, needed a great deal more time to study my tapes and to formulate a feasible language. I wanted to bring him into the circle earlier, but Reverend Abbot thought it unwise to allow too many people to be aware of the Chaos Chip.
>
> I was impatient and unwilling to wait for Brother Gustav. I decided to transmit two sentences in English so at least the extraterrestrials could recognize that it *was* an alien language, and two simple mathematical formulae. I chose $X=S+3$ as a crude way of saying that we inhabit the third planet from our star, and Einstein's energy mass

equivalence equation: E=MC². The aliens must know that energy equals mass times the velocity of light squared. I inserted the message into the transceiver with an instruction to repeat it once every sixty seconds for five minutes and then wait thirty minutes for a reply. This process will be repeated constantly. I also included a replay of their transmission with the hope that the extraterrestrials would repeat my transmission back to me so I can verify that I am receiving a response.

I have written all of this down for you so that my place in history, if indeed I have one, will perhaps be based on an accurate knowledge of my introspection and motivation. Reverend Abbot has shared the knowledge of the Chaos Chip with his friend, Richard Laplatenier, who was formerly an intelligence officer in the Swiss Army, and who is now the station chief in Munich for Veritus International Investigations. I have met this man, but I do not know him well. He holds his cards close to his vest. Reverend Abbot told Richard about the break-ins at my factory in Oregon. Richard insists that I may be in serious danger of losing my life. I find that hard to believe, but—just in case—I have written this tome for you so that my months of cognition and introspection shall not be lost. I hope God will forgive my sin of vanity.

The professor sat back, lit his pipe, and put his feet up on a stool. The aroma of vanilla filled the room. It occurred to him that the transceiver might still be transmitting and recording. He wondered whether anyone had checked it since Stephen's death. A reply this quickly would be alarming. It would mean that they're very close to Earth—possibly within our solar system. Outside, evening shadows were lengthening, and it was bitter cold. He tried to relax but curiosity got the best of him. He inserted the second floppy disk and brought the file up on the screen. After several pages of scientific jargon, the professor noticed a shift to private thoughts.

I have reached the final phase of my attempt to make contact with extraterrestrial intelligence. You may ask why would a rich man become a monk and devote countless hours and tens of thousands of dollars in a search for what may not be? The answer is quixotic. It's the quest—the pure and simple passion for knowledge—the sheer thrill of probing the unknown—my relentless need to learn. The quest itself transcends all pragmatic objections, fires my imagination, jerks me from the routines of monkish life, and compels me to imagine the unimaginable. I became a monk because I believe it is God's will that my quest be not merely physical science, but that it also be contemplative. The world must face the moral consequences of what I find.

I have named my invention the Chaos Chip because it is designed to interpret the chaos from space and deduce intelligence. My people in Oregon have manufactured three copies and shipped them to me, and on November 9, I have installed one in the transceiver located in the antenna shack on the east side of the mountain. Tomorrow I shall test it and, hopefully, put it to use.

The professor recalled that it was November 9 that Stephen had phoned him in Oregon and had told him that a ticket to Munich awaited him at the Portland International Airport, and that a room had been reserved at the Zugspitze Hof Lodge. Stephen had given no reason over the phone; the professor's curiosity would prove compelling enough.

On Monday, November 10, the test circuit confirmed that the chip was operating within tolerances. I programmed into the device the start-up frequencies Michael recommended. He called them *frequency variators*. I think he made the word up. I turned on "search a sequence" and started the recording machine. Later this afternoon I returned to the antenna shack, changed the recording tapes, and brought the first one back to my room. When I placed them in my playback, what I heard excited me beyond description and convinced me that God had placed me on this Earth for this purpose. At first I assumed that what I heard was an alien intelligence broadcasting a message at us. But after studying the recordings more carefully, I became convinced it was not. There is a strong probability that it was dialogue — a brief sentence or two — talking among themselves. It appeared that I was hearing only one side of a conversation. Is this wishful thinking? Am I hearing what is not there? Is my mind playing tricks? Is what I heard really language? Brother Gustav must listen and give his opinion. I shall prepare a message and transmit it toward them on the same frequencies tomorrow. If I can detect a response, I will know. And they will likewise know we're here.

I confided in the Reverend Abbot. Brother Martin asked whether I was absolutely certain. There is scarce absolute certainty in science. Martin's expertise is theology where absolute certainty abounds. I am reasonably certain that what I heard was intelligent conversation. Martin and I understand that, if I'm correct, there is great political and social significance. What we learn from extraterrestrials may change the life of every person on Earth forever. Such information must be managed. He asked me to keep it secret until the Brotherhood decides who shall know first. I am determined that you, Professor Klugman, shall know. Reverend Abbot is not convinced that we should confide in you because you are not a Christian. But I have prevailed. I argued successfully that your writings on ethics in science and your secular approach will help us gain perspective regarding the potential impact on the nonreligious. What if we learn that Christ appeared in another world? What if they have no concept of God? What if they believe in demonic gods? What monsters of the mind may I turn loose?

The professor wondered what Stephen could transmit that extraterrestrials might understand. Certainly they wouldn't speak English, or any other earthly language. The memoirs digressed into a report of a lengthy discussion between Brothers Stephen and Gustav on the rudiments of language which might be fundamental to all communication and which might be recognized by an alien intelligence.

⇥ 41 ⇤

As he had promised, Sascha came back for Allison and placed her in a cell separate from Murdock and Rudi. The cell was no better — dark, damp, chilling, and smelling of excrement and decay. Other than water dripping and her own breathing, Allison heard no sound. With her left foot she cautiously felt around the floor in expanding circles until she came to the wall. She detected no chair or bed, but the center of the floor was reasonably dry so she sat there, pulled her knees to her chest, and wrapped her arms around her legs. Shuddering, a deep, piercing, forlorn, hope-defying chill went through her. Hours passed. Determined to keep a clear head, she fought mind-numbing loneliness, fearing it would lead to despair. She fretted for Murdock and Rudi, wondering whether they were still in the cell — whether they were still alive. Standing, she reached for the ceiling but couldn't touch it. She needed to urinate. Badly. She couldn't bring herself to do it on the floor. *Later, when I have no choice. Have I any choice now?* She craved a human voice. "Please God," she said out loud, her words echoing up and down the pit, "I've never asked much from you. I've got to ask now. Please get us out of this." She listened, half expecting a reply. "For Jesus sake," she added, aware that the magical incantation of his name would not invoke deliverance, but that is how she had been taught by her mother to end a prayer.

She heard footsteps cautiously descending the spiral stairway. The beam of a flashlight appeared. The footsteps stopped outside her cell door, and her craving for a human voice was ironically satisfied when Sascha cursed, his key sticking in the lock. Opening the cell door, he ordered Allison to follow him. She obeyed, retching at his stench. They ascended the stairway, Sascha dragging Allison by the hand.

"Who are you?" she asked, as calmly as she could muster.

"Sascha," he replied gruffly. "You know who I am. I told you in the van."

"I mean, your last name."

"If I had one, I don't remember. Who gives a shit?"

"Sascha, please wait. I have a problem."

He stopped, turned around, grabbed her wrist tighter, and directed his flashlight into her face. "What problem?" he demanded.

"I need to urinate. Now. Very badly. Please." She dropped into a squatting position.

He wrenched her arm roughly, jerking her to her feet. "Sorry, nice lady," he said scornfully. "Do not piss on steps. Please to hold. In little while you have better place. You will see." He croaked, "Sascha will see, too." The pit resounded with his demented laughter.

"I'm really not sure I can hold it," she whimpered.

He didn't respond, but gripped her wrist more tightly. They continued ascending the stone stairs and presently they came to a landing. He shined the flashlight on a solid steel cell door, chose a key from a ring attached to his belt by a chain, unlocked the door, and opened it. With a filthy forefinger he pointed inside and motioned with his head for her to enter. She hesitated. He nudged her inside. "Because I like you, nice lady, Sascha must teach lesson for your good. You look. Then you think of other friends, still living." He directed his flashlight to the far wall. There lay the body of the Baron, Rupert Karl Hermann Otto von Richter, lying on its back, naked, its legs spread apart, its genitals missing. Her horror was uncontainable. She screamed. Her bladder partially released. The scream reverberated up and down the staircase, echoing back again and again. Sascha moved the light slowly around the rim of the cell until it found the missing body parts, lying in filth on the floor.

Sascha grinned, exposing his missing teeth, saliva running from the corner of his mouth. "I sorry that he die. He not stop bleeding. I give him rags to stop the blood, but he too weak, not press hard enough, and cut too ragged — my knife not sharp enough to make clean cut. Take good look. You must do everything Sascha tell you. See." He held her head by the hair and forced her to look again. "If you obey, the same not happen to your friends. Understand? Yes, of course you do. You smart lady."

Fear sucked at her insides. Her neck throbbed. She looked into Sascha's face in the half-light. *His eyes are black and sharp, and lighted with the fires of hell.* The energy of hating overwhelmed her — an emotion she had never experienced before without a feeling of guilt. But now she felt no guilt. The hating seemed lawful.

Sascha pushed her out the door and dragged her by the wrist up the stairs. "Nice lady, you learned good. Yes?" His roaring laughter filled the room as the stairway opened into a guardhouse. He stopped and held the flashlight so she could see the room. "This is *my* room. See? That is *my* bed." He pushed her over to it. "You like?" Allison observed a dilapidated frame supporting rusted springs and an old army mattress with stuffing bulging through rotted holes. Numerous white spots, the origin of which Allison shrank from speculating, stained the blanket. Never had she experienced anything so foul smelling. Her flesh crawling, she pictured herself lying on that bed. The walls around her were covered with magazine cutouts of nude women, many in explicitly erotic poses. Sascha grinned as he studied her face. "Later," he said, "but now you must come quickly." He grabbed her wrist again and led her through the single door and into the warm night air. Across a garden she saw a spacious villa. She relished the clean smell of the sea. Her delight in being free from that terrible cell was tempered with concern for Murdock and Rudi.

Entering the house through a back door, they proceeded down a dimly lit hallway and entered a large bedroom with a high ceiling. Sascha switched on a dim table lamp. Allison noticed scant furniture other than a circular king-sized bed, tastefully appointed. Sascha picked up a chair, turned it around, placed it five feet from where she was standing, and sat on it backwards, his arms resting on top its back.

"Now, nice lady, please to take off your clothes."

Allison noticed the room had an attached bath. "Please, Sascha, I really must go to the bathroom. I can't hold it much longer. I don't want to urinate on this beautiful rug. You don't want me to, do you? Please let me go."

"I sorry you suffering, but it is good for you that Sascha teach. You learn much from suffering. Do not piss on rug or your friends will drink mine. You understand, lady. You nice lady. I like you. I want you to live. Yes. I teach you to live with suffering. Sascha knows. You suffer a little longer. Then I let you piss. First you learn real good to obey. Never question Sascha. Always do what Sascha say."

She stripped down to her panties and bra. "Is there a dress you want me to wear?"

He pointed a filthy finger at her. "Take off them too, nice lady."

"I can wear them under most any dress. Let me see it. I think they'll be okay."

"Not okay. Don't question Sascha's orders or I not feed your friends today, or maybe I fix **Murdock** so he sits down to piss." He laughed, and then turned serious. "And Sascha does not sterilize knife. Besides, your panties are soiled. You pissed in them a little, I think. Come here. I feel."

She walked over to him and he thrust his hand on to her crotch and squeezed. "Wet," he said, wiping his hand on his shirt. "That is not good. Need clean, dry panties. Take off now," he commanded, grabbing her crotch again and tugging them downward. She helped them over her hips. "You do it," he commanded. "I watch. Why not? Be nice, lady. Why you want to hide good stuff anyway?"

She turned her back to him. Her panties fell. She struggled to find the hooks on the bra strap. She felt herself losing control. She fumbled and failed. *Settle down, Allison. Better do it yourself before he decides it would be sport to rip it off*. She found them, fumbled two more attempts and then succeeded. The shoulder straps slid down her arms and what remained of her modesty slipped to the floor. Sascha walked over and picked up both items, and stuffed them in his pants pocket.

She stood naked with her back to him. When she turned and faced him, his eyes bugged. His mouth opened but no sound came out. She contained her bladder with all her strength. He stared at her body. She was afraid to move.

"Without your gun," she said, "you look as naked as I am."

"I don't need gun now. You have learned discipline, and you want friends to live. I see you have all finest equipment. Sascha very pleased."

"A decent man wouldn't have looked," she said imprudently.

"Ha," he roared angrily. "Do not call me names. An indecent man would grab tit with both hands and squeeze until you scream, and maybe give quick prelube so to make customer's entry easier. But no. I, Sascha, am gentleman. But a man must look. Maybe tomorrow I bring video camera and you undress again. You pretty lady. I sell many copies. Many men will want you. Maybe we become business partners. Make much money. You like money? I like you, nice lady. You listen to Sascha. Trust me. Tomorrow, you and I make love for first time. Maybe, if you promise to do what Sascha likes best, I take bath first."

She resisted the dry heaves.

He noticed beads of urine on her thighs. "You have learned discipline well," he said. He got up from the chair and motioned for her to follow him into the bathroom. Opening the shower door, he motioned for her to step inside. Her whole body felt obscenely filthy. Never had she held her body in such low esteem. She reached for the valves.

Sascha screamed, "No. Not yet."

Before he could finish the sentence, she released. Urine gushed down her legs and over her feet and down the drain. Sascha stared wide-eyed, his mouth open, grinning a foolish little-boy grin.

"Never see woman piss like that. Tomorrow you sit on carpet few hours and drink much water, and then repeat for Sascha's video camera. Maybe put camera on tripod and I get in shower and we piss together."

Someday I'll get even with this son of a bitch.

She showered. Never had a shower felt so good. A fragrant bath oil was provided along with soap and thick, rich shampoo. He commanded her to use all of them. When she stepped out and toweled, Sascha handed her an exquisitely thick, full-length Turkish bathrobe with a shawl collar and broad belt. She felt clean again, but violated. He led her onto an outside porch, dark except for a candlelit table. At Sascha's command, she seated herself. Allison was startled as, out of the darkness, another man suddenly appeared, dressed in a tuxedo. She relaxed as it became obvious that he was a waiter with a cart. He laid out a full-course meal. Composing herself, she settled down and began eating. *This is gourmet quality. American beef. Fresh vegetables and fruit. Carefully prepared. Absolutely delicious.* The table was appointed with the finest linen and genuine late Renaissance sterling. She guessed that the silver creamer and salt and pepper shakers were priceless. She devoured the meal, almost forgetting where she was. Sascha was sitting somewhere in the darkness, far enough away that the sea breeze dispelled his odor.

From out of the darkness he commanded her, less gruffly than before: "Open front of robe. I watch them in candlelight." The word *them* she thought was crude, but she accommodated. He moved his chair closer, just into the candlelight. His eyes looked like those of a little boy looking through a store window at a toy his parents couldn't afford to buy.

After dinner they returned to the bedroom where he commanded her to take off the robe. Laid out on the bed was a full-length ruby-red silk ball gown, the bodice decorated with dozens of pearls. *I could never afford to own such a gown, she thought.* "Where are the undergarments?" she asked.

Sascha roared with laughter. "What you want? You want panties? You don't need panties. You want bra? I watched good. You nice firm. You not wear them long anyway — they only get in way. Why you play dumb with Sascha?" He growled angrily. "Sascha no fool. You think Sascha a fool?"

"No. No. Please. You are not a fool. I'm sorry. I'm not accustomed to so much attention. I guess I just need your guidance, Sascha. Help me learn to do things properly."

He grinned. She counted four teeth missing, and the others were decayed and rotting. His bloated unshaven face reminded her of the grinning devil in Dante's Inferno. Allison slipped into the gown and stepped in front of a full-length mirror. She knew she looked stunning. It fit her perfectly. *Either they have a wide selection of sizes or a resident seamstress, she thought.*

"Hurry," he commanded. "It is time. We do not want honored guest to fall into asleep before he has you."

Sascha took her almost gently by the hand and led her into the hallway, where he stopped and pointed toward a door. Speaking softly he said, "You must be very good to honored guest. You understand? Any complaint will cause one friend piss sitting down. You very smart lady, I think. Not virgin, so relax. Sex real good. Love honored guest now." He tenderly patted her buns and nudged her toward the door.

"God, it looks like you're my only chance. Please, if it be your will, let this horror pass from me, but, if it be your will that I must suffer at the hands of these men, first send your Holy Spirit to strengthen my faith. Without that strength, I may not be able to endure.

She knocked. After several seconds the door opened. She looked over her shoulder. Sascha had disappeared. A handsome man with Iberian features wearing half-glasses, looked into her face, obviously pleased at what he saw. He reached for her right hand, took it gently, and led her in.

"Please be seated," he said, nodding toward a tall, Renaissance high-backed chair. When she was seated, he released her hand. "I was enjoying some Greek wine. It is red and very dry. Please, will you join me?"

So this is what it's like to be a whore for the rich and powerful. One needs a touch of class. I can ooze class if that's what it takes to keep Murdock and Rudi alive until we can figure a way out of here. "Yes," she whispered with downcast eyes. "You are very kind. I would enjoy that."

She felt vaguely uncomfortable and vulnerable without undercloth-ing. She wondered if he knew. *Is this the way women are traditionally presented to Mr. Big Bucks? Does this add to his excitement—knowing that she has nothing else on?*

"Please excuse me," he said seating himself next to an end table covered with documents. "I didn't expect you quite so soon. I must read these first. It will not take long. But please make yourself comfortable while you wait. There are magazines. I do not mean to be rude, my dear. Business comes first."

"Please don't be concerned," Allison replied as she sipped the wine. "Nothing compels us to hurry."

"Thank you. You are as gracious as you are beautiful."

He became engrossed in his papers. She watched from under lowered lashes. *This one works up his passion casually. Does he expect romance? That might be difficult. I make a lousy hypocrite. Can I fake romance? I must try. Actresses do it. I'll pretend he's Jerr. Or Murdock.*

A thought struck her. She panicked inwardly. *I'm probably fertile. I've had no reason to be on the pill. I've saved myself for Murdock, but he treats me like an old buddy. There isn't a man this side of the dungeon who cares whether I get pregnant or what would happen to our baby. But I must please this man. It'll buy time. If we can all stay alive a while longer, we'll find a way out.* Frenzied thoughts raced through her head. *The little creature would be my baby too—maybe the only one I'll ever have. I couldn't kill it. If they plan on keeping me, I doubt they would give me a choice. I'd lose my figure, so they would abort me. Would a professional do it? Someone they trust? Someone who'd keep my slavery secret? Would these men do it themselves? Would Sascha use his knife? What if he mutilates me? Oh, God. I've got to get control of myself. We'll get out of this if we keep our heads.*

She composed herself, but she couldn't help staring at the man so nonchalantly seated there, reading and sipping his wine. *What if he wants oral sex. I can't get pregnant that way, but I've no experience. Jerr never asked for it. I might be awkward and displease him. I've got to try. Murdock's and Rudi's lives depend on me. It's that simple. Where there's no love, it usually doesn't last all that long, unless he's cruel and enjoys prolonging cruelty. But this cool character calmly sits there reading. I can't let him complain to Sascha.* She surveyed the room. It was on the second floor, and the windows were barred. *Even if I could escape from this room, how could I free them? There's great wealth here. For the price this man's paid, he may expect both vaginal and oral sex? Or something else. How many things can a guy do? Face it, girl. He doesn't give a hoot what happens to you. What he wants is fun fucking. Period. Plain and simple.*

He finished reading, placed the documents neatly on the nightstand, turned toward her, and sat pensively watching her. "Why so quiet?" he asked.

"We've never met," Allison replied awkwardly, forcing a smile. "I don't know the name of this dashingly handsome man with whom I'll spend the night. May I know who you are?" Boldly, she raised her wine glass and extended her arm toward him. He smiled and half filled it.

"Of course." He stood and bowed. "I apologize. I am Jose Enrique Perez-Krieger. I am from Chile. As you have guessed, I am a businessman. I am bewildered by the obvious quality of the woman who has so graciously joined me. I would be very pleased if she consented to stay the night, as she suggested."

Allison's eyes widened. "*You* are Enrique?"

Startled by her response, Enrique paused in the middle of pouring wine into his glass and looked up. "You have heard of me?"

Allison pointed to the ceiling and made a circle with her finger.

"Ah," he said, understanding. "There are no bugs. I've tested."

"I'm Allison Spencer."

He dropped the wine glass. It shattered on the floor. "Murdock's friend?"

"Yes."

"Why did we not meet at dinner? Why does a woman of your quality not appear until now? Do you work for Boris? Are you one of his . . . No. You couldn't be. That is impossible. Excuse me for thinking so, even for a second."

He appeared embarrassed. Fear gripped her. *Have I been foolish? Things are not going as Sascha would want.* She knew the penalty. She resisted panic, but just barely. "Please, Señor Perez-Krieger, do not let my friendship with Murdock interfere with our pleasure."

Enrique kneeled down in front of her, took her hands in his and attempted to hold them. She jerked them back convulsively. "Sorry," she insisted.

"Señora. Please be quiet for a moment. I touched your hands out of desire — but not the desire you think. I touched out of desire to know whether you are here voluntarily. Your body replied."

Her intuition told her to gamble. "I *must* please you. I've been ordered to please you. If I disobey . . ."

"You are forcing yourself to accept me because you are afraid. When I look at you I don't see a lover; I see a woman protecting someone she loves. No woman has ever loved me as much as I see in your eyes. Is Murdock here and in trouble?"

She froze, confused, her mind swimming. For several seconds she couldn't speak. "Please, Señor Perez-Krieger," she begged. "It's okay to do it. Really."

"Or tell them I did?"

There was a long silence. She wondered what game he was playing. *Was the question some sort of test? Why does he have to mess with my mind? Why all this mock concern? Are these the games that rich men play with helpless women to torment them? Does the helplessness make it more fun?*

Do it, she commanded — her lips moved but no words escaped. *Maybe it's the game that turns him on. I must play the god-awful game but I don't know the rules. He doesn't seem turned on yet. If I can't turn him on, Sascha may kill Murdock or Rudi.*

He repeated. "Or tell them that I did?"

She stared at him, her eyes pleading.

"Or tell them that I did?" he persisted.

"Yes!" she wailed. *Oh, God. What have I done?*" A deep, anguished sob burst from the depth of her throat, choking her, and uncontrollable tears flowed. She pressed her knees together. He leaned forward and held her in his arms.

"Where is Murdock?" he whispered softly in her ear.

"You don't know?"

"I don't know."

Enrique took his handkerchief and dabbed her eyes, and then hugged her tighter. She sobbed convulsively. "They have Murdock and Rudi Benzinger."

"Do they have them in the crusaders' dungeon?"

"Yes," she sobbed, recklessly abandoning all pretense. "And they've already brutally murdered Baron von Richter."

Enrique was stunned and appalled. He released her, sat back on his heels, and stared into her face. "And Boris is using you with a promise to keep them alive?"

"Boris?"

He whispered close to her ear. "Listen carefully, Señora. I have a gun. I always have a gun around Boris. I spent three years as an officer in the Chilean army. I know how to use it. Truly, we will free them." He gently wiped her eyes. "And you do not have to pay for it."

She looked into his eyes. "They may kill you," she sobbed, trying to get control of herself.

He gently kissed her forehead and hugged her again. The tenseness of her body began to relax. "I have faced death before," he whispered. "Believe me, it is better to die than to live without honor. God has granted me an opportunity, and made clear to me how evil this Boris is before I have done business with him. Linda, my assistant, was right about Boris. His slime would drip onto me."

She stopped sobbing. "I'm so embarrassed, Señor."

"Please to call me Enrique and I shall call you Allison. Okay? Yes, of course you are embarrassed. And, Allison, I am embarrassed too. It is proof of your quality that you were willing to suffer humiliation for the sake of your friends. Remember, Señora, from this day forward, that you have done nothing tonight that you need to be ashamed of, and I have done nothing to you. In some happier time fate may bring us together again under different circumstances."

He helped her to her feet. "This is not a traditional way of beginning a friendship," he said, "but let us be friends anyway. We must help our friends in the dungeon. Boris Romanovsky, who is your captor, once gave me a tour of the ruins of the old crusaders' castle. I saw the dungeon. I know where the cell keys are hung. There is an airplane within walking distance ready for takeoff. I am a competent pilot, and I under-stand that Murdock is too. But we must wait." He pointed to the door. "The room is relatively soundproof. They cannot hear us talk, but over the next few hours you must scream loud enough to penetrate the walls. They understand brutal pleasure. By 2:00 A.M. we will let them assume we have fallen into an exhausted sleep. In the meantime, between screams, we will make a plan and execute it at 3:00 A.M. They will not expect another sound from us until after sunrise. By then it will be the guards who scream when Boris throws them in the dungeon. In the mean-time you must remove that dress. I will give you clothing, and we will need to run. Disrobe in the bathroom, please. I will bring some of my extra clothes to you."

Monday

November 24

⇥ **42** ⇤

The hours passed slowly. At 3:00 A.M., Enrique and Allison carefully retraced the steps that she and Sascha had taken. They removed their shoes as they approached the guardhouse. Enrique pointed to a window. They crept up to it cautiously and looked in. The full moon lighted the filthy mass that passed for Sascha's bed. He was sleeping, his gun clearly visible on a table next to him. The door was bolted from the inside. Enrique whispered: "We've got to get him to open the door. When he does, I don't want to shoot him. It'll arouse the others. I'll need to sneak up on him from behind and hit him on the head. I don't need to tell you what you can do to distract his attention."

"Yes," she whispered. "I know exactly. I'll cross the room, turn and face you, so his back will be toward you.

Enrique smiled and nodded. "Hopefully I won't have to hit him hard enough to kill him. When you hear a thud, get out of the way. Let's move."

Allison undressed, put on Enrique's bathrobe, and knocked on the door, softly at first, and then with increasing vigor. Sascha sat upright, shook his head, and tried to focus his eyes. "Who in shit's name is it?" he demanded angrily.

"Allison Spencer," she replied, moving in front of the window so her form would be silhouetted by the moonlight. Sascha was startled. He quickly picked up his gun, unbolted the door, and pulled it open.

"Why you here?" he demanded, his eyes fixated on her breasts.

Allison entered, walked across the room, turned and faced the door. "He wasn't much of a man," she complained. "He laid me once and told me to come back in the morning. I want a real man to give me what I want." She dropped to her knees. Her robe slipped to the floor. He froze as his little-boy eyes feasted on his new toy. *What the hell is Enrique waiting for?* "Come to mamma."

Sascha simultaneously dropped his pants and his gun. Without stepping out of them, he waddled toward her. Tripping over his pants, his hand grabbed his manhood and gave himself a quick prestart, just as Enrique's gun butt landed. Sascha fell in a heap. Blood ran down the side of his head. He moaned.

Enrique handed her the clothes she'd left outside. She dressed quickly. Enrique could find no rope, so he tied Sascha as best he could with Sascha's belt. He thrust Sascha's gun into Allison's right hand. "He's not tied very well. If you think he's awakening, hit him again. As a last resort, shoot the son of a bitch. I'll get your friends." He grabbed the keys from a hook on the wall, picked up Sascha's flashlight, and disappeared into the darkness of the spiral staircase. When he reached their cell door, he unlocked it and threw it open. Both Murdock and Rudi were awake. They had lost all sense of day and night. Enrique shined the light on his face.

"Enrique!" Murdock shouted in disbelief.

"No time to explain," Enrique insisted. "Allison is upstairs. She's safe. Come quickly. We can talk later. There's a Cessna 310 on the landing strip, and I know where the stupid pilot hid the key. It's nearly 4:00 A.M. and we need to get to the aircraft and start those engines before anyone knows we're missing." He noticed Rudi had a splint on his arm. "Can you move okay?"

"Ja, ja," Rudi said. "We go fast."

"You sure Allison's all right?" Murdock asked.

They started up the stairs. "Allison is all right in more ways than one, but the Baron's dead. Right now it's Sascha who's in danger."

As they reached the guardhouse at the top of the stairs, Allison gave Sascha another whack on the head and joined them as they ran out the door. Enrique led. The pathway through the gardens wound upward toward the landing strip. They ran crouched down in the moonlight. As they approached the top, an alarm bell sounded.

"I should have hit him harder," Allison exclaimed, short of breath.

Floodlights came alive all around the house and on the landing strip. Enrique stopped at the top of the hill where the pathway met the airfield.

"Murdock, untie the aircraft and remove the rudder block." Enrique was feeling around in a bucket of sand. "Here's the key. We have plenty of damn light now, so do a quick walk-around preflight check."

Murdock grabbed the key and Allison's hand. Together they ran over to the airplane. He passed the key to her. "Unlock the door and put it in the ignition. I'll remove the wheel chocks and the tie-down ropes.

Rudi waited at the trailhead with Enrique. "Quickly, give me your gun," Rudi commanded. "Someone is coming up the path."

"Not with your gun hand in a sling. I'm a good shot. Get in the plane." Rudi hesitated and then bolted for the aircraft. Enrique fired once in the direction of the footsteps and dropped to the ground. A bullet whizzed by his left ear, and he fired again down the path. Two more

bullets whizzed over his head. Fifty feet distant, Allison helped Rudi into
the rear seat. "To hell with the preflight," Enrique shouted. "They're
coming." He fired again down the trail. "Start the engines," he shouted.

Murdock ducked inside into the pilot's seat, switched on the magne-
tos, pushed the fuel mixture controls to full rich, and the propeller controls to high RPM. He eased the throttle for the left engine forward and
hit the left starter button. The engine cranked over three times and
caught. *Power on the left. Please, God, give us power on the right.* He
pushed the right throttle forward and hit the right starter button. It
cranked but it didn't fire. He tried again. No joy. *These 310s don't take off
very well on one engine. It's an invitation to death.* He tried again.

Allison saw Enrique bolt for the aircraft, and Sascha's face appear
above the crown of the hill. Sascha stopped, took aim, and fired twice.
One bullet struck the aircraft, the other struck Enrique. Enrique tripped
and dropped his gun. Sascha fired again, striking the dirt next to Enrique.
Enrique got up and ran in a crouched position. Allison, standing on the
wing, wondered if she had counted correctly. Did Sascha need to reload?
She gambled, climbed onto the wing, Sascha's gun still in her hand, stood
upright, raised her right arm, steadied it with her left, took aim and fired
one round. Sascha dropped his weapon, grabbed his crotch with both
hands, and fell to his knees, howling like a wild dog. As Enrique leaped
onto the wing, Allison fell backward into the rear seat so he could jump
into the front.

"You missed his heart," Rudi said.

"I'm a sharpshooter," Allison reminded him. "I hit what I aim at."

The right engine was still cranking. Theo came over the crown of
the hill, stumbled over Sascha, fell, and dropped his gun. The right engine caught. Theo crawled toward his gun. Without waiting for the engines to warm, Murdock pushed both throttles to the fire wall, and the
aircraft surged onto the runway in a cloud of dust. Theo grabbed his gun
and fired randomly into the cloud. Murdock heard a bullet strike the airframe. He didn't know where.

"I can't help," Enrique shouted to Murdock as he struggled to close
and lock the cabin door. "My shoulder's in a bad way. I'm losing blood."

A row of tall trees stood just past the end of the runway. They
loomed larger every second. Another bullet struck the airframe. Murdock
pulled back on the yoke. The aircraft rotated, its nosewheel lifting off the
ground. *You've taken us this far God, now we need a . . .* The main gears
left the ground, and the aircraft took flight, barely clearing the trees. Murdock's right foot pushed the left rudder pedal to compensate for pro-
peller-induced torque. *The cable controlling the elevator's working, but
there's a rough spot. I hope a bullet hasn't nicked it. If it has, God, please*

let it hold together 'till we get back on the ground. I've never flown with-out an elevator. He shook his head. *It'll be a miracle if we make it.* Mur-dock wondered how one would distinguish between a miracle and dumb ass luck. He raised the landing gear lever. The aircraft dipped slightly from the added drag of the three gear doors opening to receive the two main gears and the nose gear. The altimeter needle read one thousand feet.

"Keep low," Enrique shouted. "Keep under their radar."

"I intend to," Murdock replied, leveling the aircraft. "I don't know this area. Do you have a recommendation as to heading?"

"Two-eight-zero."

Allison released her seat belt and leaned forward. Using both hands and her handkerchief, she applied pressure on Enrique's wound. "The bullet went clean through," she said. "It didn't hit an artery or a vein. The bleeding looks worse than it is. Use your right hand to apply pressure from the front. Rudi, use your good hand to apply pressure from the back. I saw a first aid kit somewhere behind me. Your biggest danger is infec-tion."

"Why two-eight-zero?" Murdock asked. "That puts us out to sea with no landfall for a long haul."

"You're right," Enrique responded. "About four hundred miles to the coast of Crete. We're in danger anywhere on Cyprus, and they'll expect us to head for Turkey because it's close."

"Why Crete? Why not Egypt or Greece?"

"I have a friend there — Homer we call him because he's a poet. He owns more companies than I, so he can afford to be a poet. I recommend that our destination be his private landing strip." Holding pressure on the wound with his left hand, he fought the pain, reached into his back pants pocket, and pulled out a phone.

"We may be too low and too far out to use that," Murdock said.

"No. It bounces off a satellite." He pushed a key. After several sec-onds he spoke into the instrument. "Sorry to waken you at this hour, Linda, but I've got trouble. You were 100 percent right about Boris. Mur-dock McCabe, Allison Spencer, and Rudi Benzinger are with me in the Cessna 310. Boris was holding them prisoner, and I've helped them es-cape. We're flying low and heading for Homer. Ask him to turn on his locator beacon. We'll arrive around sunrise. I'm wounded. I'll need a doctor. Tune in 122.9, the aircraft to aircraft frequency. Listen on this phone but pretend we're conversing on the aircraft radio. If Boris is lis-tening, he'll think we've got more altitude than we have. On the radio I'll indicate we're heading for Adana in Turkey. If they try to intercept, they'll start out in the wrong direction. That'll buy us time."

He tuned the radio to 122.9 MHz and performed the charade.

Murdock checked the fuel gauges. Enrique turned on the automatic direction finder and tuned it to 560 KHz. "What's that?"

"Radio Helene at Terápetra on the island of Crete. It's a broadcast station. It'll help zero in on Crete. When we get within twenty-five miles of Homer's landing strip, we'll pick up his radio beacon. Then the ADF needle will point directly to the runway."

"We're thin on fuel," Murdock said. "Aux tanks are empty. The main tanks are less than half full. At this low altitude we're running rich and burning gasoline like crazy. It would help to gain altitude as soon as possible so I can lean her back. The DME indicates we have some tailwind. We might find a stronger tailwind at higher altitude."

Enrique shook his head. "I don't think so. I saw my pilot's weather chart yesterday. There's a cold front that should be crossing the heel of Italy about now. At higher altitude the winds aloft may switch to the south and give us a crosswind. That would waste fuel."

Murdock adjusted the directional gyro so that the indicated heading conformed to the compass. "That bad weather is too close for comfort. Storms usually develop four or five hundred miles in advance of a cold front. The sky could get rough before sunrise."

Allison found antiseptic and applied it to Enrique's wounds. "I haven't found any life preservers," she said. "If we're low on fuel, maybe we should go back to Limassol or Nicosia."

Rudi objected. "I agree we're not safe there. Boris owns some powerful policemen. We can use seat cushions for flotation, can't we?"

"Not these," Murdock replied. He turned his head toward Enrique. "We're thirty miles offshore. I'll let it drift up to 1500 so I can lean the mixture a tad."

"No higher, yet," Enrique urged.

The engines sounded rough. Murdock adjusted the RPM controls to synchronize the propellers. "When you're out of sight of land," he said, "engines seem to go instant ruff." He trimmed the aircraft to hold altitude at 1000, sat back, and tried to relax. "What time does Radio Helene come on the air?"

"Six."

Murdock cringed. They could drift off course by then. And he knew that Enrique knew it too. "I think we're getting a little crosswind from the right rear. I'm going to change our heading to two-eight-five to correct for wind drift."

"I agree," Enrique said.

Allison finished with the first aid kit and returned it to its rack. Turning to Rudi, she helped him adjust his sling. "How did you get the splint for your arm?" she asked.

"From the wisdom of Murdock," he said with as much cheeriness as he could muster. "He made a deal that he would tell them what they wanted to know if they provided medical attention for me immediately and promised to release us all unharmed. Within the hour a doctor appeared. Theo assured us you were having dinner in a luxury apartment. He took us upstairs and let us watch you through field glasses so we could feel that you were safe."

"You saw the candlelight meal on the porch. Did you figure what it might foreshadow?"

"Yes. Murdock informed them that Brother Stephen had developed an advanced, super-fast computer chip that would revolutionize computing. The plans that the killer obtained from the body of Brother Stephen, he told them, were flawed decoys. Brother Martin had given Murdock the real plans to protect, and they were in his safe deposit box at a bank in Munich."

Allison turned to Murdock. "I didn't realize you are such an artful liar."

"Thank you," he said, looking over his shoulder, his face pained. "I'm sorry, Al. I couldn't prevent your ordeal. Theo would only guarantee your life and your release. I compromised. Really sorry, but I thought at least you'd live through it."

"As it turned out," she said, "they gave me to Enrique who was a perfect gentleman. That turned out to be their mother of all blunders."

Rudi interjected. "Murdock agreed to obtain the true schematics for them if they released you and me in front of the bank in Munich today. That confused them. Should they believe Murdock's story? Could they afford to turn us loose? Could they afford not to obtain the schematics for the super-fast chip? They needed a plan to have us killed in Munich immediately after the turnover — before we could identify them. They couldn't rough up Murdock because he had to look natural to the bank clerk. Murdock's story bought us time."

An hour passed with little conversation. They had gradually climbed to five thousand feet. Suddenly Murdock turned to Enrique. "Did you see that?"

"Yes. Lightning on the horizon at twelve o'clock. That's not good."

Murdock reset the directional gyro to correct for precession. "Our fuel situation is a stretch. I hope we don't have to divert for heavy weather." He checked the automatic direction finder. "The needle's come alive. Turn up the volume and see if you can confirm it's Radio Helene."

Enrique turned the knob. "It's the Greek national anthem. The station just came on the air. We'll have an ID soon. There it is. It's Radio Helene."

Murdock checked the needle. "The wind must have shifted to the south in advance of the cold front. We've drifted north of course. If we miss Crete, we'll run out of fuel before we see land. I propose to correct our heading to two-seven-zero—due west."

"Or two-six-five," Enrique suggested.

"You're probably right." Murdock applied pressure to the left rudder pedal and turned the wheel in the same direction. The aircraft went into a coordinated twenty degree left turn. He rotated to straight level with the gyro indicating exactly 265°. "One of the bullets may have grazed the elevator cable. Have you ever tried to fly an aircraft without an elevator?"

"No. It might be tough." Enrique checked the altimeter. "From this altitude we should be able to raise Homer on 122.8 MHz in a few minutes."

Allison tapped Enrique on the shoulder. "What if Boris's jet took off and they're looking for us? Won't they hear your transmission? What if they have a direction finder on board?"

"We should be well over the horizon from them. Radio waves from these very high frequencies head straight for the horizon and off into space. They don't bounce off the ionosphere like Radio Helene."

Murdock pointed out the forward window. "There's a lot of lightning zapping around between two-five-zero and three-one-zero. We may need to divert several miles south of our course. I hate to waste the fuel, but flying into the teeth of a thunderstorm is foolhardy. We're going to arrive before sunrise, so I hope he has runway lights."

"He has." Enrique set the frequency on the communications radio to 122.8 MHz and keyed the mike. "Homer, this is Enrique. Do you read?"

After several anxious seconds, the speaker came to life. "That's affirmative, Enrique. What is your position, ETA, and type aircraft?"

"I estimate thirty to forty miles east in a Cessna 310—a piece of cake for your runway length."

"Runway length is fine but we have a rapidly approaching squall line about two miles west and moving eastward. I expect severe vertical wind shear. It looks like a very, very dangerous storm. Judging by location of lightning, the southern edge is ten miles south offshore. I recommend that you monitor our radio locator at 410 KHz when you come within its range, and enter a holding pattern fifteen miles south."

Enrique's and Murdock's eyes met. Enrique clicked the mike button again. "Thank you, Homer. We have no joy on fuel. We'll hold as long as we think wise, and then turn north—fly directly at you." Enrique glanced at Murdock, who nodded in agreement. "We're at five thousand, so if we lose power, we should be able to glide to within a few miles of shore. How heavy are the seas?"

"Sorry, my friend. I don't think I could find volunteers to go out in a boat right now. And that condition won't improve rapidly after the squall line passes. Surviving a ditching in seas this heavy will be difficult if not impossible. I just looked outside. Very heavy rain and severe vertical wind shear are approaching the western end of the runway. Rather than holding, consider looping around the backside of the squall line, and pray that it passes before you get here."

"We'll do that," Murdock shouted.

"Homer, that's affirmative."

Murdock picked up the mike and shouted: "When we leave the holding pattern, we'll loop around behind and approach from the west, if we can."

The speaker was silent for several seconds. Then Homer's voice came on again. "That'll be a hell of a tailwind landing."

"We know," Enrique replied. "We'll be eating a lot of runway. We may overrun. Please have your doctor close by."

And we've never tried the brakes, Murdock thought.

"Roger, Enrique. I have a doctor present. Linda warned me about your wound. I've just looked outside again. There's at least an inch of water over the entire runway. Brakes won't help. You'd hydroplane. I recommend that you consider a gears-up landing. It'll bend the props but you'll stop before you roll off the end of the runway. God be with you. Homer over and out."

"Thank you. Pray for us. Enrique out."

Murdock tuned 410 KHz on the radio direction finder. "The needle's all over the place," he said. "The lightning is screwing it up. I'm going to take a heading directly toward the southernmost lightning sighting and slip as close around the outside edge of it as I can. If there's not enough fuel for a holding pattern, I'll get behind the squall line and head north for the runway and land this sucker, come hell or high water."

"We may get both if you don't hold your altitude," Enrique suggested. "You're drifting downward."

"Thanks." Murdock trimmed the nose up slightly. If we make the runway under power, I'll pull the fuel mixture control as soon as we touch down. If we hit something, I'd rather not have the engines sucking gasoline."

Allison and Rudi remained quiet.

"Check your seat belts," Murdock commanded. Turbulence buffeted the aircraft. It felt like the aircraft was jouncing across a washboard."

Homer's voice came over the speaker. "Severe vertical turbulence along entire runway. Hold offshore if you can."

Enrique keyed the mike. "Can't do." He turned toward Murdock. "Visual contact," he shouted. "There's the light beacon at three o'clock." He keyed the mike: "Field conditions, please."

"No change," Homer replied. "Storm is directly over the runway. It's ugly."

Murdock knew that a severe downdraft during a low approach could slam them into the ground with force sufficient to disintegrate the aircraft. He checked the fuel gauges and shook his head. "No joy on the fuel gauges, Enrique," Murdock shouted, repeating the obvious. "I'd recommend that God improve conditions within the next few seconds. In the absence of that, there's no fuel available for a holding pattern. I'm changing course for the light beacon now, and, unfortunately, we're going to shave the backside of the damn storm."

Enrique keyed the mike. "Homer, we're inbound for landing."

"Roger, Enrique. Again, I strongly recommend a gears-up landing to slow you down quicker. There's so much water on the runway, you don't need to worry about sparks."

"Negative," Murdock shouted. "I want to try for rudder directional control on the ground. If we land on our belly, we could spin out of control, and if we hit something, centrifugal force could break everyone's neck. Help me watch the turn and bank ball." He put his right hand on the prop RPM controls. Either engine could run out of gas any second. If an engine quit, he needed to feather the prop immediately. Even a few seconds of drag from a windmilling prop could cost him altitude when he needed it. And he had to be ready for the second engine to quit too.

No one spoke. Sweat ran into Murdock's eyes. Enrique was bleeding again. Directly in front of them a bolt of lightning struck the ground. Vertical wind shear bumped them up several hundred feet and suddenly dropped them again. Murdock struggled to maintain direction of flight and hold the aircraft on a steady glide slope. "We're on borrowed time," he shouted, "but we've got the field made. We can glide in from here. I'm reducing power now. Standard rate of descent—more or less—difficult to control altitude in this turbulence. Turning on runway heading." Murdock's hand nervously held the fuel mixture controls, but he knew that, if they ran out of gas, the controls would be irrelevant.

"God is good," Enrique exclaimed. "The trailing edge of the heavy rain is already at mid-runway."

Murdock shouted, "We've got the glide path nailed. We're lined up with the center line as good as we're ever going to be."

Enrique warned, "We're coming in hot."

Murdock lowered the landing gears, eased the flaps into their full down position, and raised the nose to bleed off speed. Murdock, speaking calmly, announced: "Put your head between your legs and your feet flat on the floor. If we land hard, it's easier to walk away if you don't have broken ankles. I'm going to need that fence at the far end of the runway to slow us down."

In front of them the runway numbers — a big 09 — were racing toward them. The main gears touched just past them. He pulled the mixture controls and eased back the yoke to maximize the flaps as air brakes. He saw people standing in the rain to his right. *Still too much water on the runway. If I apply mechanical brakes, I may spin into the fence out of control. Better to hit it straight on—nose high. I've still got sufficient speed for directional control from the rudder but not for much longer. Here comes the fence.* As they rolled off the runway into the field grass, he quickly scanned the control panel and noticed that the magneto switches were still on. *Don't need any sparks.* As he whacked both switches into the off position, the aircraft hit the chain-link fence, ripping it out of the ground. Dragging fence with it for another twenty feet, the aircraft came to a stop, upright. After several seconds of silence, Enrique said quietly: "God is merciful."

Light from a flashlight from outside the cabin caught a slow grin crossing Murdock's face. "Either that, or we had a pilot highly skilled in crash landings."

Allison released her seat belt, leaned forward, and planted a big kiss on Murdock's right cheek. "I suspect it was a big dose of both," she said.

⇥ 43 ⇤

The professor hadn't slept well. He awakened at 4:00 A.M. Anxious to return to his computer, he put on his robe, turned up the thermostat, switched on the computer, and sat down before it. Brother Stephen's narrative continued.

On Wednesday, November 12, I had to subdue my excitement. The tapes disclosed what I thought was a echo of the message I had sent. Were they repeating it back to me? Or passing it on to someone else? I couldn't be certain. Their response, if that's what it was, was communicated beginning on the base frequency *variant* that Michael gave me. Michael had indicated that there was a high probability that this approach would work. But I know he was certain. The man is amazing. He must have an IQ near 200.

The promptness of the reply is troublesome. Traveling at the speed of light it would take at least eight years for my message to get to and a response to come from a planet around the nearest star other than the Sun. It would unless the universe is made of stranger stuff than I think. Assuming for the sake of argument that it isn't, and assuming that what I've seen and heard *is* a response, they must be quite close — perhaps just outside our solar system traveling toward us. If that's true, how long have they been en route? Have they discovered a means of navigating straight lines through some wormhole in the curvature of space so that time and distance is minimized? If they're on their way at all, their science must be more advanced than ours. Their society would have adjusted to thousands of scientific discoveries that we have not. How will we deal with such a deluge of knowledge?

The professor didn't have an answer. He had not ever planned to face the problem. *And therein lies the difficulty. No one has.* He scrolled forward to another page.

Brother Antonio senses our excitement and so in turn is excited himself. He can barely contain himself. He's like a little boy waiting to go to a carnival. That concerns me. He is eager to know to what use his software has been put. He suspects. He is a bright man. Hopefully, his imagination is not big enough. He has accepted our Reverend Abbot's decree that he wait until the meeting of the Brotherhood on Tuesday. Even then, hopefully, he will not know the whole truth. *I* may not know the whole truth.

I have recommended to Reverend Abbot that, except for Brother Gustav, Richard Laplatenier, and you, we keep all of this secret until we have confirmed that the signals come from extraterrestrials, and until we have effectively communicated with them and learned their purpose. Then we will be in a better position to recommend a plan to manage the information.

The professor agreed that management was necessary. He knew that if any government learned they had made contact with extraterrestrials, the politicians and bureaucrats would descend upon them, promulgate rules, take command, and find ways to invest taxpayer's money in the project so they could funnel it to their friends. He turned another page.

It is Friday, November 14. It has been a discouraging day. I have listened to the tapes of the last twenty-four hours and heard nothing. If they're there, are they waiting for me to make the next move? If they are scientists, they should be anxious to make contact — unless they're obligated to first report to some political authority — or unless, God forbid, they're military.

It is now Saturday, November 15. I am looking forward to your arrival on Monday. I feel that you should be present at the meeting of the Brotherhood on Tuesday. Reverend Abbot is not convinced.

For the last forty-eight hours the tapes have remained silent. It's as if I interrupted their conversation and they stopped talking. Have they changed the base frequency code? I wish Michael were here.

His entries have become laconic. He's not writing all that's in his mind.

It is now Sunday, November 16. I fear that my work has come to naught. This morning Reverend Abbot preached on Ruth 2:12 — "The Lord recompense your work, and a full reward be given you of the Lord God of Israel, under whose wings you have come to trust." My reward is in pleasing God. I believe He is pleased that I search for others of His creatures in the universe. I trust Him. I must be satisfied with both the gifts and the burdens He gives me. His is the success. The failures are mine.

Alas, Brother Gustav has come out of two days of seclusion and rendered his opinion. He cannot conclude to a reasonable degree of certainty that the sounds recorded on my tapes are speech. He believes that there is some evidence of intelligence, but he opines that the sounds may be something similar to the Morse code, but with inflections. He suggests that, if it is intelligence, it may be a broadcast, like we on Earth broadcast into space. If that is true, the message, if there is one, could have been on its way for hundreds of thousands of years, and the civilization that transmitted it could have disappeared long ago. Perhaps I have been swept away by wishful thinking. Gustav urges me to obtain a second opinion. I shall. But Gustav is highly respected in his field. I thought we were at an ending, or at least a new beginning, but I fear there is much more work to do. Years, rather than days, of patience may be required. But if they're there, and if they're broadcasting for the purpose of discovering life on other planets, why are they using complex variations of frequencies that discourage detection?

My work must be kept secret from the world until secrecy is no longer morally defensible. Secrets are better kept by few than many. Martin is determined that the Brotherhood deal with the problem, but he has agreed to couch it in a hypothetical parallel.

To borrow from Tennyson: That which I have done, may God within Himself make pure.

I am anxious to talk to you. There is much more for you to know than I have written — or than I have told anyone.

The professor found it difficult to understand the psychological process that conditions people to crave divine acceptance.

One last page contained writing.

It is Monday, November 17. You will arrive this morning.

I fear the cat is out of the bag. Can't tell whether it is all the way out. Reverend Abbot has received inquiries about my work from one of the richest men in Germany, the Baron von Richter, and from one of the richest men in the world, Jose Enrique Perez-Krieger. Who has leaked? What was leaked? Brother Antonio is a child of enthusiasms. His heart is pure, but he may have said too much to his family in Spain. I don't think he's guessed that my goal is to make contact with extraterrestrials. Or has he? I shall prepare a decoy and advertise to him that I am sending my secret off to my plant in Oregon. I shall take the decoy to the village this afternoon and post it. We'll see what happens when it arrives in Oregon.

The memoirs ended there. The professor shut down the computer, relit his pipe, and stared out the picture window. The sun had disappeared behind clouds, and a very light snow was falling — just like the day he had arrived a week ago. *Last Monday at this time, Stephen was probably still alive. Later that same day on his way to post the decoy, he died of foul play in the meadow of the Liederbach Creek. Could Antonio be the killer? Stephen felt he was pure of heart. Martin is protecting him—keeping him somewhere. Is Martin clean? I must share the information from the memoirs with Murdock when he gets back today. From what Georg Brüner told me, Murdock's lucky to be alive. In the meantime, I must go to the antenna shack and check the recording devices.*

The professor took the floppy disks to Herr Bayer's office and locked them in his safe deposit box. Herr Bayer was curious but accepted the explanation that the disks contained complicated scientific formulas. Anxious to check the recording machine in the antenna shack, the professor considered walking, but that was out of the question. It was too far and there was a cold north wind blowing upslope. No roads led there — only trails. To his disappointment, Herr Bayer indicated that all of the snowmobiles had been rented for the day. As he was about to return to his room, he remembered that when he had lunch yesterday with Diana Crenshaw, she mentioned that she'd reserved a snowmobile for today. "Herr Bayer," he exclaimed, "have you seen Miss Crenshaw?"

Bayer pointed toward the coffee shop. "Ja, ja. A few minutes ago I saw her having breakfast."

"Thank you," he said, and walked across the foyer and into the coffee shop. Diana was sitting alone at a table near the center of a mostly empty room. She saw him and waved.

"Good morning," she said cheerfully. "Please join me."

"Gladly, gracious lady," he replied, bowing with mock eloquence. He seated himself. "But I must warn you. I come begging."

Diana poured a cup of coffee for him. "Begging? Friends don't need to beg. They simply ask. What can I do for you?" She handed him the cup of coffee. Their eyes met. She smiled.

He sipped the coffee. "You mentioned yesterday that you had reserved a snowmobile for today."

"How unromantic. Do you need one?"

"More than that. I'm not very good with such contraptions, and I need to ascend some rather rugged trails, so . . ."

"So I shall take you. I'm quite good with them. Where are we going?"

"To an antenna shack. I need to check some equipment?"

"Equipment?"

"It is part of a scientific experiment in which I am interested."

Their eyes met again. She didn't press.

*   *   *

Meanwhile in a private hospital in an eastern suburb of Zürich, two men sat — one propped up in the bed — the other sitting on the chair. The one in bed stared at the far wall, processing with what remained of his mind, the patterns on faded wallpaper. The room was cold. The other man, in a green nylon ski jacket who had been sitting in the chair next to the bed, arose and adjusted a blanket. "Please, Antonio," he pleaded, "you must try to remember who it was that you told." Brother Antonio's lips moved almost imperceptibly, but no words came.

⇥ 44 ⇤

Linda sat back, munched on a celery stalk, and studied Murdock's face. The jet was level at twenty-seven thousand feet, heading northbound. Coffee and sandwiches were laid out on the conference table.

They—Linda, Murdock and Allison—would be on the ground at Garmisch-Partenkirchen within two hours. Enrique and Rudi were in a hospital on Crete. If all went well with Enrique's wound and Rudi's arm, Linda planned to return in two days and retrieve them. Allison was sleeping in the aft cabin. Linda offered Murdock a stalk. He accepted.

"Do you feel up to talking about a few things?" she asked.

"I feel wonderful," Murdock responded enthusiastically. "Yesterday morning things looked pretty bleak. During the night, Enrique turned it around. What luck to find him there."

Linda smiled. "I suspect that many gifts of God are attributed to luck."

"You have a point."

"There are some things you need to know."

Murdock's expression turned serious. They were on board Enrique's jet. This woman was Enrique's administrative assistant. He remembered the reports from the FBI and Diana's confirmation. *I need to be cautious. Nothing is what it seems in this case. Maybe the whole thing was set up to fool us, but von Richter's dead. That's real.*

Linda's eyes met his. She spoke slowly and softly. "Two days ago—Friday—the director of the FBI in Washington was given certain information by one of his subordinates who, incidentally, is a member of Plato."

She awaited a response. His eyes narrowed. "Carl Sutherland? Jerr's friend?" he asked.

"He was our mole in Joe Carlyle's camp."

"Was?" Murdock asked. "What happened to him?"

"I'm coming to that. On Friday—three days ago—as a result of information provided by Carl Sutherland, the Director of the FBI organized a special task force. They obtained a warrant for the search of Joe Carlyle's house in Virginia. The affidavit supporting the warrant alleged that a gun and documents would be found under floorboards in the master bedroom, all having to do with the death of your wife. The warrant was executed. A gun was found and dispatched to the state police crime lab in Richmond."

"That was a good move," Murdock injected. "The state police lab has the bullet that killed Karen. Joe has camp followers in the FBI forensic lab. The evidence could have been compromised there."

Linda picked up the satellite phone, punched in several numbers, and handed it to him. "Jerr's waiting in Washington for your call."

Murdock took the phone. "In Washington?" Linda nodded. Jerr answered. A puzzled look crossed Murdock's face. "What are you doing in Washington?" he asked.

"Carl caught me on the cell phone on the way back from Des Moines on Saturday. The Director knew you and I were close friends. He had a plane waiting for me at Omaha. I joined the task force."

Murdock interrupted. "I hear you've got the gun that killed Karen."

"Yesterday, we learned that it was *not* the gun that fired the bullet that killed Karen. We did, however, retrieve boxes of documents. Joe was one of those people with a sense of history—people who keep copious records no matter how naughty they've been—like the Nazis and the Brazilians. There was a diary. I reviewed it. Because none of the guns used in the raid by either side fired the bullet that killed Karen, Joe always said there was a fourth kidnapper who escaped. The diary discloses that Karen was indeed shot by the fourth kidnapper who conveniently escaped seconds before Joe's agents appeared at the scene, leaving the dummies she'd hired behind to die in the gunfire. The fourth kidnapper was the brains of the operation—the woman called Patti Dale."

Murdock clenched his fist. "Jerr, do you believe Patti Dale killed Karen?"

"There's no doubt in my mind. Apparently the rumors about her and Joe were correct. But it wasn't sex like Carl thought. Joe wasn't screwing her. Joe was being controlled by her. This Dale woman has big money behind her and so big power. Joe hid some big bucks—a secret Swiss bank account with over a quarter million in it. He was selling classified information to her about our investigations of the international illicit weapons trade. There are references to a furtive organization called Traction. Has Enrique mentioned it?"

"Yes."

"Karen broke its code. She decoded their messages off the Internet. She phoned Joe to warn him that there was a mole within FBI Headquarters. She didn't know he was the mole. Patti Dale and Joe manipulated the fact that you were going to testify against the mob bosses and made Karen's kidnapping appear to be a mob hit. We believe the Dale woman is a power in Traction—if not *the* power. We know precious little about her. We know precious little about Traction. None of our contacts have met her. Have you?"

"No, but I'd like to. Moira—one of our operatives—has met her."

"Please talk to Moira and share the information with us. Joe Carlyle was trying to get some leverage on Patti Dale. He asked his buddy—your favorite district manager, Harvey Specter—to investigate her connections with gunrunning in Munich. That's why Moira was assigned."

"Unbelievable!"

"There's more. Joe Carlyle is dead."

"Dead?" Murdock exclaimed.

"Dead. His body was found yesterday by National Park Police in Fort Marcy Park — an apparent suicide."

Murdock's jaw dropped. "Joe killed himself? Are you certain it was suicide? Hard to believe. I suppose he thought it was better than spending the rest of his life in prison."

"That could be a reason," Jerr interjected. "Apparently he knew why Carl went into the director's office."

"Thanks, Jerr. And thank Carl Sutherland for me. My mind won't rest until we've got Patti Dale behind bars, but now at least I know that Karen's death wasn't accidental. That never fit."

"We've put out an international APB on Patti Dale. The Virginia police picked up a warrant this morning charging her with murder. I wish all this could bring Karen back, Murdock. I truly do. At least our sense of justice is partially satisfied. We just need Patti Dale."

"Have them send notice of the warrant to Rudi. We'll get her."

"Will do."

"Jerr, thanks again. You're a real pal. And please thank Carl for me. And the director."

"Surely. Is Allison okay?"

"She's sleeping in the aft cabin. She's fine."

"I lost her, old Pal. Don't you lose her too."

Murdock decided not to touch that. "Did you talk to Mr. Gregory — the original owner of Veritus?"

"Yes. Just before I received the call from Carl. The buyer was a Kurt M. Braun. Gregory thinks he was German, although he spoke near-perfect English. The sale was for cash — a cashier's check drawn on a CitiBank account in New York. Gregory described him as a tall, confident, muscular man, balding, with a heavy black beard and the beginning of a beer belly. Braun hadn't participated in the negotiations. Gregory first met him at the closing in Chicago. Gregory didn't ask questions. He was interested in the money. That's about all I have, my friend."

"That's a whole heap. You've been a great help, Jerr. Thanks a million."

"May I give you a piece of advice, Murdock?"

"Absolutely."

"Have a heart-to-heart talk with Linda. See ya." Click.

Murdock returned the phone to Linda. Neither spoke. Murdock collected his thoughts. Moira must be warned. Patti Dale has already killed once. Linda placed a call to Moira, but she couldn't be located. She tried the professor. He had left with Diana on a snowmobile. A call was placed to Brother Martin. Murdock took the phone.

"I am delighted to hear from you," Brother Martin said. Newscasts reported that all of you had been missing. Foul play was suspected. What's happening?"

Murdock ignored the question. "Please meet me at to the Zugspitze Hof Lodge. I should be there about 11:30 A.M. Wait in the foyer until I arrive."

Martin understood Murdock's reluctance to say much on a radio telephone. "I'll be there. In spite of what you have been through, you are a fortunate man. Someone else will be waiting for you. The professor told me that he had lunch yesterday with that intelligent and attractive young woman, Diana Crenshaw, and that she had many kind things to say about you. In fact, I understand that you were their main topic of conversation."

"I must confess that that isn't bad news."

"It shouldn't be. I shall see you soon. For now, *auf wiedersehen*, and God be with you."

Murdock placed the phone on the conference table. Linda poured a cup of coffee for him. "So," she said, "your plate is full?"

A wry smile crossed Murdock's face. "This has been one of the more interesting days of my life, and it isn't half over." He buttered a croissant and added jam. His appetite had returned in spades.

She smiled ironically. "You had many doubts about Enrique and Plato. Are they satisfied now?"

He hesitated. She was staring at him. *My God, she's an attractive woman. She dresses so businesslike, I hadn't noticed before.* He finished his croissant. "There are things about Enrique that I wish I didn't know." He searched her face. Her eyes were steady. She folded her hands and placed them firmly on top the conference table.

"Do you mean the child sex information? The little girl who died?"

"You know about that? How can you work for him?"

Her eyes fixed on his. "I can work for him because I believe in him. I believe he is a generous, honorable, honest man. I'm proud to be his assistant. I probably know him better than anyone knows him. Every human being is part enigma, but I find Enrique mostly transparent."

"If he hadn't learned about us in the dungeon, would he have . . ."

Linda interrupted. "He *is* a man. Yes, he would have had sex with your Allison, but he would never have raped her. He would never have permitted her in his room if he had known that she was there involuntarily. You may rest assured of that."

"Were you with him on the trip when he took those young girls?"

She laughed with no sign of a smile. "You graduated from law school. You know your question assumes a fact not in evidence. There is no evidence he did these things — only allegations. Has your FBI ever suspected a person who turned out to be innocent?"

"Naturally."

Linda smiled. "There are powerful people who would, at any cost, destroy the faith in him held by the members of Plato. That would destroy Plato and the economic stability it seeks to achieve. Instability is profitable for merchants of death. The world is full of scum. You know that from your years with the FBI. I'm confident that sometime today Jerr or Carl will confirm that Joe Carlyle manufactured the information in the FBI report on instructions from Traction."

Murdock's eyes met hers. "You're pretty articulate on the subject."

"It's part of my job to sort truth from fiction. You know the fiction. It's been spoon-fed to you."

"There's no truth in it?"

"There's *some* truth in it. The truth is that young girls were brought to Enrique's rooms in both Bangkok and Manila. In Manila, for example, right after he checked in, he found a naked twelve-year-old in his bed. He never touched her and checked out immediately. If Plato is to continue its work, Enrique must appear pure as the driven snow. I can categorically say he has never had sex with a child."

"How could you possibly know?"

"I am almost always with him, not inside his bedroom door, but constantly close enough that I would know. He keeps precious little from me. The rest I accept on faith. Do you believe me?"

"I'd like to, Linda, but over the two years since Karen's death, I've become damn cynical. I'm not proud of it. My own employer — my government — was responsible for Karen's death by letting slimy bums like Joe Carlyle rise to high positions while competent and dedicated agents rot in lesser jobs. As a kid I was patriotic, but in the highest echelons of my government I found men and women who would tell any lie and sacrifice any person for the sake of grasping raw power. It wasn't pretty. Blind trust went out the window."

Linda smiled. "You seem to trust Diana, and you have known her for barely a week. Do you trust God?"

"I went to church with my mother and occasionally with Karen."

"You're a bright man, Murdock. You know what I asked you."

He fidgeted with his hands. *She's pretty damn nosy but Jerr wants me to listen to her. Besides, after two years maybe it's time to face my demons.* But he hedged. "The truth is I just don't know. I surely don't need all that church stuff."

"Church stuff?"

"You know, rituals and hymn singing and all that." He caught himself wringing his hands.

"What's the matter?" Linda asked softly.

"There's no room in me for God right now. I'm filled with too much hate."

Sweat ran down his forehead. He knew that at that moment, if he had Patti Dale's neck in his hands, he could kill her and think nothing of it. His face convulsed. Linda took his hands in hers, her eyes soft, met his. He hadn't found compassion in her before. "I am a lawyer, not a psychologist," she said quietly, "but I think you need closure. You're cynical because you feel that your boss and your government have let you down . . . that with their help, Karen was torn from you in her youth. Hate makes things simple, doesn't it? Hate and cynicism stun thought. Did you *ever* believe that governments were perfect? Of course not. Can you afford to be a purist in an impure world, and judge that everyone else's sense of honor is less virtuous than yours?"

Murdock cocked his head. "A purist?"

"Aren't governments made up of people — all kinds of people — from people whose hearts are pure to people whose hearts are rotten? Generalizing just lumps the innocents with the guilty. You can't have closure on Karen's death by wallowing in cynicism. Believe in something or someone."

"You want me to believe in Enrique?"

"And me. Enrique saved your skins. Did he have a deeper, even more sinister motive that he's about to spring on you? What do you think? Decide. Can you believe in a God who watches over you? You found an airplane this morning with exactly enough fuel to fly from Boris's airstrip to Homer's, and land downwind on a short runway during a raging storm, through severe vertical wind shear and touchdown on a runway covered with water so that brakes were useless. The bullet-damaged elevator cable held long enough for you to steer the aircraft down the runway, and you struck a fence nose high with just enough force that the plane didn't flip over. Do you attribute all that to your skill? Come on! Do you trust me? If you do, I can help you. If you don't believe in anyone, no one can. I understand that your world has been cockeyed since Karen's death, so cockeyed that you're blind to the woman in the aft compartment who loves you. You impress me as a man whose — for lack of a better word — *soul* is in jeopardy. You need to trust. Everyone does. Try us. It's possible, you know, that even newfound friends can care about you deeply. Your kind of genuine article doesn't show up every day."

Murdock searched her eyes, convinced that he'd recognize insincerity if it were there. He saw none. "Thank you," were the only words he could find.

"Begin by disbelieving the offensive things you've heard about Enrique. Then ask yourself, 'Where does that take me?' "

Murdock slowly withdrew his hands from hers. His were steady now. "You don't mince words."

"Did Karen mince words?"

"No."

"Can you imagine Karen telling you what I have?"

"Yes, but why should *you*?"

"Because we consider you a friend. Friends don't mince words. Enrique has many friends, but few close ones. When he makes a new friend that he would like to be close to, he begins instinctively. He instinctively trusted you. You're genuine, honest and you have a virtue that's so rare these days — a sense of honor. He wants you to be a close friend."

"But we're a mismatch. He's rich and I'm far from it."

"Nevertheless, you've passed through the eye of his needle. For me, I fire straight from the shoulder. You can accept what I've said or forget it. Your choice. Decide. Enrique and I both want to be your friend. I can imagine the uncertainty in your mind today — the struggle you're going through. We care about the outcome."

She's not going to believe ill of Enrique. No point trying to convince her. But my instincts are tugging at me to believe her. She's right about Karen. Karen would have said the same things about faith and trust. And Joe could easily have faked the information in the FBI report. Okay. So I believe her. Now what? Where does that leave me? Murdock sat back and closed his eyes, his thoughts churning. He folded his hands on his lap. Linda remained silent. He heard the engines spool down. The aircraft, high over the northern Adriatic Sea, had begun a descent for Garmisch-Partenkirchen. One thing that bothered him. *Why had von Richter's staff been so foolish as to release their flight arrival time? They knew the situation was dangerous and should have known that it was safer to arrive without fanfare. If it was his staff.* He couldn't remember telling anyone other than the professor. He turned the events of the last week over and over in his mind. He remembered the sentence from the notebook found on Brother Stephen's body. *"Odin has found the wolf, and its name is Hecate."* It seemed meaningless. Nothing that he'd learned about Brother Stephen suggested that he would write something meaningless. *Why the mixture of German and Greek myths? Had Stephen intended to obtusely identify someone who was interested in such things? Hecate was a feminine name in ancient Greece. Could Stephen have meant Patti Dale? She keeps popping up, but I've found no evidence that Brother Stephen knew about her, or had any contact with her, or that she or Joe Carlyle had any interest in Stephen. How could either have gotten wind of the chaos chip? Who might have put them on to it?*

Linda turned toward her laptop. Out of the corner of her eye, she saw Murdock sit suddenly upright, his eyes wide.

"Oh my God," he exclaimed. "I've been blind. And I've been brilliantly misled. Please, Linda, get me St. Luke's Monastery on the phone immediately."

She pulled the number onto the screen and auto-dialed. "Do you wish to speak to Brother Martin?"

"No," he exclaimed. "Brother Gustav."

⇥ **45** ⇤

A light snow was falling. Slick spots speckled the highway. *That winding road leading to the lodge might be a bit tricky to navigate on the return trip, Moira thought.* She was still two kilometers from the airport. *They might already be there waiting. I don't like to be late, but Allison phoned me on short notice.*

She was frustrated and hadn't had a full night's sleep. Kitten's husband was leaving on still another business trip tomorrow, but Moira didn't foresee any chance of her getting back to Munich, at least not for a few days. And Kitten couldn't come to Zugspitze Hof Lodge without tongues wagging and a political price to pay. *It's bad enough that she got into politics, but it's downright inconvenient that she was appointed to a prominent position in the state government. I detest the idiotic slag of pretense people contrive when they enter public life. The wives of the party leaders would turn on Kitten if they knew she had a woman lover. But even if she weren't a government minister, she'd need to keep our affair from her husband. But for all I know, his business traveling could mean he has access to women's beds all over the world. Or men's. That would be delicious.*

Moira turned off the highway onto the road that leads to the general aviation terminal. Allison and Murdock were waving from the doorway. They looked a bit strange standing there without luggage and wearing clothes that didn't fit. Moira pulled up beside them. Allison entered the front passenger side and Murdock took the back. As they exchanged greetings, Moira pulled back onto the highway. Traffic was moving slowly.

"Do we have a plan?" Moira asked.

Allison responded. "We need to meet with Professor Klugman as soon as we arrive at the lodge."

"I haven't seen him today," Moira said. "I inquired about him. Herr Bayer said that he had remained in his room until mid-morning, studying some scientific book. Shortly before lunch he saw him leave with Diana Crenshaw on a snowmobile."

Murdock leaned forward. "Have you seen Patti Dale since Friday?"

Moira squirmed. "I haven't seen her since lunchtime yesterday."

"Where?"

"In the restaurant at the Zugspitze Hof Lodge."

"Was she alone?" he asked.

"Your friend, the professor, was with her. Some friend." Moira searched Murdock's face in the rearview mirror. He didn't seem surprised, as she thought he would.

"Al, let's try Brother Gustav on the cell phone again. He should be back from the village now." She dialed and activated the speakerphone. Murdock leaned forward between the two front seats. Gustav answered. "Good afternoon, Brother Gustav, this is Murdock McCabe. How are you?"

"Ah, Mr. McCabe. Good to hear from you. I am fine. Sorry I was not here when you phoned earlier. I'm glad you are safe. How can I help you?"

"I need your advice."

"Me? I must confess that I am probably the least consulted member of our brotherhood. How could I possibly help you?"

"You were a professor of ancient classics and linguistics, were you not?"

"Yes. What is it that you need to know?"

"Among the myths and legends in ancient Greek literature, I believe there was a character named Hecate. Is that correct?"

"Oh yes. She was a deity. Pretty big stuff indeed."

"What can you tell me about her?"

"Well, to begin, she was a chthonic goddess . . ."

"Chthonic?"

"Sorry. I sometimes lapse back into my professorial lecture mode. Chthonic is synonymous with infernal. Hecate was an infernal character — deadly dangerous — eminently evil. Even the other gods feared her. Actually, she was a multiple character. Today we would probably diagnose her as having multiple personality disorder, you know, like the Three Faces of Eve in the old movie. Hecate could transfigure herself — or perhaps perform a metamorphosis is more accurate — into either the benign Artemis, goddess of domestic animals and of the hunt, or into Selene, the moon goddess to whom lovers paid homage. But why do you ask?"

"A small notebook was found on Brother Stephen's body. After they dried it out, the forensics people deciphered a message: 'Odin has found the wolf, and its name is Hecate.' What do you make of that?"

Several seconds of silence followed. "I find it quite curious," Brother Gustav responded. "It's probably nothing that will help you. In college Stephen had read and enjoyed the classical myths and legends. He made sport of tantalizing me with cryptic messages in which he inserted mythical characters like Hecate. He'd challenge me to decipher them. The message might be an invitation to lunch in the village. He often commuted names. Hecate could mean someone else. But he never mixed German and Greek myths."

"I suspect *this* was not an invitation to lunch."

"It *is* interesting," Gustav admitted. "The mixture is odd. Odin is a character from the Norse and German legends, but Hecate is Greek. Odin was the warrior king of the German gods. Stephen often would playfully sign his notes 'Odin.' As I said, it's a playful way that two monks amused themselves. In the Odin myth, there was a prophesy that, on the last day of the world, Odin would do battle with and die in the jaws of a gigantic, horrible wolf, but the wolf's name was Fenrer. I know of no connection between Fenrer and Hecate. They were not counterparts. It could be said that the wolf was an infernal deity, like Hecate, but there the comparison ends. Of course, Stephen didn't believe in such deities. The sentence is probably a metaphor intended to puzzle me — a mind game. He died before he could give it to me."

Murdock leaned further forward and raised his voice slightly. "We *are* dealing with infernal powers, even if they're not deities. Perhaps this was not a mind game, just a mixed metaphor. Maybe it was something written in haste when he realized who was a threat to him. Was there a Roman goddess who was a counterpart to Hecate?"

"I don't recall one in her personality as Hecate, but in her personality as Artemis, her counterpart in Roman mythology was the goddess Diana." There was a long pause. "Now really, do you possibly think that . . ."

"Yes. I'd say there's a high degree of probability that we need to explore. Thank you," he said as he reached forward and pushed the off button. Murdock was on his knees between the two women. "Speed it up," he urged.

"The road is slippery in spots," Moira cautioned.

"Try," he said as he poked Georg's phone number into the keypad. "The professor may be in danger. You saw him having lunch with Patti

Dale yesterday, and we know that today Diana volunteered to take him
to the antenna shack." Georg answered. "This is Murdock McCabe.
Quickly. Come to Zugspitze Hof Lodge. Bring help. I may have solved
the murder of Brother Stephen. I'll explain later."

"I cannot obey your order," Georg replied coldly and officiously. "I
need authority."

"Did Rudi call you? Do you have the number in Crete where he can
be reached?"

"Yes."

"If you place any value on human life, call him immediately and tell
him that I'm asking him to order you to do what I requested." He hit the
off button. "Damn, I've been blind. Friday, I thought Diana was in Frankfurt. I now believe she was in Munich as Patti Dale threatening Moira.
The real downer is — I was falling in love with the woman who killed my
wife."

Allison turned toward him. "You think that Patti Dale and Diana
Crenshaw are the same person?"

"The probability is overwhelming. The child sex intelligence on Enrique came from Joe Carlyle through the FBI report. Carl is convinced
that Joe and Patti are in bed together, figuratively if not literally. I believe
it was misinformation, but Diana confirmed it. I'm convinced that she
knew that Brother Stephen had developed a remarkable computer chip
that could be worth billions. In her façade as Diana, she'd befriended
Brother Antonio and his family and won their confidence. Antonio must
have inadvertently and innocently — I hope — tipped off his sister Maria
Rosita or Diana herself. Last week Monday, Diana may have learned
from Brother Antonio that Stephen was taking an important package to
the village to post to his staff in Oregon. She intercepted him on the trail,
killed him, and stole the plans — albeit the flawed ones. She remained at
Zugspitze Hof Lodge, using her entertainment of Enrique as a cover until
she could confirm what she had acquired. Later in the week she probably
learned she had been tricked, and she wanted the real documents. She
played up to me because she learned of my friendship with Rudi, and I
would know the progress of and be able to influence the murder investigation. As long as I responded to her romantically, she could feel safe.
When she realized that I was not likely to reveal confidential police information, she jumped onto Moira as Patti Dale. She may have a big
weapons deal pending in Munich, and she doesn't want to run if she
doesn't have to. Most likely she was convinced that there was some obscure purpose for Stephen's computer chip, because Antonio or Maria
Rosita believed that it was bigger than big, and because Stephen was
fearful that it might fall into the wrong hands. She decided the right

hands were her own. When she learned we were heading to Boris's domain, she hired Boris to squeeze that information from us. Diana knew we were flying to Cyprus, and she knew our ETA."

"This is all conjecture," Allison said. "Do you think Seneca Financial is a fake?"

"Maybe not, but I think her job there is at least a convenient cover."

Allison shrugged. "Until yesterday you believed that Enrique was a bad guy and Diana was a good one. Now you've inverted them. Why?"

"I decided that Linda was straight arrow. Once I decided not to believe anything contrary to what she told me, the sky opened. If Linda was telling the truth, then Diana had lied. I asked myself, why would she lie? Why would she tell the same lie that Joe Carlyle had inserted into FBI records?

Allison's eyes met his. "What could the child sex story possibly have to do with the murder of Brother Stephen?"

"I believe it had nothing to do with Brother Stephen's death. Enrique is the leader of an organization. He and other wealthy people invest in a private mutual fund called Plato. Their purpose is to expand economic stability among Third World nations by investment in them. Joe and Diana — Patti — have been involved with an organization called Traction. Its purpose is to destabilize and encourage revolutions so they can sell arms to either or both sides. Enrique's being here at the time of Brother Stephen's murder may have been arranged by Diana so as to place her close to the monastery and to give her cover until she possessed Brother Stephen's secret."

"That's still conjecture," Allison insisted. "The logic fits only if you first assume that Diana and Patti are the same person. Diana's being gone from the lodge the same night that Patti met Moira in Munich could be sheer coincidence."

Murdock leaned forward and turned his head toward Moira. "Diana is about 5'10", neatly packaged with a pleasant face, a slim figure, blonde hair, fullish lips that gleam red without lipstick, and bluish hazel eyes. Her cheeks are naturally pink. She uses little or no makeup, and her nails aren't painted. How does that match Patti Dale?"

Moira thought for a moment. "Patti's hair was dark brown and her nails were long and painted purple to match her lipstick. The rest checks. Your theory could explain why Patti Dale was so interested in the investigation. She needed to know whether her disguise was threatened. As Diana, she could discredit Enrique by confirming the false story. Diana, as Patti, ordered the story to be placed in the FBI files. Then through you, Murdock, the files of Veritus International would be infected with the same misinformation. Many Plato investors use the services of Veritus.

That information smoldering in our files could lead to the demise of Plato if it knocked Enrique off his pedestal."

Allison turned toward Moira. "Are you convinced that Diana and Patti Dale are the same?"

"It works."

"Ha," Murdock exclaimed. "Which is the masquerade? If Diana is really Patti Dale, is Patti Dale really Patti Dale? No wonder Jerr and Carl couldn't trace her. She doesn't exist. Does Diana Crenshaw exist? I doubt it. We have no idea who this woman really is. Traction is real. Talk about a *femme fatale*."

Allison glanced out the front window as they approached the road leading to the Zugspitze Hof Lodge. "You two are the experienced investigators, but you're playing hunches, and you could both be wrong," she reminded them. "We have no hard evidence. I've still heard nothing but conjecture."

Murdock sat back in his seat. "Are you arguing against the logic, Allison?"

"I don't wish to risk the reputation of Veritus by accusing someone on conjecture alone — assuming I still work for Veritus and have anything to say in this matter."

Murdock hesitated for several seconds. "I'm sure Moira agrees, you're our boss."

Moira nodded in the affirmative. "Absolutely. Screw Harvey. He never told me not to follow your orders."

Murdock continued. "Allison, try this on for size. Saturday Diana told me that Enrique asked her to obtain virgin girls for him. She told me that he takes extreme pleasure in luring women who have moral compunctions against sex-for-hire, or sex outside of marriage, by offering them ever-increasing sums of money until the woman breaks. Then he ravishes them and humiliates them. Does that sound like the man you met in the bedroom at Boris's villa last night? Could the man you met believe that every woman is a whore at some price?"

Moira turned up the winding drive. Allison thought for a moment. "No," she answered. "But Diana might have told the child sex story out of spite because she couldn't land him as a client for Seneca Financial, or because she found his first cash offer for her body too low and insulting."

"One other thing," Murdock said. "Diana was interested in Karen's notebooks. She offered to review them for me to see if she could find the reason for Karen's murder. She was rabid to get her hands on them."

Allison smiled. "Perhaps because she was falling in love with you. That wouldn't be difficult. But you weren't worth having until you found closure on Karen, and she wanted to speed that along. You're never going to convict her of murder using conjecture based on conjecture."

Moira slowed for the sharp curve just past the bridge crossing the Liederbach Creek. "It may take another death," she offered.

Allison shrugged. "I'll play your hunches. We shall proceed, using the assumption that Diana and Patti are one."

Murdock tapped Allison's arm. She turned toward him. "Good decision," he said. "Thanks to Jerr and Carl, the FBI has evidence that will convict Patti Dale of the murder of Karen. That's closure. You know what would be nice, Al?"

"What?" she asked, taking the bait.

"It would be nice if, when all of this is over, we could learn who our client has been, and if it isn't Top Dog, why Top Dog is so interested in a dead monk."

*   *   *

The antenna shack, side walls and roof, was constructed of reinforced concrete mounted on steel posts anchored in the granite of the mountainside. Next to the shack a dish antenna was mounted on a tall tower, designed to withstand an avalanche but never tested. A much smaller antenna mounted lower on the structure was directed toward the monastery. Stephen had used it to transmit warning signals if equipment failed. A single overhead electric power line was strung on wooden poles that reached from the darkness of the forest to the shack, but there was no telephone line.

When they reached bare rock about two hundred feet from the shack, the professor and Diana dismounted the snowmobile. "I must confess," he said, "that it was indeed a pleasure to have my arms around a beautiful young woman again, even if it were only to keep me from falling off the machine."

Diana smiled adroitly. "That was a nice compliment," she replied.

The professor looked down the slope. It was a cloudy day. Scattered snow showers blocked the view to the north, but eastward visibility was good. They were above the tree line. Below them, the conifers had taken on a new mantel of snow overnight. They looked like an army of great white ghosts surrounding and protecting the peak. In the cold clear air he could see several miles into Austria. *Stunning. If there had been a god who created all this, he would have my compliments.* A fresh wind made it bitter cold. Above them a huge accumulation of snow overhung a rock ledge, but it appeared to be stable. He noticed a jet airplane break through the clouds and descend toward the airport. He pointed to it. "That might be our friend Murdock returning from the warmer clime. Are you familiar with Enrique's airplane?"

"That could be it," she replied.

The village, far below, had also been blanketed with new snow during the night. He could make out the highway that led to Garmisch-Partenkirchen winding like a black snake across a white blanket. He turned toward the antenna shack, extracted a key from his coat pocket, took the padlock in his hand, and unlocked it.

"May I come inside?" Diana asked.

"Of course, my dear. I wouldn't want you standing out in the cold. Are you sure you will feel safe with me alone in there?"

"I'm betting that you don't want to freeze your buns anymore than I do."

The professor laughed good-naturedly as they stepped inside. "Actually, as you can tell, this shack is electrically heated — it maintains 60° at all times so that the equipment will function properly. If it falls below that, an alarm rings at the monastery."

"Is there any other communication with the outside world?"

"No, so you couldn't phone for help if I tried to ravish you." He closed the door behind them. "It's nice and warm in here. So you see, freezing buns is not what restrains my masculine ardor in the presence of your youthfulness and beauty. The problem is old age and a surgeon who probably needed to make a payment on his yacht. Otherwise, I would be gentlemanly and flatter you with a pass."

"Why you naughty man. I can understand how you sweet-talked Clarissa."

"How do you know about Clarissa?"

Diana laughed. "Have you forgotten the stories we told about ourselves at Enrique's dinner party?"

"Oh, yes. You have a good memory for names."

"I *do* pride myself. She had two daughters, and your favorite is named Amy. She lives in Cannon Beach, Oregon, near you."

"Amazing."

"Do you communicate with her frequently?" she asked in a businesslike tone.

This sounds like more than idle conversation. Why is the hair rising on my back? He decided to hide the fact that he'd sent her a package last week. He lied. "No. We aren't close."

Diana smiled wryly. "I got the impression that you two were quite close. I am not sure whether Amy has guessed the reason."

The professor stared at her blankly. He shook his head. He had become determined to confound her. "Or, perhaps you have guessed the wrong reason."

"I seldom do." Their eyes met. "You and her mother made poetry together, didn't you?" she asked coyly. "And is not Amy the resulting ballad?"

"Touché. Now please excuse me for a minute. I must change some tapes."

"What do they record?"

Lying did not come easy to the professor, but he felt uneasy with Diana today, and he couldn't quite put his finger on the reason. In any event, there was too much at stake to tell the whole truth to anyone. "They record digital information from a satellite — scientific jargon that the monks use."

She pointed to a transceiver. "Is that the unit that reads the satellite?"

"Yes, I suppose it is."

"It's a surprisingly small unit, isn't it? For such an important task. I could hold it in my hand. Is there something uncommon about it?"

"Oh, my dear lady, radio is outside the scope of my expertise."

"But you *do* know the answer to my question, don't you?"

"Brother Martin has simply asked me to change these recording tapes. I'm just a mule . . ."

"A lying mule. It doesn't become you, professor. But you have answered the question in part by playing dumb."

His eyes widened. She was holding a Smith and Wesson .32.

"Yes," she said, "in case you're wondering. This is the gun that killed the monk. You might be interested to know that this is the gun that killed Murdock's wife. It can also kill a professor. The question is: Do you want to die in this remote shack on the side of a huge, cold rock and never see your Amy again — the young woman you are not close to. Would she miss you?"

She's pretty as Clarissa was and, until a few minutes ago, she'd made me wish I were young again. But she's a fake—an old fool's fraudulent dream. What seemed genuine is really delusion. He put a stop to his reverie. "What do you want?" he demanded firmly.

She pointed to a brown box on top a table connected to a recording machine. "I believe there is a futuristic central processing chip in there. Tell me what's special about it?"

"Special?"

"Yeah, special. It's more than just super fast, isn't it? What more? I have experts that can find the answer, but *you* tell me. That information will save us time and money, and it will allow you to live."

"I'm not a fool, young woman. I'm never going to walk out of here alive. You can't afford to let me live. Not after you've confessed to two murders."

Diana laughed almost gently. "My dear old man. I like you. I really do. But you are naive. You know nothing about me. I don't exist. My face, my manner of walking, my manner of speech — it's all illusion. I'm an actress made up for a performance. When I leave you, Diana will disappear forever. She'll cease to exist unless I decide to resurrect her."

"The sad thing is you're going to kill me, and then spend weeks trying to discern a secret that isn't there. How unfortunate for both of us."

She smiled slyly. "It won't work, professor. Please strip down to your underwear, *now*."

"Tell me why I should," he demanded.

"Because, as I said, I like you, and I'll give you a chance to live. Tell me what's so special about the chip that Stephen was willing to die rather than disclose it, and I'll let you live. I'll take your clothes with me so you can't walk down the trail in the freezing cold. That'll give me the time I need to disappear. Eventually, Brother Martin will send someone looking for you, or your friend Murdock will appear. In the meantime you'll be reasonably warm."

"You're a master of ruses, Diana, or whatever your name is. You're trying to delude me into thinking that I can survive this encounter. I know that I can't, so you're powerless. I'm not going to take off my clothes. Take off yours. Pit vipers are supposed to be naked."

Diana's face twisted in anger. She raised the gun and pointed it at him. "Watch your mouth. I've already killed five times. People are incredibly easy to kill."

"I can see that, but your problem is that I'm not afraid of death. I've already lived a long time. I've searched for truth. It's given my life purpose. There's no immortality except to be remembered for the contributions we've made to uplifting the human spirit. I have no fear of hellfire and damnation because I believe in neither. You've chosen a path that demeans the human spirit. The Diana I knew was a delightful person — a person who deserved respect and honor. Was she the fake? Or is what I see today the fake, driven by some compelling ambition for wealth and power?"

"Your problem is that I don't believe that there's any moral law imposed by some god who wields divine retribution. A moral law with no god to enforce it is a law without teeth. I haven't the slightest compunction about killing you. Assume that the Diana you knew was the fake, and give me the information within the next ten seconds or you'll learn whether you were wrong about the nonexistence of an afterlife."

"Oh, but I'm *anxious* to know whether I'm wrong. For you, the sad truth is that there's nothing sensational or even exceptional about any chip in this brown box, that I know of. You're not going to believe me, so you're going to kill me."

"You are correct, professor. I don't believe you."

* * *

When Allison, Murdock, and Moira arrived at the Zugspitze Hof Lodge, Brother Martin was waiting for them in the lobby. He saw them coming and met them at the door. Murdock shook his hand and without pleasantries asked: "Has the professor returned from the antenna shack."

"No," Martin said, troubled. "He should have been back by now. Do you suppose something has happened to him?"

"Yes. Take me there as quickly as you can."

Allison interrupted. "I'm coming with you. I see the Bayers' snow-mobile outside. I'll take it. Moira, you talk to Herr Bayer. Tell him I've taken his machine. Ask him for a map of the mountain and have him indicate the location of the antenna shack. When the police arrive, have them join us there."

"If they arrive," Murdock said. "Georg doesn't like me." He phoned Georg and reached him on his cell phone. Georg had not been able to reach Rudi yet. He reported that another jet had landed at the airport shortly after they had, its flight plan reporting Limassol as its port of embarkation. Georg had gone to the airport and, while interviewing Linda DiStefano, he had seen one man exit the second jet. He had been picked up by a chopper. Georg had seen Boris Romanovsky before. It was not he. "Please," Murdock pleaded, "if you value human life get out there immediately with a half dozen men. I'm going to try to save the professor's life. Goodbye."

He stared at Moira, frustration written on his face. "We're going to need police firepower," he urged. "I don't know how hard Georg is trying to reach Rudi. He resents me. He needs someone to give him an order."

Moira grumbled disgustedly. "Its not unusual for policemen to resent private investigators, especially when we're more diligent than they. We can't count on him. How about Rudi's superior, Commander Weiss? Would he give the order?"

Allison rejoined them. "I've just tried to reach him by phone. All I get is a song and dance. He's too important. They won't put me through."

They walked outside. Martin fired up his engine. He would lead. Murdock and Allison mounted Bayers' machine. Murdock started its engine. Moira awaited instructions. Allison shouted over the noise. "Why don't you jump on Brother Martin's machine?"

"Go without me," Moira suggested. "I'll get ahold of the Bavarian minister of justice. She'll give the order, and Georg will jump out of his shorts when it comes directly from her."

"Are you sure you can reach her?" Allison asked.

"Count on it."

Murdock looked over his shoulder. "I don't think its a good idea for you to come along, Allison."

"Get this contraption moving," she ordered. "Why should you investigators have all the fun?"

"By the way," Brother Martin shouted, "what is the professor's danger?"

"He accepted a ride from Diana. I believe she murdered Brother Stephen. She knows something about the chip, and she wants it."

Martin frowned. "Does she know what it is?"

"I think not. Not unless she's tortured it out of the professor. We must hurry."

Martin zoomed off toward a trail through the dense conifers. Murdock and Allison took chase. After fifteen minutes, as they approached the tree line, the trail became rougher and more difficult to manage. Martin slowed. Murdock followed suit. About two hundred feet from the shack, Martin stopped. "Best to walk the rest of the way," he said. "There are more rocks than snow ahead. We could damage the machines."

They dismounted. Martin pointed to snowmobile tracks made earlier, leading both to and away from where they had stopped. "It looks like they've been here and gone," Martin said. "We've missed them."

"Let's check the shack," Murdock suggested.

They climbed the remaining slope. The door was locked. Martin unlocked it. Allison grabbed Murdock's arm and pointed downhill. Near the tree line about a half-mile east were two people standing beside a helicopter. The engine was shut down. Brother Martin saw them too. He extracted field glasses from his backpack and focused on the pair. "The woman is Diana Crenshaw. I don't recognize the man."

He passed the glasses to Murdock. "I can't tell . . . not under that hood with sunglasses on."

"Let me see," Allison urged. Murdock passed the glasses to her. She focused on the man. He turned his back to her as he extracted something from the chopper. He placed it on his shoulder and removed his sunglasses. "That," she said, "is our friendly priest — Father Theo — Sascha's keeper. I can't tell what he's placed on his shoulder."

Murdock grabbed the field glasses. "My God! It's a rocket launcher," he screamed as a streak of fire shot upslope, followed by a loud explosion. Snow and rocks surged downward with a horrific thundering roar, accumulating huge chunks of the ledge that had been thrown into the air by the explosion. Brother Martin threw open the door of the shack.

"Quick, inside," he shouted as he pushed them in. Martin pulled the door closed as tons of snow and rock buried the shack. A boulder struck the roof. Chunks of concrete and concrete dust descended upon them and choked them. The roof cracked, sagged, and shifted, but the steel reinforcing bars held. The heater stopped and the lights went out. In the last light, Murdock caught a glimpse of the professor, lying on his back, a bullet wound in his lower chest. He heard Brother Martin groan and fall to his right. He felt Allison moving, under him. When the roar of the avalanche ceased, it became very quiet. *Quiet as a tomb, he thought.*

Tuesday
November 25

⊰ **46** ⊱

Back at the lodge, Moira heard the far-off explosion. Her instincts ignited. She calculated that her phone call to the justice minister would have borne fruit by now. *Kitten reacts quickly.* She phoned Georg. He, contrite, was on his way to the lodge with several subordinates. Moira shared her concern with Herr Bayer who also had heard the explosion. He had served in the army and recognized the sound of ordnance. He believed it had come from the antenna shack. Convinced that military equipment had been used to destabilize snow, he attached a trailer to Frau Bayer's personal snowmobile and loaded it with picks and shovels. With one of his employees hanging on his waist, he roared off.

Moira heard the drone of a chopper approaching from downslope. *It can't be the police. They're coming by road.* Frau Bayer indicated that she didn't expect any guest arriving. Moira rushed to her car, opened the glove compartment, and extracted a pistol. Concealing it in her ski jacket, she walked toward the landing pad. The chopper hovered overhead. A straight-out wind sock atop a tall pole indicated a strong wind from the northwest. Another windsock, lower on the pole, below the tops of the trees, indicated lesser wind but more variable in direction. The machine hesitated. She tried to make out the occupants, but swirling ground snow made it impossible. Back in the United States she had begun flying lessons in a chopper, but her transfer to Germany had interrupted them. *I would have to be pretty desperate to attempt a landing under these conditions. The tall trees are too close for comfort in this wind.* The registration letters on the aircraft indicated that it was Swiss, and a company logo suggested it had been rented in Zürich. She heard a change in the pitch of the rotor blades. *My God, he's going to attempt it.* She stopped, fearful of getting closer in the event of a crash and explosion. The chopper settled downward, the pilot skillfully manipulating the foot pedals to adjust tail prop torque, holding its nose into the wind, and manipulating the cyclic pitch stick to compensate for wind drift. As the machine descended below treetop level and encountered ground effect, it gained stability and in a few seconds was firmly positioned on the ground. *I could never have done that, Moira thought..* The pilot chopped the power as two groundskeepers ducked under the decelerating blades to tie the aircraft down. Moira noticed the door open on the passenger side. Her index finger touched the safety on the gun. A man in a green nylon jacket exited, scanned the small group of gawkers, noticed Moira, and began running toward her. She froze.

*   *   *

The antenna shack was buried under tons of snow and rock. It was impossible to tell how deep they were buried. No amount of joint effort could open the door. Murdock found and opened a small window about seven inches high and eighteen inches wide. They could use melting snow for drinking. Brother Martin stuck his hand through the opening and dug out a cavity, but he had no sense of being near the surface.

Murdock lit a match. His watch read 7:31 P.M. The professor, his head resting on Allison's lap, suggested that Murdock use matches sparingly. They needed the remaining oxygen for breathing. Their capsule was roughly ten feet square. At the professor's suggestion, Murdock searched the wall with his hands and, on the second circuit, found an electrical conduit that extended outside. On his tiptoes and without a wrench, he struggled to remove a length of it. The professor theorized that it carried electrical cable to the antenna. Hopefully it had broken above the snow cover, and hopefully the electrical cable had snapped so they could pull it through and use the metal conduit as a breathing tube. The professor, convinced he was dying, urged them to smother him, because the oxygen he was breathing was wasted. No one agreed. Brother Martin covered the professor with his coat. Murdock's fingers were raw from trying to loosen the retaining nuts. Brother Martin joined him. Together they broke the pipe loose. Martin unscrewed the connector. A segment, which ran from the point of entry to the floor, came undone. Anxiously, Murdock and Martin together pulled the wires inside. One broke loose. They pulled it through. Murdock wet a finger and placed it near the conduit. He felt no movement of air.

The building, covered on all sides with snow, remained reasonably warm. "Snow is a good insulator," Brother Martin suggested.

The professor shifted his weight to become more comfortable. "Do you feel like talking?" Allison asked.

"Yes," he replied, "if you don't mind the ramblings of an old man."

She felt his forehead. He was sweating. She found her handkerchief and wiped it dry. "You said that Diana took the transceiver. Will she be capable of using the chaos chip?"

The professor tried to laugh. "What she took was a variable frequency transmitter combined with a broadband receiver. It's designed to receive a whole host of frequencies in a quiet area of the radio spectrum, surrounding a median frequency of 1420 MHz, the frequency of the hydrogen atom in space. She didn't get the chaos chip. It's not in the transceiver. It's connected inside the larger contraption — the device with the recording tapes, which was too big for her to carry. It receives the broadband scan, identifies the proper frequency sequences, and records the result on the tapes. So she's done all this for nothing."

"We need to stop your bleeding," Allison urged.

"The effort is entirely otiose," the professor said. He caught himself. "Sorry. I used to salt my lectures with obscure words so my students might think I was smarter than they. It's entirely useless. It's gone too far. Transporting me to a hospital would kill me. Listen, Murdock. I don't know whether a dying man's declaration can be used as evidence in a criminal trial in Bavaria, but Diana confessed to me that she murdered Brother Stephen . . . and . . . sorry . . . your wife too, I'm afraid."

"Thank you," Murdock replied. "Even if it can't be used in Bavaria, it can in Virginia where Karen died."

If I can keep him talking, Allison thought, maybe it'll keep him from giving up. "I'm sorry I didn't meet you in happier circumstances. Please tell me about yourself," she urged.

"Okay, but just the good stuff," he said. "When I was young, I had a repetitive dream."

"Could you remember the dream when you awoke?"

"Oh, I never experienced it when I was sleeping. It was a daydream. I was enchanted by the thought that our minds are simply parts of a pure intellective power that permeates the universe. I thought that, if I tuned my mind in properly, I'd find a singularity that would unlock all the secrets of the universe. I dreamed that my mind was one of billions of inquiring minds on billions of planets. But I never found that singularity — never quite tuned it in. But the hope of finding it kept me inquiring, and the enchantment it generated made life continually exciting. Now the dream is over and the enchantment dissolved."

"I know it sounds trite," Allison said, "but you mustn't give up hope. Now you have the chaos chip. It may tune you in."

"It's too late. I'm dying now. I know it. It's all right."

Allison wiped his forehead again. "Perhaps there really is a life after death, and you'll find all your answers," she said.

The professor's voice became less audible. "It's eternal silence for which I hope. I'd hate to die and find I'd been wrong and have some spiteful god eternally punishing me for my impertinence."

"But with Brother Stephen's discovery, you may be very close to achieving your dream. Hang on. Wouldn't it be a shame to come so close and let up just before the finish line? Wouldn't it make you happy to contact some being on another planet?"

The professor chuckled feebly. "Don't expect too much from life. Give it all you've got. You'll get more back than you expect, so you'll always find happiness."

There was a long silence. The professor drifted into unconsciousness. Except for an occasional moan from him and the sound of four people breathing, they heard nothing. Murdock sat down next to Allison, his back against a wall, his shoulder touching hers. He could hear Brother Martin's breathing coming from the wall opposite them, the professor's from her lap. Awkwardly, he found her left hand and held it in both of his. "Allison, there's something I need to say." There was a long, uninterrupted silence. "We all know that we're facing oxygen depravation. There's a formidable pile of snow and rock for our rescuers to dig through. I only state the obvious when I say that we may die in this place. Wouldn't that be ironic, just a day after escaping death on Cyprus and over the Mediterranean? I'm not afraid to die. Hopefully, there's a better world on the other side. Our situation may make what I'm about to say melodramatic. It's not easy to speak my mind, although now I think I've finally put Karen to rest."

"Murdock," Allison interrupted. "Let me say it. Other than Jerr, you're the only man in the world I've loved since that day on campus in Buffalo when Jerr introduced us. I loved Karen too. She was my closest confidante. If I'd met you before Jerr and before I introduced you to Karen, our lives might have been different. But I didn't. In spite of the divorce, my life has been reasonably happy."

Murdock squeezed her hand. "Thank you. You said it much better than I could. Other than Karen, there is no woman I've ever loved except you. I've been reticent because you're Jerr's ex . . . and my boss."

Allison squeezed Murdock's hands. "Jerr's found a woman with a career who can follow him. What's ahead for us?"

They heard a clanking sound followed by something rubbing against metal. Murdock took a length of conduit and banged three times on the conduit that exited the wall. Three clanks answered. The rubbing sound was coming from the antenna wires. Someone was pulling and releasing, pulling and releasing. Murdock pulled on the wires. They had been cut free. He pulled them through. Some air descended through the conduit, but very little. He put his ear to the tube. He could make out a voice but couldn't tell who it was or what was being said.

He shouted into the tube: "We have a man shot in the chest. He needs help desperately." He heard words, but they were inaudible.

Allison felt the professor's head rise from her lap. Words gushed out of his delirium: "If superstrings can exist in the tenth dimension, what else can exist in dimensions that we can't perceive? Spirits?" His words became unintelligible and, drifting back into unconsciousness, his head lowered onto her lap again.

Murdock turned to the direction from which he had last heard Brother Martin's voice. "What did you make of that" he asked.

"He's still searching," Martin replied. "Maybe in his delirium he's starting to find."

Allison felt the professor raise his head again. "I removed the chaos chip and destroyed it," he shouted. "Last week I mailed a copy . . ." His head fell onto her lap again.

"He's fading," Murdock whispered. "Maybe you should say a prayer for him, Brother Martin." Martin didn't reply. The professor moaned. Murdock felt blood running from the corner of the professor's mouth. Allison's lap was soaked. A minute passed that seemed like five. Brother Martin broke the silence.

"He's *your* friend."

"But you're a monk," Murdock insisted.

"He's *your* friend," Martin repeated, firmly. "You pray for him."

"I'm not even sure that I believe in God," Murdock protested.

"It's your call," Martin replied. "Every believer, unless he's blind to the world, is on the edge of doubt. Every nonbeliever, unless he's blind to the universe, is on the edge of faith. What does your inner voice tell you? What are your mother and Karen telling you, or aren't they here?"

There was a long silence. The professor moaned softly. A sharp cracking sound came from the roof, and more concrete dust fell on them. The steel reinforcing bars held. "But I don't think the professor would want anyone to pray for him," Murdock protested.

"A man does what *he* feels he must do, regardless what another man wants or doesn't want."

"Would it make any difference?"

"Listen to your inner voice."

Another long silence. The roof creaked again. More dust fell.

"It's worth a shot," Murdock replied.

"Just talk," Martin urged. "There aren't any magic words."

He took the professor's hand. *This mass of flesh, Murdock thought. This bleeding man with a bullet in his chest. That's what she's reduced him to. How can God permit a woman so evil to destroy a man so good?* The professor half-cried, half-moaned.

"There's little dignity in dying," Murdock remarked.

"Sometimes none at all," Brother Martin agreed, "but it's the *last* indignity."

Allison reached for and found Murdock's arm. "Go ahead," she said. "Say a prayer for him. If it helps, say what you think Karen would have said."

There was a long silence. Water dripped from melting snow at the open window. The professor's breathing became shallow. A gurgling sound came from deep inside him.

"God," Murdock began, "my friend, the professor is in tough shape, but you already know that. Please be merciful to this old man. He hasn't really denied you, Lord. Just the opposite. He spent his life searching for you. It's just that wherever he looked, he couldn't find you. He was a scientist who needed physical proof — maybe some mathematical formula that could be tested. When his formulas didn't reveal you, he just reached the wrong conclusion. I'm a poor one to ask favors. I've not paid much attention to you since Karen was murdered, but you *did* answer my prayer today. You pointed me to her killer. Now grant this old man in death the answers he couldn't find in life, and please don't fault him too much. Neither of us deserves your favors, but my mother taught me that that's why Jesus died — so that those of us who deserve nothing can receive everything for his sake. I ask these things for Jesus sake, if it's your will. I don't know what else to say except amen . . . whatever that means."

The professor, coughing like a man choking on fish bones, tried to speak. His words were garbled.

"What did he say?" Murdock asked.

"I'm not sure," Allison replied.

"He said thank you." The words came from Brother Martin.

There was a long silence. The professor moaned softly. Another sharp cracking sound came from the roof. They were showered with concrete dust again. "Lord," Brother Martin said ignoring it, "thank you for giving us this day a man who showed us how to pray."

Allison turned toward Brother Martin's voice. "Why do you think he never found God?"

"The professor never looked in the right place. Rather than looking outside himself, he needed to listen to the deepest silence within himself. When a person shuts out the world, all that remains is God's voice gently calling. Sometimes people despair that they have fallen so far from God that they're unworthy of His love. I suspect that we're closest to God at the precise moment that we feel that we're furthest away."

No one spoke for several minutes. They could hear digging above them, but it was still far away. The warmth from the heater was long gone, and their cell was becoming very cold. Allison broke the silence.

"Do you enjoy being a monk? If that's a fair question."

"It's a fair question. Yes, I do. Do you enjoy your employment?"

Allison was silent for several seconds. "I'm not certain that I'm still employed. Our district manager has probably fired me by now."

"I wouldn't worry about that."

"Easy for you to say."

"Still, I wouldn't worry."

"Have we met before?" Allison inquired.

"I think not," Brother Martin replied.

"Are you sure? Your voice sounds so familiar, but I can't place it. I'm almost certain that we've talked before."

"That we have. We've talked on the telephone, but we've never met."

"Recently?"

"Quite recently. Are you familiar with the Stasi?"

"Yes," Allison replied. "They were the East German government's secret police."

"I was one of their agents in West Germany. Before the fall of the Berlin Wall, I was given money and instructed to purchase unobtrusively in my name, Kurt Martin Braun, several businesses in the West. One in particular, my superiors thought, could be developed as an instrument of intelligence gathering. I purchased it from an American, Howard G. Gregory of Des Moines, Iowa, and . . ."

"Veritus!" she exclaimed. "That's it! You bought Veritus. You're Top Dog! Oh, I'm sorry."

"Sorry that you called me Top Dog? Don't be. I rather like it. It tickles my staid Prussian nature. Please don't be concerned about your employment. We need a take-charge person as dedicated as yourself. Harvey won't have power over you. I have other plans for him."

Murdock interrupted. "Now I understand why I was thrust into the investigation of a missing monk. Was that why Richard gave me the expense-paid trip to the Zugspitze Hof Lodge?"

"No. That was a fortunate coincidence. We didn't anticipate the tragedy. And," Martin added, "now you must understand why I became a client of my own agency. With Stephen dead, I became fearful for the life of Brother Antonio. He went into shock when he learned of the murder. I asked Richard to go undercover and take Antonio to where he could recuperate and be safe."

"Shh," Murdock said. "I think I heard something above us." They fell silent. Nothing. Their breathing was becoming deeper and faster. Each knew what it meant. Too much carbon dioxide. As each minute passed, it would get worse. Brother Martin crawled toward the table containing the recording device. "Under the table," he said, "is a first aid kit. It contains two small oxygen tanks that we keep for people affected by altitude sickness. They won't last long for four of us, but they will buy us a little time.

"Three," Allison said softly. "God's finger has touched the professor and he sleeps. I wonder if now he's debating the existence of God with the angels."

A long silence followed. Each, thankful but gripped by guilt, knew his death would conserve oxygen and slow the accumulation of carbon dioxide. Murdock broke the silence.

"Can an atheist go to Heaven?" he asked.

"He wasn't an atheist," Brother Martin offered. "Why search so hard if deep down you don't believe there's something to find. He was God's vagabond. Has God let him into Paradise? I'm reminded of a sentence from C. S. Lewis: 'We need to adore that Love which will open the high gates to a prodigal son who is brought in kicking, screaming, resentful, and darting his eyes in every direction for a chance of escape.' "

Allison moved out from under the professor and laid his head gently on the floor. "Heaven's got to be different for each of us," she offered. "For one person it might be a cellar filled with fine wine. For the professor I think it is a classroom in which he is an eternal student and angels are the professors."

Murdock chuckled: "Angels lecturing on the superstring theory and explaining how they, and he, can exist in the thirtieth dimension, or some such thing."

Martin touched Allison's arm. "Here's an oxygen tank. Put the mask over your mouth and nose. Inhale five times and pass it on," he suggested.

Through the small window, they heard the sound of digging. "They're coming down at the wrong place," Murdock said. "We can't get out that window."

"But we can get air through it," Allison added.

A soft glow began to illuminate the room. A cold draft followed as snow fell in. A flashlight entered, followed by a hand, and then an arm clothed in a green nylon sleeve. Above they could hear voices.

"You've found the window. The door is over here." It was the voice of Georg shouting. "Be careful. That's all unstable. We don't want to bury them again."

The air coming through the window was frigid. Reluctantly Murdock and Brother Martin removed their coats from the professor's body and put them on.

"Be patient." It was Brother Gustav shouting to them. "It may be an hour or more before we can clear the door. Is everyone all right?"

They looked at one another. "Yes," Brother Martin shouted. It was the simplest answer.

*   *   *

Above them a crew of police and emergency medical people, aided by Richard Laplatenier, Moira, and Herr Bayer, had been digging for an hour. Food and warm coffee, which Herr Bayer had sent for, arrived from the lodge. Richard and Moira took a break — their first. Richard half unzipped his green nylon ski jacket. Moira's mittens were tattered from friction with a shovel. Georg brought them both coffee. "I don't like the look of the part of the ledge that survived the blast."

"It looks very unstable," Richard agreed.

Moira looked downslope. Two choppers awaited, their engines running and rotor blades spinning. *Can we outrun another slide and get to them? she wondered.* Trying to calm herself, she turned to Richard. "Did you leave Brother Antonio in Zürich?"

"Yes. He was not ready to be . . ."

"Run," Georg shouted. "It's coming!"

An avalanche of snow and granite boulders thundered toward them. They ran. The choppers lifted off the ground to avoid being caught up in the charging mass. A boulder struck the partially exposed roof of the antenna shack and was redirected to the left of the runners. They heard a man's and a woman's muffled scream from the direction of the shack. The onrushing snow caught them and the rest of the crew just before they reached the ladders dangling from the choppers. But its energy had dissipated. Knocked to the ground, they tumbled a few times, but no one was seriously hurt. Georg leapt to his feet, grabbed a ladder dangling from a chopper, and motioned the pilot to take him back to the shack. Richard motioned to the other chopper pilot to do the same.

"It could be very unstable," Georg shouted to him after they both were airborne.

"I know, but they're my friends," Richard shouted back.

Moira was frantic. She tried to grab onto Richard's ladder but missed. She struggled on foot upward through the loose snow.

*   *   *

The steel reinforcing bars held fast, but the bars in the roof were not welded to the bars in the walls, nor the bars in the walls to the bars in other walls. When the granite boulder struck, the roof shifted. The wall on the downslope side — the wall that contained the door — broke loose from the connecting side walls and was cocked to an 80° angle. The roof at that end dropped into the shack. The screams had come from Allison and Brother Martin — Allison from fright — Brother Martin from pain as the slab crushed his left leg and pinned him. Murdock had instinctively thrown himself on top of Allison. Concrete dust filled his nose and covered his hair. Snow poured in. When the shifting concrete and snow settled, he and Allison had not been injured, but there was little maneuvering space. Dim daylight seeped in. Murdock struggled into a crouch position, and put his back against the roof slab. It didn't budge. Martin swallowed another scream. Allison rolled onto her back, pulled her knees to her chin, and fixed both feet against the slab. She and Murdock pushed with their combined might. The slab moved ever so slightly. Brother Martin screamed in pain. He was still pinned. "Please try again," he pleaded. "I think the blood is cut off from my foot. I'm afraid I'll lose it."

Murdock whispered to Allison: "If the snow above us slides any more, we could smother."

* * *

Richard and Georg assessed the problem. They could see the caved-in roof and the snow that had fallen in. Richard got down on his hands and knees and shouted: "Murdock, can you hear me? This is Richard. What's your situation down there?" He heard Murdock's muffled voice coming from beneath the snow. He began frantically digging at the point from which the voice seemed to come. Georg joined him. They reached the top of the front wall. The crew arrived with shovels. Quickly they cleared the snow and rock from on top the roof, the lower-most point of which was separated from the ground by Brother Martin's left foot. Georg stared at it. Richard grabbed his hand radio. "Do you have a heavy line?" he asked the pilots above him. His twenty years as a Swiss army officer had given him command bearing. Georg didn't interfere. Both pilots affirmed. A crew member of the one directly above began unreeling a heavy hemp rope. Back on his hands and knees, Richard shouted: "Murdock, can you hear me clearly now?"

"I hear you fine," Murdock shouted back.

"What's your situation?"

"Allison and I are unhurt. Brother Martin is pinned, and he's worried about getting blood to his left foot. The slab is resting on it. Professor Klugman is dead."

"I'm digging with my fingers between the roof and the east wall. Can you see light now?

"Yes."

"Good. I'm passing a line down to you. There. Do you have it?"

"Affirmative."

"Pull about ten feet of it through," Richard suggested. "I'm going to dig over by the west wall now. Will you be able to get over there and push the line up toward me?"

"No, but I think Martin can, if shock doesn't get him. He's asking for the rope. He says he's digging toward you with his fingertips, but he's not sure there's enough space for the rope to pass."

One of the crew stuck a crowbar between the sagging roof and the west wall. Georg helped. "Not too much," he commanded. "Just enough to get the rope through. We don't want this whole slab falling in on them."

The west wall moved, but not much. "Just enough for the rope," Brother Martin shouted. He forced it upward through the narrow gap between roof and wall. Richard grabbed it and pulled it through. Tying a Swiss army hitch, Richard shouted into the microphone: "Move away far enough for the second chopper to drop a line. We need two lines before we try to move it. Yanking with one line could drop the other end in and kill them all." The second chopper hovered nearer, and the second line was secured. "He keyed the mike again. Now I suggest you both lock your lines and make them taut . . . easy . . . good. Number one," he commanded, " carefully now, ascend about ten feet to level the slab."

The edge of the slab that held Brother Martin's foot moved upward.

"His foot is free," Murdock shouted. "I'm afraid to move it."

"Don't," Richard shouted. He keyed the mike again. "Both of you now . . . climb gently about twenty feet . . . good . . . good . . . number two a few more. Excellent. Now both move slowly westward." The pilots acknowledged and increased power. The choppers were dangerously close to each other. Both moved cautiously westward. The police and medics had joined them on foot. Richard motioned for the people on the ground to get on their bellies at the east wall and shouted downward: "As soon as the slab clears the top, I suggest that Allison and Murdock get to the east wall where the crew will pull you out. The medics and I are coming down for Brother Martin."

As the rotors increased in RPM, the slab rose unevenly. Georg shouted to his men, "If it tilts too far, we've got trouble. Grab the edges. Push it westward. Quickly. If the lines break or the hitches give, it'll fall on those people."

Night had fallen. Bright spotlights from the choppers flooded what remained of the antenna shack. Allison and Murdock saw the hands of their rescuers, Richard along with a medic, grabbed them, and in seconds were out. Richard looked up, hunting for Georg. "Is the slab still a factor?" he shouted.

Moira, who was standing on the edge, said calmly: "No. It's clear."

"Throw my kit down," the medic commanded. He turned to Brother Martin. "I'll give you an injection to relieve your pain and immobilize your leg and foot before we move you."

On top, Murdock, Allison, Richard, and Moira joined in a bear hug. Richard stepped back. "You shall all have a bonus," he promised.

Murdock roared with laughter. "Like the bonus ski vacation you gave me at the famous Zugspitze Hof Lodge?" Allison and Moira joined the laughter.

After a few minutes, the crew brought Brother Martin up. He was strapped to a litter, his left leg immobilized. When he saw them, he gave a thumbs-up signal. The police connected the litter to lines from one of the choppers, and Brother Martin straightway disappeared into the spotlights.

Murdock turned to Richard. "So you were the man in the green nylon jacket. Dinner's on me tonight at the lodge, folks. I think our Sir Boss has a story to tell us." Allison and Moira nodded in agreement.

Richard smiled cheerfully. "If you're buying, I'll be there."

Herr Bayer interrupted. "You are *not* buying. After what all of you have been through, dinner is on the house, along with the best wines in our cellars."

"That's not necessary," Murdock insisted.

"Not necessary? You do not know Frau Bayer as well as I do. She would skin me if I do not insist. Please. Save my life and be our guests."

"But first," Murdock said, "we've got to intercept Diana Crenshaw."

"Please do not concern yourself," Georg replied. "With information provided by Miss Zawadska, Moira, I ordered the airport police to arrest the occupants of the helicopter when it returned. Diana Crenshaw is in custody along with a Greek Cypriot character whose name is somewhat ambiguous. But come now. We must leave before we are all buried by another slide. There is still unstable snow and rock above us."

They thanked the crew that had gathered around them and, together, all cautiously descended the icy granite slope toward the tree line where snowmobiles were waiting. Murdock looked back. Medics were retrieving the professor's body.

Murdock turned to Moira. "When I phoned Georg, he spurned my request. How did you get him to respond?"

An cryptic smile crossed Moira's face. "I phoned the minister of justice."

A slow grin crossed Murdock's face. He gave Moira a hug.

"I think she's the one who needs the hug," Moira responded, nodding toward Allison who was walking alone.

Murdock joined Allison. They walked downward arm in arm. He smiled his big, boyish grin. "It's good to be alive," he said. Allison put her arm around him. "Yes," she affirmed, "very good indeed."

Tuesday
December 23

⊰ 47 ⊱

Signs of Christmas were everywhere. Every shop in downtown Munich was decorated. Last night the streets had radiated with colored lights. It was Tuesday morning, December 23rd. Pedestrians on the street seemed friendlier. Even the snow seemed whiter. Murdock planned to spend the holiday skiing at the Zugspitze Hof Lodge. He loaded his ski gear into his five-week-old BMW 528i, and lowered his six-foot-two frame into the driver's seat. His boss, Richard, had scheduled another bonus week for him at the Zugspitze Hof Lodge. The previous one had lasted only one afternoon. He wiped fingerprints from the broad walnut door trim with his coat sleeve and unconsciously ran his hand through his thick mop of red hair. The morning rush hour had passed. Traffic was moderate. Once outside the city, he accelerated to 120 KPH. The car held the road beautifully. He was looking forward to a pleasant day. Brother Martin had invited him to the annual Christmas party at the monastery this afternoon. Allison, who had checked in at the Zugspitze Hof Lodge yesterday, was also invited, along with Moira, Rudi, Angelika, Enrique, and Linda.

It's a reunion of sorts. And a first meeting of trustees. Three weeks ago Allison had opened the envelope that the professor had left with her. It contained the professor's will, which she forwarded to an attorney in Oregon for probate. Among the other papers, Allison found a letter addressed to Murdock, Brother Martin, and Allison. It read in part:

> I have had many good friends. Most are dead. I found none with more strength of character than you three. Please forgive me for imposing on you. You are named as trustees in my will. Serving should not be burdensome. My estate is worth about one and a half million dollars. One million is to be held in trust for my late friend Clarissa's daughter, Amy Gallagher. She is 32 now. All current income goes to her. You may also use principal for her benefit, if you judge it necessary. The other half million shall be devoted to genuine research in physical science. Murdock knows what I mean by genuine. Let Amy suggest the project. She majored in planetary

astronomy. If she selects one of her own projects, and if she personally benefits from it, that's okay. If she makes no choice, please devote it to SETI — the search for extraterrestrial intelligence — perhaps to the perfection of Stephen's chaos chip, if it needs perfecting.

There is another duty. Amy does not know I am her natural father. Clarissa and I confirmed that genetically. Amy loved and has fond memories of the man she thought was her father — Clarissa's husband. Amy will wonder why my trust has provided only for her and not for her sister. Please tell her the truth only if you decide it will not destroy her memories of her parents.

The letter troubled Murdock. Brother Martin and Allison had already agreed to serve as trustees. He would too, but he was confident that the responsibility for dealing with Amy would fall on his shoulders, even though Allison had offered her help. The murder of the monk had set in motion interrelationships that he realized wouldn't end readily. He looked forward to meeting the professor's only daughter.

Snow showers were dusting the road, but traction was good. The farmland changed to grazing pastures. A lumber mill passed on his left. On the right the waters of the picturesque Starnberger Sea were frozen over. Swirls of snow devils danced across the ice like playful winter spirits. The stubble of dead plants, which had punctuated both sides of the road on his last trip, had given way to an unbroken white wasteland. That in turn soon surrendered to the tall conifers that announced the foothills — the prelude to the Alps.

Brother Martin — wearing his other hat as Top Dog — had announced he would take a more active role in the management of Veritus. Murdock was pleased that the profits would be managed by Plato and used for economic development in the five states that had formed the former East Germany. It would benefit the taxpayers whose money had funded the purchase of Veritus.

Murdock was not displeased that several people were changing positions the first of the year. Harvey was going to Nairobi in Kenya. His challenge was to develop business in central Africa. He wasn't happy about it. Terry was given an opportunity for promotion to assistant station chief at Katmandu, should he choose to accept. Having never heard of Nepal, he hadn't decided whether to accept it. Richard was taking Harvey's place as district manager in Frankfurt. There had been no word whether Allison would replace him in Munich. She wasn't certain she wanted to. She had lived outside the United States long enough to suit her. Germany was fine, but there was nothing like America.

Murdock turned onto the narrow side road that led to the Zugspitze Hof Lodge. He slowed. At this higher altitude, more snow had accumulated, and the meanders and tortuous twists were becoming icy. Where the road narrowed into a one-lane bridge, he slowed almost to a stop. Cautiously, he navigated the sharp, blind curve just beyond the bridge. Beneath the bridge the fast falling waters of the Liederbach Creek had not frozen. Just past the curve, at the wide spot in the road, he paused for a moment and looked over the bluff into the meadow below. Only five weeks ago Brother Stephen's body had been found there. It seemed a lifetime. He couldn't make out the creek. *It must be frozen over. There's no contrast. But somewhere down there, Diana shot Brother Stephen. Now she sits in a Bavarian prison. If she ever sees the United States again, it'll be from the window of a prison cell in Virginia. One copy of Stephen's chaos chip is with Brother Stephen's manager in Oregon, and the other the professor sent to Amy Gallagher. And hopefully, we'll soon confirm whether or not Stephen made contact with another world. That would be the enduring testimonial to his life.*

He paused, sitting in the car, the window rolled down. A gentle wind stirred the snow-laden branches of the tall trees. The air was frosty. Murdock inhaled deeply. He killed his engine. Outside, he heard only the sound of water falling and splashing upon rocks below. He strained to listen as if the silence itself had something to say. It did. As he peered down into the lonesome meadow where Brother Stephen's body had lain, his mind's ear heard the words: "Life is fragile." A chill ran up his spine. He decided to move on. Allison would be joining him for lunch. He anticipated that with pleasure.

*   *   *

Later that afternoon Brother Martin, deftly maneuvering his crutches, ascended a stage that had been erected at the center of the long northern wall of the monastery's assembly hall — a hall that had never witnessed a Christmas party such as this. Brandy, wine, and cognac were in abundance. Camaraderie was enthusiastic, and spirits were high.

"Please," Brother Martin said loudly so that several dozen monks and guests could hear, "gather around this stage." A ten foot pine tree stood at its center, decorated with apples, pieces of unleavened bread, and electric candles.

"We are pleased," Martin began, "to have with us this year our special guests." He nodded toward them. "We welcome you, and we are indeed honored to have each of you with us. Please step up here as I introduce you so all can see you. My brothers, meet Jose Enrique Perez-Krieger — a name renowned throughout the world who needs no further introduction." The monks applauded. "And Herr Rudi Benzinger of the Bavarian State Police, and his wife, Angelika." More applause. "And also my good friends, Allison Spencer, Moira Zawadska, and Murdock Mc-Cabe — all from Veritus International. These three call me Top Dog." The monks roared with laughter. "I knew it was a mistake to tell you this."

One of the monks stepped forward. "Shall we call you Reverend Top Dog, or would you prefer Reverend Abbott Top Dog?" They roared again.

Martin joined in the laughter. "I fear that once again I suffer from foot-in-mouth disease. Oh well, it's Christmas. As you know, it was Mister McCabe who solved the mystery of the death of our brother, Stephen. We are grateful to him." A hearty round of applause clattered across the assembly hall. "And last but not least, most of you have already met another man from Veritus, my old friend, Richard Laplatenier." Another hearty round of applause followed. "Richard is called by the other three 'Sir Richard the Boss.'" Another roar of laughter. "For most of his career, Richard was with the Swiss military intelligence, and after his retirement he accepted a position as our station chief at Munich. When Stephen was killed, we feared for the life of Brother Antonio — both from the killer of Brother Stephen, and from himself. Antonio was despondent and went into shock. His sister, Maria Rosita, is involved in political causes in Spain, and he feared that he had said too much to her about Brother Stephen's projects. He feared that Spanish political figures may have tried to kidnap Stephen. But his family was not involved. Antonio had also mentioned Stephen's work with Diana Crenshaw, who had become a confidante. But with Stephen dead and Antonio the next most knowledgeable, and suffering from severe shock, I feared for his life. Richard immediately fell back into his cloak-and-dagger and secretly whisked Antonio to a hospital in Zürich under an assumed name. Antonio is progressing very well. He will return to us tomorrow — Christmas eve." Applause again filled the hall. "He will be God's Christmas present."

The entrance door opened and a woman stepped through. As she walked toward them, Brother Martin shouted to her: "Please join us on stage," and, turning to the audience said: "Although I have not met her, I believe this is Linda DiStefano, Señor Perez-Krieger's good right hand."

"You are most certainly correct," Enrique said exuberantly, leaning over and offering his hand to assist her.

The audience applauded, led most vigorously by Murdock McCabe. As she took her place on stage, Linda noticed the evergreen.

Brother Martin shook her hand and said: "I see you've noticed the tree."

"Your decorations are a mite curious," Linda replied.

Martin raised his arms until the room quieted. "Miss DiStefano thinks my decorations are curious. They are, but they tell a story. Two millennia ago the ancient Germans lived in a dense forest. All central Europe was dense forest. They were tree worshippers. Around the winter solstice, when the periods of daylight were very short — like today — they placed pine trees in their barns and homes to repel the demonic spirits that they believed wandered the woods — the spirits that created the long darkness. They celebrated, like we are, knowing that, after these celebrations, the daylight would grow longer each day. When Christianity came, they preserved the tradition with some modifications. The day before the Christ Mass, or Christmas, was the feast of Adam and Eve. In the early Christian era each family decorated an evergreen tree as you see here, except the candles were not electric. They called it the Paradise Tree. The apples represented the Garden of Eden and man's falling into sin. The bread represented the body of Christ in the Holy Eucharist — the means by which mans' sins are forgiven. The candles represented Christ, the light of the world. Later Germans transformed the Paradise Tree into the Christmas tree which is more familiar to us. I decorated this tree in the ancient tradition, because I regret that so many fine traditions die from neglect. End of lecture. A hearty meal — not monks' meat — will be served in one hour. In the meantime, please mix and be joy filled."

Brother Martin, Brother Gustav, and the special guests seated themselves at a large round table and quickly engaged in spirited conversation.

Rudi laughed. "Murdock, I shall never forget that bad landing that you made on Crete."

"*Bad* landing?" Murdock chided. "That was a good landing."

"What? I received three stitches in my forehead. How do you define a *good* landing?"

Enrique interrupted. "A good landing is any landing you walk away from."

A roar of laughter circled the table.

"If you think that's funny," Enrique said, "here's one for you. Linda was late because we received a phone call from Boris Romanovsky. Tell them about it, please."

Linda raised a pitcher of beer and poured one for herself. "Boris called while I was driving here from the airport. He wondered if Enrique had had time to read the proposed contract. He insists that he is still the best man to introduce us into Russia."

Murdock roared with laughter. "The unmitigated gall. After what he did?"

"Boris assured me that he didn't," Linda continued straight-faced. "He claims that Theo was acting on his own account. Boris says he had no idea what was going on in his dungeon. He never went there. Theo, he claims, was paid five hundred U.S. dollars to find a classy whore for Enrique. Boris was surprised, he says, when he heard the alarms and the shooting. He forgives Murdock for stealing his Cessna 310." She turned to Enrique. "He assures me that the replacement cost of the aircraft will not be hidden in the agency contract. He's anxious to get started and awaits our reply."

Allison put down her glass. "And chickens have teeth," she said. "Did he mention my friend Sascha?"

"Oh yes. Your bullet created some damage. Sascha had to be repaired like a girl, as Boris put it. Sascha's in police custody, charged with the murder of Baron von Richter. Boris said that he personally directed the recovery of the Baron's body, had it flown to Regensburg at his expense, and turned it over to the family. Boris has fixed it so the police will not need to talk to you, Allison. He attends to detail."

"Will you answer him?" Murdock asked.

Enrique leaned back in his chair, swishing brandy about in a snifter. Linda didn't speak. A sly smile crossed his face. "It's not an easy call," Enrique said. "Possibly he is innocent as he claims. I have engaged your office in Cyprus to check that. Russia is still worth doing. Can we find anyone less soiled than Boris in the Russian morass, or anyone who is more pragmatic and has better connections? If we cannot, then we must decide whether he is the devil, and whether we will deal with him in order to achieve the greater good. Can we be *in* his world without becoming *of* his world? Linda thinks not. We shall see."

Rudi interrupted. "I spoke with Colonel Constantine last week. He is my counterpart in the Cypriot police. He assures me that Boris Romanovsky is beyond suspicion."

Murdock chuckled. "Do you believe him?"

"I believe that is the official position that they're taking, and we have no direct evidence to contradict it. The Cypriots want Theo what's-his-name when we're finished with him. That may be a long time. We've charged him with illegally firing a rocket launcher and the attempted murder of Murdock, Allison, and Brother Martin. Forensics has identified fragments of the rocket and identified his fingerprints on the launcher. We've offered him some consideration if he'll testify against Diana Crenshaw."

"Will he?" Murdock asked.

"No. I think not. He says that, if he testified against her, he would feel safer in prison."

Murdock turned to Angelika. "It's good to have you back with us this Christmas."

"After sleeping for two years, at least I've had plenty of rest."

Allison asked the question that had occurred to all. "Did you dream?"

Angelika thought for several seconds. "Yes, I believe so."

Allison smiled. "Can you remember what you dreamt?"

"Yes. I was swimming—breaststroking—through a foggy fluid of white light, ascending, getting away from something, but I felt no urgency. I'd been awestruck by something. I could never quite remember what it was, but I wanted to leave it behind. Other creatures were around me—or it seemed they were. I couldn't see them. The light was brilliant. Perhaps they washed out in the light. They were more a presence than things. It was radiant, but I wanted the dream to end. I remember an awesome, unnatural silence. I wanted to speak, but it seemed improper. I wanted to touch something, anything. The dream was always the same."

Brother Martin urged, "Please go on."

"The dream always began with a brilliant ball of swimming multicolored thread-like things vigorously vibrating irregularly. The ball would float about randomly. The individual threads constantly changed their colors and configurations."

"Was it a large ball? Did it grow?" he asked.

"No. Always the same size—the size of a basketball. I know this sounds silly, but I remember feeling vaguely comfortable when the ball appeared—as if I were meeting an old friend. The ball would become suddenly larger, and the threads would congeal into a man. He would step out of the ball and smile at me—an avuncular smile."

"Can you describe him?" Murdock asked.

"Yes. He was somewhat taller than you, but with blond hair and blue eyes, and muscular. He stood erect. His skin was milky white, like mine after our long Bavarian winter."

"Did he speak?" Enrique asked.

"Never. But *he* changed too, like the ball had. As I watched him, his features would fluctuate—become less muscular, shorter, slighter, almost feminine, but always the same eyes and the kindly smile. Sometimes I was less certain that the figure was male. It seemed as if gender was inconsequential, just like the absence of firm patterns in the ball threads had seemed unimportant. He, or she, would hold out its hands to me. I needed to sit up and take them, but I couldn't. When I didn't, it would dissolve into a ball again, and the ball would disappear."

Brother Gustav interrupted. "How often did you dream this?"

"I had no sense of time. Maybe a hundred times. Maybe once. Maybe not at all."

Rudi interrupted. "Tell them about the last time."

"The last time, if there was more than one time, I was convinced it was male. He walked over to me and took my hand and held it. I felt warmed, as if I had been cold for a long time and now was warm. Then he released my hands, turned and walked away. I didn't see the ball when he left. I felt like I would not see him — or her — again for a long time. The next thing I remember — and I don't know whether it happened immediately as the dream ended, or weeks later — I awoke and saw Doctor Kohl who told me that a man had just left my room. What do you think this dream meant?"

No one spoke. Presently Brother Martin broke the silence. "I think it means that each of us has to search our hearts and rediscover the forgotten knowledge that we're never quite alone."

Murdock turned toward him. "Do you believe in guardian angels?"

"I believe that intelligence exists in dimensions other than the four we're familiar with. The rest is semantics." Weeks later Brother Martin would read Stephen's memoirs and learn his opinion of Michael.

There was a long, thoughtful silence. Angelika broke it.

"We may have some news. Commander Weiss will retire in March. Rudi is being considered for his position. We are hopeful."

"He'll receive the appointment," Moira said.

Allison added quickly: "Moira is our fortune-teller. Her intuitions are seldom wrong. I know of no one more qualified than you, Rudi."

"Thank you," Rudi said. "Perhaps you have drunk too much beer."

"Rudi!" Angelika scolded. "Allison has never drunk too much beer."

"Not since college days," Murdock inserted, grinning.

Brother Martin laughed. "Changing from my monk's cowl to my Top Dog hat, we are offering double promotions to Allison and Murdock. We would like you, Allison, to accept the position as district manager for the American Pacific Northwest. The office is in Seattle. It covers Washington, Oregon, Idaho, and Montana. Please give it some thought."

"I accept," she said.

Brother Martin was taken back. "Well," he said, "we offered it because we thought you capable of making decisions promptly. You prove us right." Everyone laughed. He turned to Murdock. "And we offer you the position of station manager at Portland — in Oregon."

"May I have Moira as my assistant?"

"I think that can be arranged."

"Then I accept," Murdock replied.

Brother Martin brought out the brandy and poured a snifter for each of them. "A toast to their success — Rudi, Allison, Moira, and Murdock." They all raised their snifters and drank. "And," Brother Martin continued, "to our absent friends — the professor and our sainted brother, Stephen." Again, but more soberly, they drank.

Murdock took Allison aside and put one arm around her. "We'll be close together: Seattle and Portland. I'll like that."

She put one arm around him. They stood looking out a window at the fresh, new snow. "So will I," she replied.

As the afternoon wore into evening, Murdock separated himself from the crowd, stood by a window, and stared out. The setting sun tinted the snowcapped peak of the Zugspitze bright red. The shadow of the mountain had already captured the woodlands. Soft lights, camaraderie, and a brandy-induced glow had utterly relaxed Murdock. He turned, leaned his back against the window, and surveyed the tables of convivial people. Enrique and Brother Martin were laughing. Moira and Rudi appeared to be confiding some secret. Murdock sat down next to Allison who was engaged in an animated conversation with Angelika and Linda. Allison's hand lay on the table. Murdock gently placed his hand on hers. Hers didn't move. *In Portland I'll be near Allison, but she'll still be my supervisor. I'll also be near the professor's daughter, Amy Gallagher, and both copies of the chaos chip, along with its design documents. It's difficult to know whether this party is the conclusion of an adventure, or a pregnant intermission.*